"A miracle; an exquisite story exquisitely told. This glorious novel, big-hearted and clear-eyed, features the most uncanny incarnation of our sixteenth president since Daniel Day-Lewis strode onscreen in *Lincoln*. If you love Jane Austen, or *Hamilton*, or fiction—of any era—that transports and transforms in equal measure, look no further."

—A. J. Finn, bestselling author of *The Woman in the Window*

"In his ninth novel, *Courting Mr. Lincoln*, Louis Bayard dramatically re-creates the months after Abraham Lincoln's 1840 winter arrival in Springfield with delicious detail and diligent diplomacy. Alternating between the disparate voices of Lincoln's future wife and Lincoln's best friend, Bayard offers an insider's view of just how much the two may have influenced the awkward, often ill-mannered country lawyer as he began to inch his way up the political ladder. Bayard does an exceptional job of keeping readers engrossed as he weaves fact and fiction in this intriguing tale of intimacy between Lincoln and his two closest confidantes."   —*BookPage*

"Bayard has made a career of working in different genres and styles, and his writing has always been stellar throughout. Bayard's descriptions of the characters and the dialogue he creates are delightful. What Bayard has accomplished is to take popular figures in U.S. history and not only make them more real—if that is possible—but humanize them to a level where we all can relate to them. *Courting Mr. Lincoln* is engaging because Bayard has such a fine way with words. The result is a triumph of a novel and an unforgettable read that is a true page-turner."   —Bookreporter.com

"An exquisite novel about how Lincoln's courtship of the brilliant, complicated Mary Todd intersected with his long and very (possibly VERY) close friendship with Joshua Speed. *Courting Mr. Lincoln* is so subtle and human and heartbreaking, infused with sly wit. I loved every word of it, and the end is note perfect. My heart broke for both Joshua and Mary, and at the same time, they were lenses that let me think about my favorite president in new ways."

—Joshilyn Jackson, *New York Times* bestselling
author of *Never Have I Ever*

"Was Abraham Lincoln gay? The question, not a new one, is delicately and touchingly presented in *Courting Mr. Lincoln* . . . Tenderly told."
—*St. Louis Post-Dispatch*

"*Courting Mr. Lincoln* is a fascinating (and partly fictional) exploration of not only the sixteenth president, but those enamored by him." —Advocate.com

"In this sparkling tale of strategy and desire, Louis Bayard renders the origin story of the Lincoln-Todd marriage with a wit worthy of Jane Austen and the keen political insight of the best presidential biographers. When it comes to bringing our most revered historical figures to vivid life—and returning to them their full humanity—Louis Bayard has no peer. He is, quite simply, a master of the storytelling art." —Liza Mundy, bestselling author of *Code Girls*

"In exquisite detail and luminous prose, Louis Bayard has taken what might have been a footnote in the history of Abraham Lincoln and made it the story. It is as if there was a secret door in Lincoln's life and Bayard has opened it and walked inside. Suddenly all the pieces fit. Utterly fascinating and brilliantly convincing, this is a terrific book that people will be talking about for a long time." —Mary Morris, author of *Gateway to the Moon*

"Superb, witty, gorgeously written. For the length of this dazzling, subversive novel, I was plunged so deeply into the sitting rooms and muddy streets of mid-nineteenth-century Springfield, Illinois, that I too had fallen in love with and had my heart broken by the awkward young lawyer from Kentucky. *Courting Mr. Lincoln* is an essential read: it makes the past a human place."
—Christopher Bollen, author of *The Destroyers*

"With a masterful grasp of its characters, this moving reflection on Lincoln is an elegiac, illuminating portrait of love." —*Foreword Reviews*

"At its heart, *Courting Mr. Lincoln* is an intimate portrayal of this complicated and compassionate romantic triangle. By the end of the novel, who's courting Lincoln remains a delicious mystery." —*Shepherd Express* (Milwaukee)

"WONDERFUL . . . SUSPENSEFUL
AND REVEALING."
—*Minneapolis Star Tribune*

"An e   site historical reimagining of a love acknowledged—and a longing
deni   —*People* (Book of the Week)

"[P   n   s] extraordinarily gifted at blending provocative fiction with his-
r   details of [Mary Todd and Lincoln's] courtship are lovely to read,
            ln's time with Speed is much more riveting. At book's end, who's
cou.   Lincoln remains an enticing mystery."   —*The Washington Post*

"A h   divided against itself cannot stand, Abraham Lincoln warned us. But
a boc   vided against itself stands up quite nicely in Louis Bayard's wonderful
Court   Mr. Lincoln . . . Suspenseful and revealing . . . It's a tribute to Bayard's
entert   ng novel that he has imagined a love story for Abraham and Mary
Todd   coln that embroiders the truth but that also fits perfectly with what
we know about these very famous figures."   —*Minneapolis Star Tribune*

"A rich fascinating and romantic union of fact and imagination about young
Lincol , the woman he would marry and his beloved best friend . . . *Courting
Mr.   oln* is intimate, warm and, above all, compassionate. Bayard is
conc   with the possibilities of the human heart, and he presents an
enig   Lincoln seen—and loved—from two other points of a romantic
triang   . The greatest triumph of *Courting Mr. Lincoln* is how effectively
Baya   ates suspense, even when we know how the story ends. Love is
love   e, after all, and he invests us deeply in the moving journey of three
extra   nary people."   —*Newsday*

"[A   cute and passionate portrait . . . In Bayard's skilled hands, three compli-
cate eople groping toward a new phase in their lives is all the plot you need."
—*Kirkus Reviews*, starred review

"With wit and charm that only Louis Bayard can deliver, *Courting Mr. Lincoln* transports readers to nineteenth-century Springfield, Ill., to view both the romance of Abraham Lincoln and Mary Todd and the intimate friendship of the future president and a dry-goods merchant named Joshua Speed . . . Those familiar with Bayard's work will appreciate his sterling dialogue and ingenious humor. Bayard's masterful command of language enchants and thrills; his meticulous, almost otherworldly understanding of his historical subject awes and inspires. When that all comes together, *Courting Mr. Lincoln* is Bayard at his absolute best. He offers more reasons to love one of the most admired presidents in U.S. history and proves yet again why he himself is one of the nation's greatest literary gems." —*Shelf Awareness*, starred review

"A wildly clever imagining of Honest Abe's complicated personal life. In *Courting Mr. Lincoln*, Louis Bayard, an accomplished historical novelist, breathes life into the massive cultural icon whom we know so well, but really don't have much of a clue about. Read the book. You'll thank me." —*Washington Independent Review of Books*

"Thoroughly researched and thrillingly plotted . . . Filled with rich historical detail and compulsively readable, *Courting Mr. Lincoln* is a story of a best friend, a future wife, and the political legend that they came together to create, each leaving an indelible mark on the man that would one day become president. Fans of historical fiction will be up late into the night to uncover the next chapter of this fascinating time in history." —*New York Journal of Books*

"A gripping historical thriller . . . An entertaining novel by a gifted storyteller." —*The Washington Book Review*

"Bayard fictionalizes the early days of Mary Todd and Abraham Lincoln's relationship in this delightful embellishment of American history. This charming love story delicately reveals the emotional roller coaster of two inexperienced adults traversing the unknown realm of love while trying to meet the demands and expectations of society." —*Publishers Weekly*

COURTING MR. LINCOLN

COURTING MR. LINCOLN

A Novel

Louis Bayard

ALGONQUIN BOOKS OF CHAPEL HILL 2020

Published by
ALGONQUIN BOOKS OF CHAPEL HILL
Post Office Box 2225
Chapel Hill, North Carolina 27515-2225

a division of
WORKMAN PUBLISHING
225 Varick Street
New York, New York 10014

First paperback edition, Algonquin Books of Chapel Hill, February 2020. Originally
published in hardcover by Algonquin Books of Chapel Hill in April 2019.
Printed in the United States of America.
Published simultaneously in Canada by Thomas Allen & Son Limited.
Design by Steve Godwin.

LIBRARY OF CONGRESS CATALOGING-IN-PUBLICATION DATA
Names: Bayard, Louis, author.
Title: Courting Mr. Lincoln / Louis Bayard.
Description: First edition. | Chapel Hill, North Carolina :
Algonquin Books of Chapel Hill, 2019.
Identifiers: LCCN 2018028814 | ISBN 9781616208479 (hardcover : alk. paper)
Subjects: LCSH: Lincoln, Mary Todd, 1818–1882—Fiction. | Lincoln, Abraham,
1809–1865—Fiction. | Speed, Joshua F. (Joshua Fry), 1814–1882—Fiction. |
Courtship—Fiction. | Springfield (Ill.)—History—19th century—
Fiction. | GSAFD: Historical fiction. | Biographical fiction.
Classification: LCC PS3552.A85864 C68 2019 | DDC 813/.54—dc23
LC record available at https://lccn.loc.gov/2018028814

ISBN 978-1-64375-044-6 (PB)

10 9 8 7 6 5 4 3 2 1
First Paperback Edition

Courting Mr. Lincoln is a work of historical fiction, which means that, where necessary, I have reshuffled chronology, speculated, and invented. At the same time, I have hewed as closely as possible to the historical record and to the documented psychology of Abraham Lincoln, Mary Todd, and Joshua Speed. The quotations from Lincoln's letters to Speed are drawn from original documents.

I hide myself within my flower,
That wearing on your breast,
You, unsuspecting, wear me too—
And angels know the rest.

I hide myself within my flower,
That, fading from your vase,
You, unsuspecting, feel for me
Almost a loneliness.

—EMILY DICKINSON

COURTING MR. LINCOLN

PART ONE

Mary

ONE

———

Her journey from Alton to Springfield should have taken no longer than two days, but as the stage driver himself said, "That's no more 'n a hope." At any second of any hour, they might have to pause for a fox or a passel of wild hogs. One morning, it was a pair of rattlesnakes, sporting themselves in the sun. Two hours later, a pile of bleached bones, uncertain in provenance.

Wagon tracks would end without warning, or the old Indian trail they were following would fade back into prairie. More than once, the path would vanish altogether beneath stagnant ponds, obliging the passengers—men and women alike—to walk ahead, with gnats and horseflies for companions.

Farms were few here. Look to every quadrant, there was no signpost, no settlement. Only grass, rolling on like a tide. Higher than any man, pawing at the windows, swallowing whatever it absorbed. Bucks disappeared all the way to their antlers. An entire flock of prairie chickens could feed unseen and then, startled into flight, blacken the sky with their wings.

And as soon as the sun dropped, the prairie wolves began to howl. The sound didn't bother her so much at first—she made a point of using the word *charming*—but on the third evening, the calls began to coalesce, as if the wolves were solving a problem amongst themselves, and she began to wonder how many were out there. A hundred? A thousand? Were they even now circling the stage?

She awoke the next morning with a start, convinced that something was grazing on her shoulder, but it was just the slumbering head of a Presbyterian deacon's sister. This lady until now had kept a cool tone with Mary, but the duress of the journey must have loosened her tongue for, later that day, the woman gave a light rustle to her traveling dress and asked: "Are you coming to Springfield for a visit?"

"Something between a visit and a stay."

"Depending on how it goes, you mean."

Mary flushed. "How is it *supposed* to go, I wonder?" Thinking, as she spoke, that her companion would retreat into convention, but the woman's dry contralto began to quaver with purpose.

"I'll tell you how. You're to find a husband, that's how. Pretty girl like you, it shouldn't take you long."

"You're very kind," Mary answered, faintly.

"You have family, then. Waiting for you."

"A sister, yes. Elizabeth Edwards." She glanced at the older woman, waiting for a gleam of recognition. "Her husband is *Ninian* Edwards." Still waiting. "The son of the late governor."

"I do apologize," said her companion. "I can't be trusted with the names of this world."

On the fourth day, Mary awoke to find a jaybird perched on the lip of her window. Miles from any tree, what had possessed it to travel so far?

The words came back to her then, unbidden. *Tell-tale-tell.*

Blame it on Sally, the Todds' nursemaid. She used to tell the children that jaybirds were Satan's messengers, flying down to hell every Friday night to recount the sins they'd witnessed. "Down in that bad place," said Sally, "there's a little devil setting up on a stool so high that his tail don't touch the floor. *What's up, Mr. Jay?* he says. And Mr. Jay twitters, *Well, for beginners, Mary hid Sally's slippers when Sally was trying to rest her feet in the garden.* Old Man Satan bellows, *Write that down in your big book, little son. Who else?* So, Mr. Jay twitters, *Well now, Elizabeth helps Mary in all her mischievous doings.* And Satan says, *Write that down, too. Careful. Don't trust nary a thing to your remembrance.* So then Mr. Jay says, *Miss Ann hollered when Sally curled her hair. . . .*"

It was dazzling to think how many sins could be committed by a brood of six children—and how stingily Satan's messenger could hoard them in his brain. One summer morning, Mary found a jaybird sitting in a tulip tree and began calling up to him. "Howdy, Mr. Jay, you are a tell-tale-tell. You play the spy each day, then carry tales to hell."

Just then, the bird flashed its wings in a crack of air. The upper beak parted from the lower, and a thick suety maw opened before Mary's eyes. At the sound of her scream, Sally came limping over. "Child," she said, gathering her up, "that bird can't do a thing to you 'less you let him."

Gazing now at the jaybird on the other side of her window, Mary could afford to smile at the memory. Only the smile soon faded, and with a vigor that startled her fellow passengers, she began pounding on the window until the bird flew away.

For the rest of the journey, her mood was black. She spoke to no one and grimaced at every shudder of the coach's frame as it toiled over the swells. When at last they crested the final hill and began the slow descent into Springfield, the view that rose up before her was a match for her mood. Streets treacled with mud and horse dung. Unpainted mud-daubed cabins. Steers and hogs and the noisiest wagons in creation, piled high with corn and turnips. Shoeless farmers and their shoeless wives and children. Not a sidewalk, not a streetlight. The mud so thick the stage could barely pull through. An ugly, raw, primordial town.

What had she done? Why had she left behind the four walls she knew? The people who loved her? Father and Sally and Nelson and Madame Mentelle and Mrs. Ward. She had thrown them all away on a bet.

"Now now," said the deacon's sister, resting her hand on Mary's. "Why should you be crying, dear one? You're going to your future."

TWO

Living in a frontier town, Ninian Edwards liked to say, was no different from living anywhere else. You just had to find a way to rise above.

In a town like Springfield, you might start by shaking off your fifteen-by-eighteen cabin for a two-story frame house with wooden paling. From there, if you were feeling bullish about your prospects, you might graduate to something in the Greek Revival style, with as many as four rooms upstairs and another room in the attic and a back stairway. This stairway would necessarily consume part of your kitchen, which would then require you to eat all your meals in the dining room. From there it was a short step to the cherry dining table with the turned legs and thence to the French bedsteads that sold for ten dollars. Why stop there? Why not build a wide hall with parlors on both sides? From there, you would necessarily have to hire servants to clean all the rooms and to spare your wife, in her newly minted role as hostess, the labor of cooking and laundering and child rearing.

But finally, the best way to stand out among your fellows was to move skyward. It was, thus, the impulse of Ninian Edwards—an impulse very much encouraged and, one might even say, fomented by his distinguished wife—to buy the first plot and to build the first house on the elevation known (with some bitterness and only by those who did not live there) as Quality Hill.

This being Illinois, it could scarcely be called a hill, but the house was pitched at least thirteen feet above its nearest competitors and boasted two floors and five servants and a dizzying fifteen rooms, including bedrooms for the master and mistress. But where the house particularly excelled in the eyes of the Springfield gentry was in its front parlor, which ran for an unprecedented forty feet, making it longer than most flatboats and giving it the capacity to hold as many notables as Ninian Edwards, in his position as lawyer and state representative, could cram inside.

For his wife, Elizabeth, however, the room that bore the most strategic value was the spare bedroom. Here she had resolved to install each of her younger sisters until such time as they were carried off by husbands. Frances Todd was the first beneficiary of that campaign and was claimed—within a year and to a mostly lukewarm response—by William Wallace, a genial, impoverished doctor and drugstore proprietor who harbored dreams of land speculation.

Now it was Mary's turn, and her pride bridled not just at being second but also at being so scarcely concealed a burden. Ninian, for all his upward aspirations, had weathered setbacks in the panic of thirty-seven, and with his liquidity strained by the cost of entertaining, he was not eager to add more debits in the form of Todds. But he himself had a young cousin he was preparing to bring into the world, and after weeks of remorseless negotiations with his wife—waged in each of their fifteen rooms—Ninian agreed that Mary could be sent for.

Never was there a question of whether she would come.

At the time of her summons, she was working as an apprentice teacher at her old school. She had taken the job on the premise that teaching was a perfectly honorable profession for an unmarried gentlewoman and that there might be worse ways to fill one's days than helping Mrs. Ward herd a pack of Lexington girls from grammar to arithmetic to history to plain sewing. Yet she couldn't escape the feeling that every time she read aloud from Miss Swift's *Natural Philosophy*, every time she encouraged some tin-eared ten-year-old to plump up her French vowels, she was being measured for a coffin. Her father was more than usually absent from home—the state senate, the branch bank, and the family manufactory all claimed their pieces of him—and Mary had little to do with her spare time but quarrel with her stepmother and pick her way through the thickening ranks of Todd brats. Springfield, Illinois, may have been on the edge of civilization, but it had the advantage of being there and not here.

So, in the fall of 1839, she came.

Her new bedroom was small but well proportioned, with all the accouterments of an indefinitely temporary guest: a canopy bed, a carpet from Lauderman's in St. Louis (Elizabeth said Springfield carpets were too drab), a bureau, a wash-hand basin, a looking glass. When she retired, a freshly tended fire was waiting for her; when she awoke, she found a pitcher of fresh water. The only thing she could think to complain of was the jarring sound of carts carrying stone to the new capitol . . . but she commanded herself to think of it as the price of progress.

And was she not progressing, too? *Going to her future.* Until, without warning, the future came rushing at her.

It happened on her twenty-first birthday, a few days shy of Christmas. Elizabeth had commemorated the occasion by giving her sister a dry embrace, a new pair of shoes, and a cake. It was only when Mary was reaching for a second piece that Elizabeth leaned in and whispered: "You mustn't panic."

Which, up to that moment, she had felt no inclination to do. It was true that Kentucky girls married young and Todd girls younger—Elizabeth herself was barely nineteen when she snagged Ninian. There was at least a perverse comfort in the counterexample of Mary's stepmother, who had been written off as a lost cause until the newly widowed Robert Todd came a-calling. To hear people talk, Betsey had been anywhere from twenty-five to twenty-eight, though it was impossible to know because she had destroyed all the records. "Birthdates," she used to say, "are never etched in stone. Not even *tomb*stone."

At face level, such vanity was ridiculous. With her marriage, Betsey had inherited half a dozen children from a dead woman and had then popped out another nine of her own in nearly as many years. She was constantly ill, eternally vexed. Any accents of spring had long since vanished from her face and figure—and still she carried on as if she were a woodland nymph. Only now could Mary see the advantages. Imagine being whatever age you chose! Suppose, she thought, she were to declare herself four. Mama would be alive, and so would Baby Bobby. Grandmother Parker would still live just up the hill. She would still be Mary *Ann*, infinitely better than Mary.

Suppose now she were twelve. Running so quickly the three blocks uphill to school that a Lexington watchman once reported her for eloping. Reciting from *The Ladies Geography* and wearing a chaplet of flowers to the May Day parade.

Suppose now she were seventeen. Fresh out of finishing school, a prized dance partner, fluent in flirtation, gazing down the rest of her life as if it were a flowering prairie, extending in every direction.

How had it become so quickly a peninsula? Today, if she were to call the roll of her old classmates at Madame Mentelle's, she would have to add to every girl's name, except hers, a man's surname. Even the least likely of prospects had gone at matrimony with a grim and single-minded resolve, and they now had the carriages and summer cottages to show for it.

And what had she to show after four years of tea parties and late-night suppers? Four years of flirting with the same Lexington boys with whom she'd once picked blackberries along Upper Broadway. Four years of French swiss and pianofortes and blushing for the homesick students of Transylvania University.

After all this time, she had begun to wonder if, unbeknownst to her, she harbored some constitutional flaw. An innate faltering, perhaps, that manifested itself at *le moment critique.* Looking back at the swains who used to crowd around her on the herringbone floors, she could see how easily she had wielded her power over them, had guided them to the brink of infatuation. Yet each time it had come to naught. And each time—here was the insight that had until now eluded her—*she* had been the one to take the step back.

Often without intending to. All it needed, in the end, was a passing gibe, a bit of playful sparring that devolved into quarrel.

Take that sweet young Mr. Broadhead, the Massachusetts theology student whom Father had engaged to tutor the younger Todds. Anyone could see he was besotted with her. Always clearing his throat when she passed. Engaging her in the fine points of Episcopalian liturgy. She had given him just enough encouragement to awaken hope. Then, over breakfast one morning, for reasons she still couldn't understand, she had called him the one word she knew he couldn't abide. "Do *Yankees* know how to dance, Mr. Broadhead?"

Rather than simply have her joke and fall back into silence, she had pressed on. "Is it true Yankees bathe in molasses?" "I've read that Yankee drawing rooms are fairly bathed in spittle." Every word wreathed in laughter and striking so deeply that, by the end of breakfast, he had quite gone off her, never to be coaxed back.

Why had she done that to Mr. Broadhead? Why had she teased Jedediah Fowler about President Jackson? Why had she chided Alexander Chaney for chewing too loudly and laughed when John Wilkes got a kernel of corn stuck between his teeth? She had meant no harm—no conscious harm—and still she had managed, in the space of a few seconds, to deaden every last ember that stirred in their hearts.

It had to be that, in her soul, there lay some rebel contingent. Lying in ambush the whole while and rising up at the first suggestion of romance. But if so, what was it rebelling against? Or holding out *for*? Something better, was that it?

"There *is* nothing better," said Elizabeth. "And many things worse." She gave Mary the lightest of boxes on the ear. "It's only a matter of time, puss. At least you still have your bloom."

The very thing you told a woman on the verge of losing it.

Every morning now, she stood before her looking glass, canvassing her assets as pitilessly as a butcher. Arms: shapely. Shoulders: smooth. Complexion: good. Forehead: too broad. Cheeks: too ruddy. Face: a touch too round. Hair: chestnut with a hint of bronze. Eyes: blue, shading toward violet. Eyelashes: silky. Nose: straight. Lips: curled. Teeth: small. Figure: full, with the tiniest suggestion of stoutness.

She could not reckon herself a beauty, but she felt entitled to the claim of prettiness, and from experience, she had learned it shone brightest in social settings. Under Madame Mentelle's tutelage, she had mastered the waltz at fifteen, and men who might never have given her another glance changed their minds after watching her on the dance floor. The sway of hoop under lace, teasing glimpses of silk-sheathed ankles . . . here and here alone she was confident in her own spectacle.

"And don't forget," said Elizabeth. "You're a woman."

Mary had considered this self-evident until the night of her first Springfield cotillion. Coming down the stairs half an hour into the proceedings, she heard fiddles striking up a three-quarter tune. She saw the long wavering lines cast by the candles across the marble floor. For a few moments, she paused on the next-to-last step to better savor the spectacle—only to realize that a dozen men in black wool were converging on her. The suaver ones asked if she had a place on her dance program; the others simply stared. In every eye growled the same hunger. How could she not think of prairie wolves?

"Gentlemen," crooned Elizabeth, "please don't crowd Miss Todd. We have all night to grow acquainted."

Back in Lexington, eligible men were so thin on the ground that it was not uncommon to see girls finishing out balls in each other's arms. There was no such danger in Springfield, where males outnumbered females two to one. To be a young woman in the young capital of a young state was to enjoy an immediate fame.

"It's like this," her new friend Mercy told her. "When menfolk start in to settling a place—clearing their trees, I mean, and fighting their Indians— they're perfectly happy with whores. It's all they're fit for. But once a town gets up on its feet, as Springfield has, well, then they start aspiring to something more. The kind of girl you can take out on your arm."

Or, as the minister at First Presbyterian liked to put it: "It's never too late to help some poor fellow fight the battle of life."

Mercy had already found hers. A lawyer: amiable, devoted, attractively sardonic, but ever on the circuits, chasing judges from county to county. A "Gone-Case," Mercy called him, but she treated his absences as an excuse to be the unattached girl the world assumed her to be, and she and Mary spent many an idle hour that fall, keeping a running tally of Springfield bachelors.

"Mr. Billings?"

"Gracious, no. That ghoulish smile."

"Mr. Edmund?"

"Too fond of his own jaw."

"Mr. Douglas, then."

"One's husband should never be shorter than oneself."

At some point, the discussion always broke down in laughter, but even at her giddiest, Mary was alive to her injustice. Was she not *small*? To be dismissing, in a few hard words, men who had done nothing more than show an interest? Did they not deserve better?

And at the back of those scruples lay another question, posed by that rebel contingent of her soul. Did *she* not deserve better?

In January, Elizabeth, sounding moderately impatient, said: "You need a fallback."

There was no point protesting for Elizabeth had already found a candidate: Edwin Webb.

A Whig lawyer and state representative. ("I know how soft you are for politicians.") A trusted ally of Elizabeth's husband. ("Ninian says he could be governor one day.") And crucially: in a lonely cast of mind, having just lost a wife.

"Of course, he has charming manners," said Elizabeth.

"I have seen his manners."

"He owns a two-story brick house, and Ninian tells me he is unimpeachably solvent."

"Solvent? Is that now enough to recommend a man? Why not declare him bipedal? Air-breathing?"

"You're missing my point. He is intended as an insurance policy."

"In the event nobody else comes along. Thank you very much."

They were silent for a time.

"Perhaps," said Mary, "you might tell me where Mr. Webb resides. When he's not legislating."

"In Carmi."

"Where on earth is that?"

"South," said Elizabeth, waving her hand vaguely at the parlor window.

"How far?"

"A few days by stage. You'd be much closer to Father."

Mary cast her eyes down at the mess of blue yarn in her lap. It had started out as a mitten but seemed to be venturing toward mantua.

"Carmi," she muttered.

"They say it's famous for its hospitality."

"If by hospitality you mean whiskey, I've no doubt. A girl need never fear coming down with the *ague* in Carmi."

They were silent again.

"I don't suppose it matters," said Mary, "that Mr. Webb is twenty years my senior."

"Fifteen," said Elizabeth softly.

"And has two children."

"I am told they have a sweet character."

"Yes. The sweetest little objections you'd ever hope to find."

The subject remained closed for the rest of the night. Which meant only that Elizabeth had been driven underground. The very next evening, Mary was invited to dinner at the Jayneses and was unsurprised to find Mr. Webb, in a rather dandyish striped waistcoat, waiting in the drawing room. At the sight of her, he leaped to his feet and began scratching his scalp.

"Miss Todd! Aren't you a sight for sore eyes?"

"You are quite a sight yourself."

From across the room, Elizabeth stared daggers.

"Please," said Mr. Webb, drawing out an armchair. "Won't you sit down?"

At dinner, they were seated next to each other, but as luck would have it, the conversation was animated and general enough to deter side conferences. Railroads and tunnels. General Adams and Dr. Henry. The minutes fairly winged past, and all she had to do, really, was fix her gaze on whoever was speaking at any given moment to forget the entire reason she was there. It wasn't until dessert arrived that Mr. Webb leaned into her and murmured: "I see you follow the political circus."

"A family obsession."

"But how rare to see such a discriminating intelligence wrapped in a—a package so . . ." He faltered. "Such lovely hands you have."

"Thank you."

"Lucky the gentleman who gets to hold them."

"Well," she said, "perhaps, upon my death, I shall have them severed and bequeathed to you."

It was out of her mouth before she could call it back. His response was a laugh so piercing that every head swung around.

"Pardon me," he said. "Miss Todd has struck straight to the funny bone."

Then he laughed again, his jaws flapping open to reveal a great expanse of gray tooth and pink uvula and, beyond it, only blackness. And from the blackness, the sound of flapping. A bearing down of wings.

"Did you hear that?" she cried.

"Hear what, Miss Todd? Are you quite well?"

THREE

No QUANTITY OF merino could have prepared her for a Springfield winter.

She'd wake up of a morning, thinking she was in the heart of May: the sky clear, the streets dry and hard trodden, sunlight pouring through every door and window. Then, a few minutes before eleven, the mercury would dive for the cellar, and an armada of frost would come sailing in from the south, and merino was nothing.

In late January, there came a long stretch of mild weather, beguiling enough to make her think spring had muscled its way to the fore. Following hard on, a perfect torrent of snow. Between supper and dinner, a good foot and a half of it, piling along the streets in thick dull ramparts. Elizabeth dragged all the quilts from her trousseau, the servants kept the fires blazing in every room, and still the windows sheathed over with ice, and still the cups froze to the saucers. A roast chicken sprouted a layer of frost as it sat at the breakfast table.

The horses stayed in their stables, wreathed in blankets. Steamships ceased to travel on the upper Mississippi and—an occasion of equal significance—Ninian and Elizabeth ceased to entertain. What was the point when no one would venture abroad? Mary did as much needlepoint as she could, perused the local papers, read great quantities of nonsense verse to her niece and nephew (when she could keep them still), and when all that began to pall, she set herself the project of translating the latest Balzac. Line by line, she plied herself, imagining the day when she would fling the completed pages at the author and cry: *"Voyez! J'étais fidèle!"*

But no matter how many projects she took up, the gloom crowded round. Night flowed indistinguishably into day, sounds echoed queerly down every hallway. Even the tolling of the clocks took on a strange asymmetry. De-*don*. De-*don*. She was saved from madness by her uncle, who drove up the hill one afternoon in a horse-drawn sleigh. "Who's for an adventure?" he called.

Mary ran next door to summon Mercy. The two women climbed into the sleigh, wrapped themselves in buffalo robes, and they were off.

The way was hard through the city, but once they had climbed out of the valley, the horse took new heart, and the grass that would have slowed their passage in warmer times lay hard packed now under a bed of snow, which eased the runners over every slough. Everywhere she looked, Mary saw boundlessness.

"Lovely," she murmured.

Half a league outside Springfield, Uncle John drew the sleigh to a halt and pointed toward a nearby walnut tree, where a strange, gray figure stood shimmering in the dusk. Like a charcoal drawing, she thought, bleeding off the page. In fact, it was a doe, trapped in the snow and ice. Straining every limb to be free and only imprisoning itself more thoroughly. It was so mesmeric a spectacle that Mary never saw her uncle reach for his rifle. Not until the stock was pressed to his cheek and his finger poised on the trigger did her hand, without any command from her, grab for the gun. The barrel jerked straight toward the sky, and the ball went roaring into the snowy wastes.

"Have you taken leave of your senses?" Her uncle turned on her. "Do you want to get yourself killed?"

"But you can't," she whispered.

"And if I don't, she'll starve to death! Is that what you want?"

Mary's face must have composed some reply, for with a clench of fury, he flung down his rifle.

"That's what I get. Bringing along a pair of girls."

They were quiet, the three of them, all the way back to town, although it seemed to Mary that, even from a great remove, she could still hear the thrashes of that trapped animal. *Dying*, in increments of terror. She pressed her gloved hands to her face as the cold began to coil round her. She should never have come to Springfield.

Fifty yards shy of Quality Hill, the sleigh caught in a culvert and took a sudden lurch to the right. The horse staggered, briefly lost its footing, and for a second, the conveyance threatened to tip over altogether. Mary's hands groped for Mercy's, and together, they sat teetering on some unseen fulcrum.

At last the carriage resolved into stillness. For some seconds the three of them sat there, collecting their wits. Everything around them was the soul of silence—until, from behind, came the sound of feet crunching in the snow, gradually accelerating in the manner of a predator converging on prey.

"May I be of help?"

A gentleman's voice, robed in Kentucky vowels. Uncle John whipped his head round and squinted into the dusk.

"Why," he declared, "it's Mr. Speed! Aren't you an angel of mercy?"

"No such thing," answered the stranger, drawing up alongside them. "Just a pair of hands, ready to work."

From her tottering vantage, Mary could see no hands, only a bundle of scarves and a top hat. Whatever face was concealed therein was already inclining toward her uncle.

"This *is* a bit of a pickle," said the stranger. "We must get the ladies out, but we mustn't risk tipping the sleigh over."

After some consultation, it was decided that Mr. Speed would attempt to hold the sleigh in place while Dr. Todd, with great care, extricated himself. The resulting shift in weight sent a rather terrifying tremor through the springs, but the runners held firm, and the two men, digging in their heels as best they could, contrived to drag the sleigh, inch by inch, to level ground. From there it was short work to extricate the women. Mercy, being nearest to the street, was the first to come out. It was Mary who, being second, hesitated.

"Up we go," said Mr. Speed, extending his arms toward her.

Down he meant, surely. But, in that first instant she *did* rise—in an utterly pure way, the weight of her own body left far behind and the stars rushing toward her. A second later, she was back on Earth, and Mr. Speed was saying what a near thing it was. Later, much later, she would be able to break down his face to its component parts. The chin, etched to a taper. The nose, sensitive and rather agreeably long. The mouth, generous. Eyes of the most candid and guileless blue. But in that first encounter, she could reliably speak only to the corporate effect. It was simply the most pleasant face she had ever seen.

Even as her mind voiced the word, she winced at its mildness. How could *pleasant* begin to describe a face of such patent and palpable affability? A face that bent its every last ray on you. *Shone* on you, yes. With a start, she realized that she had been gazing at him rather longer than was strictly necessary. "I do thank you, sir," she murmured. "We were most fortunate to—although I don't suppose we were in any great—"

But he was already looking past her. "Here now, Dr. Todd! Your sleigh is in a bad way, and these womenfolk look chilled to the bone. Mightn't we convey them home?"

"By great and good fortune, they live just up the hill."

Mr. Speed followed the trajectory of Uncle John's figure to the Edwards manse, then turned his head slowly back round.

"Why, you're Miss Todd."

In that moment, it was if that doe had never been trapped, as if Death had never breathed on them.

"May I?" said Mr. Speed, holding out his arm.

Uncle John offered his arm to Mercy, and the four of them picked their way up the hill. Their progress was slow for the snow had been crusted over with a new coat of rime. Once, just once, Mary slipped—and was astonished to find Mr. Speed's arm already reaching around to secure her, so nonchalantly that he seemed scarcely to notice it had happened.

"My, but there are a lot of you," he said.

"A lot of . . ."

"*Todds*, I mean. A friend of mine says you can't swing a dead cat without hitting one."

"How colorfully your friend expresses himself."

"It's true," answered Mr. Speed with a laugh. "He knows his way round the vernacular. But I fear, at this rate of influx, we shall have to change the town's name ere long. *Todd*field, perhaps."

"I'm not sure that has quite the ring."

"What of Todd*ville*, then? Todd*opolis*?"

"I'm more inclined to Toddington."

"Great Toddington. . . ."

"*Hot* Toddington!" she cried, and heard the peal of her laughter ringing off the house fronts.

"That has charm," Mr. Speed conceded. "But it doesn't do justice to our winters."

She pulled her buffalo robe closely around her. "Perhaps some hot springs will be discovered before too long."

Then she blushed, for it seemed she had overstepped in some way. Yet he was no more or less agreeable at the top of the hill than he'd been at the bottom.

"Good night," he said, folding her one hand between his two. "I'm so glad I could be of service."

Later that night, she was drying her gloves on the parlor fender when Elizabeth wandered in. Hoping, from the looks of her, to find the room empty. She had just finished nursing, and the faint aroma of milk clung to her as she eased herself onto the parlor chair and closed her eyes. Once, just once, Mary had found their mother in the same attitude. Asleep in the front hall, her head lolling, feet splayed in the least ladylike of fashions. Baby George clamped to her breast like some monstrous succubus. . . .

Unexpectedly now, Elizabeth spoke. In a sleep-glazed voice.

"What have I done," she said, "to be cursed with Irish servant girls?"

"You have crossed the Ohio River," said Mary. "If you had wanted the likes of Nelson and Sally, you should have stayed in Kentucky."

In fact, Elizabeth, upon her marriage, had brought two family slaves with her, although she declined to call them that except on census forms, where, together, they counted as six-fifths of a person.

"Dear Mary," she said, "I believe I hear a note of reproach in your voice."

"Hear what you like."

"I suppose you'll do quite without Negroes when you are mistress of your own house."

"That is the plan."

"Irish girls, too."

"That is also the plan."

"Well, good luck to you, then."

Things might have escalated into quarrel, but Elizabeth was too tired. Instead, she gave the bridge of her nose a rub and pried her eyes open.

"I hear you had quite the excitement this evening."

"I don't know about that. We did encounter a Mr. Speed."

"Ah." Her sister's brows made the tiniest of ascensions.

"And how am I to interpret that? Is there something you wish to tell me?"

"What do you wish to know?"

"Whatever you think useful."

"Well then." Elizabeth kneaded her neck. "He is well named."

"How so?"

"He *speeds* from girl to girl. Without ever entangling himself."

"So his heart barely quickens."

"Something like that."

Mary stood for a time, listening to the hiss of the oak logs.

"He is twenty-two?" she guessed.

"Add four, and you're closer to the sum."

"Not another widower?"

Elizabeth gave a soft smile. Not quite readable. Then shook her head.

"What about family?"

"Kentucky gentry."

"Occupation?"

"He keeps a shop."

"Keeps or owns?"

"Owns. With the help of a cousin."

"Christian name?"

"Joshua."

Mary watched as one of the logs split open and sent up a geyser of sparks.

"Can it be?" said Elizabeth. "You mean to set your cap for a merchant?"

"Father's a merchant."

"As a means to an end, yes."

"Then grant me the means, and I will figure out the end." She could feel the color rising up her neck. "And what do I *care* if he's a storekeeper? Or the King of Prussia? He need only be . . ."

She was on the verge of saying *good*, but she knew Elizabeth would sally right back with *Good for what?*

That night, long after everyone else was slumbering, she was emphatically awake, turning back and forth under her eiderdown, trying to decode that moment in the street when Joshua Speed had . . . Well, there was the trouble.

What had he done? She could remember every gesture, summon back all the words down to their very inflections, and yet she had no thread to bind them together. The only thing she could attest to was the pleasure she took in watching him—or, more precisely, watching him watch her. The soft electric thrill of being claimed. *You're Miss Todd.*

FOUR

—

THE NEXT SUNDAY, as she was leaving First Presbyterian, she saw him strolling down the opposite side of Fourth Street with a decidedly unreligious air. Walking alongside him: none other than Edwin Webb, whose face broke out in a satyr's grin at the sight of her. Joshua Speed's features, by contrast, betrayed neither delight nor dismay, although he was courtly enough to wait until she had nodded before nodding back.

Oh, she thought, *a cool one.*

The next sighting was of a different character. Out of sheer boredom, she and Mercy had attended a performance of the Springfield Thespian Society—a temperance melodrama called *Fifteen Years of a Drunkard's Life*. The theme of the evening must have stayed with her, for as she came out of the American House and saw Mr. Speed striding past, he looked to have the deep self-engrossment of the very drunk. Only his path was straight and his gait steady. Did he simply have something on his mind? As she watched him enlarge the distance between them, it occurred to her to call out, but Mercy gave her an admonitory squeeze on the wrist.

By late February, the weather had broken enough that she could walk through town again. "Come," she told Mercy. "I know just the place."

Through discreet inquiries, she had learned that Mr. Speed's establishment was located at the corner of Washington and Fifth. Their first disappointment upon arriving was this: The place was called Bell & Company. Mr. Speed's name, for reasons uncertain, was nowhere in evidence. A greater disappointment: It was not even a shop at all but a dry-goods store, large and boxy and plebeian, with just the faintest note of aspiration in its gilt lettering. A quick window canvass revealed only tiresome plenitudes: hardware and books, medicines and mattresses, all tagged and organized by some unfussy hand. Mary's instinct was to turn right back round, but Mercy was already whispering in her ear.

"Let's go in."

"And what?" retorted Mary. "Ask for French chalk? The latest Thackeray?"

"For all you know, he has them."

"I couldn't possibly behave in such a desperate manner."

Still they loitered. In the hopes that Mr. Speed might—what? . . . Spy them from the vantage point of his counter and come running? Offer them a *discount*? For some minutes, they lingered, of two and possibly three minds, until it dawned on them that they were becoming objects of curiosity.

"Dear God," said Mercy, clapping a hand over her mouth. "They think we're plying our trade."

With a shriek, they gathered up their skirts and sped home—laughing so gaily that the incident seemed already to be passing into lore. One day, thought Mary, she would be able to tell Mr. Speed just how close she had come to compromising herself on his behalf. He would chuckle, surely, to hear it. But when she thought back to that solitary figure hustling past the American House, laughter seemed to be the last thing on its mind.

IN MARCH, ELIZABETH and Ninian announced plans for a spring-solstice ball. Over the next two days, the Brussels carpets were beaten senseless and every tallow candle switched out for sperm oil. It took nearly as long to decide whom to invite. In the end, the guest list was a useful map of the Edwardses' ambitions, embracing as it did both Whig and Democrat, banker and judge, farmer and speculator. At some risk, the editors of both local newspapers were invited, with the injunction that they were to stay twenty feet apart.

Frances Todd Wallace was so eager to show off her new gown (though both her sisters understood that it was simply a new bodice laid over last spring's skirt) that, after some discussion, it was agreed that Frances's husband might come, too (for all that he'd been recently dismissed by the Mercantile Company). Much to Mary's surprise, even the Gone-Case had vowed to come. "Now you mustn't expect too much," Mercy cautioned. "He's just a little above the common grade." In fact, Mr. Conkling (for that was his name) was several notches beyond agreeable—and a far more useful fount of information than Elizabeth, who considered it vulgar to gossip about guests until after they had left. "It's not proper *ton*," she liked to say. (And if ever there was a word that defined Elizabeth, it was *ton*.)

Mr. Conkling had no such compunctions. "That one there? James Forquer. His father was the first man to put a lightning rod on his house. Funny story for another occasion. Oh, and *that* depressed specimen is the architect of the new capitol. Rumor says he'll be thrown out within the month. I mean to say, the thing won't get finished! That thin-blooded specimen over there by the sconces? Patrick Henry's grandson. Traveled here from St. Louis."

"Give me liberty of *him*," said Mary. "He looks icy to the bone."

"He may warm up at the sight of you," said Mercy. "Or else your dress."

The gown, it was true, was fresh from Canal Street in New Orleans. Watered silk with embroidered strawberries and a lace flounce collar. Mary had pinched her cheeks into ruddiness, brightened her eyes with drops of lemon juice, and threaded a spray of silk roses so tightly through her hair that she felt like an arbor. No guest was more transported than Mr. Webb, who arrived in mud-caked boots, the consequence of a balky horse, and left a trail across Elizabeth's marble.

"You are a vision, Miss Todd! Imagine my happiness at learning I am written down for your maiden dance."

Swallowing down her alarm, she snatched up her dance program. *Edwin Webb*. In a hand not her own.

"So you are," she said.

There was this further surprise in store: The Fallback was good on his feet. Treating three-quarter time with the same nonchalance as four-quarter, he glided her in and out of the orbiting couples without collision—a success that only emboldened him toward further conversation.

"What are your thoughts on the coming election, Miss Todd?"

"My *thoughts*? Surely, that depends upon what you are asking. If you mean will General Harrison unseat Mr. Van Buren, then I offer you a provisional yes."

"I am glad to—"

"If you are asking *how* he will do it, I will also tell you. He must nullify the chief argument against him."

"The chief—"

"I advert, of course, to his *age*. The general has passed sixty-seven winters on God's earth. That is too many."

"But he—"

"—is a man of great virility, yes. The key, however, is to force the issue *back* on Van Buren. Younger in years he may be, but he has been exhausted, *enfeebled*, by the labor of propping up a corrupt regime. His ideas, his aspirations, his vision—everything about him reeks of age."

"To be sure, that is—"

"Surely, you have heard the slogan making the rounds. 'Van, Van, Van's a used-up man.' I assure you, if you hired choirs to chant that litany at every Democratic rally in the land—everywhere Mr. Van Buren so much as peeps his head—it will stick to him like a limpet. President Jackson has many ills to answer for, but if he taught us nothing else, indisputably it was the importance of political theater. That is the route to the heart, Mr. Webb, and the *heart* is the organ that drives the common man to the polls, not the brain."

Mr. Webb was blinking rapidly.

"I beg your pardon," she said. "I have a habit of keeping *up*."

Elizabeth's usual practice was to invite a surplus of guests on the assumption that some would beg off, but tonight close to a hundred citizens thronged into the parlor, the library, the living room, the halls. Some of them even spilled upstairs into Ninian's bedroom, where the bed had been dismantled for just this purpose. In short order, the house began to swelter, and the stores of hard cider purchased in honor of General Harrison were drained dry. Unsuspecting dancers came staggering off the floor to find only scattered bowls of grog and ginger beer. Men clawed at their collars and, in every room, women could be seen covertly dabbing each other with talc. More than one guest was heard to pine for the lately departed winter. Mary, for her part, longed only for *air*—with an intensity that was, under the circumstances, nearly erotic.

"Come!" she cried, grabbing Mercy by the hand. "Keep me company."

The fullness of their skirts prevented them from walking abreast, but they held hands for dear life and made a thousand apologies to the guests they were inconveniencing and so found their way to the kitchen, where the Edwardses' cook was even now boiling wine sauce for the carrot pudding. The heat was even more intolerable here, so the two women skipped out to the back veranda and closed the door after them. For some time they stood, feeling the flesh goose up on their necks. The only signs of life were the nightjars, flapping their wings and chirring like locusts. The stars still had the jeweled hardness of January.

"Do I look a terror?" she asked Mercy.

"No. Do I?"

"Of course not."

They were both lying. Mary could feel the wilt in her hair, the film of sweat along her neck and cheeks. The bone weariness.

"I know it sounds strange," she said, "but sometimes I feel as if we are soldiers."

"Because we wear armor?" Mercy sketched the pleats of her bodice.

"Because we seek to vanquish."

"Better than *being* vanquished, surely."

Mary gave a twitch of her shoulder. "That's just the trouble. Say we vanquish them—subdue them by degrees. What do we win? Our own surrender."

"Why, Miss Todd, you are being quite the rain cloud."

But it was only her rebel contingent, she wanted to say, rising up once more. Making her question the underlying logic of things. Wasn't it entirely possible that the finest qualities in any man would never be discernible to her but would be merely immanent—*germs*, waiting to be coaxed into seed, thence into flower? And that being the case, how to know they were there? Had every man to be taken finally on faith? Was there a faith so capacious?

On impulse, she teased one of the flowers from her hair and proffered it to her friend, bowing as low as she dared.

"Wilt thou marry me?"

In repose, Mercy's features were no more than regular, but laughter had a charming way of disrupting them. Her nostrils flared, her teeth blazed, her irises flashed, and you wished her to keep laughing forever.

"Give the Gone-Case a few months," she said. "And try me again."

THEY HAD A notion of running upstairs to Mary's bedroom and mending themselves before the looking glass. But the back stairs were blocked by kegs, and Mercy was anxious about leaving Mr. Conkling alone for too long, and so they were just inching back into the main hall when a gentleman guest, leaning indolently against the wall, chose that moment to swivel round.

"Why, there you are," he said.

Joshua Speed's coat fit him as lightly as feathers. His boots looked as if they had been blacked at the door. But what struck Mary most forcibly was his hair, which had lain hidden from view during their last encounter and which now rippled in chestnut waves down to his collar. A prodigal mane that had the effect of both lengthening and poeticizing his face. Yes, she thought, this must have been how Lord Byron looked, training his gaze upon some Alpine lass.

"Good evening," she remembered to say. She slid a damp tendril off her face and glanced into the empty space where Mercy had just stood.

"I fear I've come too late to make it onto your program," he said.

"Oh." She stared at the tiny book still dangling from her wrist. "I believe I have a waltz open. . . ."

"Then," he said, "the night is not lost." He bent over the program, wrote out his name in a light, casual hand. "How those flowers become you."

"I regret to inform you they are silk. Give me a few more weeks, and I shall have real ones to conjure with."

"I hope you will set one aside for me, then."

She smiled and shifted her eyes just to the west of him. An attitude of maidenly abstraction, refined over some years, that had the usual effect of calling out another compliment, more lavish than the previous. In this case, Mr. Speed said only: "There's someone you should meet."

He swung his head around in an arc of expectation—only no one was there. With no great delicacy, he leaned in the direction of the foyer and beckoned with his arm. Against all expectations, a figure came lumbering toward them.

Her first impressions arrived singly, refusing to be reconciled. An El Greco frame, stretched beyond sufferance. A mournful well of eye. A face of *bones*, all badgering to break through.

From here, all was confusion. Mr. Speed, who gave every sign of wanting to remain, was being called away, and Mary was reaching out a hand to stay him, and at the same time, this *other* man's hand—massive and elemental—was extending toward her, and it was *this* hand in which her hand now unaccountably rested, like a starfish on a boulder, and Mr. Speed was already slipping from view, and Mr. Speed's friend, scarcely audible, was saying something to her. He was saying . . .

"I know who you are."

But the effect of being recognized was not so tonic as it had been with Mr. Speed. Now it only discomposed her.

"You must forgive me," she said. "I failed to catch your name."

"Lincoln."

"Ah."

Her brain went scrambling; her smile, by way of compensation, stood still.

"I believe you are known to me as *well*. By repute. . . ."

Think.

"I mean my *cousin* has spoken of you. John Stuart, yes?"

He nodded, with such an emphatic motion that his chin came nearly to his chest.

"You . . ." She ventured an inch further on the limb. "If I'm not mistaken, you are partners, are you not? In Cousin John's law practice. . . ."

"Guilty." He was silent for a time, then roused himself enough to add, "I'm glad you mention Congressman Stuart. I owe him a great deal."

"Well, he—speaks very highly of you, Mr. Lincoln." Was that true? "He tells me . . ." What? "He says you are quite the *force*. In the courtroom, I think."

"Oh. Well." He gave the punch bowl a stare. "I don't have a great deal of book learning, so I expect I'm able to speak to juries at their own level."

"Ah."

The silence came rolling back. Sulfurous.

"But of course," she rallied, "my cousin is a fine judge of *character*, so it may be that you . . . you under*value* yourself. . . ."

Perhaps Cousin John had actually said that.

"Isn't it funny?" she said, galloping ahead. "We have never met before and yet you—you surely live here in Springfield."

"That is so."

"And I have been in your charming city since only—"

"Last fall," he said.

"Well, yes."

He studied the flounce of her dress. "The thing is, Miss Todd, I'm on the circuits quite a bit."

"Oh, yes. Like Mr. Conkling."

"And then, you know, I've got that pesky body politic's interests to attend to."

It was such an oblique way to come at the subject that she was a long time following him there.

"Of course," she said, with something like release. "You are one of Ninian's comrades in arms. In the statehouse."

"Guilty again."

"I believe, in fact, you are a member of the Long Nine."

The first stirrings of a smile on his face. "The *longest* of the nine."

"So I see," she answered, in a lighter voice. "It seems that, whenever I pass our new capitol, I shall have you to thank for bringing it here."

His head tipped toward his shoulder, and the words came scattering out like loose pennies.

"I'm sorry?" she said.

"I said it was a whole *team* of oxen. Dragging that particular plow."

"Ah, well. Let us hope we can"—she plucked softly at her throat—"devise a better metaphor for you, Mr. Lincoln, than oxen."

"I think the plainer you come at me, the better."

Silence once more. A great cloud of it, leaching out their last native spark. He had just enough volition left to mutter the words "very pleased to" . . . but not enough to finish them. With a bow, he angled his body away and then left the room, maneuvering around each guest in the manner of a barge navigating sandbars.

Elizabeth sidled up a minute later, her arm softly hooking through her sister's.

"I despair of you," she whispered. "You turn up your nose at a Webb and take up with a Lincoln."

"Take *up*? Heaven shield me, I was making conversation. Under great duress, I might add."

"I have told you before that, if you don't wish a man to be your suitor, you must confine yourself to the fewest possible words."

"And so I did."

"Let us hope so."

With a single motion, Elizabeth unhooked her arm and tacked straight for the foyer. Leaving behind a trail of some mystery. Why was she being so preemptive? Had Mary missed, perhaps, some essential fact about the stranger? A foundational bit of gossip? Were the hens of Springfield even now clucking in timbres outside her range of hearing?

For the next two hours, she alternated between dancing and eyeing the periphery, waiting for the Longest of the Nine to rise up once more, but he never reemerged. Impossible, surely, that he should be able to conceal himself. More likely that he had hied himself home. Wherever that was.

Mr. Speed showed up promptly for his dance at seven minutes to ten. There was a touch of self-mockery, she thought, in the way he bowed his head and led her to the floor. She had deliberately left open the waltz to see how he would respond to close quarters. But if his hands were longing to tighten their grip on hers or curl more tightly around her waist or draw her closer with each measure, they held off. The only suggestion of pleasure she could find was in his eyes, which were as agreeable as at the moment of their meeting.

"What did you think of Lincoln?" he asked.

She pondered for three turns before answering.

"I can only hope that, his waters being so very still, they also run deep."

She could not tell if she had erred, for Mr. Speed said nothing.

"How is it that you are acquainted?" she pressed.

"He sleeps in the room over my store."

"Does he? And is that fit lodging for a state legislator?"

"I keep a clean inn."

Again, that light note of self-deprecation, not at all unattractive.

"It does sound like a peculiar arrangement," she allowed. "But I suppose you should be grateful for having such a quiet tenant."

"You haven't heard him snore."

Then, quite unexpectedly, Mr. Speed laughed. Not a giggle, not a guffaw, not a snort. A perfectly polished and calibrated sound that extended so far and no further and left them just four measures short of the waltz's end. When at last the strings died out, he asked her if she would take refreshment, and when she declined, he conducted her back to her seat and said, "Thank you, Miss Todd, for this great honor." She bowed in reply and was about to turn away when he added: "If it's agreeable, might we pay you a call?"

MARY HAD ASKED Mercy to spend the night, the better to run through the evening's events. So it was that, as the midnight bells struck, the two young women were in upstairs seclusion, unlacing each other from their corsets.

"I don't understand," said Mercy. "You said Mr. Speed was the most elegant dancer out there."

"So he was."

"And perfectly congenial."

"In the manner of a nephew with his doddering aunt, yes."

"Well, that's not so bad for a first dance. You wouldn't have wanted him to be forward, would you?"

"I should have liked to see him manfully suppressing the temptation. God knows Mr. Webb did."

"But what was the last thing he said to you?"

"He asked if he might pay a call."

If *we* might. . . .

"Well," said Mercy. "That's not nothing."

"It is perilously close."

Mary was silent for a time, undoing the outer petticoat, then the middle, then the inner. A mound of corded cotton and horsehair billowed around her.

"What do you know of Mr. Lincoln?" she asked.

"Only what I hear from the Gone-Case. Great native ability but *rough* around the edges. Rough *beyond* the edges. The lawyers of Springfield have given him an Indian name."

"Which is?"

"Raised by Wolves."

Mary smiled, peeled off a stocking.

"Were they *Illinois* wolves or . . ."

"Kentucky, originally."

"Which part?"

"Not any part you've ever traveled, I promise." Mercy gave her bare toes a luxuriant rub. "I will say this. He gets less ugly with time. But Mr. Conkling says there's not a dime there."

"It's of no concern to me if he has a penny. He him*self* is of no concern."

"No?" Mercy unbunched the chemise from around her waist, lazily drew it over her head. "Are you telling me, then, that you *don't* have Mr. Speed on the brain?"

"What if I do?"

"Then you might consider making an ally of Mr. Lincoln."

"Because he is Mr. Speed's tenant?"

"Nearer than that. Where one goes, the other is bound to follow. It might take a woman just to pry them apart."

FIVE

To a Springfield newcomer, the first few weeks of spring were the cruelest of feints, for at no time of year were the streets so impassable. Frost bled out of the ground, and the valley's snowmelt washed down in gullies and ruts, swelling the town branch past its bounds. For whole days, the city lay under a lake of opaque water, acrid with pig waste, circled by grackles and nuthatches. Only a long stretch of dry weather could make the water subside, and it invariably left behind a choking cloak of mud, deep enough, it was said, to swallow a horse and its rider. This was mud such as Mary had never seen: black and thick with a *permanent* cast, eradicable only through the combined efforts of sun and shovels. Until then, it was impossible for the ladies of Springfield to venture safely out of doors, at least not in the satin slippers that fashion dictated.

The resulting confinement was especially hard on someone of Mary's roving disposition. All about her, nature was shaking off its torpor. Rosebuds and dogwoods were coming to flower. Frogs were tuning in an evening choir. From her bedroom window, she could see buttercups and bedstraw and dogtooth violets. The sky deepening with each passing day, the sun dangling that much closer to Earth.

Oh, she might, if she liked, open her windows as far as they would go. Lean out as far as she dared. Even make an occasional foray to the base of

Quality Hill, right to the point where the mire took, and stand there waiting, her fancy conjuring the most banal of rescuers. (A barge. An ark. Mr. Speed, why not? On a white palfrey.) But the rest of the town remained as closed to her as if it lay under quarantine.

With each successive day, her mood blackened. She grew negligent with her toilet, left her hair papers in, stayed in morning dress well into the afternoon, declined to show for meals. She ignored Elizabeth's children, gave not a second glance to the newspapers, and once, in a particularly aggravated pique, tossed her Balzac translation into the fire. Which would break first, Mary wondered. the weather or her mind? Then, one Monday morning, over breakfast, she heard Elizabeth complaining about a day laborer who had disappeared on an extended bacchanal and left behind a pile of unused wooden shingles.

"*Still* there," her sister added. "Rotting away by the privy. No use to anyone."

Just like me, thought Mary, silently counting the cracks in the ceiling joist. In the next second, a spark was tossed into the darkness. Ten minutes later, she was knocking on the Leverings' door.

"Mercy!" she cried. "We are going to town."

"You're mad."

"My dear, I have calculated. It is but nine blocks to the courthouse square."

"It might as well be nine miles. The mud is too thick."

But Mary's scheme was both simple and, to her own mind, ingenious. They would gather up enough shingles to create a chain of stepping-stones that would carry them all the way to town and back, utterly dry and intact.

"What?" cried Mercy. "You mean leap from one lily pad to the next?"

"When necessary. Is it not better than being shut in all day?"

"You will have to go it alone, dear one."

But decorum would not allow for a solo expedition, and the prospect of being confined a second longer was more than Mary could bear. She pleaded. She railed. Yet, in the end, she could find no better epithet to fling at her friend than . . .

"Stick in the mud!"

The pun, unintended, caught them both in the midsection. By the time she had finished laughing, Mercy was enlisted.

With no small trepidation, they traveled down to the brink of Second Street. From there, they each flung down a shingle, hoisted up all three layers of petticoat, and leaped.

The shingles held.

"Again!" said Mary.

And so they went, hopping down the road, laughing like crickets. Now and again, one of them might briefly totter, and the other might put out an arresting hand, but they honed their technique as they went and grew in confidence. Indeed, so intent were they on their progress, and so completely was the view obscured by their bonnets, that they scarcely registered the eyes that were even now turning on them. Farmers, mostly, hauling their potatoes and beets, pausing in the midst of cracking their whips to gaze upon these leaping lady-birds, with their snow-white feathers.

"Go it, gals!" somebody shouted, but Mary and Mercy never heard—any more than they noticed the clouds massing over their heads. The first drops began to land just as they reached Sixth and Monroe. Shivering, they darted for the first cover they could find: a niche carved out by the courthouse's hip roof. With dismal hearts, they watched the rain slice down and the streets disappear once more in an unquiet black broth. Half an hour later, each one of their shingles lay submerged.

"I told you this was madness," said Mercy.

"Nothing of the sort," declared Mary. "We want only a conveyance."

The rain by now had dwindled to a mist, but the streets remained stubbornly empty, save for a pair of querulous hogs, sunk to their knees, and a single goose, flitting from post to post. Too proud to relent, Mary kept her face turned to the square and was rewarded, after a space of ten minutes, with the sight of a horse-drawn dray, slogging through the trackless wastes.

"You there!" she called.

Startled, the driver drew up the reins. "What on airth," he muttered.

"Good sir, it seems you are heaven-sent!"

His face clouded, and in a mournful voice, he replied: "Wasn't heaven sent me. And there's hell to pay if I don't deliver on time."

"Such native *wit*," she cooed. "Kind sir, tell us your name."

"Hart. Ellis Hart."

"Mr. *Hart*. Would you be so good as to bring your cart round?"

"For what reason?"

"Why, to ferry us home. We are two lost lambs, you see!" Finding no change in his expression, she added, "There's a quarter in it for you. A half dollar."

"But. . . ." His face seemed to fold in on itself. "There's nowhere up here for you to sot."

"In the *aft* section, perhaps."

Dazedly, he swung his head around. "Oh, no, miss, it's powerful dirty back there. Straw and stone dust and the whatnot."

"Yet it is dry, I am sure! Thanks to your ingenious tarpaulin."

He took off his hat. Gave his forelock a hard twirl. In a voice that tasted already of defeat, he said: "I ain't never carried a lady before."

"Then there is no time like the present!" Ablaze now with triumph, Mary reached for her friend's hand. "Come, dearest."

"I won't," hissed Mercy.

"There's no other course."

"We shall be a public spectacle."

"I sincerely hope so."

But her friend's Baltimore-gentry roots had dug too deep. With a narrowed eye, Mary turned on her heel and, in a tone of mock aggravation, called: "Here now, Mr. Hart! We don't have all day."

Sulking the whole way, he brought the dray round. Even unhooked the iron pin that fastened the dray to the harness so that she could walk straight up. Once ensconced, she gathered her skirts about her and gave her friend—faithless friend!—a wave.

"Goodbye, my dear! I shall send a carriage for you."

As the dray lurched forward, Mary cast her eyes upward, expecting—longing, even—to see windows flung open in every house and establishment. But the upper realm of Springfield was as impassive as ever. Search as she might, she could find only an orange tabby, lounging on a flower box and indolently swishing its tail. She was about to turn away altogether when she caught the faintest glint of something in the second-floor window of the courthouse.

A man—coatless, hatless—his face shaded from view. She wouldn't have granted him another second of attention had it not been for the way he seemed to tower within the window frame, to *subdue* it. He drew closer to the glass, and his identity was borne home.

Mr. Lincoln.

Exactly where one might have expected to find him: in the law offices he shared with her cousin John. At the sight of him, though, all gaiety vanished, and propriety crowded round. How to explain it? Looking at her from such a height, he seemed to epitomize Judgment itself, preparing to rain down upon her. Already, she was repenting her rashness. Already, she was wishing she had stayed behind with Mercy.

But then something surprising happened. Lincoln, in one crisp motion, raised his hand to his brow and snapped off a military salute. And with that single act, he managed to transform her rashness into heroism, and she no longer feared judgment or ridicule or anything the world had to toss her way. She was free now to *laugh*—so richly and boisterously that the sound became its own engine, guiding the cart home.

THAT FRIDAY, ELIZABETH came down to dinner with a copy of the *Sangamo Journal*. "Shall I read you something?" she said.

No mistaking the ominousness of her tone. Mary set down her fork.

"I know," she said. "I have seen it."

"But it is *poetry*. It must be read aloud."

"Then by all means," she muttered.

"Ahem. . . ."

> As I walked out on Monday last
> A wet and muddy day
> Twas there I saw a pretty lass
> A riding on a dray, a riding on a dray.

The doggerel went on for five verses, the lass never named but her identity unmistakable from the moment she climbed into the wagon to the moment the driver rolled her off like a load of turnips. Elizabeth made a special point of slowing for the final quatrain.

When safely landed on her feet
Said she what is to pay
Quoth Hart I cannot charge you aught
For riding on my dray.

"Well, *that* part is true," said Mary. "He wouldn't take a penny."

Elizabeth set the paper down. Folded it like a napkin. Folded it again. Then, with a slow intake of breath, she dipped a ladle into a tureen of oyster soup.

"I had no notion that you were such a local luminary. Even our sister Frances has heard tell of it, and she doesn't even subscribe."

"Does she disapprove? Do *you*?"

Elizabeth carried the ladle toward the bowl at her left hand. "I am only recalling our stepmother's advice on the subject of public scrutiny."

"You cite her as an authority?"

"The principle stands." She poured the soup in a slow, smooth cataract. "A lady is in the newspaper but three times in her life. When she is born—"

"When she marries and when she dies, yes. Much as I hate to disappoint the *both* of you, I intend to be in print dozens of times before I'm played out."

"Then," said Elizabeth, lifting the ladle, "do it in some other paper." She passed the bowl to Mary, poured another for herself. "Traipsing about in a stranger's cart. Ladies have lost their character for smaller indiscretions."

"I requested a ride, I did not flash my gaiters."

"It is this very tone that fills me with foreboding. I do not want you mistaken for a brazen woman."

"Then perhaps," said Mary, rising to it, "I should have pretended to faint. Had them carry me home on a litter. *Fluttering* my handkerchief the whole way. Honestly, sister, if I'd known you wanted a *mouse* for a tenant. . . ."

"I believe the word *tenant* implies compensation. Or, at the very least, gratitude."

The heat climbed straight up the back of Mary's neck. By the time she was master of herself, her voice had dropped nearly out of hearing range.

"You should never have encouraged me to come."

Something extraordinary then: Elizabeth rested her pale hand on Mary's wrist.

"I am only looking out for you because *she* can't."

At once, tears sprang to Mary's eyes, and she was obliged to turn away, for the years were burning off, and she was once again that six-year-old child, watching her mother's coffin lowered into the earth. Listening to those first clods of clay on the wooden lid and turning in wonder to her older sister. "But how shall she come back to us? If they put all that dirt on top?" Elizabeth folded her into an embrace and held her there, for some interval, before saying in the softest of voices: "She is an angel now. She will come *flying* back. Whenever we have most need of her."

How long had Mary been waiting for that prophesy to hold true?

The next morning, she forbore even to get out of bed and might have gone without bread and water had not Johanna, Elizabeth's Irish girl, come knocking sometime before three in the afternoon.

"Please, miss. There's a pair of gentlemen wishing to see you."

"Who?"

"I couldn't say."

"Where is my sister?"

"She's with them, isn't she? She says you're to come down at once."

Fifteen minutes later, still adjusting her shawl, Mary ventured into the drawing room. Two men rose to greet her. First, Mr. Speed. And then Mr. Lincoln, who, in these domestic confines, looked almost prohibitively large. Like a pine tree, she thought, preparing to burst through the ceiling.

"Why, there you are," called Elizabeth. "It seems two acolytes have come in search of their muse."

Smiling tightly, Mary lowered herself onto the couch next to her sister.

"It is true," said Mr. Speed. "Since Friday's article, Miss Todd is spoken of in every household."

"I've no doubt," said Elizabeth icily. "It was quite the *coup de théâtre*."

Mary folded her hands into a penitential attitude. "Gentlemen, you will allow me, I hope, to express my contrition. It appears my innate exuberance must have overwhelmed my better judgment."

"Nothing of the sort!" declared Mr. Speed. "Across town, we have heard nothing but huzzahs."

In the way he spoke of her, she at once discerned a new color. Formality had been replaced by something more genuine. He was interested.

"Why," he went on, "Miss Todd's spirit and pluck—her resourcefulness—they seem to many of us to exemplify the best qualities of the Modern Woman. Is that not so, Lincoln?"

The sound of his own name, far from freeing the other gentleman to speak, seemed to demoralize him beyond all telling. He pinioned his arms behind his back and knit his hands together as if he were trying to tie himself into a bow.

"We might still be in the shank of April," continued Mr. Speed, "but there is already talk among the citizenry of declaring Miss Todd our very own Queen of May."

"Queen of *Dray*. . . ."

The witticism emanated from somewhere in the vicinity of Mr. Lincoln, but the rest of Mr. Lincoln seemed already to be disavowing it.

"How *amusant*," said Elizabeth.

"Among other distinctions," Mr. Speed said, forging on, "Miss Todd should know that her heroics have prompted a robust discussion of internal improvements. As we all know, the state of Springfield's streets are a disgrace to the name of Capital City. . . ."

From there, he was off. And here a new talent revealed itself: the ability to discuss public affairs without ever being—exactly, precisely—dull. Indeed, as the minutes ticked past, the fluency of his speech began to exert a magnetic pulse quite apart from its content.

"Yes, ladies, I tell you it is time, it is long past time, to speak of *sidewalks*, of planking, underground drainage, water rediversion. Why, just the other night, Mr. Baker raised these very topics during his address to the Young Men's Lyceum."

She waited until she was sure he was done. Then, as lightly as she could: "May I ask, gentlemen, if there is a Young *Women's* Lyceum? Since our sex does not appear to play a part in your deliberations?"

"Oh, on that account," said Mr. Speed, "you must consider yourself blessed, for you would find the whole business dreadfully dull."

"But we already experience gentlemen's dullness in our drawing rooms. It is nothing less than our daily diet. Why should we not go abroad for more?"

"You were not to know, gentlemen," said Elizabeth, swiftly interposing, "that Mary has the most amazing constitution when it comes to political talk. I have seen her sit two, even *three* hours—without complaint, without redress—listening to some hapless candidate or other *drone* on."

"I can well believe it," said Mr. Speed.

"No matter how prolix or tedious, she swallows it *down*, as the baby robin its worm. How I wish I had her endurance! Last November, I remember, I had to sit in the courthouse square for some ungodly interval, listening to— oh, what was his subject?—the politics of our time, the condition of our country. . . ."

Tiny fissures appeared in the placid surface of Joshua Speed's face.

"Don't misunderstand," Elizabeth hurried on. "He was effective in his way, but he did ramble on, and his anecdotes were of the coarsest, most homespun variety. Fine for the rank and file but not for the cognoscenti. The minutes fairly crawled past."

"That was me," said Mr. Lincoln.

The only thing Mary could say afterward in her sister's defense was that, in the exact *moment*, Elizabeth's cheeks had colored. Either she had miscalculated or she had overstepped.

"Surely not," she murmured.

"It wasn't one of my best."

"Oh, no, Mr. Lincoln, I have done you a great dishonor. I have utterly confounded you with some vastly inferior orator who—when, of all *people*, Mr. Edwards tells me you are the soul of *eloquence* on the statehouse floor. . . ."

"Does Ninian say that?"

For the second time now, Mary caught the faintest note of mirth in his eyes. Perhaps it was to draw out that note that she leaned forward a fraction and curved her lips a quarter-inch north.

"You must tell me the next time you are to speak, Mr. Lincoln. I am a devotee of both the coarse *and* the homespun."

"You may depend on it, Miss Todd."

From there, the conversation straggled into pleasantries. But the words— prosaic, forgettable—were merely a kind of cape thrown over the rage of Elizabeth Edwards. To the untutored eye, her poise had not ebbed by one degree. It took a sister to see the squaring of the jaw, the rather too pronounced staring, the tiny pauses before speaking. At last, with a half-stifled yawn and a chagrined smile, she rose.

"I must beg your pardon, gentlemen, it is time to see to the children's supper. Of course, I implore you to *stay*, as I'm sure my sister would be only too glad to. . . ."

"Not at all," said Mr. Speed, jumping to his feet. "We have taken too much of your time as it is."

"And Miss Todd's," said Mr. Lincoln, himself rising, by slower degrees.

Elizabeth, with persuasive signs of regret, handed them their hats and conveyed them with all due deliberation to the door. "Mr. Edwards will be *so* sorry to have missed you. Next time, I will insist upon his inviting you *himself* so you may be certain of a fitter reception. We must spare you another afternoon with two *females*, who are so removed from the world's strife. Can there *be* more impoverishing company? No, don't you dare disagree, Mr. Lincoln! But tell me, have you both retrieved everything you came with? You are sure? Every last handkerchief?"

Safely deposited on the landing, the two men doffed their hats, and the mighty door closed after them, with no less a personage than Elizabeth driving it home. She paused there a second, then made a glacial turn.

"Queer sort of visit."

"If you say so."

"And queer *strategy*," Elizabeth added. "Are they *both* vying for you? Or is one of them propping up the other?"

"They were paying a call," muttered Mary.

Elizabeth's mouth rose a fraction at one end. Then, with a hummed snatch of melody, she swept down the hall. Stopping only to call back: "His cuffs were a disgrace. I know you noticed."

Here was her shame: She had.

But as she thought back to that scene in the drawing room, she remembered the strange contortions by which Mr. Lincoln had done everything in his power to conceal those same cuffs. Surely, if he could have made every last segment of his upper appendages disappear, he would have. It struck her then. *He* had noticed, too.

SIX

FATE HAD DENIED Eliza Francis children of her own, but by way of compensation, she had made surrogate children of the neophyte Whig legislators who arrived punctually in Springfield at two-year intervals. The greener they were, the more rapidly they were conveyed to Mrs. Francis's parlor, where, under the combined influences of her encouragement and her whiskey, they emerged hours later as brighter, more hopeful specimens. Going forward, they might get their marching orders from Eliza's husband, the bearish and fractious editor of the *Sangamo Journal*, but it was Mrs. Francis who kept their feet marching.

Her maternal offices were not confined to men. If one of these young Whigs chanced to bring with him a wife, that young lady would spend her own afternoon in Mrs. Francis's parlor and come home ready to sacrifice herself on the altar of public service. If, by contrast, the Whig came unattached, it became Mrs. Francis's mission in life to find him the loyal helpmeet who would cleave to him through every election cycle. She kept perforce a running and constantly revised tally of eligible Springfield girls, the better to pair them all off at some later date. Which made it perfectly natural that, in the spring of 1840, her eye should come to rest on Mary Todd.

It required no genius to see the young woman's advantages. She had at her back an entire dynasty—Scots Covenanters, Revolutionary War heroes, veterans of the Indian wars, a Michigan governor, a United States congressman. Not to mention a father who had diligently climbed the ladder from city magistrate and sheriff to state assemblyman and state senator and had become, through force of character more than intelligence, one of Kentucky's great men. Mary, from the hour of her birth, had imbibed politics like mother's milk, and she was now, like any young woman of good sense, seeking a politician of her own. In short, she could be *helped*.

As a consequence, Mary, starting in late April, began to receive regular weekly supper invitations to the Francis home. Her only concern at first was to hold her own against the great tide of talk, but any fears she held on that score were put to rest on the third night.

"My dear!" said Mrs. Francis, drawing her into the hall. "How well you have applied yourself to the Illinois question. You must be a studious reader of our newspaper. And if I'm not mistaken," she added, "the competition's newspaper."

Mary flushed. "You must blame my father for that. He has always emphasized the importance of knowing the enemy."

"And he is right! But let us speak no more of enemies, for I am quite sure we shall be great friends. In which case, I hope you'll call me Eliza." The older woman squeezed her hand and, for a couple of uncomfortable seconds, gazed into her face. "Oh," she said, "to be a rose once more."

It was true that Mrs. Francis was now two years shy of forty, but the rose had never quite left her cheeks, which were ruddy in all weather and at all times of day. Some said the coloring was a natural emanation of her heart. Others whispered that she tippled. Still others whispered that she painted, and indeed there lingered about her person the suggestion of old excesses—those days, not long gone, when ladies puffed out their sleeves like pig bladders and piled their hair à la giraffe and did everything in their power to touch up Nature's canvas. Like the other women of her circle, Mrs. Francis had adopted the more subdued stylings of the current age, but she had never resigned herself to them, and behind those rosy cheeks lay the unspoken hope that women might once more curl their hair and show their clavicles.

"I nearly forgot," she said, curving her hand round Mary's wrist. "We're having a dance next week. *Everyone* will be there!"

"Everyone" meant, as Mary well knew, a relatively select few, but that list included her sister Elizabeth, who approached other women's entertainments in the manner of a general scouting enemy fortifications. "Remember," she said on the carriage ride over. "They're Yankees, so expect the food to be plain.

Boiled ham and boiled turkey, with some sort of pudding. If their past fetes are any guide, the horns will be out of tune, and there won't be any domestics to take your shawl, so you'll just have to find the nearest cloak pin. From there, it's *sauve qui peut*."

All those predictions were eventually borne out, yet the part that Mary couldn't have anticipated was the feeling of well-being that enveloped her from the moment she arrived. Mrs. Francis gave her a sisterly embrace; the normally scowling Mr. Francis managed a smile; and before she had traveled ten feet, she was hailed by nearly as many friends. The last being Mercy, whose radiance she attributed to the proximity of Mr. Conkling.

"You're just in time, Mary. The first dance is five minutes off."

They found their chairs in the long hall and sat, lightly fanning themselves, while the young men of Springfield wandered north and south, screwing up their courage. These days, it took a particularly courageous fellow to approach Mary Todd, for she had rapidly attained to a *noli me tangere* caste, but in a short time, she had scrawled four names into her program. It was then that a great shadow descended upon her. Looking up, she beheld the frowning spectacle of Mr. Lincoln.

"Miss Todd," he said, "I'm quite hopeless at this whole business, but . . . I'd like to dance with you in the worst way."

He was not even looking at her as he spoke—a fact that should have irked her but, for reasons unclear, had the opposite effect.

"I believe I have the *third* dance open," she ventured. "If you would be so good as to wait."

He nodded and stalked away.

There was always the possibility, of course, that he would vanish, as he had done at the Edwardses' ball, and she had to admit some part of her hoped for that outcome. Lacking Mr. Speed to intervene and interpret, she wasn't sure she could bear another halting conversation. But at the appointed time, Lincoln was there, and as they processed to the floor, she had just enough time to notice that his cuffs were unsullied.

Mr. Lincoln's mistakes on the dance floor were, to nobody's surprise, several but were also for the most part minor—rushing the tempo, failing to properly swing the corner, taking three steps instead of two—and since the dancers moved singly, nobody was too incommoded. Thank God, thought Mary, for the great equalizer of the quadrille, in which the stout and the slender, the light and the ponderous might all co-exist. She did have a brief moment of terror when, at one point, he came bounding toward her, but her toes emerged unscathed, and the promenade-all section was, on the whole, a success.

Then—just like that—the dance was done.

She looked up, expecting to see relief etched across his face, but he was frowning all the harder.

"Maybe you'd care for victuals?" he said.

"Thank you, no."

"Then I guess . . ." He swiveled his head from side to side. "Where were you sitting again?"

With some care, he led her back to her seat.

"I thank you so much," she said.

"Well. . . ." His frown skewed halfway toward a smile. "I'm just glad I didn't harm anybody."

And what surprised her more? The remark itself or the tiny contraction it produced in her throat?

"No one was in any way harmed, Mr. Lincoln. Only *charmed*. . . ."

He bowed his head and, with something like reluctance, edged away. It was only when he was out of view that Mercy and Mr. Conkling gave free vent to their hilarity.

"Shame on you both," said Mary.

"I *am* ashamed," said Mr. Conkling. "Truly, my admiration for the fellow knows no bounds, but damn me, on the dance floor, he looks like Father Jupiter, peering down from Olympus."

"Still," conceded Mercy, lowering herself back into her seat, "he was a perfect dear. And it cost him so much to ask. *I'm quite hopeless at this whole business, but . . .*" She hitched up her shoulders and stared hard at the ground. "*I'd like to dance with you in the worst way.*"

"And that's just how he did it," said Mary.

She had her reward: a rout of laughter, she herself laughing the hardest. How to explain the wretchedness that swept over her once the laughter had cleared? Her gibe was no different from the countless others she had made at suitors' expense, yet she couldn't escape the feeling that she had failed some elemental test of character, the nature of which she had yet to realize. And so, in the interregnum between dances, a new resolution began to form in her mind. She would not risk another dance with Mr. Lincoln, but she would seize the next opportunity to *shine* upon him, in the hopes of expiating her crime.

Only her chance never arose. Mr. Lincoln ventured no more onto the dance floor, and she rarely had cause to venture off. Periodically, she would glance over to find him rooted in some corner—no longer a solitary pine tree but part of the local grove—and always fast in conversation. Whether it was with the Francises or Ninian or Mr. Elkin or Mr. Dawson, his affect was one of solemn and unsurprisable wakefulness. He listened without ostentation—listened, in fact, more than he spoke—and when his time finally came to answer, something curious happened. His interlocutors would at once leave off speaking, the better to catch his words.

How she envied him those thronged corners, for her dance partners that evening were a dismal lot. A myopic state's attorney. A voluble lobbyist. A Mechanicsburg farmer who feared that the coming railroad would scare all the milk out of his cows.

"And where am I, then?" he kept asking.

For the waltz, she was trapped in the arms of Billy Herndon, a twenty-year-old settlement rube who spent most of the time apologizing for his clumsiness before letting slip that he was chief clerk to none other than Mr. Joshua Speed.

"Is that so?" she asked, endeavoring to cloak her interest. "I trust he is a benevolent employer."

"He pays out seven hundred a year," answered Billy with a grin. "I call that benevolent."

"You must know Mr. Lincoln, then."

"I know his *snore*. He and Speed sleep in the same room as me and Charlie."

Mary tried to cram all four figures into the same mental frame—and failed.

"It sounds most cramped," she murmured.

"Oh, no, there's more space than you'd think! Why, Lincoln and Speed can stay up half the night sometimes talking, and Charlie and me, on the other end, we never hear a word. Oh, but Miss Todd, the way you *move*? So easy, like?"

"Yes?"

"It reminds me of a serpent."

Something must have flashed from her eye for he at once backpedaled.

"I don't mean the *bad* kind. . . ."

"Of course you don't, Mr. Herndon. I'm sure the ladies of the German Prairie *settlement* would relish such a ghoulish metaphor. You must try them and report back to me."

Thank God for Mr. Conkling, who got her through the last dance, then went back to his Mercy, while Mary, with a wheeze and a sigh, collapsed into her chair and closed her eyes. From the fog between waking and sleeping, she heard a voice say: "The wages of beauty."

Mrs. Francis stood before her, grinning.

"I do apologize," said Mary. "I was just . . ."

"I don't blame you, my dear. I must say, however, that while you dance like a dream, I sometimes believe you are wasted on the parquet. I don't know if I *mentioned* . . ." The older woman heaved herself into the adjoining chair. "Mr. Francis hosts a weekly gathering at his offices. Every Thursday night, after the paper's been put to bed."

"So I have heard."

"Then you know it's nothing too fancy—people say what's on their minds, that's all—and if you *dare* to call it a salon, I shall be very cross. All the same, you might find it amusing."

"I should find it much more, I am sure. May *women* say what's on their minds, too?"

"There'd be hell to pay if they didn't. So you'll come? I'm so glad. Why don't I call for you Thursday at seven? Oh, and don't even think of gussying up, my dear. A simple walking dress will do. Wait, I nearly forgot!" cried Mrs. Francis. "There's our speaker."

Mary followed her friend's gaze to the foyer, where Mr. Lincoln was now standing side by side with Joshua Speed. The two men actually pressing shoulders, as though, between them, they'd been tasked with bearing up a joist. Their wardrobes may have comprised the same articles, but on Mr. Lincoln, they amounted to a hair shirt, whereas Mr. Speed's waistcoat and frock coat and cravat looked as though they had showered down on him, *flowed* round every limb.

"I've no doubt you'll find him a most stimulating orator," said Mrs. Francis.

Mary turned to her. "Mr. Speed?"

"Don't be silly, my dear. The dazzling ones never have overmuch to say. Now, if you'll excuse me, Mr. Francis looks like he's going to club one of our guests to the ground."

SEVEN

ONCE, WHEN SHE was fourteen, her father had taken her to the pressroom of the *Louisville Daily Journal*. She arrived in rapture, for in her short time on Earth, she had handled many reams of readyprint and had come to believe that journalism was the holiest of callings. What a shock, then, to find—not priests—but a clutch of emaciated consumptives hunched over dusty cases of type, loath even to raise their eyes for they were paid by the thousand ems. For weeks afterward, she could not read a newspaper without feeling herself guilty of a crime.

She understood, then, why Simeon Francis kept the *Sangamo Journal*'s pressroom from public view and hustled all visitors straight to the ventilated air of the second floor (when he was not herding them next door to his own home). Tonight's guests comprised a smaller, more concentrated version of the Edwardses' guest list, shorn of Democrats. Edward Baker was here, and so were Archer Herndon and Stephen Logan and Usher Linder and Hiram Thornton.

And Abraham Lincoln, who was, in this very moment, coming toward her.

She considered it a sign of progress that she no longer feared for her feet, and that her hand did not instinctively retreat from his (though it was as substantial and gnarled as the root of a chestnut tree). And that she had sufficient leisure to appreciate his eyes, which formed soft points in a hard face, even as one of them tipped slightly out of orbit.

"Now then, Miss Todd," he said. "Color me surprised."

"I don't see why you should be. A girl without a lyceum of her own must take her chances as they come. Especially when she may be the audience for a distinguished speaker."

"Distinguished? Is that what they're calling him? Standards have lowered."

"Mine haven't."

He paused. Looked away as if he were preparing to leave and then said: "I wonder if you'd mind offering me your opinion afterward. Your honest opinion, I mean."

"I should be happy to."

In the silence that came rushing back round them, she thought of asking him where Mr. Speed was. Only Simeon Francis was already windmilling his arms.

"Lincoln! Come forth, my lad!"

"The condemned man," he muttered.

Which was exactly how he looked as he negotiated the eight yards between her and the front of the room. Like a French aristo, she thought, bound for the Place de la Révolution.

"My friends," said Mr. Francis, tucking his thumbs behind his lapels, "it has come to the attention of this newspaper that the—the *Locofoco* contingent in our General Assembly . . ." Light groans. "Yes, sir, our Democratic friends have encountered one fellow whom they positively *hate* squaring up against." A knowing titter. "I am told that each of their encounters with this fellow describes the same bruising arc. Our Locofoco friends begin—always—by underestimating him. They then take up the business of insulting him. They then endeavor to shout him down." A chorus of answering boos. "What do they get for their troubles? My friends, at the end of the day, they are *hoarse*. . . ." A bubble of laughter. "They are *befuddled*. . . ." A swell. "And they are *defeated*!"

A commotion. In the face of that sound, Mr. Francis smiled thinly, then tweezed off his spectacles.

"Now far be it from me to follow their example," he said, "or to do this fellow the opposite disservice of *over*estimating him now. I will only say what I've said before. Our friend here carries the true Kentucky rifle, and when he fires, he sends the shot home. Gentlemen and ladies, I give you Abraham Lincoln."

She wasn't ready for it: the cry that went up in that tightly packed room. Less a sound, she thought, than a velocity, registering specifically in her spine. The only one in the room who seemed unaffected was Mr. Lincoln himself, who stood exactly where he had been, waiting for the noise to die down.

"Well now," he said, "that's likely the nicest reception a hayseed could ever ask for. Makes me think you mistook me for some other poor fool."

He smiled now, just a fraction.

"I'm reminded of an incident that transpired—oh, not so very long ago. Way out in Sucker country, it seems, there was a lynch mob. And one night—in the very *dead* of night, I should say for the point of the story—they went and grabbed a man out of his house for stealing a mule. They didn't waste a minute but hanged him to the nearest tree. It was all very efficient, I tell you, and they were pleased with their work. Then, come dawn, they looked up and they—they *concluded* that they had gone and hanged the wrong fellow. So they went back to the man's widow, looking all sheepish. And they said, *Guess the laugh is on us.*"

There was a gasp or two. Then an aching silence, as if all the listeners were huddling, baffled, over what they'd just heard. Her face burning, Mary cut her eyes away and waited for some kind of deliverance, but Lincoln's reedy voice was already sailing on.

"Yes, my friends, that's how it stands when a no-account like me stakes a claim on your notice. I figure either I'll get hanged or the laugh will be on me. So I'll take it as a good harbinger that the room is now quiet. Because it seems to me that it's in *times* of quiet—when no common danger presses—that a free people naturally divide into parties. At such times, the man who is of neither party cannot be of any consequence. Therefore, *we*—those of us joined tonight and those of us joined in the coming elections—*we* are of a party. . . ."

In this very nearly incidental manner, the speech was joined. If speech it was, for his voice, to Mary's ears, never lifted into an oratorical register; he brought with him no notes; he merely *talked*.

"Even in the act of cohering, we do well to mark the example of Mr. Clay, whose deep devotion to the cause of human liberty—whose strong sympathy with the oppressed everywhere—knows no rival. He has been a great partisan. He has been a greater American. He has loved his country, but his feeling and his judgment have ever led him to oppose extremes of opinion, in whatever camp they fall."

Lincoln neither lingered nor hastened. He spoke of Tyler, of Tippecanoe, of the United States Bank and the Illinois State Bank, of public education, of minority interests vis-à-vis majority tyranny. Exactly the themes Mary would have expected from an election-year address, yet it wasn't the content that struck her so much as the delivery—the sense of a mind calmly decanting its contents.

"With these principles foremost in mind, let us therefore cultivate reason. Let us cultivate general intelligence and sound morality. And in particular, let us cultivate a reverence for the Constitution and its laws. Upon *these* let us mount our platforms of the soul and of the spirit. We are Whigs tonight. We are Whigs tomorrow, next week and the month after. Come December, we are Americans."

Even here, his tone never rose above the conversational, so that no one was immediately sure the speech was finished. He had to take a step back and lower his chin, at which there began a slow, rhythmic clapping, gaining in intensity without gaining in volume until the listeners had formed a kind of rampart around the speaker, with only his head protruding.

Mary was relieved to be free of that first wave. Her instinct, when called on to deliver an opinion, was always to shield herself, at least initially, from the opinions of others. But Mrs. Francis's glittering eyes were already upon her.

"My dear, what did you think?"

She heard herself utter the least interesting reply imaginable: "Interesting."

"By *that*," said Mrs. Francis, sweeping on, "you probably mean not in the traditional style of oratory. Of course, I quite agree with you. It is wholly self-made—just like him. Our Lincoln has worked himself up from a poverty such as—well, such as you and I have never known. No education to speak of. No advantages. Just a mind and a soul."

It was, thought Mary, as if she were being shown a house.

"They say suffering makes a man stronger," she ventured.

"They say that, and they are wrong. Suffering makes a man narrow and petty and crippled by resentment. *Him* it makes large. I can't explain it."

"Well, it is good to know that he has found such a generous and eloquent advocate in you."

"He is his own best advocate. I am . . ." Mrs. Francis frowned into her empty wineglass. "It's just that I feel protective of him."

"Oh," answered Mary, with a laugh. "I don't suppose there is any need of that. He is surely grown enough to handle himself."

"I fear you misunderstand me," said Mrs. Francis, with a faint tinge of frost.

"I understand you well, I promise. What I meant to say is you needn't protect Mr. Lincoln from *me*."

Expecting some larkishness in response, but the older woman's reply was the height of solemnity: "I will hold you to your vow." And only then did Mrs. Francis drag a smile across her face. "As you see, my dear, I am not particularly reasonable on this subject. Now then, I don't know about you, but if I have to listen to another minute of male prognostication, I shall go mad. May I refresh your glass?"

MR. LINCOLN'S LOWER lip was already plumped out in apology when at last he approached her.

"Grant me this," he said. "It wasn't two hours."

"Nowhere *near*," she answered. "Why, you were done before I had a chance to blink. And but the single homespun anecdote!"

"Oh, yes. That one died like a quail, didn't it?"

Nobody was harmed. . . .

"Don't worry," he said. "I'm keeping most of my homespinning in reserve for next month."

"Next month?"

"The Young Men's Whig Convention. You'll not want to miss that, Miss Todd. Every log-cabin float in the *land* will be there. Some with actual smoke coming out the chimney."

"It sounds terrifying. Will you be a speaker?"

"One of many. I'm the . . ." A corner of his mouth hitched up. "I'm the one who feeds the lions their raw meat."

"For what purpose?"

"So they don't devour the other speakers."

She nodded slightly and smiled. Quiet enveloped them.

"Perhaps I have already mentioned," she said, scrambling. "Mr. Clay is an old family friend of ours."

"I thought he might be. I do envy you the association. Mr. Clay is . . ." Lincoln cast his eyes down. "Well, I consider him my *beau idéal*. Did I say that right? What a relief."

Again, that strange contraction in her throat.

"I should confess to you," she said, "that I once proposed marriage to him."

"Good thing he didn't take you up on it. Being already married."

Laughing, she turned half away. Relishing, if only for a moment, the lightness he had produced in her.

"Well," she said, "I was just twelve at the time. Father had bought me a new pony from a troupe of strolling players, and I wanted Mr. Clay to be the first to see it. Because, of course, who better? It never occurred to me, really, that he might be indisposed. Or have better things to do. No, all four feet three inches of me, I rode straight to his house."

"Ashland."

"You *are* an admirer. Ashland, yes. A mile outside of town. I remember I had on this ruffled white sunbonnet, and in my hurry, I had failed to tie it properly so it kept—flapping down my back. I knew that if I came back home with sun on my face, there'd be no end of grief from Ma, but I was twelve, I didn't care.

"I came at last to the gravel driveway and—oh, it was an old butler came out. I announced to him that I wished to see his master, and he said Mr. Clay was busy entertaining five or six fine gentlemen. I said, *My father is as fine a gentleman as they are.* Well, the butler went inside and came back with the same story. Mr. Clay was too occupied to attend to some little lassie. So I threw back my head—flapping sunbonnet and all—and I said, *You tell him Mary Todd wishes to see him this very moment.* Oh, I know, Mr. Lincoln. You're thinking what an impossible child I must have been."

"Not at all," he assured her.

"I cannot defend my conduct, I can only say it achieved my end. Mr. Clay came out not long after—if only to be rid of me. Of course, he knew my family well, and he couldn't have been kinder. He said I had the finest pony he had seen in all his born days. And he was *highly* impressed by my pony's one and only trick."

"Which was?"

"What *was* it? I think . . . standing on its hind legs."

"Ah."

"So I graciously thanked him, and I was about to ride away when he told me I was expected for dinner."

"And how did Mrs. Clay feel about that?"

"I believe she must have put him up to it, for I was seated right next to him. Pride of place. I remember saying what a tragedy it was, not having a father who was running for president as Mr. Clay was. Because, you see, I wanted to live in Washington. And he laughed, and he said if ever he became president, I should be one of his very first guests. And then I . . ."

"What?"

"Oh, it's . . . no . . ." She shook her head. "I can't."

"You're too deep now."

"Very well, I said . . . I said, *Mr. Clay, if you were not already married, I would happily wait for you.*"

It was the first time she had heard Lincoln laugh.

"Go ahead," she said. "I am sure *they* were laughing, too, behind their sleeves. No doubt they found me quite the divertissement. But that day, in my own mind, I was—Lord help me, I was a queen of some sort. A *conqueror.* I don't think I'd ever felt so . . ."

She couldn't finish the sentence, so he finished it for her.

"Noticed."

She made as if to nod, but her composure had altogether failed her now. For some several seconds, she stood there. Then, fumbling through her reticule for the handkerchief that wasn't there, she said, in a determinedly light voice: "I don't know why I told you that ridiculous story. I have never told anyone else."

"Your ridiculous story is safe with me."

She laughed then, because it was either that or go full bore in the opposite direction. And the thought of weeping—with Springfield's Whig elite for an audience—was more than she could stomach.

"So sorry to interrupt" came a familiar voice. And there was Mr. Speed, gingerly stepping toward them. His hat in hand, his baritone as cultivated as his tresses.

"You missed a brilliant speech," Lincoln told him.

"I caught the last five minutes. Perhaps Miss Todd would care to summarize the rest."

The frank curiosity with which both men now looked at her left the words dry in her mouth.

"It was . . . of course, stimulating. . . ."

"She's too well bred to give the truth," Lincoln answered.

"And *we*, of course," said Mr. Speed, "are too well bred to demand it. Alas, Miss Todd, there is this much truth to impart. Mr. Lincoln and I are expected elsewhere."

She looked from one man to the other. "Another speech?" she guessed.

"*Many* speeches," said Lincoln. "A horde of us like to gather nights round the hearth. Back of Speed's store. We call ourselves the Poetical Society, on account of how we ain't."

"Fellow Whigs?"

"With some Democrats thrown in for spice."

"If there's one thing the men of both parties share," put in Mr. Speed, "it's the desire to show each other how little they know."

"Coupled," she said, "with the desire to exclude women from their deliberations."

She had the pleasure now of seeing surprise flare in both men's eyes. No, something beyond surprise. Something closer to panic.

"Well now," said Lincoln, "I won't do you the disservice of saying you'd be bored, Miss Todd. But I do believe, in that blazing fire, you'd be good and smoked."

"Like a side of bacon," added Mr. Speed.

"Ah," she answered. "Is it not like men to excuse all their offenses through humor? And is it not like *women* to excuse them? Very well, then. Off with you both."

They nodded in tandem and turned away. It was Mr. Speed, surprisingly, who swung back in her direction.

"I promise you, Miss Todd, we have no intention of being exclusive. In fact, I hope you'll do me the honor of visiting my store sometime. In broad daylight."

I already have, she thought. And how long ago it seemed, that ludicrous outing with Mercy.

"We have yards and yards of calico," Mr. Speed was saying. "Irish linen. Plaid linsey-woolsey. You'd be right at home."

She could feel the gorge rising within her—and, rising in parallel, a new understanding. Mr. Speed, she suddenly saw, was not insulting her, or not *merely* insulting her. He was raising a barricade, and it was composed of, yes, calico and linen and linsey-woolsey and whatever else he kept at hand, whether it be on his store's shelves or the shelves of his mind. And behind that barricade, he was even now disappearing—and taking Lincoln with him. And she was left there, like a child in the forest, wailing her abandonment.

"How very kind of you," she said. "I fear, however, that with so much happening on the political scene, I have no time left for frills and furbelows. Unless, of course, you are in want of business, in which case I shall encourage all our friends to come to your aid."

Nearly impossible to read the expression in his blue eyes.

"What a pleasure it's been, Miss Todd."

EIGHT

IN THE FOUR weeks that succeeded the Francis soiree, Mary Todd was invited to six suppers. At each of those occasions, Lincoln was present.

Of course, Springfield high society was small and exclusive enough that the same ladies and gentlemen might nod to each other several times in the space of a week, but Lincoln had, by his own inclination, abstained from that world. How to explain, then, that he was *here*, night after night, in the same swallowtail coat, the same black waistcoat, the same black neckerchief? He expressed no surprise at the sight of her, nor did he waste time with unnecessary formalities but spoke as if they were picking up a conversation left off a minute ago. Again and again, the same question rose up in Mary's mind: What was this *wind* blowing them together?

It couldn't be Lincoln himself. Bless him, the fellow could barely polish his own patent-leather boots. Mrs. Francis was a candidate, but she was present at but one of the occasions and exhibited not a sign of complicity. As for the hostesses themselves, they seemed entirely impervious to schemes. Mary and Mr. Lincoln were rarely seated together and had time for only the most glancing of exchanges before their respective sexes diverged.

Yet even these brief crossings were informative in unexpected ways. One night, she remarked on his abstinence principle.

"Oh." He shrugged lightly. "It's not on principle. I just never learned the taste."

"For liquor, you mean. What of tobacco?"

"That, neither. I fear now you will write me down for a Puritan."

"On the contrary, I will write you down for a—safe bet. Safe as a *church*."

"Another word you should probably never put next to my name."

On another evening, just before escorting her into the dining room, he asked her, apropos of nothing, what her favorite Shakespeare play was.

"*Much Ado about Nothing*," she stammered.

"Mm." He nodded. "I'm partial to *Richard II* myself."

A second surprise.

"Dear me," she said. "You have just named my most abhorred character."

"More than Richard Three?"

"Infinitely more. Richard Three knows what he wants. Richard *Two* is such an unattractive mixture of arrogance and indecision. A dreadful king, a *more* dreadful prisoner. No, I don't care for him at all."

"But it's in prison that Richard discovers his true self. Too late to save himself, of course."

"And too late to save *us*," she retorted. "Four acts have already crawled past."

With a half smile, he closed his eyes and began to intone: "'I wasted time, and now doth time waste me.'"

The words produced a light tingle in her neck. The man was quoting Shakespeare.

"Very well," she said. "You may keep your Richard. At least time with *you* is not wasted."

And even as the words came out of her mouth, she was inspecting them. Were they not a form of encouragement? Did she expect him to answer in kind? Once more, she felt herself being blown in a direction she had never consented to.

The same wind seemed to have blown Mr. Speed far out to sea, for he was absent from all these suppers. So, too, was Elizabeth Edwards. Far from noticing the slight, however, Elizabeth seemed relieved that someone else was taking responsibility for her sister's entertainment. Had she known that Mary was being thrown into regular company with the same gentleman—a gentleman, moreover, who had never received her matrimonial endorsement—Elizabeth would have taken swift and decisive action. But in her innocence, she carried on as before, scientifically surveying the available male population and returning at regular intervals with new candidates.

"I don't know that you've met Mr. Trumbull," she said one afternoon.

The two of them were alone with their needlework, and Mary made a point of finishing her stitch before answering.

"I don't believe I have."

"He's a very promising lawyer from Alton. Or is it Belleville? There's talk of him being made secretary of state if the planets align."

"Well," Mary heard herself say, "that sounds promising."

Elizabeth studied her, then went on.

"I will not go so far as to call him handsome, but his face has a lively intellectual *cast*. Of course, he is Yankee-born, but he has spent a sufficient amount of time in Georgia to nullify that handicap."

"I look forward to meeting him."

Elizabeth studied her some more. "You *are* being agreeable."

With great care, Mary drew out another length of yarn. "I cannot seem to keep on the right side of you. If I resist your suggestions, I am branded ungrateful. If I do not resist, I am met with suspicion. Kindly tell me what course I am to take in the future so we may live once more in comity."

Her tone was chiding but only *lightly* chiding because she felt, beneath every word, something mysterious: the urge to laugh. Was this the natural consequence of keeping a secret? That being the case, what *was* the secret? She had lifted nary a finger . . . had at no point been compromised . . . was as far from losing her head as she had ever been. She was merely—and how the thought amused her now—following the prevailing winds. And what power had she over the weather?

THEIR NEXT MEETING was at Dr. Henry's. Lincoln was the first to rise when she came into the drawing room. The first to insist she get the seat nearest the fire, though there were older women present and the room itself positively roasting. The first also to offer his arm when the call to supper came.

Once again, they were seated at opposite sides of the table, and if Lincoln was marking her through the course of the meal, he did an exemplary job of concealing it. Only once did she feel a sea change. Dr. Henry—still smarting, perhaps, over his loss in the probate-judge election of thirty-seven—had launched an attack on political symbolism. He wanted his guests to know that log cabins and hard cider were all very well, but log cabins fell down over time and cider turned to vinegar, and if the American electorate was fed a steady diet of either substance, their mental organs would rot in short order. It was left to Mary, the youngest of the group, to pose an objection.

"Forgive me, Dr. Henry, I am not versed in Greek as you are, but it is my understanding that the word *metaphor* translates as—'carrying *over*.' Am I correct? If so, then I believe we must see these symbols as—as *bridges*. To bring people across. People who may have no clear sense of what a usury law is or an internal improvement, but they have grown up in a cabin and they have drunk cider, and they feel in their souls that whoever has done these things likewise, *he* will have their interests at heart. And in this way—perhaps this way *only* . . ." She could feel the blood seeping into her face. "They discover what those interests truly are."

In the silence that welled up, she turned by instinct to Mrs. Henry, the eldest woman in the room, who said, "There, Miss Todd! What a marvelous statesman you would make."

The voice was warm, and so was the laughter that welled up around her. Dr. Henry confessed himself routed—he in no way believed it—and a few jokes were raised about granting her the right to vote. It was, she realized, the most humane way they knew to overlook her outburst, and only when she was returning her attention to the scalloped oysters did she feel Lincoln's gaze settle once more upon her.

After dinner, the Henrys took the radical step of keeping both sexes in the same room but for the rather dreary purpose of playing *tableaux vivants*. At once three guests set to work re-creating the image of Washington crossing the Delaware. Excusing herself from their pose striking, Mary sought refuge by the hearth, where Lincoln was once again (unaccountably) waiting.

"The role of General Washington is still open," she advised him.

"I think I would just tip the boat over," he said.

"Not if you stayed very still."

He screwed up his eyes, as though peering through a telescope. "It's no use. I only know my way around flatboats."

They stood for a time with their backs to the fire.

"I would like to know how you came by it," he said.

"What?"

"Your affinity for politics."

"I believe you mean *affliction*," she said, casting her eyes down.

He huddled over that word for a time. "If you like."

"Many women, as you know, suffer from it."

"Many affect to. Your sister, for instance."

"My sister," she said, a little stiffly, "is a devotee of Ninian. Hence, she is a devotee of politics."

"That's just it, you see. There's a syllogistic progression at work. She thinks, *If A, then B*. You, Miss Todd, go straight to *B*."

Had there been world enough and time, she would have told him how it all began. How her father, as a state assemblyman, spent his winters in Frankfort and how, upon returning home, he would stagger straight to his room with a bottle of bourbon. None of his children was allowed in, but Mary, characteristically, took the prohibition as a challenge and decided to smuggle herself in by garbing herself in politics. It began always with a gentle knock. "Father?" Receiving no answer, she would continue speaking through the keyhole. "Did they give you an *awfully* hard time about that clerkship?" She had been reading the newspapers for at least three weeks and would have chosen the topic most likely to stir his emotions. Even if his answer was only a grunt, she would take that as license to open the door a crack. "I thought those Democrats were perfectly shocking the way they spoke of you in the press. *You* can't help being on the Banking Committee." Suppose his next answer extended to three syllables. This she would translate into three more steps. "And who better to oversee the Lexington branch, I'd like to know? Someone who has seen banks rise and fall and knows all the perils." This might elicit a full sentence. And in that space, she would have traveled all the way to his Windsor chair. By the time she was done, she was in his lap. A spellbound audience for his tales of deals struck and calamities averted. In this manner, the two of them might while away an entire afternoon, while the rest of the Todd children bitterly bided their time.

The memory of it fairly overpowered her now. The drawn blinds. The candle-light glancing off her father's tumbler. The smell of bourbon on his breath. . . .

"Are you all right?" she heard Lincoln ask.

"Of course." She endeavored to smile. "I am so sorry—I just realized I'm expected home. . . ."

His eyes and mouth squeezed down. "I wasn't—I mean, I wish you to know I was *complimenting* you. You don't put anything *on*. . . ."

She nodded faintly, felt the color rising in her cheeks.

"You know, Mr. Lincoln, I have often jested that the man who wishes to woo me will send neither flowers nor chocolates but *election* returns. Precinct by precinct. Tied in a beautiful bow."

He stood for some time, watching the other guests oar themselves across the Delaware River. "Duly noted," he said.

AT DR. HENRY's suggestion, Lincoln escorted her to the carriage, a duty he took up with no sign of either joy or resistance. Just as he was about to hand her in, though, he stopped.

"I'm not sure when our paths will cross again, Miss Todd."

"Some future supper, I've no doubt."

He shook his head. "Come Monday, I'm bound for Decatur. Then Tazewell County. Not sure when I'll return."

She would later wonder if it was embarrassment that forced her hand. The sight of that defeated countenance or the prospect of some more protracted or formal adieu. Or maybe it was just the prevailing winds.

"Miss Levering and I are hosting a little picnic tomorrow. I am sure you would be most welcome."

The words come boiling out of her in such a sluice that she had to gather them again and replay them in her mind.

"Miss Levering's brother will be there as well," she quickly added. "And his wife. And Mr. Conkling."

Lincoln scowled down at the carriage wheel. She assumed he was working up some conjugation of regret until he said, in a small voice: "I would be glad to come."

"Well," she answered, "that's fine." She was already backing into the carriage, reaching behind her for the seat. "Sometime around three, shall we say? In the green by Dr. Houghan's."

He nodded. Doffed his hat. Then, just as he was about to shut the door after her, he leaned his head into the compartment.

"Might Speed come?"

Curiously, the name didn't even resonate at first. "*Mr.* Speed?" she said at last.

"I think he'd enjoy it is all."

With that, the whole complexion of the event changed. Joshua *Speed* would be there—exposed, as it were, to the elements.

"Yes," she said, in a voice not clearly her own. "Tell Mr. Speed we should be delighted."

NINE

It was Mercy who had come up with the picnic idea. She had hoped that the combination of proximity, mild weather, and food might move the Gone-Case closer to formalizing his feelings and move her brother that much closer to tendering his blessing. And when the next day dawned bright and unretractably fair, it seemed possible that both women might achieve their objectives.

Certainly, they had chosen a charming glade: willows and roses growing in profusion, all the rawness of the prairie banished. They laid down their blankets under an old oak and had just enough time before the guests arrived to immerse themselves in the day's allure. The velvet lawn spreading before them. The bright foliage cupping the light. The charmed hum of insects. Mary was beginning to repent of sharing any of it, but already Mercy's brother and his wife were stalking toward them, in variations of black and gray. Both declined to sit; neither spoke unless spoken to. Their presence seemed to have a dampening effect on Mr. Conkling, who came soon after with a bouquet of spice pinks, which he handed rather sheepishly to Mercy. Conversation moved in spasms, and even the full force of Mary's gaiety could not lift the talk much above real estate.

The sun was just dipping behind the oak when the last two guests came striding down the lawn, shoulder to shoulder in matching burgundy vests. Mr. Lincoln carried an armful of snowball flowers, but it was Mr. Speed who had entered more than anyone else into the spirit of things: a pitcher of sassafras tea, a bag of horehound drops, and, rather surprisingly, a banjo.

"We shall have a grand time," he declared, and Mary discovered in him that day a previously unsuspected power: the ability to make everyone converts to an occasion. Every time she looked his way, he was at *work*. Setting up the campstools for the ladies. Adjusting the angles of their parasols to keep the sun off. Pouring tea and carving venison and chasing away the odd mosquito. Laughing at every joke, no matter how mild, and filling every yawning silence.

"Mrs. Levering, I do believe your gate has the most beautiful moss roses in all of Illinois. What do you mean you planted them yourself? Why, you must harbor some ancient horticultural arcanum to which no one else has been granted entry. Although I bid fair to say that if you need advice on *lilacs*, you might consult Miss Todd. Does anybody wear that particular color more becomingly? I wonder she doesn't wear it night and day, it suits her so. . . ."

Mary knew, of course, she was being flattered, but each time he teetered on the brink of excess, he fell back, with the most self-deprecating of smiles, as if to say the joke had been all on him. Of all the guests, he seemed both the busiest and the most at ease, so that when the Leverings at last excused themselves, shortly before six, it was Mr. Speed they were least willing to part with.

Their departure, at least, was a deliverance for Mr. Conkling, who at once demanded another slice of dried-peach pie. It was not too long before Mr. Speed was coaxed to take up his banjo, which he did with becoming modesty. He played stiffly at first, but his fingers soon found their way and began to pluck out tunes like "Jump Jim Crow" and "The Pretty Ploughboy."

"Well now," said Mary, her fingers tapping along on her collarbone. "There appears to be no *end* to your talents."

Mr. Speed expressed only the hope that others might join in, and the group's spirits were high enough now that, upon recognizing a particular tune, one of them might, without too much embarrassment, start to sing along. Upon which Mr. Speed would immediately adjust—even to the point of transposing on the spot—until a small, if scratchy, choir began to form, right there on the emerald lawn.

Some voices were easier to hear than others: Mary's schoolgirl treble, for instance, had a way of floating above, like a descant. But, at particular intervals, even Mr. Lincoln's scratchy tenor could be heard, feeling its way along the melodic line like a child on a creaking branch. For something like an hour, they sat there, all self-consciousness eroded. The glade's bees hummed in tune, and in the nearby stream, a dragonfly darned its needle back and forth into the water's fabric.

Where did it begin to go wrong? Was it when a wasp found the tiny crevice between Mary's glove and sleeve? Was it when Mr. Speed, for reasons unclear, retreated into obdurate silence? Perhaps it was when Mr. Conkling refused to release the lightning bug he had captured, even in the face of Mercy's protests, and then launched into one of the half-jesting, half-belligerent rants that Mary recognized from Lexington taverns.

"Worst thing a man can do is become a lawyer. *You* know what I'm speaking of, Lincoln. Spend your days hustling from county to county—saddle sores to prove it—licking the boots of some rascal of a judge, and for what? Because some *good* might come of it? Well, not for us, my brother! Every day, we become smaller."

"Conkling. . . ."

"I ask you now," he said, lurching to his feet. "What keeps a real man in a place like this? He should be lighting out for the next *frontier*. Staking claims, killing Injuns, and—ha!—bedding squaws."

"Mr. Conkling. . . ." Mercy, pale, rose from her stool.

"What I wouldn't give—what I wouldn't *give* to go hunting right now. When was the last time you fired a gun, Lincoln?"

"I was eight."

"You're having me on."

"I've never shot anything bigger than a turkey."

Mr. Conkling's face formed a shell of horror, then sprang open. "Ha! You don't fool me with this lily-livered talk. I hear tell you're the best wrestler north of the Ohio."

Mr. Lincoln smiled, shook his head. "I'm not even the best this side of the Sangamon."

It was here that Mr. Speed chose mysteriously to awake from his torpor. "He's lying, of course. There's only one man alive that's wrestled Lincoln to a draw. Everyone else . . ."

Conkling was breathing heavily now. "I—must—see—this."

"No," said Lincoln.

"A demonstration, that's all."

"It's not the right place. . . ."

But by some inscrutable male logic, the challenge had been laid down, and nothing was left now but to determine the terms. After some back and forth, it was decided that Mr. Speed would take on Mr. Lincoln, but only if the latter consented to have his arm tied behind his back.

"Don't be ridiculous," said Mary. "Someone will get injured."

The someone, of course, being Mr. Speed. There seemed no other possible outcome, and it was an outcome she could not even romanticize. Again and again, she pleaded for cooler heads, but the two combatants were already taking off their coats—Mr. Speed had to be helped out of his—and Conkling was solemnly binding Lincoln's left arm.

"Doesn't hurt, does it, old fellow?"

"Not yet."

"Gentlemen," said Mercy, her jaw hardening. "This is not becoming."

"Square off now, boys!"

Shaken by premonition, Mary began to stumble down the green, but the sounds followed her. Animalistic grunts. Slap of limb on limb. Heels digging in the sward. "That's it!" cried Conkling. "Keep him off! Don't let him at the legs!" From the woods lot, a murder of crows came slanting down—dropping in slow arcs and then, at the sight of her, gathering into a chevron and bearing down. With a stifled cry, Mary turned and ran back toward the oak tree. Her slippered foot caught on something that she later identified as Mr. Speed's banjo, but she kept moving and, as she ran, saw, like a dreadful collage, Mercy's sagging mouth and Conkling's blood-grin and Lincoln's long arm curved around Speed's neck—and behind her that sound—inescapable—the flap of wings, folding round, until the only way left to breathe was to scream. Right into astonished faces of everyone gathered.

"Stop it! Stop it at once!"

THE THREE GENTLEMEN made their muffled goodbyes. The Levering domestics came for the picnic's remnants, and the only task left for Mary and Mercy was to walk home, which they did at their leisure.

How calm the night seemed of a sudden. The moon new, the air warm. The stars with that curious shimmer of summer, as if they were being daubed onto the sky's canvas. At the top of Quality Hill, Mary reached over and squeezed her friend's arm.

"I *am* sorry, Mercy."

"Don't be silly, they deserved it. Two pretty girls for company, and all they can think to do is toss each other around like kindling. Did you hear what the Gone-Case said when I was chiding him? *Why do women have to spoil everything?* Very *well*, Mr. Conkling. If *that's* how you feel!" Mercy let her gaze trail back down the hill. As if, even now, her lover was laboring toward her to make amends. "I think it's time to go home," she said.

"But we're already . . ."

Too late, she grasped the direction of Mercy's thoughts. Back east. To Baltimore.

"Dearest," she began, "your Conkling may—"

"He may be *many* things, but he is assuredly not ready."

"He could be. Before long."

Mercy shook her head. "Not until he knows what he is missing."

"And what if . . . ?"

The question hung there.

"Then Baltimore has bachelors of its own," said Mercy. "Far more civilized ones, I might add."

It caught Mary then—like a hook in the belly. The sudden, piercing thought of Mercy gone. Joining that long and dismal progression of Gone-Cases.

"But what shall I do?" Mary said, softly. "I shall have nobody."

"Why, you'll have your public." Smiling, Mercy chucked her under the chin. "Remember who you are, dearest. The Belle of Springfield."

IT WAS MEANT as a consolation, she knew, but that night in bed, it took on the bitterest of aftertastes. *La Belle? On whose authority?*

Tomorrow—the day after—some prettier, younger girl, every bit as vivacious, would swan onto the scene. The prairie wolves would come flocking, and where would Mary be? Entering the vale of spinsterhood. A stalwart aunt. A reliable presence at town functions. Wool and bombazine.

The next morning, she left strict instructions not to be disturbed, but at the Edwards house, her wishes never had the force of commands, and a little before noon, Johanna the maid came loudly knocking.

"Just thought you'd want to know. A gentleman came to see you."

"When?"

"Not fifteen minutes ago."

Helplessly, Mary cut a glance at the looking glass. To see what spectacle she would have presented.

"You told him I was indisposed, I hope."

"I did." And still Johanna remained in the doorway, glowing with secret knowledge. "He was a *tall* sort of gentleman. Taller than Mr. Edwards, even."

Mary turned her head to the window. Said nothing.

"He left you a little trifle," said Johanna.

"Is that so? I wonder what it might be."

"I couldn't even say, miss."

"Because it is wrapped?"

"Because I've never seen anything quite like it."

Mary forced a smile. "Why did you not bring it with you?"

"Oh, but, miss, you said you didn't want to be disturbed."

"And yet you have disturbed me in the act of telling me."

Conscious, as she spoke, that her mask of indifference was crumbling.

"Please," she said, "bring it to me."

She had just enough time to recompose herself when Johanna sauntered back in, bearing not flowers but a flower basket. In which was set a scroll of paper, entwined in pink ribbon.

In a spell of enchantment, Mary pried the scroll from its ribbon. Unfurled it and found, staring back at her, three rows of humble print:

SANGAMON COUNTY
ELECTION RETURNS
6 AUGUST 1838

Down the left side of the page ran the precincts: places like Wolf Creek, Rochester, and Upper Lick Creek. Across the top: the names of every Whig candidate in the field. Baker. Dawson. Edwards. Elin. Fletcher. And there, on the right side of the page: *Lincoln*. Lightly circled in charcoal.

Her finger moved vertically now, tracking the column of vote totals—18, 12, 49, 6. Finishing at the very bottom on the number 2,326.

Two thousand three hundred and twenty-six: the total number of votes by which, nearly two years earlier, Abraham Lincoln had secured reelection. A sum greater than any other candidate's totals.

There was one last discovery. At the bottom of the page, etched in the crudest of strokes, a charcoal heart.

She was calm for the entire time it took her to scroll the sheet back up and return it to its osier basket. Then, bleeding tears, she lowered her face into the waiting platform of her hand.

"Well now," said Johanna. "*That's* a queer sort of gift to leave a lady."

"Isn't it?" she managed to say.

PART TWO

Joshua

TEN

——————

IT WAS EVERYTHING you'd expect of a wedding. The air thick with lilies and gladioluses. Candles gleaming from every sconce and niche. The parlor furniture in clean rows, and supper still warm in the adjoining room. Why, then, was everyone so sad?

Friends from earliest boyhood. Relations long departed. Mother, sitting downcast in an armchair. Father, glum in his best silk coat. Everywhere Joshua turned, he found a pall: black wool, black crepe. Even the bride stood, with her back turned, in a black gown and veil.

But as he traveled down the aisle, every face in the room suddenly turned toward his and gathered into a smile. How pleased they were to see him! The bride no less so, for she was turning toward him now in the tiniest of gradients and, at the same time, reaching for her veil, and the news was striking home with the force of a lance.

This was *his* wedding. His and no one else's.

Sweat spangled his brow as a great fog began to roll through the room, shrouding all the guests until the only thing remaining was the bride. Lifting her veil, inch by inch.

HERE WAS WHERE he always woke up. Sometimes in a great gasp of relief, but more often with shreds of the dream still clinging to him. On those evenings, he would have to lie awake for some time, reconstructing the particulars of his own life. *You are Joshua Speed. You own a dry-goods store in*

Springfield, Illinois. Your life is peaceable and requires no change. You have never been married. You have no plan to be married. . . .

It was a curious process—like untying the noose from around his own neck—and it left him a little queasy that he could be so unmanned by an illusion.

Unmanned even more by the idea of sharing it with some other. That's how he knew things had changed between them. Because, one night, as they lay in bed, he at last spoke of his dream. Trusting, perhaps, in the concealment of dark.

"Huh," said Lincoln after a moment of silence. "I get that one, too. All the time."

THE TALE OF how they had come to share lodgings was by now an official part of Springfield lore. So often were they asked to tell it—over whiskey, over cards—that it had graduated into a performance, with each man faithfully executing his part.

LINCOLN: You have to understand. This was thirty-seven, and I was riding into town on a borrowed horse. No client, no money. A thousand dollars in debt. That's how low I'd fallen.

JOSHUA: Listen to him! A *second*-term legislator. The highest vote tally in Sangamon County out of seventeen candidates. You can't trust this one to tell the story right.

LINCOLN: You can trust this. I was a piece of floating driftwood.

JOSHUA: Floating in a particular direction.

LINCOLN: If you mean toward Bell and Company, that was pure accident. It was the first store that presented itself.

JOSHUA: So you say.

LINCOLN: The horse needed to drink. I had some dust to shake off. Into Mr. Speed's store I went.

JOSHUA: He's not lying about the dust.

LINCOLN: My entire worldly belongings consisted of two or three law books and a pair of saddlebags, in which were all the clothes I owned in the world. Except what was on my back.

JOSHUA: And much to my dismay, he set those two filthy bags on my freshly waxed counter. No greeting, no pleasantries. The first words out of his mouth were . . .

LINCOLN: *How much for a single bedstead?*

JOSHUA: So I took slate and pencil, and made the calculation, and I told him the sum would amount to seventeen dollars in all.

LINCOLN: And I said, *Well, that's probably cheap enough but . . .*

JOSHUA: *But cheap as it is, I don't have the money to pay.* The thing every shopkeeper longs to hear.

LINCOLN: But then I said, *If you'll credit me till Christmas, and if my experiment here as a lawyer is a success, I'll pay you then.*

JOSHUA: So there I was, weighing the odds of *ever* getting repaid, and what does this cunning negotiator do next? He says, *Of course, if I fail . . .*

LINCOLN: *If I fail, I'll probably never be able to pay you at all.*

JOSHUA: Please don't ever put this one in charge of the national debt.

LINCOLN: I lived without hope, you see.

JOSHUA: So, ladies and gentlemen, I looked up into that Lincoln *face*—behold it now—and I thought, *I have never seen a gloomier— a melancholier . . .*

LINCOLN: That's not a word.

JOSHUA: *. . . a sadder countenance in all my years on God's green earth. Surely, as a Christian, I am bound to . . .*

LINCOLN: Oh, get on with it.

JOSHUA: *. . . bound to take pity on this poor lost lamb.* So I squared my shoulders, and I said, *See here, good sir. . . .*

LINCOLN: Good sir?

JOSHUA: *If the contraction of so small a debt affects you so deeply . . .*

LINCOLN: Now you're embroidering.

JOSHUA: *. . . I think I can suggest a plan.*

LINCOLN: He says *plan*, and all I hear is *debt*.

JOSHUA: *It so happens I have a very large room, with a double bed in it. Which you are perfectly welcome to share with me if you choose.* So he says—you can probably guess—*Where can such a place be?*

LINCOLN: He said nothing, he only *pointed*. To this flight of stairs, leading to God knows where.

JOSHUA: They led to the second floor, as any fool could see. So I remained at the counter, and he went upstairs and set his saddle-bags on the floor. Then he came down a few minutes later, face all aglow. A smile such as you'd never think possible. He said, *Well, Speed* . . .

LINCOLN: *Well, Speed, I'm moved. . . .*

[PAUSE]

JOSHUA: He meant moved *in.* Which he all but was.

LINCOLN: There wasn't much of me to convey.

JOSHUA: That very afternoon, he took up residence. Never again to be dislodged.

LINCOLN: Which is how a child of dirt farmers came to share lodgings with an aristocrat. Democracy in action, ladies and gentlemen.

THEY NEVER BORED their listeners with the basic mechanics of sharing a bed—that period in which two bodies come to accommodate each other. Yet there was a bit of a story there, too, in that Lincoln's legs were longer than any bed could comfortably hold. In warm weather, it mattered less because the blankets were thrown off and he could drape his naked feet over the end. In winter, though, with the cold pressing down, he had to stay jackknifed under the comforter, his knees sharply bent. Which meant that, if you were going to share the bed with him, you were obliged to mirror his position. There was no choice.

Most nights, as a consequence, Joshua found himself staring into the back of Lincoln's head, although in the pitch-blackness of that upper room, it was hard to know there was another body a foot away. Lincoln registered less as sight than as sound. Grumbles. Snorts. Snores. And, with some regularity, a chain of whimpers that would carry on until he was actually shaken awake.

"It's all right," Joshua would say. "It's all right."

Over coffee the next morning, Lincoln might recall what he'd been dreaming about. A herd of panthers. Bears feeding on swine. The hind foot of an old nag. The taste of white snakeroot. Other mornings, he would have no memory. And there were days when he simply shrugged and said: "What *wasn't* I dreaming about?"

ONE DECEMBER EVENING, polishing their boots before the back hearth, they fell to speaking of their escapes.

Joshua told of Sangamon County belles who had clung a little too close, of flirtations that had ended (on one side, anyway) in tears. Mothers' hopes dashed, future dynasties extinguished. In the telling of it, the faces tended to blur, but the names survived—a litany of recrimination—and so did the unanswered question. How had things so gotten out of hand?

Why had Frances Goodwin, at the sight of him, run sobbing from the room? Why had Jane Bell, in a voice of choked choler, called him a liar and a cheat? Why had Emily Shore's brother made noises about a duel? With each girl, he could reconstruct his behavior down to the last syllable and find no infamy. Never once had he pressed an advantage, never once had he promised more than he could honor. He had merely been *agreeable*, which was all he'd ever been trained to be.

"The harm," said Lincoln, upon reflection, "is in being so unforgivingly handsome."

Lincoln's experiences were of a different character. No mother had ever pinned her hopes on him. Flirtation, badinage, indirection were foreign to him. His way was to blunder through, all corners—and now and then, such a man blunders into someone else. Lincoln spoke then of the New Salem matron who had tried to bind him to her sister.

"This sister," said Joshua. "What was her name?"

"Mary. Mary Owens."

"What did she look like?"

Lincoln's lips folded down. "Apple cheeks. Dark curly hair. Blue eyes. A little advanced in years—well, she was *my* age, which was near to the same thing."

"You got on with her?"

"Tolerably."

"There was talk of marriage?"

"There was *talk*, I suppose, but from my side, it was only in jest. She went back to Green County, though, with a meaningful look on her face. We exchanged a letter or two, and I very nearly forgot about her, but three years later, she was back. *Flush* with understanding."

"And how did you respond?"

Lincoln smiled grimly, shook his head. "First, I had to make sure it was the same girl. Looking on her, you see, I couldn't stop thinking of my mother."

"What, wrinkles?"

"It was more her . . . her want of *teeth* and her—the whole weather-beaten *look* of her. I tried to imagine her handsome. And the hell of it, she was! It seemed to me that no woman I'd ever seen had a finer face. I tried to convince myself that the—the *mind* was much more to be valued than the *person*. . . ."

"Oh, Brother Abraham."

"And then I just—*delayed* the matter as long as I could. Finally, there was nothing for it but to screw my courage to the sticking place and bring everything to a head."

"Which is to say you made a proposal."

"Direct."

"And?"

Lincoln folded a hand over his mouth. His eyes crinkled.

"She said no."

"She didn't."

"At first I took it for modesty. But when I came back at her, she said no with ever-greater vigor. It was no and *no!*"

Joshua smiled gently. "Poor Lincoln."

"Oh, I was mortified in a hundred different ways. To think *she* had rejected *me!* With all my fancied greatness. And to think I'd been too stupid to grasp how perfectly indifferent she was to me the whole time. And then on top of that . . ."

"What?"

"I'd begun to think I really *was* a little in love with her."

"Just a little?"

"I don't know."

Joshua lofted another log on the fire. Poked it until the sparks streamed upward in a column.

"That was quite a muddle," he said.

"Muddle is all I ever get into with women."

They sat for a time, rubbing down their boots, frowning at the flames.

"What is the moral lesson for you, I wonder?" said Joshua.

"Never again to think of marrying."

"Because you can't find anyone to suit?"

"Because I could never be satisfied with anyone who'd be blockhead enough to have me."

Joshua laughed a little. Laughed a little more. "That is a vow I can get behind."

They touched glasses.

"To bachelorhood," said Lincoln.

"To brotherhood," said Joshua.

ELEVEN

JOSHUA LIKED TO tell people it was the hemp that had driven him from Kentucky.

Every year, under orders of his father, he and his brother worked five months in the fields of Farmington, expected to do what the Negroes did and to bear it without complaint (or at least to defer complaint until they had staggered back home for their bourbons on ice). This was John Speed's way of toughening his sons for the challenges of one day running the family plantation, but nothing could have readied them for the experience of breaking hemp. And being broken by it.

The essential problem was that the stalks had to be *pounded*. Again and again, until the pollen-dust rose up in burning clouds, stinging the eyes, crawling up mouth and nose and throat. Scrub it off at night, it would be there the next morning: coating your pillow, dangling from your very eyelashes. *Invading* you. A slave who broke hemp every day would be coughing out his last fragment of lung by thirty. Even the inmates at the Kentucky State Reformatory, it was said, would sooner cut off their hands than break hemp.

"But you said yourself," Lincoln pointed out. "It was only until you reached your maturity. You weren't to be doing it your whole life."

"Once you have that smell in your nostrils, you can't be free of it. You can't look at a length of rope—a piece of cotton baling—and not shudder."

"But you keep telling me how beautiful Farmington is."

Of that there was no doubt. Orchards and songbirds and plashing streams and a moss-fringed springhouse and a shining white portico. But what kept that portico shining—what kept the whole idea of Farmington afloat—was the free-market price of hemp. ("And slaves," Lincoln liked to put in.) And it was the hemp, finally, that gave Joshua Speed the strength to leave.

The impulse had been building a long time. His earliest, or perhaps fondest, memory was of running through timothy grass. Nothing on the scale of a prairie—just deep enough to close over his four-year-old self the moment he entered. He had never seen an ocean, nor had he traveled within a week's journey of one, but he threw out his arms as he imagined a swimmer would, beating back the grass and imagining that, with each stroke, he was propelling himself deeper. Another child, perhaps, might have quailed at creating such a distance between himself and the known world, but Joshua couldn't sever the tie fast enough. How far did he travel that day? Was it Morocco who brought him back? All he could remember was the joy of disappearing.

At fifteen, he'd followed his brother to St. Joseph College, and when illness kept him from finishing out his term, he'd found a clerkship with a wholesale store in Lexington. Seven miles from home—just far enough to visit every fortnight—and when the store showed signs of going belly-up, Joshua, with a calmness that surprised him, scanned the horizons for the next escape route.

In this way he learned that a goodly number of his fellow Kentuckians were hying themselves across the Ohio River to the Sangamon Valley, where the sixth child in a brood of twelve Speeds might leave the anonymity of the middle and reconfigure himself as an only. Especially (this was the part of the tale that Joshua forbore to tell) if he had a father who would grudgingly extend him credit and a cousin named James Bell already well established in the Springfield mercantile class. Bell & Company may have carried James's surname, but make no mistake, it was Joshua's business, to nurture or kill as he saw fit.

Every day, he haggled with farmers over whether a jar of beeswax was worth a yard of calico or a pair of twenty-pound cabbages was equal to an auger. He heard himself say things like "no to the hog" (where would he keep it?) but "yes to the bushel of oats," "no to the prairie chickens" but "yes to the bag of coon skins." He accepted no promissory notes—too hard to collect on—but he extended credit to the right sorts, and if they didn't pay up, Joshua always waited a humane amount of time before turning the matter over to the courts.

His inventory was constantly refreshed by the wagons that arrived twice a week from St. Louis, bearing log chains and razors and buckskin gloves and Kentucky jeans and white lead and Havana cigars and DuPont's gunpowder by the keg. In search of new suppliers, he traveled as far as Pittsburgh, but was always glad to come home to the slovenly, upwardly striving town that had embraced him.

He was Joshua Speed now. Merchant and booster and apostle of progress. A dandyish, though not extravagant, figure on the streets of Springfield. A valued conversationalist at society functions. A figure so embedded in the local Whig establishment that the great Simeon Francis, dragging his spectacles down the bridge of his nose, had once opined that he had "the makings of a pleasing candidate someday."

Joshua grasped at once the reservations built into that judgment. *Makings*. *Someday*. Most limiting of all, *pleasing*. A pleasing fellow could *merely* please—indeed, could do nothing but. Drift outside that portfolio, he ceased to exist. Well, let it go. He had long ago canvassed his soul and found there not the slightest craving for public office. Nor fame nor wealth.

"What *do* you want?" his father had once asked, in a clench of rage.

The words were queued up on Joshua's tongue. *To be of use*. But there was no point in uttering them, for they would only invite more questions. *Of use to whom? Of use for what?* And even now, all answers died in the utterance. Looking back over his twenty-four years, he could see only a litany of negation. *No* to Farmington. *No* to college. *No* to medicine, the law, the military, the clergy. And what, finally, had he said *yes* to? The chance to own and operate one of *nineteen* dry-goods stores in Springfield, Illinois. He had not escaped the middle, he had joined it.

By now he had mostly ceased to communicate with his father, but John Speed's voice—John Speed's judgments—had a way of seeping through the letters of other family members. If Joshua's mother offered him a barrel of plantation cider, Joshua heard: *Made with no help from you*. If brother James complained about his law studies, Joshua heard: *Hard at work, making a future for himself*. If sister Mary mentioned a second cousin's wedding in Louisville, Joshua heard: *Not your wedding, to be sure*. The judgment, in every case, amounted to the same. Joshua Fry Speed was taking the slow road.

And the possibility that he *would* finish out his days as the keeper of a small store on a muddy, dog-trafficked thoroughfare, notable only for its proximity to the still-birthing state capitol, began to preoccupy him to such an extent that he would pass friends in the street without noticing them. "We waved at you!" they would tell him later. "We even called your name."

Sorry, he should have said. *I was looking for a vocation.* Who would have guessed—who would have had the temerity to suggest—that it would come in the form of a gawky, debt-ridden lawyer from New Salem?

THEY HAD TAKEN their time warming to each other. Joshua at first blamed the difference in their upbringings, but he came to see that it ran deeper, that his own reticence was in the nature of a host unwilling to presume too much on his guest, whereas Lincoln's was soul deep. It didn't matter how innocent the question Joshua lobbed his way. *How do you take your coffee? Would you care for some hardtack? Would you like Charlotte to wash your linen?* Lincoln *enfolded* himself around each query, then disgorged the briefest and least revealing of replies. Always with a faint air of regret, as if he had been tricked into abandoning his Fifth Amendment protections.

It was not caginess, it was a carapace—and Joshua could find no good way to penetrate it. They awoke at the same time every morning. They dressed by the same candle, shaved before the same glass. Drank coffee (obsidian-black) from the same pot. At Joshua's suggestion, they dined together at the Butlers' every afternoon, then returned to their respective workplaces, then reunited after nightfall in the upstairs dormitory. They made a few passing observations on the weather or local events. Joshua climbed into bed; some twenty to thirty minutes later, Lincoln climbed in, too, as quietly as he could, and pulled up the linen.

What changed it all was this: a cravat.

Half a year into their joint tenancy, Lincoln was invited to supper at John Stuart's. Had anyone else invited him, he later admitted, he would have feigned any illness, invented any emergency. But Stuart was his law partner and a candidate for the U.S. Congress and one of Springfield's great men. The doom could not be averted.

Perhaps, though, it could be deferred? Ten minutes before he was scheduled to leave, Lincoln was still only half dressed. He stood there with an air of mute expectancy—shirt sleeves unbuttoned, braces unbuckled—as though reprieve was even now winging its way toward him. Then he took a couple of wincing steps toward the looking glass. From his perch on the window seat,

Joshua glanced up from his day's ledgers. Just as he was about to lower his eyes, Lincoln's voice cut through the space that separated them.

"See here, Speed. Do you know how to tie a cravat?"

It was the tone that disarmed. Like a ten-year-old boy rummaging through his father's wardrobe.

"Oh," said Joshua, rising to his feet. "Of course. . . ."

"I know you're occupied."

"No, it's no trouble at all, it's just . . ."

"Yes?"

"Well, I need you to turn back round and face the glass. I can only do it if I pretend it's me."

"You mean like this?"

"Just so."

Coming from behind, Joshua lightly folded his arms around Lincoln's neck, gazed over Lincoln's shoulder. He watched in the glass as his own fingers, working by rote, wrapped and tied and tucked.

"It looks so easy when you do it," said Lincoln.

"Well, it's—I mean, it isn't *hard*. Once you get the trick of it. But of course," he hurried on, "you needn't bother doing it yourself. Just buy the ones that come already tied."

"That's all I've ever done," Lincoln answered with a frown. "*This* one is a gift from Mrs. Stuart."

"And you couldn't possibly show up—"

"Not wearing it. No, sir."

"In *that* case," said Joshua with a smile, "we shall have a cravat lesson tomorrow night. It won't take more than ten minutes, I promise, and you may go on pleasing Mrs. Stuart to eternity."

Lincoln's gray eyes took on a laminate of warmth, which had the strange effect of raising strawberry patches in Joshua's cheeks.

"That's mighty decent of you," he heard Lincoln say, but Joshua was already shifting his gaze elsewhere—anywhere—and it was then, without his knowing, he made a full investigation of the Lincoln ensemble, right down to the top hat that rested by his right foot.

"If I might?" he ventured.

At once the guardedness returned to Lincoln's eyes. "Of course."

"I'm only wondering if a silk hat might make a better accompaniment than your beaver one."

"Silk?" Lincoln's lips folded down. "I don't own such a thing."

"Oh, that's all right. I've got two or—or *three*. . . ."

And it was to stave off embarrassment that Joshua began striding toward the hat rack by the banister.

"But surely," murmured Lincoln. "The *size* . . ."

"Oh, make no mistake, we could never share a—a *coat* or a pair of trousers, but our *heads* can't be too off the mark, can they? For all my want of brain? Here now, try it on."

In fact, Lincoln's head was markedly larger. The hat *perched* there, like a tiny lighthouse. Lincoln's hands fastened around the brim, pulled it down as hard as they could, but there was no yielding. Joshua was already reaching for it when he heard the other man say: I like it."

"Well, it's . . ." Joshua gave a reassuring nod. "It's more in keeping with your silk coat. . . ."

Which needed to be brushed, but that was a bridge further than Joshua felt he could cross. He merely watched now as Lincoln's features softened.

"I'll tell you what, Speed. I shall come back *with* your hat or upon it."

"No," answered Joshua, with a gulp of laughter. "Not *upon* it, that wouldn't do. Now when are you supposed to be there?"

Lincoln pulled the watch out of his vest pocket. "A minute ago."

There was a final flurry of adjustment and alteration. Looking only slightly less mournful than before, Lincoln strode to the top of the stairs.

"I'm really most grateful," he said.

THAT NIGHT, JOSHUA went to bed a little earlier than usual, then awoke, sometime after eleven, to the sound of boots, trudging penitentially up the stairs. The candle flame had guttered down to the size of a fingernail, so Lincoln conveyed now as a peculiarly elongated shadow.

"How did you fare?" Joshua called.

"Well," said Lincoln, "it was superior to being eaten by boll weevils and scalped by an Injun."

Joshua smiled. "A success."

With a grunt, Lincoln slumped down onto the edge of the bed. Began prying off his boots and then, with a start, remembered the hat, which had realigned itself at a cockeyed angle, like someone in a burning house, preparing to jump.

"This was the biggest success of all," he said. "Mrs. Stuart made a point of saying what a nice hat it was."

"Well, there you are."

"She liked it so much she asked me to take it off and hand it to her so it might not suffer any harm."

"Take it *off*, she said?"

"Yes."

"That's peculiar."

"I'd say so."

Frowning, Joshua stared into the last remnants of candle flame.

"Were you . . ." He gave his throat a quick clearing. "Sorry, were you wearing the hat *indoors*, by any chance?"

"For a stretch. Otherwise, no one would have seen it." Lincoln sat there for a while. "That was wrong, wasn't it?"

"Well . . ."

"I thought, being silk . . ."

"No, it's not the—it's not the *composition*. Hats are hats, you see. In regard to the . . . the . . ."

"The rules."

"Well, yes."

"Huh." Lincoln angled his head toward the window. "I wonder if the Stuarts will ever ask me back now." His head dropped an increment. "Not that I'd mind so much, but it might be damned awkward come Christmas."

For some quiet interval, Joshua studied the hunched, angular form perched at the edge of the bed. Then, in the voice of a conspirator, he whispered: "Tomorrow night. Cravats *and* rules. . . ."

TWELVE

—•—

"Now remember," said Joshua, "before you go into supper, the master of the house must first ask you to pass in."

"Then who leads the way?"

"*He* does. Or else the mistress of the house. At any rate, you offer your arm to one of the lady guests."

"Which one?"

"The one of greatest distinction."

Lincoln chewed that over. "You mean the oldest?"

"Precisely. If she is already taken, you . . ."

"Go down the ladder."

"Eldest to youngest, yes. As best you can determine. So . . . why don't we walk through it?"

Rising gingerly to his feet, Lincoln extended a stiff arm to an invisible escort. Took a single lunge forward.

"That stride is a little long," said Joshua. "The object is to match her gait."

"Not with these feet."

"Well then, just try not to—*drag* her out of her natural cadence. There, that's more like it. Now you lead her to her chair."

"How do I know which is hers?"

"If there's no name card, the hostess will direct you."

His face a rictus of concentration, Lincoln advanced three more steps. Softly unhooked his arm from his companion's.

"That's right," said Joshua. "You draw out the chair. And when she is safely ensconced, you bow. No, not quite that low. Just a little decline of the head. She will bow *back* and—"

"Wait," protested Lincoln. "I thought she's the one to bow first."

"That's only if you pass her in the street."

"But in the dining room, it's reversed?"

"Well, consider it your way of *thanking* her for the honor of escorting her. It's the same after a dance. She has conferred this inestimable favor on you, and you are grateful beyond words, and so you bow, do you see?"

Lincoln stared helplessly at the ceiling. "This is the queerest business. It's a wonder anybody gets it right."

"Oh, very few of us get it right *all* the time. And there's a loophole, you know. When somebody gets it wrong, it's bad manners to notice."

Night after night, they gathered. Sometimes, depending on the press of their respective business, they had no more than fifteen minutes left before bedtime. Just enough time to review the usage of knife and fork or the drapery of the napkin or the proper way to get in a carriage or the best brushstrokes for blacking boots. Lincoln had no great trust in his powers of mimesis, so he forced himself to rehearse each ritual again and again. (Some nights, he was still at it well after Joshua had gone to sleep.) When it came to a rule, however, he had only to be told once to own it forever. God forbid any rule should come close to contradicting another. It was then that the full brunt of the Lincoln brain was brought down, ironing out every Talmudic wrinkle.

Sometimes, in the midst of absorbing some new intelligence, he would close his eyes and, in a wondering hush, ask, "Speed, where did you *learn* all this nonsense?" Joshua had no good answer, or at least no single answer. From his mother he had acquired the proper salutations. From his brother, the gentleman's toilet. Hunting and riding decorum from his father. Morocco had taught him how to keep his cuffs, and Mrs. McMecken, his landlady at St. Joseph College, had shown him (through trial and error) how to flirt without being forward.

He learned to dance from a squat and fiery German lady who would slap down his shoulders every time they hunched upward and cry "*Mit Leichtigkeit!*" ("With ease!") And from Grandmother Fry . . . well, she had taken him on his first *visite de digestion*. He was only eleven at the time and considered the whole business a waste of time. Calling on some Louisville matron just to thank her for throwing such an enchanting supper the Sunday previous? What a bore. But from the very start, he'd been taken by the complexity of the interactions between the two women. So deliberate, so curiously fraught. He soaked it all up as a priest his catechism, and the first thing he did upon returning home was to re-create the whole encounter.

Of course, he had always considered such knowledge fundamentally use-less—now at last he had found someone who not only valued it but couldn't plumb it deeply enough. Every night a new question. When you retire from a private ball, are you obliged to say good night to the host or hostess? Should gentlemen carry their calling cards in cases? Or were their pockets sufficient? How does one address a doctor? A general? A count? How long may one speak of the weather before graduating to another topic?

The more Lincoln learned, the more he wanted to know. The best way to begin a thank-you letter. Where to put your arms during supper and when to rise after dessert. Again and again, an upbringing that had always struck Joshua as no more than decorative turned out to have practical utility. "Escorting down a staircase?" he'd say. "Oh, that's easy. A lady always gets the side next to the wall. You present your right arm unless that puts her by the balustrade."

"And if she's to return in a carriage?"

"Why, you walk her out, and you hand her up the stairs, that's all."

"Hand her *in*. What does that mean? Show me."

Show me. That might have been the refrain of their whole apprenticeship. Show me how to keep soup off my sleeves. How to sip wine. How to pour water for somebody without spilling on the cloth. When to leave. When to come back. *If* to come back. Show me, Speed!

One night in February, they even practiced the waltz. Blame Mrs. Francis, who had told Lincoln that, if he were ever to flourish in the higher realms, he would have to apply himself to the terpsichorean.

"By which I think she means dancing," said Lincoln. "Which, if she does, I'm sunk."

"Nonsense," said Joshua. "It's a matter of repetition, that's all. Think of it as a military drill."

"I was afraid you'd say that."

During the Black Hawk War, Lincoln had been voted captain of a company of Clary's Grove boys, despite having no practice of any kind in marching. He couldn't even figure out the command for getting two platoons through a gate, so he'd mumbled something like *This company is dismissed for two minutes, when it will fall in again on the other side.*

"And I never did get any better at it."

Joshua assured him there would be no superior officers watching. "Just you and your God," he said, smiling.

"You had to bring him into it. Very well. *Show me.*"

So they waited until the night's visitors had dispersed, and they cleared some space in the store between the pocketknives and the curry combs. They sketched out a chalk square on the floor and set to work.

It was the tempo that defeated Lincoln at first. No matter how many times Joshua chanted "*One*-two-three . . . *one*-two-three. . . ." Lincoln kept adding a beat. Every circle he tried to square; every square he converted to a circle. They rehearsed him at first with a phantom partner, his arms lofted like dead branches, but his feet, despite having no toes to step on, refused to do what was asked of them.

"All right," said Joshua. "Try it with me. Until you find your way."

"We'll regret this," Lincoln said.

"Now *you* are the lead, so you will just . . . you will *hook* your right hand round my back. Like that. Now I will rest my hand . . . lightly . . . *here.*"

"This will end badly."

"Be quiet. Now . . . raise your elbows. Shoulder height, that's it. And back *straight*. And knees . . . well, you *can* bend the knees a little."

"Like this?"

"Well, no, not like you're praying."

"I am praying."

"Just an inch or two is all you need. Very good. Now bring your feet together. Fine. Now your first step is forward with—your *left* foot. Not quite so far. . . ."

There was seven inches' difference in their height, and Joshua was no better versed in following than Lincoln in leading, but the greatest danger they faced was having their eyes meet. They knew that, in that moment, the whole enterprise would dissolve. So Lincoln kept his gaze fixed on his boots, and Joshua tilted his face toward the ceiling.

"So your right foot goes . . . diagonally. Yes, just like that. Now all you have to do is bring your left foot over. Yes. And now, Mr. Lincoln, we are halfway *there*."

"If you say so."

"We move in reverse. You step back with your right—no, your *right*. That's it. Now diagonally with the left. And then bring the—yes, the *right* foot over. *Et voilà!* Back to starting position."

"Once more," said Lincoln.

So they went at it, again and again, Joshua keeping time and, without letting on, increasing the tempo. By the twentieth go-around, they were moving at very nearly a ballroom pace. It was here that Joshua chanced a glance at his partner's face and found there a look of such grave apprehension that he lost an entire beat. If Lincoln had felt the caesura, things would never have ended in disaster, but he carried on unheedingly. A second later, their legs were entwined beyond repair, and down they went with a great clatter, limbs splaying toward every compass point of Joshua Speed's store. And with that, the laughter they had been at such pains to contain came cascading out of them. For some minutes they lay on the wood planking, rib cages shaking.

"There's always the quadrille," said Joshua.

THIRTEEN

———◆———

THE FIRST TIME Joshua offered to buy him clothes, Lincoln rebuffed the idea so sharply that Joshua refrained from offering again. It was a distinction worth noting: Lincoln was open to tutelage but would close the door on charity. Clothes would have to wait until his finances were more secure.

It didn't take as long as Joshua feared. With John Stuart now running for the Twenty-Sixth Congress, the bulk of the law firm's business had fallen to Lincoln. He dutifully kept half of the retainers for his partner, but his presence in so many courtrooms, coupled with his rising prominence on the political scene, gave him the aura of a sure bet. A steady—or, at least, steadier—stream of clients began to pour into his Hoffman's Row office: abandoned wives, cuckolded husbands, brawlers, speculators, the occasional murderer. Lincoln collected their fees, rode the circuit, won more cases than he lost, paid down his New Salem debts, and in the fall of 1838, announced to Joshua that he might be open to a new evening coat.

"Only because . . . well, you've seen the one I've got. I mean, I'd take the thing out back and shoot it, but that would leave me coatless."

"Leave it to me."

It so happened that a misunderstanding with a St. Louis supplier had left Bell & Company with a surfeit of watered silk. Joshua relayed Lincoln's measurements to Kirkman the tailor. A week later, Lincoln stood before the largest looking glass he had ever encountered and watched as the swallowtail coat was lowered onto him like a suit of armor.

"Well," he said after a time, "it fits."

"And while we're here," said Joshua. He nodded to Kirkman, who, with a soft flourish, brought forth a bundle, wrapped in butcher paper.

"Buffalo hide?" guessed Lincoln.

"Open it," said Joshua.

It was a waistcoat. Persian blue, with jacquard stitching. It might have been a hunk of moon for how foreign it looked in Lincoln's hands.

"This can't be for me," he said, softly.

"Who else?"

"But it's . . . it's got color in it. . . ."

"Doesn't it?"

"I can't afford it."

"It's squarely within your budget. Now hold still."

As they buttoned it onto him, Lincoln kept angling and reangling himself toward the glass. "It seems a touch gaudy," he murmured.

"Not in the least."

But still he writhed inside that waistcoat, until finally Joshua said, "Why are you acting that way? It fits you just fine."

"I guess I'm thinking of my old friend Justice Green. He used to walk into court with just a shirt and breeches and one suspender. He didn't even wear *shoes* reliably. What would he think to look at me now?"

"He'd think you were rising in the world."

"Too fast, maybe."

Joshua expelled a sigh. "It's a waistcoat, Lincoln. Not a primrose path."

Lincoln tugged at each of the buttons, all but daring them to come off. A note of resolution began to concentrate in those gray eyes.

"If I'm to wear this, Speed, you have to be there, too."

"Where?"

"In the very room where it's taking place."

"And what will that accomplish?"

"It will give me somebody to blame."

. . .

IN THOSE DAYS, both of them bore a certain stigma in the eyes of Springfield hostesses. Lincoln, of course, because he was Lincoln. But even Speed, for all his courtliness, had, in the eyes of some injured parties, toyed too lightly with local girls' affections. As a result, neither man received as many invitations as an eligible bachelor might otherwise have expected, and the chances of them being asked to the same event were negligible. So it was with some surprise and even a bit of suspicion that they realized they had both been invited to an autumnal-equinox party at the Merrymans'.

The house, as they approached, was festooned with the dead husks of Sangamon County corn. An ominous enough décor that Lincoln asked if they could take another tour round the block before entering.

"Don't be a goose," said Joshua. "You're not marching to the gallows."

"So you say."

They walked in side by side, but from the moment the door was closed on them, Joshua reverted to the old modalities. Strode straight into the Merrymans' already rather cramped parlor and began meting out his radiance in calibrated doses. A smile, a grin, a bow, a laugh. Within five minutes, as many guests had told him how pleasant it was to see him again. Women, as ever, warmed to the ingenuous eyes, complicated by the slightly excessive length of hair, but even jealously disposed husbands—tonight, it was Lawrason Levering—could be brought in line just by Joshua clapping them on their shoulders and commiserating over the female mystery.

Some half an hour passed before Joshua turned and found Lincoln standing, alone, in the far corner of the parlor. The sight of him now—so silent, so grave—was obscurely troubling to Joshua's soul. Twice, he turned away, only to turn back. After a time, it seemed the sole remedy was to keep him company, if only for a minute or two.

"No," hissed Lincoln, putting out a forestalling hand. "I prefer it this way."

"It's just as well. I'm a bit fatigued."

Joshua spoke more truly than he knew, for as he gazed out now upon the roomful of guests—the ones he had been at such pains to conquer—they grew steadily more oppressive to his senses. The candle-painted masks of their faces, the squawk of their voices. He watched them bob and whirl and wince and cozen, and he felt himself recoiling by degrees, until the only thing sealing off his escape was the wall itself.

Why, he thought suddenly, *this is how Lincoln sees the world.*

The revelation left him even more determined to hold fast. So they remained there, the two of them, a pair of obelisks, invisible to all others . . . or so Joshua thought until, an hour or so into the evening, Mrs. Francis, looking even redder than usual in the cheeks, came sallying over to them.

"Mr. Lincoln!" she declared. "How handsome you look!"

Had she jabbed him with one of her hat pins, she could not have produced a more pained look.

"I thank you," he murmured.

"That waistcoat is particularly suiting."

"Oh." He picked at the topmost button. "That's . . . that's Speed's doing. . . ."

"Is it?" Mrs. Francis's eyes lost not a fraction of their brightness as she pivoted toward Joshua. "Then this is a happy alliance! Lincoln and Speed!"

That night, the two men took a more roundabout route home than usual—as if, by common consent, they needed more time to digest the evening's events.

"Do you know?" Joshua said at last. "I believe Mrs. Francis would marry you if she could."

"She would marry my waistcoat." There was a pause before Lincoln added, in a slyer tone: "That's a little like marrying the both of us, don't you think?"

FROM THEN ON, whenever Lincoln found a surplus in his bank balance, he set aside a certain portion for clothes, and once a month, he and Joshua ventured over to Kirkman's for some new sartorial wonder. A waistcoat with stripes. A coat of black bombazine. Nankeen pantaloons. White drill trousers. Embroidered shirts.

Lincoln always wanted Joshua to be in the room with him before he sported anything new in public. As a result, many weeks might go by before that article of clothing got its airing, and if it were inconspicuous enough—say, a pair of wool socks, purchased at discount from Bell & Company—the evening might end with nobody the wiser. But some part of the new Lincoln must have developed a craving for attention, for when no one else provided it, he would make a point of catching Joshua's glance and, with the most comically blank of faces, gesturing to the article in question. The immediate effect on Joshua was always a convulsion of laughter. The larger effect was something warmer and deeper—and for a long time, quite mysterious, for he had never experienced it before. That sensation of being enrolled in a private alliance, concealed at its core.

Nobody else knows. That was the refrain that kept singing through his brain. Every day, the list of things that only he and Lincoln alone were privy to—passing misadventures, comic leitmotifs—grew ever larger, refused to be limited, and it seemed now to Joshua that the best reason to devote all their free hours to each other was to build upon that body of arcane knowledge—to build it *high*, like some silo that only they could see.

They were now a tandem, and among Springfield hostesses, it was said that if you invited one, you must invite the other. And whenever they arrived at an event and stood shoulder to shoulder in the doorway, the shout that rose up was always on the order of "There they are!" or "They took their sweet time coming" or, more teasingly, "Who invited *them*, anyway?" Ned Baker took to calling them Damon and Pythias. No, said Arch Herndon, teasingly, they were more like Romulus and Remus (though they couldn't have been less twin-like). At table, they were routinely seated together. More than that, addressed together, interrogated together, sent out into the world together. If anything of note had taken place within the walls of Bell & Company, it was assumed that Lincoln would be the one to start telling and that Joshua would interrupt at regular intervals with corrections. If, by contrast, the tale centered on Lincoln, the process would go exactly in reverse.

JOSHUA: There were six of us, I think, riding along this country road outside Chandlerville. Wild plums, crab-apple trees. . . .

LINCOLN: He's setting the scene.

JOSHUA: Hardin was there and . . . I can't remember, was Baker there?

LINCOLN: He was.

JOSHUA: So we dismounted at a creek, and while the horses were drinking, we looked round and . . . suddenly there were only four of us.

LINCOLN: Nothing gets past Speed.

JOSHUA: We made a quick reconnaissance, and we realized that the missing parties were Messieurs Hardin and Lincoln. Who were bringing up the rear. Well, before we could even sound the alarm, Hardin came trotting up. Alone. *Come now, where's Lincoln?* we asked. *Oh,* said Hardin, *if I told you, you wouldn't believe me.* So we pressed a little harder, and he said, *Last I saw him, he was walking away with two wee birds in hand.* Well, as you might expect, we were curious to know what Mr. Lincoln was doing with a pair of wee birds.

LINCOLN: You forgot to mention the windstorm.

JOSHUA: I was getting round to it.

LINCOLN: Now would be a good time to—

JOSHUA: Very *well.* Just before we set out, there was a violent windstorm, and these two young birds . . .

LINCOLN: Too young to fly.

JOSHUA; Too young to fly . . . were blown out of their nest and left *lying* there by the side of the road. Of course, the rest of us rode right on past. It took the tenderhearted Mr. Lincoln to spy them there.

LINCOLN: And hear the mother bird's cry.

JOSHUA: So what did he do? He gathered up these two wee birds and set off in search of their nest. Which obliged the rest of us to remain by that creek an entire hour, waiting for our companion here to redress this—this *crime* against nature. And what did he say when at last he came riding up? Go ahead, tell them.

LINCOLN: I said if I'd left them there, I wouldn't have been able to sleep again.

JOSHUA: *Their cries would've been ringing in my ears,* that's how he put it.

LINCOLN: And, ladies and gentlemen, I would do the same again.

JOSHUA: Yes, but he's left out his real offense. He hasn't yet billed the mother bird for his services. What kind of lawyer *is* he?

Even as he held up his end of the narrative, Joshua noted with some delight how attuned their listeners were to the contrapuntal rhythm—attention flowing easily from one man to the other, enjoyment mounting with each interchange. Without ever intending to, he and Lincoln had created a kind of parlor theater—close enough, at any rate, to the playacting of the Illinois General Assembly that Lincoln began, for the first time, to relax in genteel company and to call upon the full arsenal of his rhetorical devices. One night, with a quiet swell of triumph, Joshua heard Mrs. Ridgely whispering to Mrs. Mather: "My dear, I had no notion Lincoln was so droll. I mean, that business about the preacher and the *lizard*. . . ."

WHENEVER THE ELEMENTS allowed, they took an evening walk. It was Joshua's favorite time to tour the city. The two men walked down Fifth Street, west on Monroe, up Fourth, west on Madison. On some nights, if the weather was fine, they'd turn their backs on the city altogether and travel north until the town melted away into a level plain. With only the moon or the stars for light, they'd pick their way along some narrow path until they reached the Northern Cross railbed. There wasn't a speck of rail to be found, and the locomotive was still a year or two away from reaching Springfield, but in Joshua's eyes, that elevation was luminous with the prospect of motion. Here the two men would stop, declining to go farther, and begin to speak of the places they'd traveled, and even after the talk tapered off, they would remain there in equable silence, neither in a hurry to return.

It was on one of these nights that Lincoln impulsively threw his arm around his friend. *Held* it there and then said, in a voice of rare warmth: "I do not lie, Speed. Meeting you was the greatest fortune that ever befell me."

To Joshua, it was the most foreign of gestures. Somebody *reaching* for him—and not in anger, as his father might have done. He had no answer for it, and it was nearly a mercy when, a second later, the hand pried itself free and Lincoln said: "Shall we head back?"

Their bedtime rituals that night were the same as ever. Joshua, in a habit imposed upon him years earlier by his mother, gave his hair three quick brushes, and by the light of a single candle, they hastened to undress—for the night was cold and the fire was out—and throw on their nightshirts. Lincoln spent his usual hour reading and, with his usual care, slid himself under the goose-feather comforter. There followed the usual rearrangement of bodies, half-conscious, and then all was still.

"Lincoln," said Joshua.

From somewhere in the darkness: "Mm. . . ."

"Did you mean what you said?"

"Uhh . . ." A stirring of sheet. "Did I . . . ? Sorry. . . ."

Joshua lay there for a while longer.

"Never mind," he said.

He assumed it would die there. Never would he have expected Lincoln to turn round in the bed, to front him in the way he did.

"Did I mean what, Speed?"

FOURTEEN

THE LETTER THAT Joshua wrote his mother every Christmas was virtually the same text from year to year, and the 1840 edition was at first no exception.

> Dearest Mother,
>
> I hope you are well. I think of you oftener than any one of the family, and even in this joyous season, I find my joy tempered by our separation. Next to seeing you and claiming and receiving from you your kiss, and your blessing, writing to you is the most pleasant way I know to spend this day. . . .

He might have carried on in just this vein, but in the midst of his dutiful scratching, a strange impulse stole over him. He slid the letter slowly away, snatched up another sheaf of folio writing paper, and began writing a new draft.

> Dearest Mother,
>
> Tell Father that I have found my vocation.
>
> Only I'm not sure it _is_ a vocation, exactly. A calling . . . a path? . . . The essential point is that I believe myself to be moving forward.
>
> Do you recall that time I was traveling to St. Louis on business and my carriage overturned and I came _this_ close to being hurled into the

Mississippi? My first thought, as I later wrote, was of you. Of course it was. But I think, if it were to happen again, my thoughts would fly to him as well—not in your stead, I mean, but in parallel flight. I would wonder who was going to keep his cravat plumb if I were dead. Who would remind him to change out his linen and nudge him awake in the mornings when he was slumbering a little too heavy? All those small considerations that he would never think of himself.

You'll like him, Mother, when you meet him. Once you get past the physical element of him—that does put some off—you'll find there is not a scrap of affectation or unnaturalness in him. He is purely what he is and thinks more deeply, more searchingly than anybody I know.

If I could contrive to bring you over on some great southerly wind, I would have you come for one of our Poetical Society gatherings. The name is ironical; there is nothing remotely poetical about it. I suppose one might call it a social club, though it has no organization, nor any fixed membership. Night after night, in all weathers, eight or ten choice Springfield spirits assemble at the back of my store. They come not to be fed, as they have already dined. Nor exactly to drink, though we supply every potable. They come to talk.

They are local eminences, invited without distinction of party. On any night, a Democrat like Mr. Douglas might light into a Whig such as Mr. Baker; Mr. Calhoun might do the same with Mr. Browning. But more often than not, politics drops out of the conversation. They speak of last week's snow or the price of pork or the exorbitant rates at the American House. At some point, however—somewhere in that interval between ten and eleven—silence will descend upon the throng and one of their rank will inevitably say . . . "What do you think, Lincoln?"

This is the question that has been bubbling beneath the surface all the while. It is, I daresay, the point toward which the entire evening has been climbing. These men, you see, have come here for many things, but more than anything, they have come for Lincoln.

You might wonder how your boy contributes to this intellectual ferment. Let me see. Before the men arrive, I arrange the kindling. I light the wood. I prepare the cider and the coffee. If I have any filberts or Zante currants at hand, I put them out. I provide cuspidors. I fill glasses, I refill them. Now and again, somebody will call out to me . . . something on the order of "Speed! Sit down for a spell. Tell us what you think." I tell them I am too busy listening. They don't know how truthfully I speak.

It is with no small reluctance that our guests finally quit our premises. Whether they have a block to walk or a half mile, whether they have wives waiting on them or merely empty bedsteads, there is a part of them which wishes to linger and cannot. But this is the tribute they pay us as they depart. They look back and they sing out: "Good night, gentlemen!" By which they mean the both of us. The one who has supplied the thoughts and the one who has supplied the conditions. We are—in this moment, at least—an alliance of equals, and it seems to me there is nothing more I need ask of this life.

Have I persuaded you, Mother? Have I . . . ?

It was his hand that faltered first. In the rush to get all the words on the page, the muscles in his fingers finally contracted into a knot. He had to flex and unflex them to get them to work again . . . and it was in this interval that the second thoughts rushed in. He recalled suddenly that the envelope, per family instructions, would have to be addressed care of his father. John Speed would be wrapping his knotty hands around his letter—tearing open the envelope—dragging the pages to the light—*reading* them, line after incriminating line.

With a drumming heart, Joshua snatched up the letter and crumpled it into a ball. He took a breath, two breaths. Then he reached for the candle and touched it to the paper. When the last smolder had died out, Joshua took a whisk broom and swept the ashes, still oily from the heat, into a can.

For some time, he sat there at the writing table, watching the morning light smear across the window glass. Somewhere toward noon, he heard a pair of feet mounting the stairs. Unmistakable, their mournful tread, even under the squeak of melted snow. He waited. Then, from the top of the steps, he heard Lincoln's hedged voice.

"Speed?"

On any other day, Joshua would have turned round, made some pleasantry. Today, the room fairly swelled with his silence.

"I understand," said Lincoln at last. "Christmas makes me morbid, too."

Joshua nodded a fraction.

"Devilish holiday," said Lincoln.

Once more Joshua nodded.

"We could walk over to Watson's Saloon," said Lincoln. "There should be quite the crowd right around now."

"Oh," said Joshua, "I think not. Or later, perhaps."

"As you like."

Lincoln took a step forward, stopped. Then two longer strides, until he was standing just over Joshua's left shoulder.

"Seeing as how I haven't said it, I should probably say it now. Merry Christmas."

Next to Joshua's elbow he set a small cardboard box, skillfully wrapped in a Delft-blue bow.

"I got someone else to do the ribbon," said Lincoln.

For a second or two, Joshua did nothing but stare at it. Then, willing his stilled fingers into motion, he unwrapped the box, reached into a cloud of crepe paper, and drew out a gold pocket watch.

Somebody must already have wound it, for even now it lay ticking in his palm. By instinct, he tugged open the cover, squinted down at the watch face. Ten minutes to twelve. Then he turned the watch over, and, from the gilt surface, an engraved monogram bodied forth.

JFS

"Please tell me I got the middle initial right," said Lincoln. "It *is* Fry, isn't it?"

"Yes."

"Well, that's a relief."

Joshua set the watch down on the desk. He rose, very slowly.

"It seems I owe you an apology, Lincoln."

"What on earth for?"

"I didn't . . . I mean, I've given you *nothing* . . . nothing at all. . . ."

A smile spread itself slowly across Lincoln's face.

"Liar," he said.

ONE AFTERNOON IN February, while carting in a load of Havana coffee that had been delayed four days by a levee break, Joshua fainted. His clerk, not knowing what else to do, propped him against a stool and brought him a glass of cider.

"Should I fetch a doctor, Mr. Speed?"

"No. No, there's . . . would you just help me up?" He felt his own brow: scalding. "I'm just going to close my eyes for a bit."

But as he climbed the steps to his room, he collapsed once more. By the time he crawled to the top of the stairs, he had voided his bowels and had only enough strength left to climb into bed.

From there, he lost all sense of waking or sleeping. He was told later that Dr. Henry had come twice to call. That typhoid and cholera had been ruled out but nothing else ruled *in*. That quinine and whiskey had failed to produce a change and that letters had been drafted for his family in the event he never emerged.

He was beyond knowing or caring. It seemed to him that he floated in a medium specific to him—somewhere between solid and liquid but refusing to resolve in either direction.

In his delirium, he hosted many visitors. First, his mother, fluttering about the bed in a nun's wimple and only stopping at intervals to press compresses to his eyes. His brother James sat quietly by the window, with a fat volume of Blackstone in his lap. Frances Goodwin floated in like some dark angel, for the sole purpose of gloating. "You see?" she cried. "This is what comes of leading a girl on."

Before too long, the dead came to call. Grandfather Speed, dragging his war-ravaged leg. Sister Ann—poor little Ann—fresh as a sunrise and wearing the pea-green silk she had worn at her funeral. A family Negro named Charles Harrison, who ran off one day and was never brought back. On his way to Indiana, that's what everyone thought. A free man. But as he now staggered toward Joshua's bed, the Ohio River puddled round each step, and his eyes were pools of white, with no irises. Joshua tried to pull the sheets over his head.

"I didn't," he muttered. "It wasn't . . ."

He lay there for four days and three nights . . . and awoke, as if to a new planet, sprawled across a bed that felt vaguely like his, with something that looked like the sun carving highways through a swirl of dust motes.

A hand was lying on his forehead. A man's voice was saying: "I think it's broken."

The fever, he meant, but Joshua, in his dazedness, began to feel about his arms and legs, searching for fissures. The ceiling drew away by degrees, and the mattress grew solid beneath his weight, and the air thinned into translucency. Somewhere above him, he found Lincoln's drawn face.

"Good morning. No, hold on," said Lincoln, pulling his watch out of his vest pocket. "*Afternoon.*"

Joshua's first thought was that he was still soiled. But the sheets that enfolded him were clean. So, too, the nightgown that someone had wrapped round him. Somewhere, incense was burning.

"The store," he said at last.

"Billy and Charlie are keeping it going."

"Um . . . there was a shipment. It was due to come in. . . ."

"Taken care of," said Lincoln.

With some difficulty, Joshua raised himself onto his elbows. Then sank back down.

"You've been here?" he murmured.

"Not the *whole* time."

"What day is it?"

"The twelfth."

He closed his eyes. Inched back through the calendar. Eleven, ten, nine . . .

"There was . . ."

"Yes."

"There was a *vote*. Wasn't there? On the bank charter. . . ."

"I'd say Illinois can get by without me for a few days."

Joshua became suddenly aware of the bed—of his own position within it—arms and legs flung to each side.

"Where did *you* sleep?" he asked.

"On the floor." A sly smile. "You *would* insist on thrashing, Joshua."

And there it was. The first time he had ever heard his Christian name on Lincoln's lips. A pocket of air lodged in the convalescent's throat.

"Brother Abraham, I'm . . ."

Lincoln leaned in, waited.

"I'm *moved*," said Joshua. Not even understanding the resonance of those words until he saw the answering flicker in the other man's eyes.

"Well, here's how it is, Speed. A fellow can't sit idle when his dance instructor has been laid low. That's against all etiquette."

Joshua must have extended his hand, for he found it, of a sudden, resting in the other man's hand. Through the half-open window, the creaking of a wagon. The grunts of rooting pigs. A dog's bark. The sounds that living things make.

"It didn't get me," he said.

"No, sir. Not on Captain Lincoln's watch."

FIFTEEN

"IT WON'T DO, I tell you!" Mrs. Francis was coming at them with her fan pointed like a rapier. "Two bachelors, holding themselves aloof! I have said it before—it is a crime against womanhood."

Lincoln, trapped in the corner of yet another parlor—in this case, Mrs. Francis's own—did what he usually did in such cases. He bowed his head and mumbled regrets, leaving the work of appeasement to Joshua, who at once assured Mrs. Francis that no crime was in progress, they were only catching up on business.

"*That* is not the business which interests me," she retorted. "I care about the business of the *heart*. When will you allow yourselves to be claimed by some blushing maiden?"

If Joshua thought Mrs. Francis would be put off by their silence, he was mistaken. She simply waited them out, with an air of martyred patience.

"You know how it is," said Lincoln at last. "I honor the female sex by leaving it alone."

"Is that the principle *you* follow?" asked Mrs. Francis, shifting her gaze to Joshua.

He could feel the color rising in his cheeks. "I can't say that I have *any* principle, really. . . ."

"You are an agnostic in love."

"If you like."

What was more troubling in that moment? The fixed, but in no way over-bearing, gaze of Mrs. Francis? Or the thin, squiggly sound of his own laughter, trying to clear the air? Long after their hostess had quit them, a crackle of disquiet remained in his skin. He might have tamped it down with food and wine, but at supper, something curious happened. For the first time in recent memory, he and Lincoln were seated apart.

To make matters still stranger, Lincoln was given pride of place along-side Mrs. Francis, while Joshua was placed alongside Judge Breese. It was, in theory, a promotion, for Breese had recently been appointed to the Illinois Supreme Court and carried himself accordingly; even his hair seemed to bil-low with consequence. The judge had just launched into a learned dissertation on whether a governor could legally remove a secretary of state when Joshua found his eyes drifting helplessly to the far corner of the table, where Lincoln and Mrs. Francis sat in rapt conversation. Again and again, over the course of the meal, Joshua darted a glance over, trying to catch his friend's eye—searching for that silent moment of communion that would allow him to laugh off the whole dismal affair. But Lincoln looked his way only once and in such a preoccupied fashion that Joshua might well have been a wall sconce.

"And now, perhaps, you're wondering," said Judge Breese, "if the secretary of state *can* be removed, may he then be replaced at the governor's discretion? Well, my young whelp, that opens an entirely *new* realm of jurisprudence. . . ."

On their way home, Lincoln said, "You're quiet."

Joshua lifted his hat, combed his hand through his hair. "I was fearfully bored, that's all."

"Small wonder. Judge Breese could put the angels to sleep."

They walked on in silence. Then Joshua, struggling to keep the aggrieve-ment out of his voice, said: "Why do you suppose she put me there?"

"Not a clue."

"I couldn't help but think she was punishing me."

Lincoln gave him a quizzical look. "Why would she do that?"

"Who knows? She's a plotter, that one. Beneath all the chatter."

They were coming round the northeast corner of the town square when Lincoln, with a sigh, declared, "If anyone was being punished tonight, it was me. Two hours of uninterrupted interrogation. I'm surprised she didn't inspect my entrails."

"They would have been tastier than the pudding," said Joshua. And was rewarded with the sound of Lincoln's laughter, easy and rolling.

Two weeks later, Joshua, entering the *Sangamo Journal* offices, interrupted a meeting between Lincoln and the Francises. A private meeting, by the look of it, the three of them leaning across a baize-covered desk, their voices scaled to the level of a chamber trio. Joshua's first instinct was to step back out of the doorway, but Mrs. Francis had already scented him.

"Mr. Speed! What a lovely surprise."

Surprise was, indeed, stamped entire onto Lincoln's features as he swung his head toward the doorway.

"So sorry to interrupt," said Joshua. "We're due at the Lyceum. Conkling is speaking, remember?"

Lincoln lurched to his feet. "Very sorry. It passed clean out of mind."

"Isn't that like men?" said Mrs. Francis. "Thank heavens for Mr. Speed, who never forgets."

The effect was the same as it had been in her parlor. A barometric prickling in his skin, as if some storm front were even now funneling down. It stayed there the rest of the evening—and then returned the next day when a servant brought a note from Mrs. Francis, asking him to tea on Thursday. There was no mention of other guests.

Joshua carried the invitation straight to Lincoln's law office. "Kindly explain."

"How could I?"

"You're saying you don't know what's at the back of her mind."

"I don't even know what's at the back of *my* mind."

Joshua frowned down at the card, traced its lavender border through three circuits. "It's most peculiar."

"Speed, you could just say no. She's not the Empress Elisabeth."

"In her *mind*, she is. She's certainly not the sort to take no for an answer."

"Then go."

"Yes, and into what trap?"

"Then don't go."

The first note of strain in Lincoln's voice. Just enough to make Joshua turn toward the window, where he stood for a minute, watching two blind horses drag a spring wagon through the muck.

"Here is the difficulty," he said. "You are one of those rare creatures who says what he believes and believes what he says. That is why you are slow to fathom those who do *neither*."

Lincoln sat back in his Windsor chair and squared his hands on his knees. In a voice lacking any inflection, he said: "You consider me slow?"

"You know what I mean," Joshua hedged.

"Not yet."

"I was adverting to your *naïveté*. . . ."

Lincoln took even longer to spin that word around. "That's a queer sort of thing to say about a lawyer."

Then silence.

An *extinguishing* silence. With a start, Joshua realized it was the first time they had ever come near to quarreling. The sensation was so strange, it was as if the air around them had cracked open. Gingerly, he took a step toward the stove. Opened the door and tossed in a log and prodded it into flame.

"I'm sorry," he said. "I don't know what's got into me. It *is* only tea."

Several more seconds before Lincoln said: "You haven't considered her likeliest motive."

"Yes?"

"She wants to apologize for her pudding."

JOSHUA SLEPT POORLY that night, his dreams filled not with Springfield hostesses but the teeming animal life of Farmington. Broodmares and colts and riding horses and workhorses. Work oxen and beef oxen. Hogs and sows and oxen. An Irish Grazier boar. They formed a tight ring around him, a mongrel horde, remorselessly trotting and, with each circuit, shrinking the circle until he could smell each droplet of their sweat.

Lincoln roused him before they could get any closer. "Dear me, Speed. I thought *I* had the worst nightmares in town."

SIXTEEN

———

In local Whig circles, it was a momentous thing to enter Mrs. Francis's parlor alone. It was here that a young officeholder (and, when applicable, his wife) received the head of steam to carry them to end times. But Joshua had entered this legendary room only in the evening, when it was thronged with bodies, and he was struck now by what different a place it was in the naked light of day, how it ached of *better* days. The carpet, with its faded tea roses. The tiny framed waterscapes, rimed with dust. Bedraggled peacock feathers sagging over the grate, and all about, a chaos of tidies and lambrequins. Joshua found his gaze particularly drawn to a knitted mass of cherry-red flax, amorphous in both shape and function, resting on the settee in a condition that would charitably be called unfinished.

"It's wretched, isn't it?" Already in full conversational mode, Mrs. Francis came sallying into the room. "I warned Mr. Francis when we married: Don't expect me to work wonders with the needle. Therein my gifts do *not* lie. Alas, women must do what society expects of them, mustn't they?" She did not stay for an answer but sat before the teapot and began to pour. "I don't know why, but I was in the mood for ginseng tea. Is that agreeable, Mr. Speed? And would you care for sweet cakes? They're still fresh." She slid the cup and saucer toward him. "I know what a busy man you are, so I shan't keep you any longer than necessary."

The cup had the tiniest of fissures on its handle but held all the same as he raised the tea to his lips. Mrs. Francis watched him drink, then, without taking a sip of her own, set her cup down and folded her hands in her lap.

"Dear Mr. Speed, before I say anything else, I want you to know how very *partial* we are to you, my husband and I. And with that in view, I hope you will allow me to speak as plainly as I can."

This was the difference, he thought, between the South and the North. A Southern woman would never ask permission.

"I suppose it all comes down to this," said Mrs. Francis. "I *believe* in your Mr. Lincoln. I believe him to be the most naturally gifted politician I have ever encountered, but more than that, I believe him to be a great man—large of mind and large of soul. I believe he has *pinnacles* in him, and I should like to do whatever I can to *raise* him there."

Joshua eyed her over the rim of his cup. "As would I," he said.

"Yes."

She studied her hands for a time, then lifted her head.

"The Greeks always spoke so highly of friendship, didn't they? *Both* kinds. In my experience, it's a more complicated business. Oh, to be sure, it can ennoble, it can inspire, but it can also"—she idly ran a finger around her ear— "*constrict*, do you not think?"

He took another sip, set his cup down. Drew back a fraction in the chair.

"You are being abstract, Mrs. Francis."

"Am I?"

"Perhaps you could favor me with specific instances."

"For now, let us adhere to the general. Sometimes, I believe, it is the height of love to—to *release* a loved one."

Joshua gave her a thin smile.

"Once again," he said, "I must beg you to be particular."

"I was hoping you would spare me that chore."

Over her face there spread now the warmest smile he had yet seen on her. It had the effect of leaving him less prepared for what came next.

"Mr. Speed, from my admittedly compromised female perspective, it strikes me that Mr. Lincoln is not permitted to move anywhere in society without you at his side."

"*Permitted*, you say." Joshua set the cup and saucer back on the table. "What a—what an uncharitable word to introduce into our conversation."

"Mr. Speed. . . ."

"From the moment he sought out my company, Lincoln has been free to quit it. The same liberty has been mine."

"Yet neither of you has made use of it." Her smile folded down. "There are different sorts of cages, Mr. Speed."

He angled his head to one side. His fingers, without his consent, began to drum along the arms of the chair.

"How tragic," he said, "that you consider friendship a cage."

"Oh, I don't believe it's that way for everybody. I don't believe it's that way for *you*."

To his ear now there came the sound of a clock—in the foyer, perhaps—balefully ticking. Each new second louder than the last. And something more mysterious: the mewling of a cat, elderly and querulous, emanating from some covert niche.

"Well now, look at me," said Mrs. Francis, in a mollifying tone. "I have set you back on your heels, Mr. Speed, and that was never my design. If anything—and I hope you will credit me on this point—I wish to *applaud* you. For the yeoman's work you have done with our Lincoln."

He had just enough presence of mind to mark the pronoun: *our*.

"*Work?*"

"Why, yes! I can't tell you how many of my friends have remarked on how much more polished and *confident* a specimen our Lincoln has become. We all recall that sweet yokel who washed up on our shores two years back, and we all relish the change that has come over him under your tutelage. Why," she added, "he even trims his fingernails now!"

That particular lesson came flooding right back to him. The penknife. Guiding him, finger by finger.

Show me. . . .

"You keep making new insinuations, Mrs. Francis. First Lincoln is my friend. Next he is my captive. Now he is—well, I hardly know what. Some sort of pet project, perhaps."

"Oh." She gave a comical shrug. "Project. Captive. Friend. We need not dwell on the *word*, Mr. Speed, only the outcome. Which has been *all* to our Lincoln's advantage. I salute you, and now I entreat you. Let me take him the rest of the way."

His mouth opened, slowly closed itself again.

"The rest of *what* way?"

"Toward his destiny."

He stared at her for a time. Then, to his own surprise, he began to laugh.

"You find me amusing?" she said.

"I find you incredible. Do you actually propose to accomplish all this single-handedly?"

"Of course not. Mr. Lincoln has many allies, as you know. Though, with the exception of you, there is none more devoted than I. The point is, Mr. Speed, that he must marry *somebody*. You know it, and I know it."

STRANGE. HE HAD assumed there would be some comfort in seeing Mrs. Francis's agenda at last laid bare.

"Why do you not marry him yourself?" he murmured. "I think you would if you could."

"You're probably right," she answered amiably. "Diamonds in the rough have always been my weakness. Oh, you should have *seen* Mr. Francis when I first got hold of him. Licking his knife, balling up his handkerchief, scratching himself at all times of day. He made our Lincoln look like Beau Brummell."

"So," he said, "in lieu of yourself, you propose some *other* candidate."

"Not as yet," she said equably. "I must first survey the field."

"And in so doing, you will find what? A limp, lisping virgin of, what, seventeen? Eighteen? Just enough brain to fit in her own thimble?"

"Oh, for the first time, I believe you underestimate me, Mr. Speed. *And* him. Do you honestly think our Lincoln could attach his fortunes to someone he couldn't talk with?"

Joshua stared at his teacup on the table. Still three-quarters full. Impossibly distant.

"He's quite hopeless at wooing," he muttered. "He'd be the first to tell you."

"Many a woman has been won without ever being wooed. I say that with some assurance, for I am one of them. And here we *are*—Mr. and Mrs. Simeon Francis!" She extended her palms to incorporate not just the parlor but, by inference, all of Springfield. "A happy marriage. Or, if you prefer, a satisfactory and reciprocal *partnership*. That is all I wish for our Lincoln. No more, no less."

He shook his head, half smiled.

"You must have great confidence in your own machinations to suppose that he will simply fall in line."

"I don't suppose anything. I merely . . ." Something swelled now in her eyes. "I ask that, whatever happens, you *allow* it to happen, Mr. Speed. As gracefully as you can."

He could feel the pulsing of blood just inside his ear, muffling his own hearing. He edged himself up in his chair.

"And *I* ask that you refrain from any more insulting suggestions."

"It is not my—"

"Your design, no. And what if I made it *my* design to speak of this conversation? To Lincoln himself?"

She stared at him now with a genuine fascination. "And what will you say, Mr. Speed? That I wish him only the greatest success? The highest happiness? Or will you tell him that a politician without a *wife*"—her head moved almost imperceptibly forward—"has not a prayer of rising in this world?"

They were silent for some time now: Mrs. Francis lightly swirling her teacup and Joshua studying his own boots, splayed across the tea-rose carpet. Once again, the mewling of a cat could be heard, like a phantom protesting behind the wallboards.

"I should have thought," he said, "that you would wait until he asked for your help."

"Men don't always know what they need. That's why God made women."

"And so you grant yourself license to weave this—this matrimonial *web* about him."

"*For* him, I think you mean. Or do you suppose him to be ignorant of my plans?"

Joshua's eyes swerved toward hers. For the first time, he could see a glint of steel in the hazel irises.

"It seems to me," she went on, "that our Lincoln has ever depended upon— ever *thrived* upon—the good offices of friends. Such as you, Mr. Speed. *And* me."

She did something startling then. She leaned over and pressed her plump hands on his. All coldness had been banished from her eyes. And from her voice, too, which was low and quick and importunate.

"You must understand this, or you will understand nothing. We are on the same side, you and I. We both want only what is best for him." Then, drawing her hands away, she settled back in her chair. "Do we not?"

THAT NIGHT, LINCOLN stayed up later than usual—he was reading and remonstrating with Fenimore Cooper—but by the time he rustled into bed, Joshua was still awake. Listening to the wind rattle the casement. The rustle of something in the eaves (bat? squirrel?). The untroubled exhalations of Billy Herndon and Charlie Hurst, fast asleep on the far side of the dormitory.

It was a function of their shared space that Lincoln, even though he couldn't see Joshua, knew if there was a conversation in the offing. In those moments, he would simply lay himself flat on the mattress and wait. And if Joshua didn't speak, he would.

"She didn't poison your tea, I see."

"No," said Joshua.

"Did she . . . ?" A light yawn. "Did she disclose her dark motives?"

Joshua took some time to calibrate his response. "She told me nothing she hasn't already told you."

They lay there another minute.

"May I ask you something?" Joshua said.

"Certainly."

"How far do you see yourself traveling?"

"Ohhh. . . ." He could hear Lincoln stretching himself out. "Petersburg, probably. Astoria, even, with a good horse. Back in time for breakfast."

"Don't be an idiot. I mean politics."

"Why are you asking all of a sudden?"

Joshua paused. "Because I never thought to ask you before."

Lincoln gave his whiskers a good long scrape with his finger. "I'd say I've hit my ceiling," he said.

"Statehouse and no farther?"

"Oh, maybe the state senate, with some help. A judgeship if the stars align."

"And that's all?"

"Ehh." A longer yawn now. "I don't know. I sometimes think . . ."

"What?"

"Well, say that, twenty years from now, Congressman Stuart agrees to retire. Say he takes pity on an old friend of his. An old *law* partner. . . ."

"And where will this old friend *be*?"

"Oh, where he's always been. Living over Bell and Company."

Joshua felt the muscles around his eyes begin to unclench.

"And how," he asked, "will Congressman Stuart's pity manifest itself?"

"Why, he'll call in the local Whig dignitaries. I have no idea who they'll *be*, but he'll call them in. He'll say, *Gentlemen, this here Lincoln, this poor cur, has been chasing his tail these many moons. Mightn't we throw him a bone and let him cool himself in that Washington kennel for a term?*"

"Just *a term*?"

"Oh, they'll find me out before the two years are done. I'll be lucky to beat the tar and feathers."

Joshua folded his hands together, rested them on his chest.

"I suppose," he said, "if you were married, it might be different."

"If I were married. . . ."

There followed a stretch of quiet so deep that Joshua began to wonder if Lincoln had fallen asleep. Only there was something stirring out there in the darkness, he could sense it. Something stirring, too, in Lincoln's voice when it reemerged.

"If I were married," he said, quietly, "I would still be the same wretched excuse for a man that I have always been."

His voice caught on the last word.

"Speed, I'm tired. Can we. . . ."

"Of course," said Joshua. "Of course."

SEVENTEEN

———◆———

THERE WAS ONE point at least on which the two men diverged: shaving.

Lincoln, like most men of his generation, never brought a blade to his own face. Instead, he betook himself three times a week to William de Fleurville, an amiable Haitian barber whose shop stood northwest of the public square just below the mayor's office. Billy was known for keeping his razor keen and his water hot and for never charging more than fifteen dollars per annum. Joshua, by contrast, had long since been schooled in shaving by Morocco, his father's Negro, and refused to subject his chin to a foreign hand. The result was this: Four mornings a week, Lincoln sat at their desk, reviewing some writ or bill, while Joshua stood before a water basin and routed every last whisker from his face. It was on one of these mornings, in the last roar of winter, that Lincoln, almost as an afterthought, asked: "Do you know of a Miss Todd?"

Joshua paused in the act of rubbing shaving soap around his jaw.

"*Mary* Todd?" he said.

"Yes."

"Why do you ask after her?"

"Oh. . . ." Lincoln frowned down at the manila paper. "She's Stuart's cousin. I figured I ought to pay her some kind of call."

"Professional courtesy."

"Mm," said Lincoln.

Joshua drew out the leather strop and ran his razor along it, back and forth, taking care to turn the blade with each stroke.

"Was it Stuart told you?" he asked.

"Told me what?"

"That his cousin was in Springfield."

"I'm sure many have spoken of her." Lincoln reached for his pen, dipped it in the inkwell. "She *is* Elizabeth Edwards' sister."

"For which she has my sympathies."

A breath of a laugh escaped Lincoln. Joshua held the razor between his thumb and his three adjoining fingers, raised it to the point just below his right ear.

"As it happens," he said, "I ran into Miss Todd not too long ago."

"Is that so?"

"Just after the blizzard. She was . . ." He lifted the blade. "She was trapped in her uncle's sleigh. Stuck in some culvert or other. I was the lucky fellow who chanced along."

"Knight errant, that's you."

"Oh, I don't know about that." He ran his index finger along the track of his cleared skin. "Though she *was* a bit on the damsel side." He gave the blade a quick wipe on his neck cloth. "Pretty enough. By starlight. I don't know."

"What don't you know?"

"I mean we spent so little time together. And there was her friend, too. Who was also obliging. *You* know the one I mean. . . ." He brought the blade back up. "That girl *Conkling* is sweet on. . . ."

"Miss Levering."

"*Levering*, that's it. Lawrason's sister."

The blade went with the grain, then—a subtler proposition—against it. The softest rasp of metal against flesh.

"She put me in mind of a wren," said Joshua.

"Miss Levering?"

"No, Miss Todd."

"Not sure I follow."

"I mean a wren that's fallen from its nest. . . ."

He might have carried the metaphor out but was stopped by the memory of those two baby birds, blown out of their tree.

"Not *recently* fallen," Joshua hurried on. "*Years* ago fallen. And squawking as if it were yesterday."

They were silent for a time.

"She was certainly agreeable," Joshua said finally.

"I don't doubt."

"Perhaps you'd care for an introduction?"

"In due time," murmured Lincoln.

THE FIRST MEETING between Miss Todd and Mr. Lincoln was indeed engineered by Joshua and, as anyone might have predicted, did not go well. In the company of marriageable women, Lincoln became, in his own mind, twice as awkward, twice as plain. The earth was suddenly too small a place to hide in. As for Miss Todd, the note of fear never quite left her eyes as she contemplated the giant fauna that had descended upon her. She did, however, put on a gay front, and when Joshua came for his dance with her, he was surprised by how surely she had taken Lincoln's measure. "I can only hope," she said, "that his waters being so very still, they also run deep." He was surprised, too, by her quickness, her raillery. *Yes*, he thought, half admiringly. *I can see why Mrs. Francis chose you.* His guard was far enough down that, when the dance ended, he actually heard himself say: "If it's agreeable, might we pay you a call?"

What lay behind that request he could not begin to say, for he had no real intention of following up on it, but Miss Todd bowed her head with the expected demureness, and once they had parted, his only remaining mission was to find Lincoln, who had ducked out an hour earlier. Joshua found him standing, hatless, on the northern side of the Edwards mansion in a grove of maples, still bare from winter.

"Sorry," said Lincoln. "It was getting hot in there."

"Like Africa," Joshua agreed.

The night, however, was splendidly cool, and free of insects, so they took their time going home, hewing to the northern perimeter of Madison. The town's last frontier, Joshua liked to think, for on the other side, all was prairie and timber, save for the Matheny farm, where a single lantern was winking from the kitchen window.

"At least Congressman Stuart will be pleased," said Joshua.

"How so?"

Joshua gave him a quizzical look. "You paid your respects to his cousin."

"So I did."

"Fulfilled your professional courtesy."

"Indeed."

They stopped now. Pulled their frock coats more tightly around them and stared off into the wilderness.

"She's prettier than her sister," Joshua allowed. "And not quite so proud. Then again, who is prouder than Elizabeth Edwards?"

Lincoln lifted his hat to let the cool air circulate round his skull. Set it back down at a slightly skewed angle.

"I like her smile," he said.

"Yes?"

"It comes slow, but it gets there."

Joshua stared down in the direction of his boots. "It's funny," he said. "I didn't suppose her to be your sort."

"I have a sort?" asked Lincoln, wryly.

"Oh, I mean she's just a touch on the rounded side, that's all. Not *Falstaffian*, of course."

Lincoln was quiet for a time. Then, with a light shrug, he said: "It doesn't matter anyway. She has no use for me."

"Oh," said Joshua, appeasingly. "I don't think she has much use for anyone."

Conscious, as he spoke, that he was falling shy of the truth. For hadn't Joshua himself felt the pressure of Miss Todd's gaze? Detected each fluster and stammer she made in his presence? The symptoms were clear enough, but the diagnosis gave him no pleasure. He knew from experience how quickly a young woman's infatuation might change to possessiveness and thence to sorrow. (*But I thought . . . I thought you . . .*)

The lightest of sighs, escaping Lincoln like smoke from a flue.

"Times like these, Speed, I wish I was a drinking man."

EIGHTEEN

A FORTNIGHT LATER, Joshua and Lincoln were carrying their laundry to Mrs. Butler's. Socks, shirts, drawers . . . whatever could survive a prolonged immersion in the Butler lye baths had been stuffed into burlap bags and slung over their shoulders. It would have been easier, certainly, to transport the clothes in a barrow or cart, but Joshua loved the feeling of striding down the street like a peddler, his wares swinging behind him, and here it was, early April, and all was well—well enough, at any rate, that he felt free to say, in a winking tone: "Have you heard the latest?"

All his customers, it seemed, were abuzz with the news of Miss Mary Todd. Who, not wishing to endanger her slippers, had taken the radical act of riding back home in the back of Ellis Hart's dray. For all the world to see!

"They tell me she was laughing the whole way," said Joshua. "Waving to every citizen in sight."

"Yes," said Lincoln, in the flattest of tones. "I was one of them."

Joshua started to angle his face toward him, then brought it back.

"You saw her?" he asked.

"Yes."

"How did you manage that?"

"I looked out my office window."

"By chance, you mean."

"How else?"

"And did she see you?"

"In passing."

Joshua swung his bag onto the other shoulder. "Well," he said, "I must have been the only one in Springfield who *didn't* catch a glimpse. Of course," he quickly added, "the old hens in the store were being awfully unchristian to her. But I said, *How else is a young woman without a carriage to navigate our streets? The fault is not in Miss Todd but in our surface drainage.* No, indeed, she need fear no judgment from me. As for her *sister*," he added, "well, that's another story. I'm sure there'll be no end of grief at the Edwards manse."

"I hope not," said Lincoln in a voice of some warmth.

They were nearly to the Butlers' when Lincoln stopped of a sudden. Dropped his sack and turned toward Joshua.

"I gave her a salute, if you must know."

"Why on earth did you do that?"

"I'm not sure. She just looked so very bold, sitting up there. She looked *free*."

"You admired her, then?"

He gave his temple a long rub. "I envied her."

LINCOLN LEFT EARLY the next morning for a Whig rally in Carlinville. Joshua, awaking an hour later, instinctively took up the one bachelor chore that Lincoln hated most: beating the bed, which had absorbed a winter's worth of dust. As Joshua dragged the mattress from its frame, a paper came loose—sailed back and forth on a trough of wind currents before alighting on the floorboards.

He picked it up. It was an order of court in petition for the *Keys & Matheny vs. Matheny et al.* case. Dated March the third. Signed by Lincoln, signed by the plaintiff's attorney, signed by the relevant judge. A dead article, in short. So what was it doing under the mattress?

On a whim, or perhaps it was presentiment, Joshua turned the petition over. Something had been scrawled on the back. He reached for a candle, and the words climbed straight toward him.

A poem, in five stanzas.

> As I walked out on Monday last
> A wet and muddy day
> 'Twas there I saw a pretty lass
> A riding on a dray, a riding on a dray.

No question who the lass was, thought Joshua. The only remaining question was the author. Clearly it was written in Lincoln's hand—no other—but the mind behind these words, *that* was not one Joshua recognized. The Lincoln *he* knew spent his days writing briefs and writs and deeds and bills and, yes, orders of court in petition. He may have waxed lyrical from time to time on the campaign hustings, but never, to Joshua's knowledge, had he committed verse to paper.

Yet here was Lincoln's very scrawl, beckoning the eye onward. . . .

> Quoth I, sweet lass, what do you do there
> Said she good lack a day
> I had no coach to take me home
> So I'm riding on a dray.

The "sweet lass" was never mentioned by name, but in the penultimate stanza, her cart came to the "Edwards' gate," where she and her "silken coat and feathers white" were rolled off the conveyance. And so it concluded. . . .

> When safely landed on her feet
> Said she what is to pay
> Quoth Hart I cannot charge you aught
> For riding on my dray.

It was impossible to credit. Lincoln, *his* Lincoln, had followed Miss Todd the four blocks home? Spied on her exchange with Ellis Hart? Grabbed a pen and the nearest piece of scratch paper and set to scribbling? It defied all sense. Yet here was the document, and here was the most dispositive evidence of all: Lincoln had hidden it.

Joshua stared at the paper—stared *through* it—as though it might be coaxed into talking. Was it to be delivered to Miss Todd in person? Or committed to memory and recited at some future crossing? Or locked for eternity in its author's private bell tower?

By the time Lincoln returned the following day, the document had been returned to its hiding place, and Joshua, in similar fashion, had managed to secrete the incident in some back recess of his mind. That Friday, though, the poem appeared, word for word, in the most public of venues: the pages of the *Sangamo Journal*.

There was at least this much solace: The attributed author was not Lincoln but Dr. Merryman. Perhaps, after all, Lincoln had simply copied out another man's whimsy and prevailed upon the Francises to publish it—as he prevailed upon them to publish so many things.

But then why not simply leave the copied lines in the *Journal* offices? Why squirrel them away?

Lincoln, at this moment, was sitting with a mug of coffee in the window embrasure, half concealed by a billowing white curtain. Joshua, keeping his motions casual, laid the newspaper on his friend's lap.

"You might be amused by this."

While Lincoln read—or affected to read—Joshua stood before the looking glass, affecting to button his shirt.

"I think Miss Todd has entered the realm of legend," said Lincoln at length.

"So it would seem." Joshua reached for his burgundy cravat, wrapped it round his neck. "Do you know I think we ought to pay her a call?"

"Miss Todd?"

"This very afternoon, perhaps."

Lincoln calmly refolded the newspaper. "Why would we do that?"

"Why, to *congratulate* her on her newfound celebrity." Joshua gave the first knot a tug. "And to thank her, of course, for her hospitality at the ball."

Lincoln pondered. "Wasn't it Mrs. Edwards who threw the ball?"

"Just so, but Miss Todd is the—the family *surrogate*. . . ."

"I thought such a visit had to come within a week of the event. Or else it would be too late."

Sometimes his mind was a little too adhesive.

"Well, yes," Joshua allowed, "that is the *rule*. But a good hostess never turns away a grateful guest."

A shadow crossed Lincoln's face. "We would *both* go?"

"Of course. Do you really think I'd abandon you?"

But that afternoon, in the minutes leading up to their departure, Lincoln was in a state of unusual anxiety.

"*This* waistcoat? Are you sure? It doesn't look too drab? Which hat, do you think?"

They were just walking out the door when Joshua glanced down at his friend's frayed shirt cuffs.

Now it was one of Lincoln's blind spots that, for all his compulsive dress itineraries, he never looked at his cuffs before venturing into the world. It fell always to Joshua to point out that a shirt suitable for lounging about Hoffman's Row would not pass muster in higher society. This last-minute inspection had become so ritualized that, if they were descending the staircase, Joshua had only to murmur the word *cuffs*, and Lincoln, without a word, would sprint back upstairs to change shirts.

Today, Joshua didn't say *cuffs*.

And as they strolled over to Quality Hill, his very silence filled him with foreboding. Just what had stopped his tongue?

Their call was, by design, unannounced, so Joshua was in no way surprised to be received coolly by Mrs. Edwards. He was surprised, though, to see the extra layer of frost she reserved for Lincoln. Perhaps she, too, had sensed something in the air, or else the shame of Hart's dray had left her ill-disposed to uncouth specimens.

By now, Lincoln had noticed—too late—the state of his cuffs. His first instinct was to hide them under his coat sleeves; his second was to sit on them. He then resorted to wrapping his arms round his back—an attitude that broadcast, in equal measures, his awkwardness and misery. Whatever remorse Joshua felt vanished in the moment that Miss Todd rather shyly entered the room. He had, after all, a job to do, and he went to it with vigor. He praised Miss Todd's spirit and pluck and resourcefulness. He called her a Modern Woman, a May Queen. He inundated her with talk of internal improvements. He smiled, he gazed, he leaned, he did everything he could think of to shine in her eyes.

It was all for naught.

Miss Todd, it turned out, was every bit as proud as her sister and bridled at the notion (a commonplace in Joshua's world) that women might be bored by political matters. As for Mrs. Edwards, her hostility to Lincoln, for reasons mysterious, continued to mount. She sneered at his jokes, mocked his speeches, *martyred* the man in her own parlor—and succeeded only in awakening Mary Todd's tenderest reserves of pity.

"You must tell me the next time you are to speak, Mr. Lincoln. I am a devotee of both the coarse *and* the homespun."

"You may depend on it, Miss Todd."

By the time Mrs. Edwards showed her callers to the door, her face was a perfect death mask. She, too, had hoped for a different outcome, but if Joshua expected a moment of silent commiseration between them, he was mistaken. She nodded curtly to each man, then closed the door on them.

They stood blinking in the rays of midafternoon.

"Huh," said Lincoln. "That went better than I thought."

THE WHEELS WERE now in motion. One could no sooner stop them than stop the sun.

Joshua was thus in no way surprised to find Miss Todd popping up at the Francises' party—or, a few nights later, at the weekly *Journal* salon. On both occasions, by quirk of fate, Joshua had been held up by work and had arrived to find Lincoln and Miss Todd already in conversation. They had even danced together, he was told, though he was glad to have missed that spectacle. Glad, too, to have missed the triumphant look in Mrs. Francis's eye. But he could not escape the change that came over Lincoln each time he basked in Miss Todd's luster. The night of the quadrille, for instance, he went on at nearly embarrassing length about her kindness, her wit, her shrewdness, and when Joshua dragged him away from the Francis salon, the first thing Lincoln said upon reaching the street was: "You were right, Speed. The baby wren fallen from its nest. But those are the ones that turn out the toughest, aren't they? The broken ones."

NINETEEN

———

BILLY HERNDON, CHIEF clerk of Bell & Company, made two rash decisions that spring: first, to get married; second, to resign his position amidst noises of pursuing a law career. This left Joshua trapped behind the store counter more than he would have liked, but he took his confinement in good humor and hired a local seamstress to sew him a hunter-green twill apron that would keep off the sawdust and chalk. It looked so dashing on him that Mrs. Iles asked where she might get one for her husband. So did Mrs. Ridgeley, who always made a point of stopping by Joshua's store every Thursday, ostensibly to buy Castile soap but really to get his opinion of her latest bonnet. It was on one of these Thursdays that Mrs. Ridgeley said, in a guileless voice: "Mr. Lincoln told us the funniest story two nights ago."

"Oh, yes?"

"About the—oh, dear, the—the family that moves so *often*, you see, that even their *chickens* know what's to happen, so they—what is it they do, they—"

"Walk right up to the mover," said Joshua.

"Yes, and then they . . ."

"Stretch themselves flat on the ground."

"That's it. . . ."

"And put their feet up to be tied."

"Just so!" cried Mrs. Ridgely. "You *have* heard it. Well, I don't need to tell you Mr. Lincoln gave us quite the laugh. Although it would have been so much more amusing with you there."

Smiling softly, he studied her.

"I'm sorry," he said. "Where was this?"

"Why, supper at the Merrymans'."

The first thing he wanted to say was there could have been no such supper. He had run into Dr. Merryman just this past Monday by the Springfield Chair Factory. Merryman had spoken of Governor Carlin and *The Saturday Evening Post* and the price of salt and . . . dear God, Joseph *Smith*. Never once had the subject of supper come up. But Mrs. Ridgeley was eying Joshua now, as through opera glasses, and there was nothing for him to do but take cover.

"I was *so* sorry not to make it," he said. "I've been spending all my surplus hours, you see, editing *The Old Soldier*." He tossed up his hands in mock despair. "All work and no play for this poor lad."

"Well, you were sorely missed. I mean to say, only two gentlemen for *four* ladies."

He paused. Then he forced his smile a little wider.

"Was Miss Todd one of the ladies, by any chance?"

"Indeed, she was, charming creature. Now I am not a gambling woman, sir, but if I were to put money on any outcome, it would be that Miss Todd will be married off before the summer is out. You may depend upon it!"

LATER THAT NIGHT, after the Poetical Society had come and gone, Lincoln sank into his rocker, chewing meditatively on a piece of straw. Joshua drew out the adjoining chair. For some minutes, they sat in silence.

"I saw Mrs. Ridgeley today," said Joshua at last.

Lincoln's rocking continued without a hitch. "Yes?" he answered.

"She mentioned that she saw you Tuesday evening. At the Merrymans', I think it was."

"Mm." Lincoln's head executed a slow forward roll.

"I admit I was surprised," said Joshua. "You having never mentioned it yourself."

"I'm sure I did."

"No, that night, you told me you had election business."

"That's what it was, really. For all intents and purposes."

For all intents and purposes. Such a lawyerly turn of phrase that Joshua very nearly smiled.

"I can see how you might conflate supper and business," he said. "Though I don't know that I would."

The air was thickening round them now.

"I was only trying to spare you, Speed. You would have found it all dreadfully dull."

It was as if Lincoln had reached out and cuffed him across the jaw. For was this not, nearly word for word, what Joshua had said to Mary Todd about the Young Men's Lyceum?

"Dull," repeated Joshua. "That is a surprisingly *interesting* word to use."

"I didn't—"

"Am I not one of the editors of the Whig campaign journal?"

"You are."

"Have I not edited *your* speeches, Lincoln? Attended your rallies and debates? Have I ever given you any sign of being bored by your vocation?"

"Of course not."

"So what else must I do? Perhaps, instead of pouring drinks when our guests come by, I should speak *up* more? Would that persuade you that my brain would not be over*taxed* . . ."

"Speed."

". . . by political *con*claves? . . ."

"Speed."

"Why, I could jawbone all night, if you'd like. Drink down all the air in the *room*, if that's what you wish. . . ."

"*Joshua.*"

It was the second time in their acquaintance that Lincoln had called him by his Christian name. They were both silenced by it.

"I meant nothing by it," said Lincoln at last. "I apologize."

Joshua rose in one smooth motion. Walked to the hearth. Reached for the poker and never quite found it.

"Have there been other suppers?" he asked.

"What do you mean?"

"I mean suppers to which I have not been invited."

"I don't know. One or two? These things happen spontaneously."

"So. . . ." A chunk of wood tumbled off the grate in a slow stream of sparks. "Am I to conclude that I have been blackballed?"

"Of course not."

"Mrs. Francis, perhaps, has—"

"Oh, Speed, enough! She wasn't even there."

Joshua's hands, looking for attachments, found the mantel. "Then explain to me what is happening," he said, in an altered voice.

"There's nothing to explain."

He heard Lincoln raise himself from the rocker. Heard him take two ponderous steps forward.

"Here I am, Speed. Right now. Nowhere else."

Surely, it was not the remains of that dying fire that made Joshua's face burn now. Nor was it the warmth of reassurance. No, he thought, this is something new. It felt perilously close to shame. *If Father could see you now,* he thought.

"You go on up," he said in a rough voice. "I'll be there directly."

He sat for upward of two hours, watching the fire die out, spark by spark, feeling the cold advance. At some point, he must have drowsed off, for he was still there the next morning when Charlie shook him awake. Someone had placed a blanket over him.

OVER THE NEXT few days, he and Lincoln were cordial and no more. When Saturday night came round, Lincoln left without even saying where he was going. Joshua had too much pride to wait up, so, after spending most of the evening with his bankbooks, he went to bed just before ten. Sometime before midnight, he was nudged awake by Lincoln.

"Speed."

"Mm?"

"We're invited to a picnic."

"A . . ." Joshua rolled himself over to face him. "When?"

"Tomorrow."

"That's . . ." He smeared a hand across his eyes. "That's soon. Who are the hosts?"

"Miss Todd," answered Lincoln, evenly. "And her friend Miss Levering. Which means the other Leverings will be there, probably. Conkling, too, though he won't be happy about it."

"How did . . . ?"

How did you get me invited? he wanted to ask, but the thought that Lincoln had been required to make some intervention on his behalf was more than he could bear, so with the awareness left him, he confined himself to logistics. Long after Lincoln himself had drifted to sleep, Joshua lay awake, planning. He had sassafras tea and a bag of horehound drops that had fallen off some supply wagon. As for entertainment, could he not drag out the old banjo that had been gathering dust in the closet? With tuning and a little practice, he might be able to call back some of the songs that Cato had taught him back at Farmington.

In the hour leading up to the event, Joshua found himself doing everything Lincoln normally did: checking and then rechecking his appearance in the glass, questioning every article of clothing right down to the socks. Twice, as they were heading out the door, Joshua turned round and ran back up the stairs—first to change his hat, then to change boots. "Speed," said Lincoln, "it's only a picnic." But the gathering had assumed a strange new urgency in Joshua's eyes. If Springfield society had turned its back on him, he would prove how indispensable he was to any social venture, no matter the scale.

From the moment he arrived, he was the soul of conviviality. He set up campstools for the ladies. He adjusted the angles of their parasols to keep the sun off. He poured the tea and carved the venison and chased away the odd mosquito. Laughed at every joke, no matter how mild, and filled every yawning silence. Caressed the vanity of each guest. *What am I doing?* he found himself asking more than once, but the reply was always prompt in coming.

Earning back your place.

And see how his efforts were bearing fruit! Miss Todd fairly blossomed when he told her how handsome she looked in lilac; Miss Levering shot him grateful looks for eliding the tensions between Conkling and her brother; Mrs. Levering was so touched that someone had noticed her moss roses (her husband never had) that she briefly lost her capacity for speech. One by one, he could feel each member of the party *turning* toward him like a heliotrope.

Only Lincoln, he noticed, remained in shadow.

From time to time, when the ladies' attention was turned elsewhere,

Conkling would fish a flask of bourbon from his waistcoat pocket and pour a dram or two into Joshua's sassafras tea, then pour twice as much into his own cup. The effect on Joshua was at first tonic, but as the afternoon lengthened, his body and spirit grew heavier. By twilight, he was sitting against the trunk of an oak, his eyes drooped to half-mast. Through the flush of bourbon, he became dimly aware that the two other men were arguing, but he scarcely attended until Conkling blurted out: "I hear tell you're the best wrestler north of the Ohio."

"I'm not even the best this side of the Sangamon," said Lincoln.

Joshua's eyes sprang open. He heard himself say: "He's lying, of course."

The two men whirled toward him. Joshua smiled blearily. Began to rise, then thought better of it.

"There's only one man alive," he said, "that's wrestled Lincoln to a draw. Everyone else . . ."

Wondering, as he spoke, who this "one man" was. Who had even told him about Lincoln's wrestling career? Surely not Lincoln himself. Joshua sat there for some time, wondering. Then, suddenly, Conkling was standing over him.

"It is all up to you, Speed!"

"What is?"

But Conkling was already drawing him to his feet. "Here's how it will work. I am going to *tie* this great beast's arm behind his back. You will then charge him."

"Charge?"

"Then the two of you will go at it like the rugged prairie men you are."

"No. . . ."

Or maybe it was the women that were saying no.

(Where *were* the women?)

"Let me help you with your coat," said Conkling. "No point getting it dirty."

Even to Joshua's clouded senses, the contradictions registered. *Go at it like men? But mind the frock coat?* Yet he gave no resistance. Even giggled as the final stretch of sleeve was dragged off him. For good measure, his cravat was stripped off, too.

"Gentlemen!" called one of the women. "This is not becoming."

"Oh, listen to her," growled Conkling. "Square off now, boys!"

Joshua's eyes started open. There, on the green, stood Lincoln, his left arm wrapped behind his back, the rest of his body tautened like a quiver. Pitched *forward*, like a bull pressed against its pen. The full horror of the situation now invaded Joshua. He and Lincoln were going to fight each other.

"Come now!" cried Conkling. "Set to it!"

Joshua felt a light push in the small of his back—enough, somehow, to overcome all misgivings and send him flailing toward his opponent. Lincoln danced out of range. Another lunge, another dance. Joshua's boots were sliding now in the still-damp grass. How ridiculous he must look! His feet scarcely able to raise themselves from the sward.

"Stop," he muttered, clapping a hand over his ear. "Stop. . . ."

From behind, Conkling called: "Go for the knees, Speed!"

Spasms of air wracked his chest. Talons of heat raked his face, his bared neck. Silently, he counted. Closed his eyes and, with a muffled shout, hurled himself into the twilit air. For half a second, it was as if he slept—in a perfect, untroubled suspension—only to be awakened by the concussive force of Lincoln's body. Opening his eyes, he found himself on his back, in the wet grass. His arm, his right arm, had magically contrived to hook itself round Lincoln's calf.

I did it!

But Lincoln's free arm had already wrapped itself round his neck like a baby anaconda. In the next instant, Lincoln's unencumbered leg pinned his two legs to the turf. There would be no escaping—not when the pressure of Lincoln's forearm against his windpipe was causing the blood to pound in his head and sending up a clamor from his lungs. Helpless, he gazed up into Lincoln's eyes but found only hollows. In the region just over their heads, a cloud swept into view, then particularized into form. A round and reddened face, choked with rage.

"Stop it!" screamed Miss Todd. "Stop it at once!"

He had to decipher her lip motions because he couldn't make out the words. But as Lincoln's arm released its grip, all the sounds of the world reemerged with a vengeance. He heard crows and lightning bugs, the rustling of grass, the whisper of new oak leaves . . . and somewhere in the weave, Lincoln's voice, tight with care.

"Is he all right?"

A third-person query, Joshua would later think. Not *you* but *he*. As if Lincoln were already pulling away.

"You should have just killed me," whispered Joshua, but no one heard.

PART THREE

Mary

TWENTY

———

"AND THIS," SHE said, pointing to the jagged white scar on his thumb. "Where did this come from?"

"An ax," he said.

"You were assaulted?"

He gave her a sheepish smile. "I assaulted myself."

"Explain."

"I was chopping wood, and the ax glanced off the wedge. I came close to losing the whole thumb."

"Poor *thumb*," she whispered, and let her lips linger there for a trace of a second. "And now *this*," she said, pointing to the cicatrix just above his right eye.

"That's a longer story."

"We have all day. Or an hour."

"I was . . ." His hand made a slow circuit of his head, as though he were dredging the memory back up. "I was traveling down the Mississippi. Me and Allen Gentry, with a flatbed cargo. Eight dollars a month."

"How old were you?"

"I don't know, seventeen? Eighteen?"

She couldn't imagine him either age.

"About six miles below Baton Rouge, we tied up the boat for the night. Out of nowhere, we were set on by—oh, I guess you'd call them bandits."

"*Bandits.*" She was embarrassed by how the word made her heart race. "How many?"

"Seven."

"You're embellishing."

"I remember each one."

"Were they armed?"

"Bandits always are," he said, dryly. "These ones had hickory clubs."

"They meant to rob you?"

"More than that."

"And what did you do?"

"Well, Gentry, he had a few years on me, so he saw the situation for what it was, and he shouted, *Lincoln, run and get the guns!*"

"Where were they?"

"That's the point, there weren't any. But once I took his meaning, I made as if to *run* for them and—oh, it was quite a *mêlée*, I guess, but we managed to drive them off. Then we cut cable and sailed downriver a ways, and it was only then I realized I'd gotten myself a clout. . . ."

His forefinger, involuntarily, sought out the old wound, but she was already moving on.

"What of *this*?" she asked, pointing to the furrow that bisected his forehead.

"That's not a scar."

"It's something."

"Then it's worry."

She drew her head back. "And what have you to worry about?"

"What do I not?" he answered, half smiling. "The election, that's up there. The practice. My bank account. The general condition of *man*." He paused. "Losing you, I guess. That would be a concern."

"And what would you do?" she asked, genuinely fascinated. "If you lost me?"

"I might have to take another ax to myself."

He laughed then, to show her he was in jest, and took her hand.

Strange to think how disconcerting that experience had been the first time, his fingers swallowing hers. Now she had come to relish the bark-like feel of his skin, the suggestion of animalism in the wiry hairs that poked out of his cuffs. Each time she met him now in Mrs. Francis's parlor, some new part of him became altered under her gaze. The outsized ears took on a goblin sprightliness. The nether lip, so hulking at first sight, became full and sensual. Even that drifting left eye began to tug at her. She followed it east and west and felt only the deepest reserves of tenderness.

Their meetings at first had been awkward, sporadic. Lincoln was gone through the bulk of May, riding the courthouse circuit. When time allowed, he debated some Democrat in Pekin or Decatur. By the time he got back to Springfield, it was nearly June, and the election season was in full tilt, which meant barbecues to attend, and log cabin rallies and hard cider rallies, and meetings of the Whig Central Committee, meetings of the Young Men's Whig Convention. Even on those afternoons when he could pry himself free, Lincoln landed in Mrs. Francis's parlor with a half-abstracted air, as if he were looking for his hat—though it sat there, always in his lap, buffed to a fine gloss by his roaming hands. More than once, he lost his train of thought in the middle of a sentence. It took all her cajoling sometimes, every last caressing fingertip, to call him back to the matter at hand.

She didn't mind. She even envied him his distraction. What must it be like, she thought, to have days so full as that. Hers were largely spent upright on a sofa, knitting and embroidering under the watchful eye of Elizabeth, who continued, with mounting impatience, to sift through the pool of eligible Springfield bachelors.

It was generally understood now that Mr. Trumbull had an outside chance, that Mr. Webb, for all his advanced years, was still in the hunt, and that Mr. Douglas had bright enough prospects to overcome the handicap of his being a Democrat. Mary neither encouraged nor discouraged their overtures. Indeed, on most evenings, in most social settings, she had enough vivacity left over to sprinkle on every male in her vicinity—young, old, comely, plain—with the result that each went home thinking he had claimed some piece of her. In truth, he was just taking his place in a long line of the claimed. If, after nine months in Springfield, Mary held any lingering doubts about her charms, it was dispelled the night her brother-in-law Ninian said, with grudging admiration: "I think you could make a bishop forget his prayers."

Yet this power gave her no joy, for she had already, in one rash leap, staked her own claim—and for a man she almost never saw.

If only she had a dear companion! Someone to reassure her or, failing that, divert her. But Mercy, precious Mercy, had made good on her vow and run back to Baltimore. Nobody could deny her strategic shrewdness. Within days of her departure, her man Conkling had grown so disconsolate that he had proposed marriage by the next post. Mercy allowed a decent amount of time to pass before consenting, and her letters to Mary now were filled with quiet triumph. *Think of it! Mrs. Conkling!*

Mary tried to be glad—she was glad—but she knew that when her friend finally returned to Springfield, it would be as a wife, or the nearest thing, and she had seen enough girls enter that amnesiac condition to know how quickly their spark was snuffed out. One had only to regard her own sisters: Frances, not six blocks away, still lodged in a tavern and sinking deeper into despond with each dollar her husband squandered; Elizabeth, the spirited lass who had all but bloodied herself in combat with their hated stepmother, hardened now into that block of granite known as Mrs. Ninian Edwards.

Would it be any different for Mary? For now, all she could reliably report was that she had a beau—though she had no one to report it *to*. She and Lincoln had instinctually embraced secrecy from the start, and their private Cupid, Mrs. Francis, had an unalloyed love for subterfuge. Whenever she found an opening in Lincoln's schedule, she would merely dispatch a lavender-scented note to Mary: *I wonder if you might join me for tea tomorrow afternoon. 4, perhaps?* It was this same card that Mary would then toss into her sister's lap with a soft laugh.

"What do you think? Shall I go?"

Elizabeth Edwards never looked down on influential connections—although she did grow suspicious when four invitations came in one week.

"You *do* see a lot of that woman."

"Oh, my dear," responded Mary, "the poor creature has asked me to help her with her fancywork. She's quite hopeless with the needle, and the more one tries to help, the worse she gets, but there you are. I feel sorry for her, really. . . ."

Mrs. Francis's embroidery was indeed locally infamous, and the explanation comported so neatly with Elizabeth's general prejudices against Yankee women that Mary never needed to enlarge upon it. She strolled the few blocks to the Francises' in the company of Elizabeth's indentured servant, Hepsey, who was quite willing to be dismissed a block shy of their destination.

Mrs. Francis was not so unmindful of her reputation as to quit the house entirely during these assignations. Neither did she greet her two visitors in person. She merely left standing orders that they were to be shown into the parlor and were not to be disturbed. Mary was usually the first to arrive, and in order to steady her nerve, she would make slow circuits of the room, mentally redecorating every corner, right down to the tea-rose carpet over which her slippered feet now paced. From time to time, she heard the supplicating sound of a cat, but the creature was either locked away in an adjoining room or hidden deep behind some upholstery, for it never emerged. At last, there came the click of the latch. Sensitive to her dignity, Mary always waited some interval before turning. By now, his hat would be in his hands, and he would be standing there, just inside the door, his eyes alight with some unstable combination of gravity and merriment, his lips already parting to form her name.

"Miss Todd."

"Mr. Lincoln."

They were holding hands by the third visit, but the formal titles persisted for quite a bit longer. She had developed, for reasons unclear, an aversion to speaking his Christian name. It didn't matter how many times she pronounced it in the safety of her own room—*Abraham, Abraham*—the name perished on her lips once they were together. When, after some hesitation, she confessed the problem, Lincoln was quick with a solution. They would call each other by pet names.

She accepted the idea on principle. But what could possibly fit the man who stood before her? In the next instant, the answer arrived: *Richard*, after the unlucky king who was Lincoln's favorite Shakespearean character. His face fairly bloomed at the idea, but he himself could devise no name for her.

"Well now," she said, after some consideration. "My friends in school used to call me Molly. To annoy me, mostly, but I came to like it."

He let the name rest on his tongue. "Molly. . . ."

Thus, in a trice, they became two other people, untrammeled by history. They met in a room that belonged to neither, and their passion was greatest when they did nothing more than sit in their respective armchairs and speak of politics.

Was this not, after all, the glue that bound them from the start? Who read more newspapers and journals than they did? Who delighted more in relaying some obscure piece of oratory or satire that nobody else could have seen? There was, in fact, no detail of the coming election—not the voter registration campaigns in the southern counties, not the fate of a canal in Carlinville, not the disposition of farmers in Dane County—that was too buried in newsprint to be hauled to the surface. Indeed, so immersed did they become in this talk that their precious hour might slip by without their knowing—at which point they would hear, on the other side of the door, the warning rap of Mrs. Francis, who always chose that moment to come sailing in with a pot of tea and sometimes a decanter of claret.

With Lincoln hewing closer to home through the latter half of June, their meetings grew more frequent. By now, they were enough of a fixture in the parlor that Mrs. Francis's cat felt free to emerge from hiding. An aged, harlequin-patterned creature with a drooping left eye and protruding tongue, she brushed against their limbs and clawed whatever section of upholstery they weren't occupying. She took a particular shine to Lincoln, who, under the creature's influence, began finally to take his ease—lounging a little more deeply in his chair, letting his hand dangle off the chair's arm or rest on an adjoining cushion.

He seemed to contemplate Mary now with a new degree of freedom, as though for the first time, ideas were coming to mind. One Thursday afternoon, he arrived in a more agitated state than usual. He had just argued his first case before the state supreme court and, having expected a round of grapeshot from the judges, was shocked to have come away with only flesh wounds.

"I didn't know what to do," he told her. "I staggered out of the chamber, perfectly astounded to be among the living. And I looked round, and there was no one there. Which was a great pity because I felt more full—more *alive*—than ever, and I knew I would bust if I didn't tell somebody all about it."

"Tell whom?"

To her surprise, the question appeared to stop him.

"You," he said, at last.

Then he passed his hand round her waist and took a kiss.

It was not exactly her first. Back in Louisville, bourbon-flushed boys had stolen their share—behind a screen or in the niche of some candlelit hallway. But this was the first time she had kissed back, her eyes sealed but her mind's eye watching.

"Richard," she murmured.

WITHIN THE BOUNDS of propriety, they were now free to explore each other. She knew the exact manner in which air escaped his nostrils. She learned how his forefinger felt when it was tracing the outline of her face. The rock-like solidity of his arms and wrists beneath their sheltering fabric. By July, with his encouragement, she was, for minutes at a time, sitting in his lap.

One afternoon, she curled her finger round that absurd ear.

"When shall we speak?" she asked him then. "To the world?"

"Of what?"

"Of us."

He was silent but not slow to glean what she was asking.

"Whenever you see fit," he said.

"Does it rest on me, then?"

"Who else?"

"I mean, do you wish to give me something to speak *of*?"

"It depends."

"On what?"

"On whether you think we're ready."

Her eyes gave a catlike flare. "Why wouldn't we be?"

"To begin with, there's the money question. The state of Illinois pays me one hundred and forty-three dollars a session. But say I lose the election come August. . . ."

"You won't."

"Now the *law* practice, that brings in somewhere between fifteen hundred and twenty-five hundred a year. But say your Cousin John's clients start to panic because he's in Washington so much of the time. Say they jump ship."

"They *won't*."

"That's not even factoring in my national debt."

"Your—"

"My New Salem debt. Still a couple hundred in arrears. Paying it *down*, of course, but . . ."

What in God's name had she wished him to say? That it didn't matter how much money he had? That he would cleave to her even if he had not a penny? Surely, by now she knew how averse he was to empty sentiments, disprovable theses. Surely, that was even part of his attraction—that those old cozening words never sounded from his throat. *The plainer you come at me, the better.* He'd announced as much in their very first meeting, and that was how he was coming at her now.

But his hand was resting on her arm, and his high, lonesome voice was crooning in her ear.

"We'll find a way, Molly."

TWENTY-ONE

MATILDA EDWARDS WAS the most beautiful girl she had ever seen.

This was not the judgment of an hour or a day, but of a second. The girl who stood in the Edwardses' foyer—her gloved hand resting lightly on a palisade of trunks, her cerulean eyes gazing out in cloudless wonder—was a perfect creation.

Only with none of perfection's coldness. There was blood—human blood—pumping behind that strawberry mouth, that polished Palmyra-marble brow. The voluptuous curves of her throat, the beautifully slender arms were all mysteriously animate, as was the soft, sonorous voice that, in this very second, was casting its enchantment over Mary.

"Miss Todd," she said, putting out a hand, "I have heard so much about you."

By now, an unequivocal frown had etched itself on Elizabeth Edwards's face. She had miscalculated.

A month earlier, when Ninian had asked if his cousin Matilda might stay with them, Elizabeth had made all the necessary calculations. The girl in question was neither conspicuously educated nor objectionably wealthy. She had grown up in the relative backwaters of Edwardsville and Alton. She had never left Illinois nor expressed any desire to. All the available reports suggested an incurious, blanching maiden, easily managed, the sort who wouldn't compromise anybody else's marital prospects.

But there had been one crucially missing piece of information. None of Elizabeth's Springfield intimates had seen Matilda Edwards since she was a stripling. In the interim, time had wrought a profound transformation, and the result now stood in the Edwardses' foyer, extending her flawless white hand.

Mary hesitated, just a fraction, for she understood just how fraught this moment was. Tack too hard in any one direction—cold or meek, haughty or cowed—she would, in the same breath, be drawing a bright line between them that could never again be crossed. Instinct—and this was all she had to steer by—told her that she must make an ally of her rival.

"Oh, my dear!" she cried, taking Miss Edwards's hand. "I've been so looking forward to meeting you. But mightn't we dispense with all formalities? You're to call me Mary, if you please, and with your permission, I shall call you Matilda, and we will become the fast friends we were always meant to be. But our most pressing business is to get you off your *feet*. What a taxing journey you've had!"

In truth, there was not a trace of tiredness about Matilda's person, and whatever dust and pollen she had carried out of the prairie had been mysteriously sloughed off by the time she was conveyed up Quality Hill. But she looked grateful for her reprieve, and even more grateful when Mary offered to escort her to her room (larger than Mary's own by a third, but now was not the time). Over supper, Mary also made a point of giving up her usual seat at the dining table and enquiring after Matilda's circumstances with such unfeigned interest that everybody else in the room—and, indeed, the room itself, the very drapes and chairs—seemed to sigh with relief.

"You're playing this well," Elizabeth murmured.

"I don't know what you mean," said Mary. "I am only being *natural*."

There was a particle of truth to this. The more she gazed on Matilda, the more she found herself wishing to be kind to her. Why this should be she couldn't say, but, in the coming weeks, she allowed not a day to go by without performing some service. She took Matilda round town, showed her which sides of the streets to walk upon, introduced her to every useful friend, guided her toward the best cobbler, the best hatter, loaned her clothes (a pelerine, a bodice), sat beside her in church, gossiped with her into the late evening.

On the night of Matilda's debut—at a July ball grudgingly organized by Elizabeth—it was Mary who set aside an additional hour to help the younger woman with her toilet and dress. Even made a point of descending the staircase with her—and became, thereby, the frontline witness to Matilda's impact. Ladies visibly shrank from her and cast worried fingers to their hair. Gentlemen who had long ago resigned themselves to a certain ceiling of beauty were shocked to see the bar so presumptively raised, and within minutes, Matilda's dance card was filled. Even those who hadn't made the cut stood staring at her from an only half-respectful distance, their eyes imbibing.

Matilda seemed scarcely to notice. Indeed, the rather distant manner with which she strolled from room to room seemed to suggest only that this was how the world worked and what could any of them do about it.

For some few hours that night, Mary lay in bed and, with a calmness that surprised her, gauged the new reality of things. If she had once been, to hear Mercy tell it, the belle of Springfield, that title had quite summarily been forfeited. The only remaining question was: How much did she care?

To speak true, she had always found it a little hot and close on that lonely eminence, and there was ever a part of her, striving within, that believed she did not belong there in the first place. And really, what right had she to draw the eyes of other men when she had found the *one* to whom she might devote all her feminine energies?

But at once, a countervailing question rose up: Were those energies producing the desired outcome?

It was possible, yes, that a few more sessions in Mrs. Francis's parlor might raise Lincoln's temperature, that another few months of solvency might embolden him toward declaration. But here it was, nine months since she had come to Springfield, and no engagement to show for it, not even the vague promise of one. Elizabeth herself growing less patient with each passing week, and an unwelcome cloud of mystery following her now wherever she went. Even Matilda found a way to notice. One evening, in the midst of coolly appraising a group of young beaux by a shandy bowl, she leaned over and whispered: "No wonder you won't be snagged."

Matilda, it turned out, had rather higher standards than one might have expected from an Alton girl. At a Whig rally in July, she was introduced to Joshua Speed, and when Mary later adverted to how handsome he was, Matilda did everything but yawn. "He's always keeping a girl at bay, isn't he? Every smile, every piece of flattery says *Stay off.*"

That construction had never crossed Mary's mind. She had been thinking only (and with some sadness) what lovely children Matilda and Mr. Speed would make together.

Though what sort of minds would those children have? Matilda's was clever and observant, but it could not be said that she sounded deeply. She read no novels or newspapers, cared little for art or music, and although her father had run for the highest office in the state, she entertained no great love for politics, either. As many a suitor would discover that summer, she had as little interest in who would be the next president as in who would clean the gutters off Chicken Row. She merely trusted that someone would do the job and forbear to trouble her further.

The one oracle to which she pledged herself with total fealty was the *Lady's Book*, which she seized the moment it arrived by post. The fiction and editorials she merely tolerated, but the dress patterns she devoured, and there was no beauty regimen to which she was unwilling to subject herself. Once a month, as a result, she found her way down to the kitchen, where, under the wary and watchful eye of the Edwardses' cook, she began to mix some enlivening new brew. July's was Paste of Palermo: soft soap and salad oil, augmented with wine, the juice of three lemons, and silver sand.

"It's divine for the hands," said Matilda, pouring a tiny pond into Mary's palm. "And perfect for erasing freckles!"

Mary paused in the act of rubbing. Why had Matilda introduced the subject of freckles? Was it because Mary herself had freckles? That night, she stood before the looking glass with a candle, remorselessly scanning every inch of skin. The next morning, blushing more than she would have liked, she drew Matilda aside.

"I say, you weren't implying I have freckles, were you?"

"Dear me!" cried her new friend. "What a silly puss!"

It became, in fact, something of a recurring pattern: Some offhand remark of Matilda's, made with no obvious trace of malice, would lodge like a canker in Mary's soul. One evening, they were dressing for supper when Matilda said: "How I wish I could get away with as many ribbons as you do!"

Mary went to the glass and examined herself with new eyes. Ribbons on her bodice, her collar, her cap. Ribbons woven into the very strands of her hair. An *insanity* of ribbons. She went straight to her room and began systematically stripping herself down. From ribbons, she moved gradually to flounces, tucks and bows—becoming, in the end, such a pall of dowdiness that Elizabeth took her aside and said, "There's no need to go dowager just yet."

And what could Mary offer in her own defense? Matilda hadn't *told* her to do it, any more than Matilda had advised discarding the bear's-oil perfume or sending a gown back to the dressmaker. She had merely said, "What a distinctive scent" and "You're the first brunette I've known who looks well in apple-green."

And, meantime, was she not affectionate? Always tickling Mary under the chin or leaning in with a conspiratorial air—even if she just wanted the saltcellar. One night, they were being handed down from their carriages when Matilda, with a wicked gleam, murmured, "Whose hearts shall we break tonight?" And then quickly added: "It's not *our* fault, puss. We are simply the means."

All in all, it seemed to Mary that she enjoyed her friend's company best when men were taken out of the picture. Those early-afternoon hours, in particular, when, lacking any other engagements, the two young women sat alone sewing in the Edwardses' front parlor. The summer heat had settled in by now with a vengeance, and they inevitably had to choose between sweltering in airless misery or opening the windows and admitting regiments of horseflies and mosquitoes. (Matilda had a special lotion for chigger bites.) Laid so bare to the elements, they were freer, perhaps, to speak of their own lives, and Mary always felt a soft pang of disappointment when her friend turned the conversation back to suitors.

"The trouble is the *interesting* ones have all been claimed. Mr. Baker, for instance, who is a rather slovenly character but his *own man*."

"Hot in the head," added Mary.

"Thrillingly so. I think he'd raze a whole building just to claim a single ember. But alas, children."

"Three, when last I checked. And a wife."

"You prove my point. Mr. Webb, of course, is a widower but might as *well* be wived, so does the old memory enchain him."

Mary felt a flush of shame at never having inquired into the late Mrs. Webb. Or taken the trouble to imagine her.

"Mr. Douglas," she ventured. "I believe *he* is quite unattached. . . ."

"Oh, puss, he barely rises to my shoulder. You'll say that doesn't matter, and I will confess that, in conversation, one feels his attraction. He seems already to be picturing you *en déshabillé*—and *liking* it. Do you suppose he makes more than three thousand a year?"

"If he doesn't, he will. And a good bit more, it's said, before he's done."

In this manner, the two women held every Springfield bachelor to the light and *peered* at him. One afternoon in August, Matilda, palming away sweat from her cheek, said: "I saw Mr. Lincoln the other day. On the way to the courthouse."

"Oh?"

"Do you know I believe he gets larger each time I look at him? Like some unstoppable tree or—*rock* face—stretching to the heavens."

Mary bent her face over her needlework.

"What a torment that body must be to him," said Matilda. "So much *limb* to reckon with. Although it occurred to me, you know, that if only his hats were a little smaller, he might look more natural in scale."

Her face was scalding now. She adjusted the thimble on her finger.

"Curious," said Matilda.

"What?"

"Whenever I bring up Mr. Lincoln's name, you fall unaccountably silent."

"I have nothing much to say, I suppose."

"You have something to say about everyone, puss."

"Very well," said Mary, with a laugh. "He is exceeding tall, as you say."

But Matilda's face was already drawing down. "Why, it's all making a pattern now," she said.

"What is?"

"Those mysterious disappearances of yours. Those visits to Mrs. Francis, or wherever it is you go. Never inviting anybody to come along."

"A girl likes to get out."

"Yes, but where does she *go*? That's the question."

She spoke in a meditative tone, as if she were the only one in the room. But once she had reached her conclusion—it was the work of no more than five seconds—it came rushing out in a spate.

"Why, you've been meeting Mr. Lincoln! In stealth! Mr. Lincoln is your lover!"

Mary never even troubled to deny it. She merely exploded into tears. In the next second, Matilda had gathered her into her arms.

"Hush now, puss."

Mary tried to calm the heaving of her chest, but it seemed to be operating independently of her. Somehow, she drew up enough air to murmur: "You won't tell? Oh, you won't tell?"

"My sweet darling!" cried Matilda, leaning her beautiful head on Mary's shoulder. "What sort of friend do you take me for? Your *grande passion* is clasped tight to my bosom. Why, though, do you make a secret of it in the first place?" But she was already following out her train of thought to its natural end. "It is your sister. She disapproves."

Helplessly, Mary nodded.

"And she disap*proves*," said Matilda, "because Mr. Lincoln is—well, terribly uncouth, of course, with the manners of a bear. But what she must appreciate, puss, is that this is *just* the thing that can be worked *out* of a man with a little effort."

Had she read that in the *Lady's Book*? Or reasoned it out in the manner of Aquinas? Either way, she spoke with unimpeachable authority.

"Mr. Lincoln is no brute," Mary answered, with a tiny surge of spirit. "He is the soul of gentleness."

"Which will make him all the more pliable in the end. Oh, my dear! How you have suffered! Holding this back for so long! Never mind, the important thing is you have a *confederate* now."

As she leaned in and folded her arm round her friend's shoulders, her eyes began to spark in a way Mary had never seen before.

"We shall make a success of this," said Matilda Edwards. "Oh, yes, we shall."

TWENTY-TWO

THEY COULD NOT trust any further discussion to the wide open spaces of the parlor—the Edwardses' servants were famous for sharp hearing—so later that night, when the rest of the house had gone to sleep, Matilda, barefoot in a high-necked cotton nightgown, tiptoed down the hallway and spirited herself into Mary's room. It had all the feeling of an assignation, particularly because Matilda insisted on lying together in bed with but a single candle for light.

"Tell me everything," said Matilda. "Has he proposed?"

"Not formally. . . ."

"Not formally or not at all?"

"Mostly not at all."

Matilda took some time to digest that.

"Has he held your hand?" she asked.

"Of course."

"Kissed you?"

"Once or twice. Perhaps a little more."

"Has he asked you to sit with him?"

Mary's eyes grazed toward the window. "Once or twice."

"You mean you have granted him all these liberties, and he has still not declared himself?"

Mary felt the reproach as a dull throb, just behind her eyes.

"It depends on what you mean by *declared*."

"Oh, for all that is holy, has he used the word *love*? In a sentence with *you* as its object?"

"Well, he's not exactly orthodox, you see. All those honeyed words—and endearments—they are not native to him. Of course, his natural *tenderness* for me is *everywhere* evident. Why, he once said he would kill himself if ever I left him!"

"What a Gothic creature."

"Oh, no, he was joking. What you must *appreciate* is that the barrier—such as there is—lies not within his heart."

"Then where?"

With a tapering sigh, Mary ran her fingers through her loosened hair. "He has had financial embarrassments."

"You mean he's a pauper."

"No! It's just that, some years ago, he owned a store in New Salem, and then, rather unexpectedly, his business partner died."

"Thoughtless."

"And Lincoln, being how he *is*, assumed the dead man's debts. Though he was in no way obliged."

Matilda lay silent for a second or two. "How deep is he?"

"Why, he's whittled it down to just two hundred! He works so very hard, you see. I scarcely saw him for all of June, he's a perfect *hive* of industry."

"And he doesn't drink?"

"Sober as a judge."

"Gamble? Chase women?"

Mary nearly giggled at that last. "I assure you," she said, "he hasn't a vice in the world. And should he be reelected in November, he'll almost certainly be solvent by the New Year."

"That being *so*," answered Matilda, "why should he keep putting you off? Surely, if it comes to it, there's enough money on *your* end?"

The bluntness gave Mary pause.

"A little," she ventured. "Although I have many brothers and sisters, you see, all clamoring for their share."

"Ah, but you are your father's favorite."

Mary lifted her head from her pillow. "Who told you such a thing?"

"Your sister, who else? The point is, there's quite enough money to go round. If you were to set up housekeeping—in, oh, some little tavern lodging across town—you could get by on four dollars a week. Board *included*, puss."

It was somehow characteristic of Matilda that she had harvested this information before landing a husband.

"Perhaps he longs for something a little grander to start with," Mary suggested. "A house, perhaps."

"A man of *his* circumstances? He should be grateful for what he gets. And in *you*"—she gave Mary's fingers a light squeeze—"he has found more than he could possibly have expected. No, puss, we must not be distracted by this talk of debt. There is some *other* reason he is putting you off." Her fingers gathered more tightly round. "We shall soon find what."

IF MARY HAD thought *we* was a formality, she was corrected two days later when Matilda found the envelope from Mrs. Francis lying on the marble table in the hall.

"So it begins!" she whispered. "Don't worry, puss, I shall escort you there myself. Who better to shield you from the prying eyes of Springfield?"

The next afternoon, she took hold of Mary's arm and set off at such a clip that her companion, with her shorter limbs, was hard-pressed to follow. "You will remember everything we've spoken of?" Matilda kept saying. "Are you sure you'll remember?" It was difficult in such moments to recall that the girl was a mere eighteen, so maternally did she impose herself—and so instinctively did Mrs. Francis greet her as a fellow doyenne.

"Come, Miss Edwards, you really must see the rest of the house."

"It would be my pleasure, of course. But we needn't drag Mary with us, need we? I'm sure she has seen all there is to see."

"You're absolutely right. We shall come find her in the parlor when we're done."

All of it accomplished without a wink or an ounce of staginess. How, then, to explain, the foreboding that gnawed at Mary as she closed the door after her? The cat, rustling through the folds of her skirt, created a layer of static that seemed finally to summon Lincoln, who stumbled in five minutes later.

"Well," she said. "You have taken your time."

Matilda waited until they had left the Francis home before laying a hand on Mary's arm. "Tell me *all*."

"There is little to tell."

"Did you inform him that there was quite enough money to go round?"

"Of course."

"What did he *say*?"

Mary tugged at the hood of her bonnet. "He said it was an easy argument for *me* to make, as I have never been poor."

Matilda stared in amazement. "The nerve of the man! Did you press him further?"

"I only asked if he had some *other* reasons beyond the pecuniary."

"And he said?"

"He only asked me if *I* had other reasons beyond the pecuniary."

With a light groan, Matilda raised her face heavenward. "God save us! Is he always so deucedly circular?"

"I don't know if he's being circular, exactly."

"Then what?"

Straight, she wanted to say. Only she didn't know how to reconcile the contradiction and found herself, instead, diverting the topic to Mrs. Francis.

"Did you sound her out?" Mary asked.

"Heavens, to hear her go on, your lover is the second coming of Zeus. The good news is that, even if she were to poison her husband tomorrow—which I don't entirely put past her—one could hardly imagine her lassoing your Lincoln and dragging him to the nearest altar. No, she will be a good friend to you both, once you are married."

"Only we are not."

"No," said Matilda, gravely regarding her. "All the more reason, then, to light a *larger* fire under this fellow of yours. And pray let us give up all thought of seduction! He would no more register a new frock on you than a change in China's climate. The solution, dear puss, is not to draw him toward you but to push him away."

"How?"

"By withholding yourself, of course. Every intimacy, every caress. The next time he desires so much as a peck from you, you must say, *Mr. Lincoln, my lips will never so much as brush against your whiskers until I have some assurances of you.*"

Three days later, in Mrs. Francis's parlor, she adopted a slightly more sub-dued version of that declaration. Lincoln's response was to draw back a space and study her with genuine curiosity.

"What do you mean by *assurances?*"

"It seems to me," she answered, with a flush of choler, "that when I use a word, you should understand what I mean."

"And how am I to understand what you mean if you won't tell me?"

Matilda gave her head a rough shake on having that remark reported back to her.

"Still circling, I see! Very well, we shall *square* him. Next time, you are to withhold *all* smiles and *all* speech."

Mary obliged as best she could, meeting every inquiry with the curtest of replies. It was to Lincoln's credit, she supposed, that he never complained of this treatment or badgered her to explain it—although he did bestir himself at one point to ask if she were ailing.

"Sore at *heart*," she muttered. "If that may be counted illness."

When Mary repeated it back that night, Matilda was sufficiently moved to leave a kiss on her cheek.

"We will bring him down yet, puss, but you must hold fast."

And so she did, going so far as to banish even politics from the conversation. The silence that rolled across that faded tea-rose carpet was now so implacable that a stranger, blundering in, might have supposed them a pair of mourners, arrived from different parts of the world. Undaunted, Lincoln stayed the whole hour, then showed up very much on time for the next meeting. Greeted there with the same wintry blast, he consented to still another meeting the following Monday.

By now, the weakness in Matilda's strategy had become all too clear: Lincoln was perfectly at home in silence. Had he not grown up in the very thick of it? Miles and miles on every side? If anything, he seized on it as a respite from the lobbyists and accused felons who were ever endangering his peace. Whereas, for Mary, each act of withholding was an affront to her very nature. Sooner ask the river to cease flowing than tell her not to speak. Not to be spoken to. Not to touch or be touched. How much she had enjoyed, for all her formal protestations, those moments when Lincoln had drawn her toward him. The sense of proximate skin—of latent power beneath respectable garments—it had the effect of spring water, bubbling beneath her skin.

By the time Monday came round, Mrs. Francis's parlor had become every bit as warm as the world outside. Lincoln, having spent many long afternoons in sweltering courthouses, knew how to relax into the dampness, but Mary could find no surcease. She mopped her brow, fanned herself for all she was worth, and felt always a little worse than before—the heat *magnified* somehow by the accreting layers of silence. At last, the words came spilling out.

"What do you want of me?"

Lincoln quietly passed her another handkerchief for her tears. Then, when she had ceased to sob, he knelt down before her.

"I want only what you have to give," he said.

"And what do *you* give? You come to this room. You *leave*. It costs you nothing."

"What does it cost you?"

She gave her head an angry shake, fixed her eyes on the floor, but he pressed on.

"What are *you* prepared to give up, Miss Todd? Are you ready to go right now to your sister? Tell her exactly how things stand?"

"My sister," she said, faintly.

"I guess you wouldn't object to that. Getting her blessing."

The look he gave her now was so searching that she felt momentarily bare before it.

"Why do you divert the subject to her?" she muttered.

"Because you always divert the subject away."

"Ah! You are unfair."

"That may be," he answered, dragging an ottoman over to her. "I'm sure we have *both* had our reasons for concealment, but if I were to say to you—right now—that the money no longer concerns me, what would you say to me? Or will you confess that the only one holding us back now is you?"

She rose at once and took several long strides toward the hearth. For some minute, she stared into the empty grate.

"You don't see it, do you?" she said. "My sister would stop us if she knew. She would!"

"You're of age. You may do as you like."

"Oh!" She waved the sodden handkerchief at him. "You talk as if it were the simplest thing in the world."

"Isn't it?"

"She would call in *allies*, Lincoln. She would find reinforcements, she would—interpose *obstacles*."

He was quiet for a time. Then he rose and came toward her.

"If these obstacles are enough to keep us apart, then it would be pointless to speak of marriage. If they *aren't* enough . . . which is to say, if they're mainly in your own mind . . ." And here he took the liberty of resting his index finger tenderly on the back of her head. "Then speaking of marriage is just as pointless."

He took her gently by the arm and turned her round. Then he angled up her chin until she was looking into his face. He folded his dark and roughened hands round hers and, in a voice of unnatural warmth, said: "Are you ready to walk in the sun with me, Mary Todd?"

How LITTLE MATILDA Edwards's stratagems had prepared her for the disorientation of this moment. For the first time in the brief history of their assignations, she left before he did. Fairly staggered out of the parlor and, without pausing for shawl or reticule, plied herself against the front door and went stumbling down the steps.

One block bled into the next. A gentleman actually stopped at the sight of her and lifted his hat, but she never quite saw him, nor did she grasp how she must have looked, wandering unescorted and disheveled. She merely walked, without application, until the ground rose beneath her and, looking up, she found the Edwards mansion. Blears of candle in every window (though there was still ample light outside) and, in the drive, a carriage, idled and horseless. Under a spell of enchantment, she crept up the front steps, turned the knob on the front door. Stood there in the hallway, drinking in the quiet.

Elizabeth was sitting halfway up the stairs.

For a second, Mary wondered if she had conjured her out of nothing. But the creature rose with all the stateliness and awe that the real Elizabeth commanded, and when she spoke, it was in Elizabeth's voice, cool and unsurprisable.

"I know," she said.

Joshua

TWENTY-THREE

In the aftermath of that disastrous spring picnic, at least three men had cause to regret. Conkling had alienated the girl of his heart. Joshua, under the sway of liquor and goading, had come close to being asphyxiated. As for Lincoln, in rashly agreeing to wrestle his friend, he had succeeded only in enraging Miss Todd, who had stormed off and taken with her the tattered remnants of Mrs. Francis's matrimonial schemes.

Yet her departure seemed not to affect him nearly so much as the sight of Joshua, lying on the green. For the whole day following, Lincoln kept stealing glances at his friend's face—checking his forehead, opening windows—asking him the most mundane of questions just to make sure of a reply.

"You don't need to lie down? A glass of water, maybe. Shall I open a window?"

Once, just once, in the ensuing week, Joshua brought up the picnic, but Lincoln calmly changed the topic, and her name was no more raised between them, even in passing.

In the second week of March, Joshua got word that his father had died.

His first response was to reproach himself for his own fallacy. Like so many sons, he had assumed his father to be eternal. It was true that John Speed had been prey to hypochondria, melancholia, all manner of minor ailments and neuroses, but the father who had for so long colonized his son's imagination was the nearly bestial specimen who swam in the coldest water, shoed his own horses, and liked the world best when he was charging against it. He treated idle workers and Unitarian preachers and recalcitrant sons with an equivalent scorn and harbored, somewhere at the back of the scorn, a grudging and doomed hope that they might all one day be brought into line.

There was no question of Joshua's going to the funeral. John Speed had already lain dead for eight or nine days, and Joshua would be as many days traveling back to Farmington. No mortal body could keep that long, which meant that, for all intents and purposes, he had been absolved of further mourning. But as he sat there at his desk, recalling all the letters he had never written, the affirmations he had never made, he realized—with a shock nearly as great as the death itself—that he no longer had any reason to keep clear of Farmington.

At some point, he heard Lincoln's voice behind him.

"Joshua, I'm sorry."

He never stopped to ask how he had heard the news. He was sensible only of the press of Lincoln's hand on his shoulder. In the next second, he was resting his own hand atop it.

VERY GRADUALLY, IN the manner of an old house resettling onto its foundations, the two men took up their former routines. The morning shave, the cups of tough coffee, dinner at the Butlers'. The Poetical Society, meeting now two or three evenings a week. Editorial conferences, Whig committee meetings.

And with the weather growing ever fairer, they went for longer and longer walks each evening. East and west they traveled—the full lengths of Jefferson and Washington and Adams and Monroe and back again—passing rosebushes and bowers of honeysuckle. Nights now were dark and warm, and the stars shimmered into some liquid status that could actually be *felt*, like a scattering of fingertips. Springfield had never looked more charming.

"Do you suppose," Joshua said one night, "that we'll be walking just like this twenty, thirty years on?"

"On sidewalks, if prayer has any effect."

"Sidewalks or no."

"Ohh," said Lincoln, with a lazy stretch, "I expect so. We'll be like those old men that townsfolk set their clocks to. *Howdy-do!*" The twang came rolling back with no effort. "*Yonder comes the Lincoln-Speed local. Must be gettin' on nine thirty-three.*"

Joshua at once recognized this for the fantasy it was. What was the likelihood that both men would even still be here two decades hence? Or that, having avoided all entanglements, they would be free to converge, in this same easy fashion, every evening? No, he thought, a Lincoln-Speed local would necessarily have to discard a great deal of cargo if it was going to arrive at such a destination.

But the world seemed once more to be clearing a path. Joshua's brief banishment from Springfield society had come to a summary end, and the same hostesses who, at the behest of Mrs. Francis, had kept him off their guest lists hastened now to call him back and even chided him for his disappearance.

"How cruel you are, Mr. Speed, to keep your qualities so hidden from view! And how dull it's been without you! Just the other day, I was saying that nobody rounds out a table like Mr. Speed. You may depend upon him for everything, and nobody has more exquisite manners. No, don't stammer, it's true."

Even Mrs. Francis made a point of going up to him at their first crossing and greeting him with unfeigned warmth.

"My dear Mr. Speed, I have been meaning to tell you what a splendid job you've done with *The Old Soldier*. To take such disparate voices and make them sing as one, what a gift that is! Now you may cherish the role of unsung hero, but I promise you that, come August, when the Whigs are swept into office, I shall be shouting your name from the very rooftops. That is my solemn vow!"

All in all, it was a bit dazzling to be gathered once more into official Springfield's bosom—and to find his old friend once more seated alongside him at table. Ready, as ever, to take up his part in their two-man production.

Have I told you the story of Lincoln and the baby birds? I haven't? Well, there were six of us, I think, on this country road near Chandlerville. Wild plums, crab-apple trees. . . .

The cues were picked up as promptly as ever. The guests followed just as attentively, the laughs arrived as punctually. One might have thought that nothing had ever parted them.

Yet something had, however briefly. And it was the memory of that rupture that imparted to even routine exchanges the air of something hard-won and precarious. One night, as they were traveling home from the Barretts', Lincoln came to a halt and rested his walking stick on a gatepost.

"There's something I'm puzzling out," he said. "Tonight, when you were telling the guests how we met . . ."

"When *we* were telling."

"There's something in the story I can't square. You say you stayed below while I went upstairs to look the room over."

"So I did."

"But then you *also* said that, once up there, I dropped my saddlebags on the ground. How could you have known that? If you were downstairs?"

The ensuing silence seemed to embarrass Lincoln more than it did his friend. He absently picked at a spray of jessamine on the trellis.

"It's a trivial thing," he said. "I don't even know why I keep rubbing against it, except you see, I brought the bags back down with me. Because I didn't want to presume that your offer still stood. And I suppose . . . Well, the way the story gets told, it makes me sound like a bit of a sponger. Moving *in* the first chance I got."

That possibility had never crossed Joshua's mind, then or now. The truth was that he *had* followed Lincoln up that stair. Had watched, from a discreet distance, as the new arrival set down his bags and tested the bed springs and peered through a windowpane and ascertained the height of the ceiling and did everything a stranger would do to imagine his way into a new space. It was such an innocent, such a curiously naked sequence that Joshua felt like a hunter stealing up on an antelope. He edged back down the stair, just in time to resume his position behind the counter.

"Bless me, Brother Abraham, I heard the saddlebags *fall*. You can't have forgotten how heavy they were, can you? Like cannonballs. And you can be sure," he hurried on, "that, when we are next asked for the history of our origins, I shall be the first to declare that Lincoln came back with his saddlebags *on*. No sponger, he!"

Lincoln's lips softened into a smile. "It was silly of me to bring it up."

"Not at all."

"I mean, how little it signifies, really. And even if . . ." He let his hand settle on Joshua's arm. "Even if things didn't go exactly the way somebody says, why, a man's entitled to his own accountings of things, isn't he? It all washes out in the end."

He uttered the words in the sweetest, most obliging of tones, and yet their import was unmistakable. He believed Joshua to be lying.

A small lie, to be sure, the lightest of omissions, but an omission all the same. And this: Lincoln had left open the possibility that he, too, was concealing something—perhaps every bit as small or perhaps larger—and was, in the same space, absolving himself. With that deceptively simple clause: *It all washes out in the end.*

Define *washing out*, thought Joshua, with a curl of lip. Define *end*. That poetical tribute to Mary Todd, the one that Lincoln had so carelessly stuffed under his mattress. Could that be said to have *washed out*? When such ill had come from it? It struck Joshua—and not for the first time—that so much of Lincoln's own heart was itself stowed away just like that poem. Chamber after chamber, locked in shadow.

As fate would have it, Joshua's dream that night took him right back to their first meeting. Once more, he was following his strange new tenant up the stairs . . . watching him set down his saddlebags to try the mattress and test the ceiling. Only this time, Lincoln unexpectedly turned. And at the sight of Joshua, crouching there on the stairs, his face contracted into a mask of disgust.

"What are *you* looking at?" he snarled.

Joshua tried to run, but there was no prying his feet from the floorboards. He could only watch as Lincoln traveled the few feet that still separated them.

"My," said Lincoln, when he woke Joshua, "that dream of yours was a thrasher."

TWENTY-FOUR

———

RIDING THE EIGHTH Judicial Circuit might have broken a lesser man.

Jolting in and out of ruts and potholes on a broken-down nag. Watching every road disappear in a swale of mud and fording swollen streams and, the whole while, praying that the papers you stuffed in your hat would still be there on the other side. Praying that enough people had done enough wrong to give you a couple of days of legal work at each courthouse. You *harvested* their sins, didn't you, like a sod farmer of the soul—their property squabbles, their slanders and libels, their debts and felonies, their divorces and bigamies, their manslaughters and assaults and batteries—squeezing as much profit from each transgression and then traveling on to the next town to reap anew. On and on through fourteen counties and four hundred miles.

Yet Lincoln was never happier than when he mounted Old Tom each spring and fall. It was on the road, he used to say, where he could be most himself, where he could swap jokes and stories, uncensored, with the judges and lawyers who formed his truest constituency. And where he could meet Illinois citizens in their purest form—which was to say, in their extremity—wondering how life could have done them such a turn.

"And none of them cares how I *dress*, Speed. I can wear my trousers too short, put on an old coat. Wear that shawl you hate so much. That's right, the one with the quilting pin! And I *still* look better than most of the judges."

So, that May, Lincoln left in his usual high spirits. And even as one court-house term bled into the next, his letters home never lost that tone of embattled cheer, so that Joshua, reading those smudged lines, ended up regretting the press of business that kept him pinned to the store. Wouldn't it have been a lark to travel out to one of those benighted courthouses and surprise Lincoln? He could just picture the stupefied grin that would break out across his friend's face. *Why, Speed*, he would say. *You have been a perfect sneak.* They could retire to whatever God-slighted tavern Lincoln had been forced to lodge in—two dozen to a room—and sit by the fire and say nothing at all, for what greater relief could there be to a man who had been living all these weeks by his wits? At some point, in the midst of his own drowsing, Lincoln might lift his head and murmur: *I'm glad you came, Speed*.

On the evening of the twenty-eighth, in the act of closing up shop, Joshua spied a lone man on the far side of the street. Joshua squinted into the dusk, trying to make out a face, but, finding nothing familiar, contented himself with a brief nod. The man nodded in return, and Joshua was about to shut the door when the stranger took a few tentative steps in his direction.

"Pardon me. Are you Mr. Speed?"

The features revealed themselves, individually, as he drew closer. Bright, close-set eyes. A hulking nose. A profligate head of chestnut hair, which had been swept back from his forehead just artfully enough to convey artlessness. The stranger doffed his hat in a smooth downward arc and said: "Someone told me Abe lives here."

Abe.

"That is so," allowed Joshua.

"What a relief! I've been tramping these streets upwards of two hours."

"Have you? I didn't know we had so many."

"Ohh." The stranger scratched his head becomingly. "More than my poor town ever had."

It was that *poor* that Joshua's ear snagged on. Edging ever so slightly toward *pore* and then edging back, as if the speaker were kicking over the traces of his own upbringing.

Just like Lincoln, he thought.

"You have the advantage of me, sir," he said. "I don't yet know your name."

"Ah! Where are my manners? Billy Greene." A thick, blunt handshake. "Abe's probably mentioned me."

The two men stood regarding each other for a moment.

"Alas," said Joshua, "you appear to have come at the wrong time. Lincoln is out of town on business."

By all rights, that should have been the end of it. The news had been imparted, and Joshua bore no further obligation except to direct his visitor to the nearest tavern or stage line. Ever afterward, he would wonder what had kept him from shutting the door. Perhaps it was the spasm of disappointment that creased his visitor's face. Or the piney musk of perspiration that rose from his damp collar.

Or maybe it was just this: A light rain had begun to fall, and there was no sign of an umbrella anywhere on the stranger's person.

"Won't you come in?" said Joshua. "Rest awhile?"

Billy Greene smiled as he fingered away the single raindrop that coursed down his face.

"I won't say no."

The day had been too warm for a fire, but the two men gathered all the same by the hearth at the back of the store. Joshua dragged a pair of chairs over, set them at angles, and poured out two tumblers of whiskey.

"Is this your first time in Springfield?" he asked, drawing his chair closer.

"My last, too, for all I know."

"How long will you be staying?"

"I wish I knew," answered Billy Greene. "A night or two? It depends on— say, are you the owner of this place?"

Joshua nodded, and Billy's eyes, enlarged by the knowledge, began to roam through the shadows, picking out the shelves and their contents.

"He's landed well," he said at length.

"I'm sorry?"

"Oh, I mean no puncheon floors. No clapboard roofs. Our Abe has gone *up* in the world. Yes, sir," he said, before adding with soft satisfaction: "He's climbed, he has."

"Well, to speak true, the roof leaks, and the floor creaks, and I feel as if I'm always one step ahead of bankruptcy."

"Oh, come now," said Billy Greene, smiling indulgently. "You're a gentleman down to your shoes, Mr. Speed. Anybody can see that. I'd wager Abe sounds a little closer to a gentleman himself, doesn't he? Bet he dresses better, too."

Staring into his whiskey, Joshua softly swirled the glass. "Abe . . ."

"Oh, apologies. That's just what we called him. Back in New Salem."

"And he answered."

"Ha! Yes, he did. Except when he was daydreaming." A rough, almost coarse laugh that gave way by increments to a sigh. "I can't believe he's not here. I wrote and told him I was coming."

"Did you say when?"

"I didn't exactly know myself."

"Well, that explains it. He's a perfect slave to the court calendars. One way or another, I don't expect him back until . . ." Saturday. "Wednesday next."

Billy absorbed the news without a word. Then he drew from his vest pocket a briar pipe. "Pardon me, Mr. Speed, do you have any tobacco about?"

In fact, Joshua's mother had just shipped him a cache. Top of the line, she said, but as Lincoln never smoked and as Joshua preferred cigars, the Farmington tobacco was kept in a Dutch oven, a few feet north of the hearth. It cost him little, therefore, to scoop a handful into Billy Greene's pipe and offer him a light.

"When *I* knew him," Billy continued, "Abe wasn't any kind of lawyer. No, sir, he could barely write a sentence. I used to help him with his grammar lessons, you know. I'd hold the book like this, so he couldn't see, and I'd say, *Very well, Abe, what do adverbs qualify?* And he'd say, *Well now, adverbs qualify verbs, adjectives, and other adverbs.* And it would carry on just like that. We'd go hours some nights. Straight through till dawn. He used to say the only reason he knew anything about grammar or mathematics was owing to me." Billy was silent for a while before adding: "Tight as thieves, that was us. Why, we even went to war together. Not *much* of a war but . . ." He drew his pipe from his mouth, frowned down at it. "Are you married, Mr. Speed?"

"No."

"Still holding out, eh?"

"I suppose."

"I held out myself. Long as I could. But once you hit that quarter-century mark, they come looking for you. They do."

"Twenty-five?" said Joshua. "That's not so—"

"Oh, I found a sweet-enough girl. We get along in a fashion. All things weighed in the balance, it's worked out. Two babes in hand, another on the way." A dry chuckle. "Who knows how many to follow?" His gaze drifted down to the neighborhood of his boots. "I remember the first time I ever saw Abe."

"Do you?"

"His flatboat had got stranded on a mill dam, right outside of New Salem. Well, that was the closest thing to entertainment we had in those days because pretty soon a whole crowd of us came round to watch. But Abe, he stayed calm through it all. Unloaded the cargo, then went ashore and borrowed an auger from—it was Onstot's cooper shop. Drilled a hole in the bow to let the water drain out and then eased it over the dam. By the time he was done, the whole crowd was clapping."

A small hunk of ash landed on Billy's coat sleeve.

"I'm trying to recall what he was wearing that day. A hickory shirt, I think it was. And a chip hat. And a pair of mixed blue-jeans pants, rolled up very high owing to the water. My, the thighs on him. Strongest man I've ever known." A moment of silence before he lifted his gaze. "Say, does Abe still wrestle? Oh, no, what am I thinking? He doesn't have the time for that now. That's a lost world, that is." He protruded his lower lip and tapped the stem of his pipe. "You say he won't be back till Wednesday next?"

"At the earliest, I'm afraid."

Joshua had thought to close off the subject for good and was all the more perturbed to see Billy's eyes brighten.

"Say now! I don't suppose I could stay here tonight?"

"Here, you say?"

"Oh, I hate like the devil to ask, but the price of hotels round here! Fifty cents a *night*, some of them."

Joshua smiled, folded out his hands. "How I wish I could manage it, but I've got two clerks sleeping upstairs as it is."

In fact, Billy Herndon had left three months earlier.

"Not to worry!" cried Billy Greene. "I'll sleep in Abe's bed. For old times' sake."

"Old times. . . ."

"Why, the two of us used to share the tiniest cot this side of the Mississippi. It got so tight in there, you couldn't even turn over without the other doing likewise. You couldn't have a *thought* without the other fella thinking it. Oh, and when that fool was *snoring*, it was—" He stopped. Groped his way back. "I guess I should just say we were most congenial."

"I've no doubt. Unfortunately, Lincoln's bed is taken as well."

Billy let the news settle over him. Then, with a flush and a pickled smile, he said: "I shouldn't have asked."

"Not at all. I'm only sorry I can't oblige."

Billy nodded to himself. Then he tugged back one of his shirtsleeves and softly stroked the square of exposed flesh.

"I'll never forget the day Abe said to me, he said, *Listen here, Billy, you need to go to university. Get yourself the education I never got.* So I went. I listened to him, and I went. Three years at Jacksonville, working like a donkey the whole time, all on account of him. Working nearly as hard today. Educating the next generation of youthful minds, that's me."

"A schoolteacher, you mean?"

"Better than that. Principal of the Priestly Academy. You probably don't know Priestly's."

"I fear not."

"It's a girls' school in White County, Tennessee. The very height of exclusivity, or that's what they tell me."

"I'm sure."

"Now don't mistake me, I'm not planning to make a career out of academia. Ha! No money to be had *there*! No, sir, my fortune will be with the railways. Mark me."

They sat in silence, looking at each other.

"Say now," said Billy, "are you *sure* he never talks about me?"

"Oh, he must have. I have a terrible head for names, you see."

"Well," said Billy. For some time, he sat there, absently scraping his lower lip with the stem of his pipe. Then, in a slightly altered voice: "I'm only glad I could be a comfort to him. Back there in New Salem. Hoist him up the ladder, as it were. Just like *you're* doing, Mr. Speed."

Joshua felt himself flinch.

"Well, yes," he rejoined. "I've always said if I could be—*useful* to some other creature, then I would consider it my . . . my Christian *duty* to—"

"Oh, I feel the same!"

And indeed, there was something beatific in the light that now welled from Billy's eyes.

"To have been a real help to somebody, that *counts*, doesn't it? Even if— even if you're no longer so *much* of a help as you once were." He paused, but his lips continued to move for another second. "What I mean is I did my duty, Mr. Speed. Just as you said. I did it with joy."

A soft thrum could be heard now on the roof. The curtains in the back window were lifting in the breeze, and a horsefly, seeking refuge from the elements, scored lazy ellipses round their chairs.

"I should be going," said Billy.

Joshua was already to his feet before he thought to ask: "Are you sure?"

Without another word, his visitor knocked the remnants of his tobacco into the fireplace and eased himself off the chair. By the time they got to the door, the rain had deepened to a downpour, and Joshua had to work against the whole grain of his upbringing to send his visitor into it. Billy Greene didn't balk. He clapped his hat on his head, and without taking his eyes off the rain, said: "When you see Abe, will you tell him Slicky Bill stopped by?"

"Slicky Bill."

"Tell him to write me. Will you do that? He knows the address. And if he ever finds himself in Tennessee . . ."

He didn't finish the sentence but took a step forward, then another, until the rain was coursing down him. Most people would have scurried for the nearest cover, but Billy reached calmly into his vest pocket and drew out a watch. Held it in his palm for a moment and then, instead of flipping open the lid to check the hour, turned it over. For some seconds, he stood there, in the driving rain, reading what was written there. Then he tucked the watch back inside his vest and strode slowly down the street.

Only when he had slipped into the darkness did Joshua feel free finally to shut and bolt the door. He had it in mind to go straight to the bed, but his feet failed him, and he sank to the floor, with only the doorjamb to prop him up. Reaching into his vest pocket, he drew out the gold watch Lincoln had given him for Christmas, with the monogram on its back.

JFS

What was Billy Greene's monogram, he wondered? Did it begin with *W* or *B*? Had the letters been worn down from hard use? Was there anything left to see?

LINCOLN CAME BACK, as expected, on the thirtieth. Trailing the usual cache of human woe. Foreclosed mortgages and breaches of promise and divided estates and infant heirs and an accused murderer and a diabolically misrepresented mare. Somewhere in that stream of anecdote, Lincoln paused and, in an even voice, asked: "Did anybody call for me while I was gone?"

Joshua, who was busy reading a consignment notice for rakes from Pittsburgh, asked him if he had been expecting anybody.

"Not particularly."

Without raising his eyes, Joshua said: "All quiet here."

TWENTY-FIVE

———— • ————

IT WAS ONE thing to close the door on Billy Greene; it was another to be shut of his memory.

I did my duty. . . . I did it with joy.

But how, Joshua wondered, would one know when one's duty was done?

Or had that time already come? Surely, Mrs. Francis had already declared as much in her parlor. Perhaps it was only a matter of time now before Lincoln found himself grasping for the *next* hand to hoist him up the ladder.

Against his will now, Joshua found himself interrogating his friend's smallest gestures. Every hesitation, every slant of eye. *Now? Is it now?* In this changed context, the tiniest things could raise alarms. A missed appointment. A swell of reticence in response to a query. . . .

Or the scent that Lincoln brought to bed with him one night in July.

It registered at first as just a prickling in Joshua's nostrils. "That's funny," he said. "You smell like rose water."

"Huh." Lincoln drew his wrist to his nose. "Mrs. Butler must be putting flowers in my drawers."

Even in the act of laughing, Joshua detected the flaw. If Mrs. Butler had been throwing roses into their laundry, his own skin would have smelled of rose water, too.

"You're right," he heard himself say. "A pox on all flowers."

It was a small matter.

Two nights later, Lincoln came to bed with the same smell. Joshua was about to make some jesting objection, but the words stalled, and long after his friend had drifted off, he lay awake, sifting through the evidence of his senses.

What did it mean that a man like Lincoln—who had to be coaxed just into taking a weekly bath—should come to bed with such a fragrance? Was he secretly anointing himself? In the hopes of making a better impression on some judge? If that were so, why not own up to it? Solicit help, even? Bell & Company had all manner of ointments, extracts. With Joshua's assistance, they could surely find a scent more suitable to a gentleman lawyer.

But here, after all, was the crux of the problem: This was no gentleman's scent.

AND HERE THE conundrum: Joshua's first impulse was to consult Lincoln.

Who, after all, would be wiser or sounder in assessing the situation? Who more likely to cut through its complexities and find the simplest of solutions? Yet there could be no sounding out the man on the subject of himself. That way lay only evasion, silence.

Nor was there any point in seeking some other confidant, for there was not a single man or woman of Joshua's acquaintance who would accept that his problem was a problem. How easily he could imagine their smiles (indulgent), their chuckles (knowing). *My word, Speed, if our boy is finding himself a little solace on the side, who are you to complain? All work and no play, old man.* He would risk many things, he believed, but he would not risk being accused, even tacitly, of hysteria. So, in the absence of counsel, he remained frozen— days and days creeping by without deed or plan. In his lowest moments, it seemed to him that the map of his future was now a trackless waste, and he himself just one more point of indeterminacy, waiting for an adjoining point to make him a segment. More points to make him a line. . . .

Then Fate sent him Eli Tibbetts.

Tibbetts had first come into Joshua's shop nine months earlier, in dire need of a dovetail saw and a miter box. He was a joiner who had lost his shop in the panic of thirty-seven and was barely getting enough from odd jobs to feed his two children (their mother having passed to her reward). He had neither cash nor anything to barter, but he brought with him a promissory note made out for the exact amount of two dollars and ninety-three cents—a sum he judged to be more than fair.

Joshua normally didn't accept notes; as Lincoln was forever pointing out, they were too hard to collect on. But there was something about Tibbetts's flat, pleated, goatish face that instilled respect. Joshua duly signed the note, and Tibbetts snatched up his saw and miter box and left the premises. For *good*, that was the likeliest possibility—but the very next morning, he was back in the store with a pair of pennies in his palm.

"That's two cents down."

The following Tuesday, it was a nickel. The Thursday after, two dimes. And so it followed. Week after week, Eli Tibbetts would take whatever surfeit of cash he had accumulated and carry it straight to Bell & Company—arriving so quietly and moving through the store so economically that Joshua wouldn't even know he was there until the coins were actually sliding across the counter.

It was in late June, with the smell of rose water still quick in his nostrils, that Joshua watched another cache of pennies gravitate toward him. "That's six cents down," announced Eli Tibbetts.

Joshua swept the coins into his till and was about to turn away when a thought crept up and caught him unawares.

"See here, Tibbetts. How much do you still owe me?"

"One dollar and twenty-three cents."

"What if you could erase that debt in a single stroke?"

Tibbetts tugged on the worn piece of corn husk that hung off his lower lip. "A job, you mean?"

"Just so."

"I reckon it depends on the job."

"I'm looking . . ." Joshua stopped, made a quick scan of the store. "You see, I'm looking for a man to . . ."

"What?"

"Well, to *follow* another man round town."

Tibbetts gave the husk a chew. "Shadder him, you mean."

"Yes, *shadow*, exactly."

"For how long?"

"Let us propose nine in the morning to six in the evening. With an hour off for dinner."

"How many days?"

"Let us propose three. At the close of the third, you may consider your debt discharged."

Tibbetts drew the husk from his mouth, rolled it between his fingers. "What's the feller's name?"

"I'll give you every other particular, but the name is of no concern."

"What are you wanting to know about him?"

"Where he goes, whom he sees. That's all."

"Has he done something evil?"

"Nothing *unlawful*, if that's your concern." Seeing how little that persuaded, Joshua added: "The truth is he's a dear friend of mine. Lives under my very roof. I just—I fear that he may have fallen in with a bad crowd."

Tibbetts put the husk back in his mouth. "Whyn't you just come out and ask him?"

"I regret to say he's not the most forthcoming of souls. He's a—he's a *lawyer*, you see."

The news produced an unmistakable ripple in the otherwise still surface of Eli Tibbetts.

"I should have guessed," he said, quietly.

Tibbetts insisted on drawing up another promissory note—this one for a dollar and twenty-three cents—which he marked with his usual *X*. Joshua countersigned and then locked the note away and ushered him to the door.

"Now your main concern here is to avoid advertising your presence, do you understand? To my friend, to anybody else. You're to be, for all intents and purposes, invisible."

Tibbetts, in that moment, came the closest Joshua had ever seen to a smile. "When it comes to that, Mr. Speed, the Lord has indeed blessed me."

TIBBETTS WAS BACK the next evening, just a little after six. Without a word, he followed Joshua into the rear office but declined the offer of a seat.

"You couldn't have sent me an easier body to follow. I could spot him halfway 'cross the prairie."

"Did you discover anything?"

"Only that you needn't fear for his soul. Best I can tell, he does nothing but travel between his office and the courthouse. Upstairs and down. When he's not breaking bread with *you*, I mean."

A knot of misgiving gathered at the base of Joshua's throat. He had never considered that he himself would be followed.

"And he went nowhere else?"

Tibbetts shook his head.

"Very well," muttered Joshua. "See what you can learn tomorrow."

But the next day provided no further enlightenment. Even Tibbetts, having been promised a certain ration of wickedness, seemed dissatisfied with the state of things.

"If there's a duller fool living, Mr. Speed, I've never seen him. He's all work-brickle, that one."

The third day, Tibbetts came back with the same report. The man he had been shadowing appeared, on the evidence, to live a blameless life. Joshua was just drawing the promissory note from his desk drawer when Tibbetts said: "He did go for a stroll. Round about four."

Joshua glanced up. "A stroll?"

"Well, he weren't in a hurry."

"Did you follow him?"

"Course."

"Where did he go?"

"A lady's house."

"But why didn't you mention it before?"

"Cause there weren't nothing wrong with it."

Joshua swallowed, twice.

"How do you know it was a lady's?"

"That's who greeted him at the door."

"Old? Young?"

Tibbetts shrugged. "In the middle."

"Where does she live, this lady?"

Tibbetts was in no position to read the street name, but he had made such a close study of the house itself—and of the *Sangamo Journal* offices next door—that, in the end, not even Thomas Cole could have sketched a finer portrait of Eliza Francis's domicile.

"How long did my friend stay there?" asked Joshua.

"A stretch."

"A quarter hour?"

"Longer."

"An hour?"

"No more 'n an hour."

"Did he leave alone?"

Tibbetts nodded.

"Where did he go?"

"Where else? Back to his office. He's a creature of habit, that one."

Joshua stared into the fire.

"Tibbetts," he said, "I believe it is time to extend our arrangement. By another week."

He reached into his waistcoat pocket and drew out a single dollar, placed it in the joiner's hand.

"I should like you to continue following him but with this proviso. The next time he ventures to this house, you're to *remain* there, do you understand? Even when he leaves, you're not to follow him back to his office but stay on your watch."

"For how long?"

"Until somebody emerges."

"Who?"

"Anybody."

"Then what?"

"Take note of them, that's all. Their age, sex. General appearance, whatever strikes the eye."

Tibbetts seemed even more skeptical about this assignment than the last, but he did as instructed. The next day passed without incident, but on the succeeding day, Tibbetts returned in a mood of vexation.

"By sugar," he said. "I hope you weren't expecting to find gamblers or horse thieves coming out of that house. It was but the two young ladies."

Joshua cocked his head. "*Two*, you say?"

"As God is my witness. Arm in arm, tight as sisters. Though they didn't much look like kin."

"What *did* they look like?"

"Fair," he said, with the air of a man who had taken time to weigh the matter.

"Can you enumerate further?"

Fortunately, Eli Tibbetts had taken as much leisure in studying the ladies as he had in studying the house. The first of them, as described, comported so closely to Mary Todd that Joshua finally cut him off.

"What of the other?" he asked.

"Oh."

This was a more halting endeavor. The girl in question was tall and slender but not too tall and not too slender. Her skin was pale but not too pale. Her lips were cherry but not too cherry. Her figure was . . .

"In short," interposed Joshua, "she was lovely."

"Enough to rile Jesus."

Joshua shook his head. It could only be Matilda Edwards, who had left men far more articulate than Tibbetts groping for words. But here was a new mystery. If Lincoln was making love to a girl in Mrs. Francis's house . . . which girl was it? Had Miss Todd somehow contrived to transfer her admirer's affections toward her cousin? Was any man's heart quite so transferable?

It was true, of course, that no man of ordinary parts could be immune to Miss Edwards's charms, but even Joshua couldn't imagine Lincoln wooing such a self-possessed creature. She was a bird who had never once fallen from its nest, or even considered the possibility. No, all things reckoned, it was far more likely that Miss Edwards was there to offer protective cover. But how to prove it?

Joshua drew another dollar from his waistcoat, laid it in Tibbetts's palm.

"You're to carry this forward, do you understand? I want you to station yourself outside the house. All day if need be. The next time those particular ladies pay a call, you're to notify me at once."

"Come here?" said Tibbetts, deepening his natural frown.

"Walk right in. If I'm not at the counter, ask for me."

"And what then?"

"We shall go back to the house together. You and I."

Tibbetts's head listed a fraction. One eye shrank down, nearly to a wink.

"You don't mean to raise a ruckus, do you?"

Of course not, Joshua wanted to answer. *I am a gentleman*. But that was a title he had forfeited, either by degrees or in one rash leap. His only reply, as a result, was to reach into the till and draw out another quarter.

JOSHUA WAS IN no particular hurry to have his suspicions corroborated, but before twenty-four more hours had passed, Eli Tibbetts was back at the store, curling his index finger balefully. Swallowing down his dread, Joshua slowly untied his apron and called out to his clerk.

"Charlie! There's a shipment from Saint Louis that's come in ahead of time. DuPont's powder, I think. I'll be back in an hour."

He was following Tibbetts out of the store when he caught his own reflection, lightly stamped by the late-afternoon sun on the shop window. He stopped where he was, the better to study those familiar features, now so estranged. The eyes, buried so deep in their sockets.

"We don't have all day," growled Tibbetts.

ON TOP OF his other virtues, Tibbetts had a knack for finding the ideal observation post—in this case, a brick garden wall with a keyhole niche that had the advantage of being shrouded from view by an overhanging willow while permitting a nearly uninterrupted angle on the Francis house across the street.

"After you," said Tibbetts.

In such close quarters, the mix of turpentine and sawdust on the joiner's skin was close to overpowering, and Joshua was about to step away to clear his head when the door to the house opened, and with a declarativeness that seemed almost fantastical, Eliza Francis and Matilda Edwards stepped in unison onto the porch.

They had brought their parasols, and looked for all the world like they were bound on a long constitutional. In fact, they traveled only so far as Mrs. Francis's sassafras bush, which inspired such an enthusiastic lecture from the hostess that scraps of it could be heard even in Joshua's hideout. "The *leaves* . . . and *this* one . . . like a mitten, do you see? . . . And *three* prongs . . . Have you ever? . . ."

The fragments wouldn't assemble into anything, for Joshua was seeing only the person who wasn't there. Leaning toward Tibbetts, he whispered:

"The other lady. You saw her go inside?"

Tibbetts nodded.

"And she is still there?"

"I can't see through walls, can I?"

Joshua stared at the door, then at the two women, then at the ground.

"You may go," he said quietly.

"You mean come back tomorrow?" asked Tibbetts.

"I mean not at all." He fished in his pocket for one last quarter, which he pressed, emphatically, into Tibbetts's palm. "Take this as a final token of my thanks. I ask only that you speak to nobody of what you have seen."

Joshua had thought that was the end of it, but a subtle transformation had taken over the joiner's face: a tapestry of rue, woven from the threads of his wrinkles. Who would have imagined that Eli Tibbetts, in the course of discharging his debt, should have discovered his true vocation?

"You mean to say it's over?" he murmured.

IN THE END, Tibbetts slipped away as soundlessly as he had come. Five minutes passed, ten. Then, like a pair of owls scenting something in the distance, Miss Edwards and Mrs. Francis swung their heads north. In that same instant, a shadow swept past Joshua's hiding place, so unexpectedly that, fearing discovery, he shrank back against the wall. But the shadow swept on, unseeing, and as Joshua peered through the willow branches, it took form.

"There he is!" cried Mrs. Francis. "Infamous dawdler!"

Far from being surprised by Lincoln's arrival, she seemed to derive some comfort from it and, instead of upbraiding him further, merely tapped him on the shoulder with her parasol.

"Go in, you beggar! And see if you're still welcome."

Joshua watched, without blinking, as Lincoln climbed the steps toward the front door, turned the knob, paused for a moment on the threshold, then took one long step into the foyer and closed the door after him.

IT WASN'T A long walk to the Edwards mansion—no more than nine blocks—but Quality Hill seemed unusually steep beneath Joshua's feet. Was it the heat, he wondered, or the clamor? The buzz of bees in the summer orchards. Geese hissing, dogs barking. A mill clacking. Off in the distance, the ceaseless clatter of carpenters and brick masons and stonecutters.

He was shown into the smaller of the two parlors, where Elizabeth Edwards stood with a pair of shears, pruning down a potted coleus.

"Mr. Speed," she said, lifting the right side of her mouth a fraction. "What a pleasant surprise."

"Is your sister at home?"

The abruptness of his tone produced the tiniest of flinches.

"Mary?" she said. "I am sorry to say she has gone to the Francises'."

"Ah."

How strangely powerful he felt in the moment. To give that single syllable such a weight of meaning that Elizabeth Edwards had to square her shoulders against it.

"She was escorted there by our cousin, Miss Edwards."

The coldest of smiles spread across Joshua's face. "At present, ma'am, I can assure you she is *not* with your cousin. But perhaps we might find some place quieter to talk."

HALF AN HOUR later, he was walking up Second Street, his mind emptied of any other mission but covering his tracks. What explanation had he given Charlie for leaving? A shipment of DuPont's powder, wasn't it? Then how to explain why he was coming back to the store empty-handed? He'd been given the wrong date, that was all. The *real* shipment was coming tomorrow. Happened all the time. . . .

Out of the column of bodies that streamed past him, one in particular impressed itself. Mary Todd. Listing past with some unstable mixture of purpose and abandon. She wore no shawl, not even a bonnet—but at the sight of her, he instinctively stopped and doffed his hat. Her eyes glanced off him without a glimmer of recognition. He turned and watched her stagger on.

Heaven help us all, he thought.

Mary

TWENTY-SIX

ONE NIGHT, WHEN they were children, Elizabeth Todd persuaded Mary to crawl out with her onto the roof of their Short Street house to howl at the moon. Mary was the third sibling to be asked—Frances and Levi had already declined—and she was conscious enough of the honor that she never once questioned the reason behind it. She paused only to ask if they were to howl like wolves or like Indians. "Wolves" was the answer. Ten minutes later, they were still howling, and it took the combined efforts of both their parents and Sally to drag them back inside.

Elizabeth Todd *Edwards*, in marked contrast, was the last person in the world to raise her voice, particularly if it meant shouting family business to the servants. At her command, then, Mary marched up the steps to the library, and Elizabeth closed the door after them.

The room held but a single candle, which rested on a credenza by Ninian's prize atlas, and the dusk inside was only a hair lighter than the dusk gathering outside the windows. With no great grace, Mary slumped into a cordovan chair and watched as Elizabeth strode back and forth like a caged catamount, disappearing into shadow only to reemerge a second later. The whisper of her slippers was so much worse than a bellow to Mary's ears that she at last broke into it.

"Who told you?"

Elizabeth said nothing.

"Never mind," said Mary, staring into uncomforting gloom. "I'm glad that you know."

"And just what do you suppose me to know? That you have, under false pretenses, absconded to Mrs. Francis's, day after day, for unchaperoned tête-à-têtes? That you have been treacherous? That you have been depraved and heartless and common?"

She resumed her stride with an even heightened intent, as if she might, with enough momentum, pitch herself straight through the walls.

"There will be words with Matilda, of course. And with Mrs. Francis. They have both trespassed upon my trust in an unconscionable manner."

"You mustn't blame them. . . ."

"Please don't misunderstand me! I reserve the lion's share of the blame for *you*. Oh, I already knew how stubborn you were—how *willful*—but I would never have guessed how duplicitous. Deceiving and conspiring against your own sister. When all I . . ." She silenced herself for a moment, the better to regather her forces. "When all I have *ever* done is for your advancement. All these months laboring to find a match for you. Watching you nod yes, and pretend to entertain all my suggestions, and the whole while, you have been throwing away your favors on another man. And *such* a man!"

Elizabeth had to travel one more circuit before she trusted herself to speak further.

"Admit it," she said. "Admit that you were in the wrong."

Mary stared down at her hands, which were still gloved. "I was wrong to conceal it."

"Then why did you?"

"Because. I knew he would not be welcome here."

"As your suitor, no. He would not." Elizabeth came at last to a halt. Rested her hand on the credenza. "But not for the reasons you imagine."

"I know you object to his manners."

"Oh, there is no question of that. How shall I ever forget my first encounter with him? Stumbling into Mrs. Lamb's parlor in Conestoga boots. Conestoga boots! And do you know the first words that came out of his mouth? *Oh, boys, how clean these girls look!*"

Flushing, Mary cast her eyes down to her lap. "He has matured. He has adapted."

"Only if, by *adaptation*, you mean acquiring a decent evening coat."

Mary gritted her teeth, gave her head a quick shake. "Monstrous," she muttered.

"What?"

"Your snobbishness."

"Is that what you call it?" cried Elizabeth, advancing once more. "I prefer the term *realism*. Your Lincoln cannot outgrow what he *is*, any more than you can. It matters nothing to me that he was poor—*our* people were poor once. It matters nothing to me that he has no education—how should he have acquired it? I care only about the chasm that lies between you."

"What chasm?"

"You come from two utterly removed spheres. There can be no bridging them. Not now, not ever."

Mary felt her jaw stiffen. "It appears you think as little of me as you think of him."

"I think more of you than you know. Of human nature, I say only what *I* know." Elizabeth eyed her a moment. "If he were a *warmer* man, perhaps, you might at least receive the attentions, the—the grace notes that a nature such as yours requires."

"A nature such as—"

"But this Lincoln of yours, he is as cold and remote and solitary as a . . ." Her hand plucked the word from the air. "A *lighthouse*."

"Not with me."

"Not yet."

Nettled, Mary raised herself in her chair. "His future is rated most promising."

"Ah."

"In the last election, I would have you know, he won more votes than any-body else on the Sangamon County ballot. More votes than . . ." *Than Ninian*, she was going to say but checked herself, knowing how touchy Elizabeth was on the subject. "Nobody has greater natural gifts for—for oratory—for persuasion . . ."

"Do you think I give a rap for politics?" said Elizabeth in a weary voice.

"*I* do," Mary expostulated. "It is something we *share*, he and I. A field of interest. A *passion*, if you like. And in sharing it, we strengthen each other. I can be of use to him, Elizabeth."

"Because he needs a wife to advance?"

"Because he needs a *companion*. He is like some—unfurnished room that is just *waiting* for an occupant to come and brighten it. To make it sweet and habitable."

Her sister scowled and turned away. Such a dismissive gesture that Mary, in a pique, called out: "You allowed *Frances* her choice!"

At this, Elizabeth turned slowly back round.

"Oh, yes," she answered in a low voice. "I let our sister follow her heart— or what she imagined her heart to be—and look what has happened to her. Financial embarrassment, social ignominy. I shall not make the same mistake with you."

WAS IT HERE, Mary would later wonder, that the transformation came over her? For until that moment, she understood only that the confrontation she'd been dreading all these months was here, *upon* her. Yet, in the same breath, her head was clearing in a way entirely unexpected. She grasped, at some buried level of intuition, that she was not the one who demanded comfort, and in the next instant, she rose and took two or three wondering steps toward her sister. Gazed into her face and, finding no resistance, reached gently for her hand.

"Elizabeth," she said. "I am no longer your mistake to make."

Her sister's eyes roved through the library's shadows, as though seeking out reinforcements.

"You are a grown woman," she said. "Is that it?"

"Something like that."

"Rather *too* grown to pitch yourself at the wrong man."

"To let a chance slip by, you mean. When it presents itself."

"No!" With a despairing cry, Elizabeth drew her hand away. "He is *not* your last chance! There is Mr. Webb, there is Mr. Douglas . . . Mr. Trumbull— any number of eligible, *suitable*—"

"I don't mean he is my last chance. I mean he is my best."

Elizabeth's eyes expanded a little.

"Then God help us all," she murmured. She stood silent for a time, fingering the red-and-gold atlas. "Oh, how I wish you could see your fate as I do. The doom toward which you are both rushing. Mark my words, you will become one of those couples—those outlandishly mismatched couples—that nobody can make heads or tails of. The world will look at you. . . . It will look at you *both*, and it will say, 'How did *that* happen? How on God's green earth did *they* come together?'"

"I don't know that I'll be able to answer," said Mary, quietly. "Except by way of happiness."

Once more, she reached for her sister's hand. Stroked it between her thumb and forefinger.

"Lincoln asked me a question not half an hour ago. He asked if I was ready to walk in the sun with him. And I realize now that I should like that very much. I should like to walk in the sun with him. If it's all the same to you."

Elizabeth said nothing.

"I shall understand," Mary went on, "if you can't see your way to housing me any longer. You and Ninian have been more than generous, and I have been such a bother, I know. There is bound to be decent lodging in town—on reasonable terms. And I *know* Father would help, and nobody would give it another thought, and you—you could have your *room* back and . . ."

She trailed off. For this was, in fact, the first time she had envisioned a life outside these walls.

Elizabeth remained silent for a while longer. Then, reassembling herself, she gave her head a toss.

"Do you sincerely believe that a Todd would throw her own sister onto the streets? As though she were an old couch?"

She gave Mary's hand the lightest tap and drew away. Strolled toward the window and stood there, staring into the gathering nightfall.

"You shall stay here," she said, half to herself. "Of course you shall."

From outside, they could hear the first stirrings of whip-poor-wills and nighthawks and owlets. The cooing of rabbits. Out toward the town's limits, a dog was barking. Elizabeth rested her hand against the windowpane.

"What would Mother say?"

It was the question she always raised when she was vexed with her sister. The only difference was that, this time, she sounded genuinely curious.

"Mother married for love, too," Mary offered.

"Much good it did her."

"It did her no harm, surely—even in those last moments—to reflect that she had given her heart to somebody worthy."

"And you think your Lincoln worthy?"

In the cleared expanses of Mary's mind, the past few weeks suddenly scrolled out. She saw Lincoln stationed like a penitent in Mrs. Francis's parlor, sitting without complaint through her piques, her withholdings. Weathering them all with a serenity that struck her now as nearly hallowed . . . And then, most shockingly of all, coming *back*—the next day, the day after, the day after that—for more of the same. *Submitting* himself to every punishment, with no hope or expectation of reward.

"He is more than worthy," said Mary. "I only wonder sometimes if I am quite worthy of him."

Elizabeth let her forehead decline, by half inches, until it was just resting against the window. Then, from somewhere deep inside her, the half-smothered fragment of a laugh jerked free.

"I do hope," she said, "that my children give me less trouble than my sisters."

TWENTY-SEVEN

No FORMAL ANNOUNCEMENT was made; no banns were published; no cards were dispatched. The only sign that relations between Mr. Lincoln and Miss Todd had reached a new level of understanding was this: They were now permitted to walk publicly in each other's company.

August brought out something kinder in Springfield. Most of the town's trees had been cut down years earlier for timber, but enough of the original groves lingered to provide oases of shade. The streets were dry, if not even a little dusty from where the wagon wheels had ground the earth down. Bees crooned in the glades. Cherries, bright as eyes, hung from the trees, and the southerly wind sent down showers of locust blossoms.

And how little of it Mary noticed during her first outing with Lincoln. Self-consciousness dogged her every step, and her bonnet—in sealing off her peripheral view—made such a perfect cameo of every passerby that she found herself helplessly searching each new face, known or unknown, to see what judgment it had formed. In the bare light of day, she felt more than ever the difference in altitude with Lincoln. Whenever he bent to speak, she had to strain her head upward to form a channel for the sound. More than once, Elizabeth's words came back to her like the prick of a hatpin. *The world will look at you both, and it will say, "How did* that *happen?"*

They took two tours of Jefferson Street, a total of eight blocks, and when they reached the base of Quality Hill, Lincoln said: "I guess that's far enough."

His head bent down once more. "Unless you'd care to see the Northern Cross Railroad?" As if to underscore, his lazy eye made a pivot to the north.

Mary declined on the grounds of fatigue, though she had walked much farther than this with both Mercy and Matilda. Lincoln acceded to her wishes and escorted her back to the house. They stopped before the door, and Mary, raising her face expectantly, was surprised when he reached for her gloved hand and kissed it.

"Till next time," he said.

On the other side of the door, Matilda Edwards was lying in wait.

"I told you! If we put him to the screw, he would make good."

She was all the more intent on claiming credit because Mary, still averse to disappointing, had neglected to say just how those final stages had played out, how it had been Lincoln who had forced the issue, not her, and how their stalemate might have carried on indefinitely had Mary not been unmasked.

Indeed, the change in the couple's fortunes had come so decisively, so fortuitously that she wondered at times if Matilda herself had been the informant. Who else, she thought, would have had the prescience to grasp what stroke was needed *au moment exact*? Yet Matilda would have been the last to conceal her genius under a shroud of modesty—and Elizabeth Edwards would have been the first to acknowledge any service done in her behalf. Whereas the relations between the two had never been icier. So ill-disposed were they to answering each other's most trivial inquiries that it often fell to Ninian to cobble together some civil reply.

"No, my dear, I don't believe Matilda will be dining home tonight, as she has an engagement with Miss Rodney and Miss Thornton." . . . "I fear, Matilda, that Elizabeth will be occupied with the Presbyterian Ladies' Guild." . . . "In answer to your query, I believe the weather today will be generally fair."

This wire-taut diplomacy made life only harder for Ninian, who objected to Mary's new alliance quite as much as his wife. He and Lincoln had always been the wariest of allies, and now that Ninian had been tossed from the August ballot, he was even less inclined to take up his fellow Whig's cause. Yet he had the sense to recognize that, in the present balance of power, Lincoln was beloved of the Francises—an unavoidable fact that demanded a brave front.

As for Elizabeth, she was, after a convalescence of several days, mindful enough of the ceremonies now demanded of her to engage in the symbolic act of inviting Lincoln to supper. But the difficulty was just beginning for, as Elizabeth and her husband both agreed, a party of four would be awkward to an indecent degree. Six would be a more pleasing number, but who to round out the table? Sister Frances, with her bibulous husband and clouded future, would set the worst possible example. Matilda was an obvious candidate, or at least Ninian considered her so, but this left open the question of which gentleman would make the ideal sixth.

The Edwardses soon eliminated anyone who had displayed notable partiality for Mary, which left out a fairly substantial portion of Springfield's bachelors. The elderly had to be weeded out on the grounds that pairing them with Matilda, if only for the length of a supper, would be an embarrassment in both directions. Whigs, Democrats, politicians, lawyers . . . Name by name, the Edwardses went, rejecting the married, the widowed, the barely grown. Then, one night, in the act of slipping off to his bedroom, Ninian called back: "Why not just have Speed over?"

The storekeeper had two notable qualifications: He was Lincoln's intimate, and he had never seriously contended for Mary's hand. Yet even so unimpeachable a candidate produced a surprising amount of resistance. Elizabeth, for reasons she declined to explain, was reluctant to bring Mr. Speed into such a triumphal gathering. Mary's reasons were no more forthcoming. She had merely concluded (if that was the right word for so indefinite a sentiment) that Mr. Speed was a rather less agreeable character while in Lincoln's presence—though not so disagreeable that his presence would detract. And it was thus through some admixture of logic and resignation that she was brought over to the idea and, in her very next walk with Lincoln, prevailed upon him to make the invitation.

"Speed?" he repeated.

"Why, who better?"

He was silent for a while.

"I don't think Speed is too socially inclined these days."

"Surely, he would make an exception for us."

But Lincoln only shook his head. "I think we might look elsewhere."

She thought at first he was joking and, when she found he was not, leaned in and gave his arm a light but importunate squeeze.

"I don't know why you are being so resistant. My sister is doing all she can to welcome us, and it seems to me we might at least meet her halfway."

She left the matter there, trusting to her own powers of persuasion. Sure enough, word came back the very next day that Mr. Speed had accepted for supper the following Sunday. Matters hit a snag when he sent a note Saturday morning, begging off on account of illness. Elizabeth, with a narrowed eye, rescheduled for the following Thursday, but over the ensuing days, Mr. Speed went so utterly silent that no one, Lincoln least of all, was quite certain he would show up at all.

"And who is he, anyway?" snarled Elizabeth to her husband. "A shop-keeper with a rich daddy."

Yet, when the night came, show up he did, smiling as boyishly as ever and carrying a bouquet of gladioluses for the hostess.

"My dear Mrs. Edwards, how kind of you to wait on me. I hope I haven't been too much of a bother. But my, what a beautiful table you've set! Those are spice pinks, aren't they? From your own garden, it must be. There can be no better assemblage of flora anywhere in Springfield, and who is a more fitting flower to be their queen?"

Elizabeth flushed, for she had consciously dressed in her plainest gray to avoid outshining her sister and had not reckoned for flirtation. Mary, by contrast, had dressed to be seen: a silk evening gown, never before worn, with stripes of cream and rose and a shortened sleeve that showed off her full white arms. She wore the flimsiest of velvet shoes and, for her hair, a fresh bunch of violets with black-lace trimmings. The only one at the table who matched her for finery was Mr. Speed, in his waistcoat of sapphire blue, perfectly fitted to his frame and artfully embroidered with velvet stenciling that, at first glance, looked black and only reluctantly revealed itself as indigo.

To look at the cut of his clothes, the smile that so proportionately divided his face, one would have thought *he* was the young man on the verge of a brilliant connection. And it was that sudden, unbidden vision—of Mr. Speed as the lover he would never be—that left a band of heat across the back of Mary's neck . . . a discomfort somehow deepened by the fact that Speed and

Lincoln were so steadfastly avoiding each other's gaze. They might have been complete strangers were it not for the uncanny echo of their movements. The light hop with which they drew in their chairs, the martial snapping of their napkins, the deliberative arc of hands toward knife and fork. Why, they even cleared their throats at the same time!

Topics were discarded as soon as they were raised, and the air itself, braised by a day's worth of sun, was thick and hot. But the claret was merely *warm*, and beneath its fumes, a kind of moderate pleasure took hold—led, as always, by Mr. Speed, who ate and drank with a gusto that belied his slenderness.

"What a bacchanal!" he cried as the roast duck and Sangamon turnips were cleared away. "However, my friends, in enjoying this splendid feast, we have been utterly negligent in our offices. We have not yet made our toast to the young couple."

He raised his glass then with such velocity that a bit of the claret spilled onto Elizabeth's tablecloth.

"To the Lincoln-Todd corporation," he said. "May it steer ever free of bankruptcy."

The words were so unexpected that the other diners—with the exception of Lincoln, who kept his eyes fixed on his plate—surveilled one another to see if some joke were being played. No wiser, they subsided into restive silence, which was broken at last by Ninian, raising his own glass and intoning: "Hear, hear."

The timely arrival of dessert—a floating island—restored some measure of spirit, and it was over the clatter of forks that Mr. Speed was heard to say: "I must set about building my *own* corporation, mustn't I, Miss Edwards?"

Matilda observed that no man could have a better head for business than Mr. Speed.

"Oh, I don't know about that," he said. "Merchandise is always slipping through one's fingers."

"Not through carelessness, surely."

"No," said Mr. Speed. "Never that."

He was silent for a while, but then came back in an even louder voice.

"Top-flight claret, Edwards!"

"I am so glad you approve," observed Ninian.

"What a cellar you must have! I should like to have one of my own, but who is there ever to drink with? I might as well join the Temperance Society."

Mary saw Lincoln set down his fork, then pick it up again.

"Yes," said Mr. Speed, "it's a fiendishly dull life. But, of course, I have only myself to blame for choosing abstemious companions. From now on, you may be sure, I will go a-*roving*." With an easy smile, he swung his face toward Matilda's. "Will you rove with me, Miss Edwards?"

"Champagne," suggested Elizabeth.

Mr. Speed was the first to embrace the idea, and, before Mary had even finished two sips, he had downed his entire glass. When he next turned to Matilda, he appeared to be rolling toward her in a slow tide.

"Miss Edwards, I wonder if you subscribe to the notion that no man is an island."

"I can only say that I have never met such an island," Matilda ventured. "Though I suppose one wouldn't, would one? I do believe I have encountered peninsulas."

"Peninsulas!" he roared. "Did you hear that, ladies and gentlemen?" He raised his empty glass, as if he were readying another toast, but his voice dropped to a near whisper. "Such a store of wit in such a charming vessel. . . ."

"Mr. Lincoln," said Elizabeth, raising her own voice a fraction. "Do tell us what you have seen in your late travels. Will the southern counties come round, do you think?"

It was a measure of her unease that she was turning the conversation toward politics, but she succeeded at least in providing a diversion. Ninian and Lincoln set straight to it, and she broke in as necessary—strictly as necessary. Mary was the only one who could not pull her gaze from the spectacle on the other side of the table. There was Matilda, receiving each advance as if she were engaged in some arcane sport. And there was Mr. Speed, his blue irises revealing, on closer inspection, a kind of glutted misery, a compounded unhappiness that lay quite apart from—and yet was intimately connected to—the gaiety of his words and gestures.

Why, thought Mary, with a soft jolt, *he is suffering*.

And suffering, she realized, toward a particular end. He wanted somebody *else* to suffer.

From there, the inferential leap was brief and undeniable: He wanted *her* to suffer. Every word, every act was meant to call out her jealousy—to make her regret, at some profound and unalterable level, her own choice.

And for perhaps the first time since making it, she did regret that choice. Why had she not set her sights on the wretch who now sat across from her, bleeding from every pore? It was more than any girl could bear, and Mary was seized with the idea of jumping from her seat and demanding that every-thing—*everything*—come to an immediate halt.

"Well, when it comes to that," Lincoln was saying, "we must solicit Mary's opinion."

Blinking, she stared at him. "My opinion. . . ."

"Edwards and I have been discussing whether the Illinois and Michigan Canal may ever be put on a sound footing. I said to myself, *Nobody's studied more on the subject than Mary.*"

It should have been a moment of welling pleasure, for this was the first time he had ever publicly addressed her by her Christian name. Yet all she could register was how unprepared she was. She stammered out a reply, cob-bled together from fragments of the past week's newspapers, but the result was so disconnected that it brought down a pall of silence, lifted finally by Ninian's deadpan voice.

"Most interesting."

From there, the men moved on without a backward glance. As did Matilda and Mr. Speed, who were sparring and gibing now like schoolboys. Mary alone sat silent. What good were words now? She had made a mistake, a terrible mistake! She had wagered everything on the wrong man, and it was too late to turn back.

"WHAT'S AILING YOU?" asked Lincoln.

They were standing together in the front hall—the others had discreetly absented themselves.

"You mustn't do that," she muttered.

"What?"

"*Embarrass* me in that fashion. Leave me so exposed."

"I only asked you what you thought."

"It was hardly the time."

"No?"

He did something disarming then. He hooked his brown finger lightly under her chin, and he said, "You mean I'm the only one who gets the benefit of you? That hardly seems fair. The rest of the world requires you, too, Mary Todd."

The tone was lightly jesting, but in his eyes, she found only tenderness. And in that exact instant, the world righted itself, and all her fevered fancies about Mr. Speed and his wounded heart were cast aside for the rubbish they were. *Here*, standing before her, was the man who loved her. How had she ever allowed herself to believe otherwise? How could she imagine any future finer than the one they would enjoy together? She laughed, then, with a startling vigor and kissed him square on the mouth—and then laughed again and drew open the door and rapped him on the temple with her fan and said, "Get out with you." Swerving her glance outward, she found Mr. Speed, standing alone in the drive, his back to the house. Like someone who been attending another supper party entirely.

Mary's first instinct was to turn away from embarrassment. Then, gathering herself, she called out:

"Good night, Mr. Speed."

Without turning round, he raised his right hand, as if to wave. Only the hand never dropped and was still hanging there, suspended, when she closed the door.

TWENTY-EIGHT

———

MATILDA CHOSE THAT evening to sneak back into Mary's room. "Goodness!" she said, drawing the coverlet over her. "What an exhibition."

Mary murmured only that it was.

"Your Lincoln acquitted himself rather well," said Matilda. "He kept his composure, at least, which, under the circumstances, was no small feat. And, you know, in certain lights, I can see now why one might be drawn to him. He stops just short of handsome, doesn't he? If you catch him right? As for Mr. Speed, he grows more intriguing the more one considers him. Pockets of mystery, puss! Places where nobody has yet penetrated. Him, least of all."

With a lingering trace of truculence, Mary said, "He seemed more than a little interested in *your* mystery."

"Ohh." Matilda let her flaxen tresses blaze across the pillow. "You needn't worry about that. If I'm to marry someone, it will be the marrying *sort*. Then again, one might have said the same of your Lincoln, and look at him now."

Once again, Mary's ears plucked out the soft lash of judgment behind her friend's words. What did it mean, exactly, that a man was not of the marrying sort? And what did that say about the girl who finally landed him? That she had gone at him so relentlessly as to break down his resistance? Or had simply waited him *out*, like a quail hunter by a copse?

And was it not the height of foolishness, finally, even to speak of a wedding when there was as yet no date? On certain subjects, to be sure, Lincoln could be more than voluble. His practice, his prospects. President Van Buren and General Harrison and, now and then, Mr. Tyler. But of marriage itself, he said precious little. The closest he came was an afternoon in mid-July when the heat left him sprawling in the Edwardses' wing chair. It was then, with the sweat pooling at his temples, that he regarded Mary with a frankness unusual to him and said, in a half-enchanted voice: "Ain't I the lucky one?"

Five words, no more. Yet, to her ear, what a freight of longing they carried. It was as if, in his long journey on Earth, he had never imagined arriving at such a destination.

She never spoke of the moment to Elizabeth or Matilda, for they would have pounced on the primitive dialect or the lack of eloquence. Lincoln, though, had something better than mere facility, he had the gift of doggedness. Which was to say he showed *up*. If anything, he was an even more reliable presence in the Edwardses' front parlor than at the Francises'. A younger girl, perhaps, would have had little use for such constancy, but in Mary's eyes, it looked like the purest expression of desire. He *wished* to be here, could picture no place better. And now and then, he would let loose with some random declaration—prefaced, invariably, with "I suppose"—that showed him to be traveling the same path as she was.

"I suppose I should get myself a new frock coat. " . . . "I suppose we'll need cutlery." . . . "I suppose I should meet your father. If he's willing."

One afternoon, in a gesture that was, by his lights, very nearly histrionic, he dropped his head back against the antimacassar. "I suppose," he said, "you'll be wanting to have your own Negroes."

It came so out of the blue that she stopped fanning herself and stared at him.

"You mean once we're settled?" she asked.

He only shrugged.

"Mr. Lincoln," she said, "Is this your circuitous way of asking me my position on a certain subject? Why do you not come right out and ask?"

"Very well. What is your position on a certain subject?"

"The institution of slavery is one that I abhor. There! Will that do?" But before he could answer, she was already moving on. "I would sooner be a slave myself than the mistress of a house with slaves in it."

She had the satisfaction of seeing his eyes swell.

"You are surprised," she said.

"I only supposed . . . since you grew *up* with them . . ."

"It is *because* I grew up with them. Sally and Nelson were as dear to me as family. Dearer, in some instances. The idea of bartering and *trading* them—like lengths of fabric—even as a child, I couldn't stomach it."

"But your father."

"He thinks as I do. Oh, he will never be mistaken for an abolitionist, but he has made his voice heard on the subject, and at no small political risk."

"Yet he keeps Negroes himself, does he not? As does your sister. . . ."

"So now you would have me call them hypocrites. Oh, I *have*," she confessed. "In times of pique. But whenever I'm inclined to dwell on—well, my moral superiority—I find that something comes along to remind of my *own* conspicuous failings." She paused. "Here is where you tell me I have none."

"Not a one."

"And here is where I affirm that I devoutly *do*. But on my list of sins, let it never be writ that I bought or sold another human being."

He was testing her, that much was clear, but she liked the way the words sounded on her tongue. More than that, she relished the space and the means he had just given her to find the words. Which was nothing more, really, than the gift of attention.

If he's not careful, she thought, *I might grow accustomed to this.*

WHILE THE WEATHER held, they still took walks together—a bit farther each time. With each tour, she found that the difference in their statures began to affect her less. She had developed a way of tilting her face toward his without letting her head drop all the way back, and with practice, she began even to take comfort in the sheer scale of him—to *lean* on him, as a pilgrim might against an oak. All his discordant elements—the angles and disproportions—began to organize themselves into a coherent whole, so that when she inspected the faces of passersby, the message she found in their faces was no longer *How did this happen?* but *Yes, it is so.*

And how quietly it had become so. Without a fuss.

Among the Springfield hostesses now, it was commonly understood that if you invited Mr. Lincoln to an event, you had best invite Miss Todd, or vice versa. Whenever they arrived at an event together and stood, arm in arm, in the doorway, the shout that rose up was always on the order of "There they are!" or "They took their sweet time coming." Or, more teasingly, "Who invited them?" Mr. Baker took to calling them Beatrice and Dante. No, said Dr. Herndon, they were more like Beatrice and Benedick. Mary and Lincoln were now routinely seated together. More than that, they were addressed together, interrogated together, sent out into the world together. If anything of note had taken place in the world of politics, it was assumed that Lincoln would be the one to start telling and that Mary would chime in at discreet intervals with her own informed commentary.

And with every glance, every smile, every shrug, the citizens of Springfield seemed to convey the same message: *This is so.*

Mary and Lincoln could be found now in church halls, in fairgrounds, in the meeting rooms of inns. Whenever Lincoln made public remarks, she was always the first to laugh at any joke (the more rustic, the better) and the first to clap hand to hand, and when the remarks were concluded, *hers* was the first reaction he sought. "Well now," he'd say, strolling toward her with his hands in his pockets. "What says the jury?"

One night, at Lincoln's special urging, they went to the theater: a piece of whimsy called *The Horse and the Widow*, mounted by the Illinois Theatrical Company. Mostly dreadful, but at the end of the curtain call, the youngest member of the company—no more than ten—stepped into the light and began reciting in his treble voice:

> For God's sake, let us sit upon the ground
> And tell sad stories of the death of kings. . . .

She recognized it at once: the third-act speech from *Richard II*.

"Why, Mr. Lincoln," she said, "I believe you have had a hand in this."

"No person shall be compelled to be a witness against himself."

"Enough of your Constitution," she said, flicking him on the wrist. "And enough of your Richard. Next time, I shall have *Twelfth Night.*"

THE SANGAMON COUNTY courthouse closed up shop on July twenty-fourth, and Lincoln proposed they celebrate by doing something they had never done before: travel outside the town limits.

The very next morning, he called for her in a rented horse and gig. Gave a deft tug on the reins, and, before she had quite gathered herself, they were traveling due north. The streets narrowed to paths; the houses and businesses gave way to farms, thick with corn. When they reached the very rim of the valley, she chanced a quick look back. In the well of rouged morning light, she could make out the Edwards mansion . . . the state capitol, even now unfinished . . . the post office . . . the power gristmill. She seemed to be viewing everything from the vantage of time—calling it back through memory, yes. *There I once lived.*

The farms they passed now were larger, more prosperous. "That one belongs to Washington Iles," said Lincoln. "*That's* Mason's. Over there is Lindsay's, and that one is Little's." The names tumbled easily off his lips, for he had represented most of them in court. He showed no inclination to linger, however, and even gave the roan a light crack to hurry it along. The farms began to fall back; the trees dwindled down until there was nothing left but a line of timber on the horizon; suddenly the prairie was upon them.

She had never seen it in its full summer immensity—grass and weeds stretching nearly as high as their box seat. The horse twitched his head clear, and the gig began to shudder over rocks and gopher holes. Faintly anxious, she glanced over at Lincoln, wondering where exactly he intended to stop. Had he some fixed destination in mind? She had about given up hope when he abruptly drew back the reins, and the gig shivered to stillness.

Just like that, the silence fell away. She could hear now the snorting of the roan, the rustling of wind, the chirring of flies and mosquitoes, the whirr of prairie chickens. . . .

"This should do," said Lincoln.

He bounded off the box and, in the next moment, began swinging his walking stick like a scythe, turning as he swung, until the air seethed with pollen and dust and fragments of goldenrod—a furious cloud that, a few seconds later, had subsided into a bright mulch at Lincoln's feet. Reaching now into the gig's belly, he drew out a gingham sheet and draped it across the newly made clearing.

"Nobody should bother us here."

"No," she murmured, with some misgiving. "We're quite alone."

From the basket, he drew out a boiled ham and a veal and a pigeon pie. Corn dodgers and chocolate caramels. A loaf of bread, a quarter pound of cheese. Spanish pickles!

"You've packed enough for an army," she protested.

Though, in truth, what surprised her more was the care with which it had all been packed. Every item wrapped in paraffin paper, and all supplemented by tin drinking cups, salt and pepper boxes, tissue-paper napkins, cheap wooden plates from the local baker—just the sorts of things that a picnicker, if pressed, might feel free to leave behind. *Why*, she said to herself, *if I didn't know better, I'd suppose that a woman helped him.*

"Milady," he said, "your feast awaits."

Winking, he drew out two parasols and, with a force that faintly unnerved her, drove their handles into the ground, creating a parabola of shade that extended three feet on each side. Then, with no discernible effort, he swung her straight from her seat. Smiling as becomingly as she could, she settled herself in the clearing while Lincoln began the work of carving—with so much vigor that her plate was full in under a minute, and only repeated protests would keep him from piling it higher. He himself took monkishly small portions—he was far more concerned with what and how *she* ate. Indeed, so nakedly did he observe her that, after a decent interval, she had to set down her plate, the ham mostly consumed and the veal only half-eaten.

"It's still early," she hastened to reassure him. "Perhaps in another hour."

"Ohh, my lady. Surely, thou hast room for . . ."

Smiling shyly, he drew from the basket's recesses a pineapple. Still clothed in its outer husk and looking, in these confines, both exotic and ungainly. With sacramental care, he pinned it to the ground. Then, reaching for the knife, he drove the blade in.

But the pineapple pushed back. Again he thrust—again—to no avail. Grunting with exasperation, he turned it on its side and began sawing off its head, laboriously, inch by inch, so that whatever savor Mary might have had for the fruit had long since disappeared by the time he dropped a single misshapen chunk in her waiting palm.

"Delicious," she whispered. But her teeth, closing round it, could make no imprint. "I wonder if we shouldn't leave it in the sun awhile longer."

"Damnation!" he growled. "They told me it was ripe."

"It doesn't matter. . . ."

"It does, it—"

His eyes ranged through their surroundings—but there was only prairie. Stretching for days.

Rising suddenly to his feet, he felt round the horse's fetlock.

"Is he bleeding?" Mary asked.

Lincoln shook his head, brought his fingers to his mouth. "Wild strawberries," he said.

He paused to absorb the intelligence. Then, a second later, he was thrashing through the grass.

"Here's one!" he cried, clutching a berry in his palm. "Here's another!"

"Oh, cease and desist!" she called after him, laughing. "You foolish man! You'll ruin yourself!"

But he kept wheeling and darting, his arm swinging like a sickle. At last, spent and panting, he stumbled back toward her and dropped his harvest onto the blanket.

There were at most a couple dozen berries. More than a few had been mashed beyond repair, and the rest were suspended in a plasma of juice and pulp. To Mary, they were the most ravishing of sights. She shoved her fingers right in, savoring every step of the berries' passage from tongue to throat. Across from her, she found Lincoln, his own fingers stained, his own lips reddened as if from a wound.

"Mary," he said, "you should know things."

She had been lying in the shade of the parasols for so long, and the breeze was whispering so softly through the grass, that a minute or two more would have brought her to the point of dozing. It was with some reluctance, then, that she dragged her eyes open.

"Things," she echoed. "Are they bad or good?"

"Oh. That's for you to say."

With his chin resting on his knee, he had about him a nearly comical melancholy.

"Pray continue," she said.

Still he hesitated.

"My *people*," he declared at last, tweezing a blade of tallgrass between his fingers, "were desperate characters. My grandfather was killed by an Indian's arrow. The same Indian would have taken my father—he was no more than six—but my uncle Mordecai ran and got his rifle and shot the Indian just as he was carrying my father away."

With a rough motion, he plucked the blade of grass from its bed, tossed it to one side.

"My parents were married by a Methodist circuit rider. Neither of them could write. They could read just a little. When Kentucky decided it no longer wanted them, they hightailed it to Indiana. They never knew anything but dirt floors and corn-husk mattresses."

Something bitter had crept into his tone.

"My mother, she was a bastard—you should probably know that, too. Her father was some kind of Virginia nobility, a word I use ironically. But she was a good woman, you'll have to take my word for it. All that I am or ever hope to be I got from her." He glanced toward Mary, as if daring her to deny it. "I was nine when she passed. The last thing she told us was *Be good to one another*."

He paused.

"Of course, being so young, I figured I was all shut of mothers. But a year later, Father went back to Kentucky and found himself a widow. *Looky here, Sarah, I have no wife and you no husband. I came a-purpose to marry you. I knowed you from a gal and you knowed me from a boy. I've no time to lose, and if you're willin', let it be done straight off*."

"And she said yes?"

"She said . . . *I got a few little debts*."

Mary covered her mouth, but the laugh had already got out.

"Well now," she said. "I applaud her candor."

"So did Father. He paid off the debts, and I got two new sisters and a brother."

"And a new mother."

"Why, yes, she was far and away the best part of that transaction." He gave Mary a quick, gauging glance and then turned his eyes toward the gig. "I tell you all this because I want you to know what you're in for. I want you to know I carry dirt on my shoes. Some blood, too."

She reached now for the blade of grass he had tossed away. Made a point of twining it round her finger.

"Very well," she said. "Since you have set us on a martyrdom *steeplechase . . .*"

His eyes blinked as if he'd been splashed.

"You are to know," she went on, "that I was not quite *eight* when my mother died. And my father waited but a sixmonth to find a new wife."

He smiled softly. "Who was the lucky gal?"

"A spinster from Frankfort. Her name was Betsey Humphreys, but we were obliged to call her Ma. To her face, anyway."

"And what did she call you?"

"Limb of Satan."

He laughed. Quick and hard.

"Was she a horror?" he asked.

"I suppose you would just call her a *wall*. I mean to say if the word *no* could be transformed into human shape, it would have looked like Ma." Mary slowly untwined the grass from around her finger. "When I was ten, I spent all summer watching the ladies of Lexington in these beautiful bouffant dresses. Swaying and billowing. Oh, I had to have one of my own, it was essential. So I made myself hoops out of a pair of willow reeds and I—I *ingeniously* inserted them into my white muslin dress and then, the next morning, I swanned into the dining room. Waiting for the world to acclaim me."

"And?"

"Ma took one look and said, *Take those awful things off, dress yourself properly, and go to Sunday school.*"

Her finger sketched a slow circle in the cropped grass.

"The hardest part? From then on, I was a family joke. I don't believe a week went by that Betsey didn't remind somebody. *Can you believe Mary stuffed those willow reeds into her dress?* It never failed to raise a laugh."

"Was she laughing, too?"

"I don't think she knew how. She has the sternest expression you've ever witnessed. There wasn't a one of us that was worth her time. She used to tell us that it takes a family seven generations to make a lady, and the Todd girls were still four generations short." Smiling grimly, she raised her eyes to his. "So you see how it was. I grew up in a brick house with fourteen rooms. We had a double parlor, a Belgian rug, imported French mahogany furniture. Argand lamps, a piano, a liquor cellar. I would have traded them all away." She gave him a slow nod. "I wanted you to know what *you're* in for, too."

The day had grown windless, but in the near distance, the grass began to rustle. Swerving their heads toward the sound, they found a doe advancing toward them in a mincing tread. With large bright eyes, it took their measure before turning and bounding into the distance.

"Don't be hasty now about trading that rug," said Lincoln.

Mary laughed then: a gay, unchecked sound. So that when he leaned over and kissed her, the bubble of her laughter actually pulsed against their lips.

"Mary Todd," he said, drawing his head back. "I believe you and I are the two brokenest birds I know."

Joshua

TWENTY-NINE

IN THE END, it had taken him no time at all to inform Mrs. Edwards of the assignations between her sister and Lincoln and then to depart, safe in the assurance that no alliance could withstand the opposition that would now be rained down on it. But Lincoln came home that evening with no sign of apprehension and seemingly no topic on his mind except what might be procured for supper.

The next afternoon, a letter arrived, requesting that Lincoln repair to the Edwards house that very night, at ten o'clock. The two men exchanged looks. At so late an hour, supper or entertainment was out of the question. But when the time came to leave, Lincoln simply clapped a hat atop his head and trudged down the steps, as if he were bound on the most mundane of errands.

"I'll try to stay up," Joshua called.

"Yes, Mother. . . ."

MIDNIGHT CAME. THEN one. Joshua, with but a single candle for company, lay in bed, staring into the vault of the dormitory ceiling. If the Edwardses had simply wanted to cut Lincoln loose, the deed would have taken no more than a minute. Perhaps they were negotiating their way out of possible scandal. Or perhaps Lincoln was even now wandering the streets of Springfield, reeling from his reversal of fortune. A little after one-thirty, Joshua heard the latch lift on the front door. Heard that first tread on the stair: slow and ponderous. With a flush of embarrassment, he blew out his candle and waited. From the darkness came the rustling of trousers, the rattle of waistcoat buttons against a chair. Only when Lincoln had tipped himself into bed did Joshua make a show of waking.

"All well?" he mumbled.

"Well enough."

An equivocal, unreadable tone.

"Anything worth chewing on?" Joshua asked.

Lincoln was quiet for a while. "It will keep."

THE NEXT MORNING was a Sunday, and Lincoln awoke with an inspiration. What better way to commemorate the Lord's blessings than by taking a constitutional?

Joshua didn't protest. To a soul as secular as his, it was a relief to escape the confines of Second Presbyterian and stroll in the broad publicity of a June morning. The sun hung fat and lozenge-like above the rim of the valley, but the air smelled of rain, and more than once, Joshua wondered if they should have brought umbrellas. He had half a mind to turn back, but when he suggested it, Lincoln flapped a hand and said, "All shall be well."

It was strange to see their evening walking routes transformed by the infusion of daylight. The accustomed shadows melted away, and Joshua could see, rolling out before them, the plain that separated town from wilderness and the farmhouses that had predated the town, stilled now under their Sabbath spell, except for the slow-moving veil of woodsmoke and the shuttling outlines of pigs foraging for food.

Lincoln was silent the whole time, his eyes fixed straight ahead, until they came to their usual terminus: the empty, pristine stretch of Northern Cross railbed. So many evenings they had, by unspoken consent, come to a halt here—quite summarily, as though any further travel were impossible. But in the thick light of morning, a new world dawned on the far side. Carpets of yellow and vermilion flowers—a grove of shagbark hickory, a bristling fringe of timber—and, hanging over it all, a sky somehow more capacious than the one they had just left.

"You should know something," said Lincoln.

. . .

IN THIS CASE, it *was* the work of a minute. The facts: dispassionately summed up, without preamble or embroidery. Lincoln and Miss Todd were engaged to be married. The Edwardses had consented to the match. The ceremony was to take place sometime after the election—perhaps even on New Year's Day. The married couple would live in temporary lodging until they were able to put money down on a house. Lincoln's political career, his law practice . . . everything would go on as before.

"Not everything," Joshua said.

He had thought he was talking to himself, but then he saw Lincoln's brows crowding together. "No," he allowed. "Not everything."

He drew from his pocket a handkerchief. Unfolded it, stretched it to its natural length, then rolled it into a ball and returned it to his pocket. Joshua had just enough presence of mind to see that he was miserable.

"What I mean you to know, Speed, is that my—my fondness for you is enduring. . . ."

I did my duty. . . . I did it with joy.

Joshua reached into his vest pocket, drew out his watch. The gold watch he'd been given for Christmas, with the monogram on its back. He stared at it for some time before realizing that Lincoln was still talking.

". . . And needless to say, Speed, my gratitude toward you knows no *bounds.* . . ."

Joshua ran his hand in front of his face. A pocket of cold condensed somewhere at the back of his head.

"You speak of gratitude," he said. "And yet you have courted this girl behind my back. You have lied—continually, *punctually*—about your whereabouts. You have played me for a fool. And now you speak of gratitude." The cold was leaching through him now. "All in all, I think I should have preferred you as an enemy. That way, I should have known to guard my back."

Lincoln bowed his head now, like a boy called to the front of a classroom. "It was never our object to injure anybody. . . ."

"Oh, just swept along, were you? Creatures of desire. Animals in heat." Slowly, with an almost predatory thrill, Joshua began to circle his friend. "Tell me, Brother Abraham, did she coo at your touch?"

"Stop."

"Did she purr? Did she *writhe*?"

"This is a little vulgar for you."

"You dare to speak to me of vulgarity? When, all these afternoons, you've been skulking over to Mrs. Francis's for your tawdry little trysts. Oh, yes," he said, catching the flash of surprise in Lincoln's eyes. "I knew. Of course I knew. I don't doubt that half of Springfield knew."

Lincoln's hands, as if for protection, dove into his pockets. "We only concealed ourselves for *her* sake. She didn't feel brave enough to tell her sister."

"And you mean to say this same sister has now accepted you?"

With an embarrassed half shrug, Lincoln inclined his head. "I won't say she's pleased about it. I know you aren't, either. I know that you don't particularly care for Mary."

Mary.

Joshua ceased his circling. Took a moment to recalibrate.

"You are wrong," he said, in an altogether calmer voice. "I admire Miss Todd. She has grace, she has wit and charm. I believe that, to some other man, she would make the ideal helpmeet. But not you, Lincoln. No. *You* she will drain dry."

Lincoln raised his head. His eyes were lightly stricken. "I don't consider that gentlemanly. . . ."

"I don't speak to you as a gentleman. I speak as a botanist. Miss Todd's type is rather thick on the ground in Kentucky society. My father used to call them the Thirsty Lilies. You think they require a few caresses, a scattering of endearments, but they need to be *watered*, yes. Told, at every hour of the day, that they are the light of your soul and the foundation of your being. That there is none lovelier, none more *deserving* of love. They will never be able to hear it often enough, and should you *ever* be slow in supplying those assurances, your reward will be bitterness and recrimination such as would stop a man's heart in its tracks."

Joshua was himself surprised by the summation. He had never thought so coherently on the subject before. Lincoln, for his part, took off his hat and gave it a slow twirl, then put it back on his head.

"Is it *this* girl you object to?" he asked, in an even voice. "Or is it any girl?"

Joshua looked at him, then turned half away.

"I thought we made a vow," he said. "Never again to think of marrying, do you remember? Because we couldn't be satisfied with anybody who'd be blockhead enough to have us. We made a toast to bachelorhood. To *brother-hood*. Do you recall?"

"That wasn't a *vow*, Speed, that was . . ." He dragged his hands down his face. "It was at least half in jest."

"Ah. Which half were you?"

Silence settled over them, and the day's first raindrop landed, like a specu-lation, on the back of Joshua's neck. He stared out across a field of echinacea. Watched, with a telescopic intensity, as a single honeybee danced from stamen to stigma.

"Tell me," he said. "Because I want to know. Is this your career speaking? Is that all this is about? Advancement?"

"You do this! You insist on—"

"What?"

"Casting me in this *role*. In this *play* you've constructed."

"So this is *my* play?"

"If you had been the one to take the jump, I would have been the first to congratulate you. I would have said, *Yes, this is what men do. Men who have reached a certain age.*"

"It is what society expects."

"Yes."

"And you wish to be like other men."

"There are times," said Lincoln, haltingly, "when that has an allure." Once more, he took out his handkerchief, crumpled it into a ball, returned it to his pocket. "I don't think you ever met my cousin Mordecai," he said.

"No."

"Curious soul. When he was a young man in Kentucky, he began to pay regular calls on a girl named Patsy. Months and months went by, and Patsy began to wonder why things weren't progressing as they ought. One night, at her mother's suggestion, she—*offered* of herself. Cousin Mord took one look and ran straight out of the house. Kept running till he hit Fountain Green, Illinois. Today, he makes coffins. And wagons and cabinets. He's got a dog, a cat, books, and a lathe. I suspect that's all he'll ever have. No more than a year my senior, and they already call him Old Mord. *Old Mord, the Woman Hater.*" Lincoln gave his head a single vigorous shake. "That's not the fate I want."

Drops were falling now with greater abandon. Joshua stared down the stretch of railbed, gray and immaculate.

"But you are prepared to abandon *me* to that fate."

"Lord above, Speed, there is no more marriageable man on God's earth. You need but snap your finger, and a dozen girls would come running, all ready to declare themselves your wife."

"What do you take me for, a Mormon?"

Lincoln coughed out a laugh, and his eyes flared with hope, as if the laugh itself were evidence of thawing. It took but one look at his friend's face to disabuse him.

"Well," he said, finally. "I just wanted you to know."

"And now I do."

Lincoln stood for some time gazing up at the hills.

"I'll certainly understand if you want me to find new lodging."

"Why should I wish that? Ours was always a business arrangement. There's no reason it cannot continue that way. Until such time as you are able to feather your nest."

Lincoln stood for a while longer in silence.

"Does it have to come to this, Joshua?"

"Have you not *brought* it to this? You yourself."

A single one of Lincoln's shoulders winced up. "I guess I was thinking there might be room. For all of us somehow."

Joshua held out his hand, watched the raindrops pool in his palm.

"And where would you put us all? In which rooms?"

He inverted his palm, watched the water tumble to the ground.

"We should be getting back, should we not?"

THIRTY

DAY AFTER DAY now, Joshua had to go down to the store and feign interest in martingales, seal caps, Tibet shawls—the daily dance of buying on credit and selling before the notes came due and tracking down shipments and catering to every last need and vanity. Each morning, he showed up a little later, having spent correspondingly less time on his toilet. He entrusted more and more of the operations to Charlie Hurst and balked at even such basic tasks as opening the window. Neither the summer heat nor the prevailing political climate could rouse him. What did it matter, he asked himself, if the Whigs failed to carry? Would his or anyone's life be appreciably different for a few hundred ballots landing in one pot or the other?

Letters from home held no more interest for him than anything else, for the remarks all bore the same burden: *Come home.* Farmington was not the same, and the whole family had now to apply themselves to the hard work of prosperity. Joshua read each letter as if somebody else's family had sent it. When a certain number of letters had piled up on his desk, he composed replies, as needed, that barely filled out a single page.

One night, in the act of getting ready for bed, Lincoln surprised him by speaking.

"See here. The Edwardses. They want you over for supper."

Joshua stared at him. "Supper."

"Yes."

He pondered this extraordinary notion for some time before he thought to ask: "Who else is invited?"

"Well," said Lincoln, cutting his eyes sideways. "Mary will be there, of course. And Miss Edwards. You know her, of course."

With a shaming slowness, Joshua performed the calculations. "So they . . . they need a *sixth*? Is that all this is about?"

"They respect you," said Lincoln, with just enough lilt at the tail of the sentence to place the sentiment in question.

"I think I'd rather not."

"It would mean a great deal to them," said Lincoln, his cheeks mottling. "And to me."

Joshua peered at him.

"You want my blessing, is that it?"

"If you could just be there."

It said something of Joshua's state of mind that he could devise no suitable objection, no plausible excuse. He could say only: "What night?"

But the next morning, he awoke with an inexpressible weight on his chest. He had just enough air left in his lungs to mutter: "I can't. I'm sorry. I'll write and . . . tell them I'm ill. . . ."

If anything, Lincoln looked relieved. But Mrs. Edwards immediately rescheduled to the following Thursday and expressed a devout hope that Mr. Speed might soon rally. *Rally*, he thought, and felt, with a kind of relief, healing drops of bitterness in his soul's desert. For if there was one person he blamed most for the current state of things, it was Elizabeth Edwards. The woman who had thanked him so fulsomely for apprising her of her sister's wanton behavior, who had declared in such unequivocal terms her horror at a Todd-Lincoln alliance . . . and who had then, by all appearances, wilted at the first sign of resistance. Weren't Kentucky matrons tougher than that?

These reflections had the perverse effect of leaving Joshua better disposed toward the dinner than he would otherwise have been. If nothing else, it would give him the opportunity to stare Elizabeth Edwards in the eye and let her know, in some wordless fashion, what he thought of her cravenness.

And why stop there? Was there not a whole roomful of people who needed to be stared down? Conspirators and co-conspirators?

That spirit of defiance carried him all the way to Thursday. Only toward the tail end of afternoon did cracks sprout in his resolve. With a sense of barely forestalled panic, he shored himself up with three tumblers of Holland gin, which sailed all the more rapidly to his brain for his having missed dinner. As he and Lincoln dressed that evening, he could hear himself actually crooning an old tune.

> Ching-a-ring-a ring ching ching,
> Ho a ding-a-ding kum larkee,
> Ching-a-ring-a ring ching ching,
> Ho a ding kum larkee.

The air was unusually hot and damp that night. As they walked over to the Edwardses', even the clouds seemed to be hanging in sodden tatters, and Joshua could feel a circlet of sweat forming where his hat pinched his head. He gave his walking stick a rapier-like twirl and, in a bright voice, asked: "Is she still in the market for a husband?"

"Who?"

"Miss Edwards. Your *complice d'amour*."

"I don't honestly know."

"She is fair, is she not? More than passing fair."

Lincoln was silent, a fact that only emboldened Joshua further.

"Have you reserved a church?" he asked.

"Why would I do that?"

"For the wedding, you goose! Oh, I know I'm getting ahead of myself, but these *are* the sorts of details . . ."

Lincoln walked on a distance before muttering: "There'll be no church."

"No? I wonder if your soon-to-be relations know that."

"I don't know what they know."

"Do they know what *I* know? About you and your God, I mean?"

Lincoln stopped. Surveyed his companion from head to foot.

"You've been drinking," he said, and began to walk at a faster clip.

"*Somebody* needs to!" Joshua called after him. "Oh, but never fear, there'll be no eruptions of *in vino veritas*. Your secrets are safe with *me*, Brother Abraham!"

Enough of a distance had opened between them now that Joshua was actually yelling the last sentence. The reverberations thrilled him, and by the time they mounted the steps to the Edwards house, it seemed to him he had never felt more alive—more in command of himself. What had he been so afraid of?

HE AWOKE LATER than usual the next morning, his head clotted, his eye sockets burning. A cup of coffee, still warm, was waiting on his bedside table, and Lincoln was dressing himself before the looking glass.

"Did I . . . ?" Joshua began to ask.

"Did you what?" replied Lincoln without turning round.

He couldn't ask the question out loud until he had answered it for himself, and that proved impossible, for much of the previous evening had been lost. He had a dim recall of making some sort of toast, though he couldn't summon the wording. He had most certainly flirted with Miss Edwards and had found her not wholly unreceptive. Or had he imagined that?

From the jumble of memory, two vignettes carved themselves free. The first was a watercolor portrait of Lincoln and Miss Todd, standing together in the doorway. Lincoln was putting on his hat and, at the same time, hooking his finger under Miss Todd's chin, and she was smiling and giving him a rap on the temple. A passing moment, no more, but it conveyed such ease, such unalloyed happiness that Joshua, viewing it from the periphery, found himself speechless before it.

The other memory was of Matilda Edwards, leaning toward him over supper and saying in that beguilingly low voice: "Never fear, Mr. Speed. You shall have your revenge ere long."

"Revenge?" he remembered sputtering. "Against whom?"

She smiled sweetly. "Why, I have no idea."

In that moment, through the fog of his inebriation, he could see that she *didn't* know. She had merely divined in him some quality that must either claim a victim or make a victim of *him*. Some animate force, perhaps, already pumping—forging its own channel. But in what direction? Toward what end?

THAT NIGHT, IN dream-memory, he burrowed back to his four-year old self. Running once more through that field of timothy grass—throwing out his arms like a swimmer and beating back the grass and, with each stroke, propelling himself farther, deeper. *Escaping*, as was his wont.

But this time, the long-suppressed sequel to that memory played itself out. He saw that same four-year-old—dirty, stained, sweaty, unrepentant—carried into the family parlor and deposited in his mother's lap. Who had found him? He had no way of recalling. All he could see now was his mother's face, collapsed with a fear that did not altogether dispel at his return. For she could see, couldn't she, that there would be other escapes, and it was *this* knowledge that lay now stamped in her face, that each step he took away from her—right up to and including the day of his departure—would be another knife in her heart.

Imagine, thought Joshua upon waking, *having such power over another*.

The morning light was still in abeyance, so he lit a candle and went to his desk. A letter from his brother sat there, recently opened. Full of the usual tedious inventories of hemp rakes and hemp hooks, work oxen and beef oxen, Irish potatoes and sugar beets. He read it now with new eyes. Then he drew out a sheet of letter paper.

My dear Philip,

　　I have been turning the question over. . . .

Mary

THIRTY-ONE

———————

That August, Lincoln was reelected.

It was a fact verified by the electoral commissioner and by the secretary of state, and it was sufficient, in and of itself, to make Mary's first response an upswelling of relief. Her future—*their* future—could now follow its ordained course.

But soon a more complicating fact came to light. Of the five Sangamon County Whigs elected to the statehouse, Lincoln had received the fewest votes.

She pored over the returns, calculating and recalculating each sum in her head. "It can't be," she said. "Two years ago, you had the most."

Had he not, in fact, wooed her with those returns? Had she not silently tallied them, again and again, in her memory? Somehow, in the space of two years, he had descended to fifth.

He was quick—too quick, she thought—to point out that he had out-polled the sixth-place candidate (a Democrat) by hundreds of votes and fallen just fifteen votes short of the first-place candidate.

"But your numbers have declined," she pointed out, "in at least three precincts. Wolf Creek, Rochester, and Upper Lick Creek."

He knew better than to be surprised at her attention to detail; he was surprised only to see it turned against *him*. He tried to persuade her that Illinois would still be safe for General Harrison come November, that he himself would be one of Harrison's electors, and with the great man ensconced in the White House, patronage would rain down on anyone who had helped put him there. But Mary was still mired in Upper Lick Creek. In Wolf Creek and Rochester. Why had they turned?

"Perhaps," she suggested, "you are tied too closely to the state bank. Or internal improvements. Perhaps we underestimated how much a seventeen-million-dollar debt would weigh on the common voter's conscience."

Lincoln was regarding her rather closely now.

"It was only fifteen votes," he said. "And I won all the same."

This was a new note in him. At first she took it for childish recalcitrance—the schoolboy being called to account. Only on further reflection did she realize that she herself was being called to account.

Can it be? she wondered. *He is finding fault with me?*

This went beyond insult; it ran against her private mythos. She had pedigree, did she not? Attractions? Not to mention an ardor for the work itself? She had attended every stump speech, cheered at every debate, squeezed every outstretched hand, expressed wonderment at every last replica of General Harrison's log cabin—today a cake, tomorrow a hat—and crooned along with every new campaign song within minutes of its composition. ("Our country calls, her banners wave, / Charge Freemen, charge, our country save.") She had shouted "Harrison and better times!" so often that she was still shouting it in her dreams. She had been more than a companion or decoration, she had been a soldier. Right there in the line of fire! Why could Lincoln not grasp his good fortune?

"Don't be silly," said Matilda, waving a hand at her. "He is only falling back on his pride. As all men must eventually. By the bye," she went on, in a brighter tone, "have you set a date yet?"

And here was the *other* trouble. The fellow could not be pinned down.

In his defense, his days and nights were full. For some four weeks, beginning in August and extending into September, he was gone entirely. Cozying up to Mr. Edwin Webb (of all gentlemen) at a barbecue in Carmi. Unspooling two-hour addresses in Belleville and Waterloo and Salem. Trotting out debate points in Mt. Vernon and Shawneetown and Equality. He wrote her faithfully while he was gone but deferred any further discussion of dates or logistics until January. *When the hurly-burly's done*, he added with a wink. *When the battle's lost and won.*

But even when he was *there*, some essential part of him seemed to have been left behind. More than once, she had to repeat herself in his presence. He always apologized but then fell back soon after into the same bank of mist. The air of distraction extended even to his dress. Each time she saw him, he looked as though he'd been rolled down the street, like a keg. Boots went unblacked; cravats took to unraveling. One morning, over breakfast, Elizabeth drawled: "You must speak to him about his suspenders."

"What of them?"

"They sag beyond repair. I cannot begin to say how his trousers stay up. Only Mr. Isaac Newton could enlighten us."

"I hadn't noticed," Mary said. Though she had.

Half yawning, Matilda reached for the raspberry preserves. "Isn't that like a man? As soon as he claims his prize, he loosens his grip. You mustn't let him get away with it, Mary."

Elizabeth was startled to find confirmation from such an unexpected quarter. It was the first sign of thawing between the two women, and before the dishes had even been cleared, they were united on a single point: Mary must demand better.

That directive coincided with her first-ever visit to Lincoln's law office. It was an occasion *he* had been putting off as long as he could, and if she had expected him to use the time to make the space more presentable, she was set wise from the moment she walked in the door. The room was as tiny as a steamboat cabin, with a decrepit old stove and a trapdoor and a bare plank table in lieu of a desk and a small cot with its bedclothes drawn back expectantly, as though any minute its occupant would return. A few loose boards, jutting from the walls, served as bookshelves, but the office's primary occupants were papers. Stacks upon stacks of depositions and deeds and declarations and praecipes and bills of complaint, piled according to no obvious system and rimed with dust of the most ancient provenance.

"It's cleaner when your cousin's here," said Lincoln.

She was sure that was true and wondered, for the first time, if John Stuart had got elected to the U.S. Congress for the sole purpose of escaping this office. She watched as Lincoln, with the back of his hand, gave a quick whisk to his own armchair and then, smiling like a plumed gallant, shoved it toward her. She lowered herself by degrees, waiting at every moment for the wood to splinter beneath her.

"Your clients come here?" she asked, faintly.

"I guess they're so desperate they don't really notice the state of things."

Lincoln took the bench usually reserved for visitors and, in the act of sitting, released a cloud of dust that, in the rays from the single window, looked like morning mist.

"Do people get so desperate as all that?" she asked.

On an impulse, she lifted her hand from the arm of the chair. Some indefinable lamina—gritty, vaguely vegetative—clung to her palm.

"Dear one," she said, giving her hand a summary wipe with a handkerchief, "I hope you will someday grant me a wife's prerogative to . . ." She let the handkerchief drop to the floor. "To effect *changes* in your *sanctum sanctorum*. Changes of a feminine variety."

"Have at it," he said.

"And while I speak of changes . . ." Clearing her throat, she fixed her face into its most winning attitude. "I wonder if I might beg a favor of you."

As she spoke, he listened with serenity—so perfect a serenity that she found herself hard-pressed to trust it.

"You mustn't think I mind on *my* account," she hastened to say. "But I am so anxious that you make the best possible impression on—well, *judges*, you know. And juries. And, of course, voters. . . ."

"Your family, most of all."

"No, no! I promise you, they are the least of it. I just believe that a gentleman as distinguished as you on the—on the *interior* should have an exterior that—that *comports* with his innumerable qualities. . . ."

He gave his neck a long, luxuriant stroke. Then he laced his hands behind his head and stretched out his legs to their full and alarming length.

"When I was ten or eleven," he said, "a rumor went about that a stranger boy had come to town with his father. And this same boy, according to rumor, *absolutely* wore broadcloth."

"Dearest, I am not sure—"

"Well, believe you me, our loftiest ambitions, our wildest dreams had never gone beyond a wool hat and a mixed-jeans coat. Oh, we'd *heard* of broadcloth. We knew preachers and lawyers sometimes wore it but only on rare occasions. But to be told that a *boy*, no bigger than ourselves, wore broadcloth, it was entirely too much. Night after night, we gathered to talk it over. Finally, we resolved that if such a wonderful thing were true, we had to see it for ourselves.

"Now we'd been told this boy would be going to a meeting Sunday with his coat on. We knew the route he would take. So we appointed a committee of three to hide behind a fence that he was sure to pass by. The rest of us were in an old mill, awaiting their report. Well, when our spies came back, we could see at once from their faces that it *was* the truth. I remember trudging back home that morning, perfectly persuaded that a superior being was in our midst."

He paused, as if in reverie. Then, with a light chuckle, he added: "The stuff that goes through a boy's head."

Mary sat motionless. Then she bent to pick up her handkerchief from the floor. Folded it and returned it to her reticule.

"Pray, Mr. Lincoln, how does this charming reminiscence relate to anything?"

"I was only telling a story."

"No, you were dodging." She could feel the simmer rise inside her. "This is not the statehouse floor and I am not one of your—your Locofoco opponents. To be fobbed off with anecdotes."

His lips curled into the most equivocal of smiles. "Is that what I was doing?"

So she left his office in a double fury: Not only had she failed to accomplish her mission, she had failed to *define* her failure. It seemed to her that a true gentleman either said what he was thinking or, better still, said nothing. The middle course was nothing but evasion—or else parable, which was evasion in another guise. It did her no good to ponder that *other* parabolist, whose listeners labored just as hard as she to gather the meaning, for Jesus was an even sorer subject.

In retrospect, it was surprising how late the subject was in coming up. Once, just once, Mary had casually suggested that Lincoln join her at church that Sunday. He had answered that it probably wouldn't work. Upon being pressed, he had said merely: "I wouldn't know how to behave myself."

Behave. Such a curious word.

"So you're a *Second* Presbyterian?" she guessed. "I assure you we don't mind. All in the family, you know. . . ."

"Neither First nor Second."

"We are equally well disposed to Episcopalians."

"That neither."

She frowned. "Methodist?"

"Nor that."

She had always been told it was vulgar to sound out someone's religious convictions, so she forbore to pry further. But one afternoon in August, over tea, she and her sister were piecing together (as best they could) plans for the impending nuptials, and the talk necessarily turned to a suitable church. At which time Elizabeth Edwards set down her cup and, in a tone of mild exasperation, asked: "But what *is* he?"

"Well. . . ." Mary's face heated a little. "He once said his people were Primitive Baptist."

The shudder caught Elizabeth at the base of her spine and traveled all the way up her neck.

"Those *foot* washers? Let us pray he has shed their example."

"I'm sure he has," she ventured.

But in favor of whom? Springfield was still a small town, with only so many churches to go round. If he could not be found in one of them, where did his heart lie? With those dismal Puritan evangelists? With the Quakers? Surely, he wasn't a Papist? There was nothing to do but ask him outright, which she did the day of his return. She feared he might take offense, but in fact, he only fell silent.

"I don't really profess a creed," he said after a time.

"You mean you don't go to church at all?"

He shrugged.

"But what do you *do* of a Sunday morning?" she pressed.

"I read, mostly."

"Tell me," she said, closing her eyes. "Tell me you at least read the Bible."

"Sometimes."

To prove it, he began spinning out a skein of Scripture. Passage upon passage, culled randomly from both testaments and delivered in the ripest of King Jamesian cadences. Two minutes later, he was still churning out verse—Job, Ecclesiastes, Corinthians, Romans—as indiscriminately as a waterwheel.

"That's all well and good," she said. "But there will come a time when you'll need to join us in the family pew."

"Why?"

"Because it's expected. Dr. Bergen expects it. Uncle John expects it."

"If they knew what was good for them, they'd rather I stay away."

Never before had she been obliged to argue on behalf of churchgoing. Nor had she ever wished to. Sunday service was, for her, the absolute nadir of the week: a pageant of petitions and psalms, ligatured in plainchant and encased in a monolithic gloom. She put *up* with it, that was all, as she put up with corsets and eyebrow plucking and the smell of woodsmoke in bed curtains. It was civilization's burden.

"I never said I was civilized," he answered.

"Please," she said. "Give me something to take back to them. Articles of faith, if you like."

This was a better tack, for he accepted it as an intellectual challenge and began, with great deliberation and maybe even for the first time, to outline his credo. He told her he did not deny the truth of the Scriptures. Nor would he ever speak with disrespect of religion in general, or of any denomination of Christians in particular. Nor would he ever support a man for office, whom he knew to be an open enemy of, and scoffer at, religion.

"And I'll make you a further concession," he said. "On the day that some church embraces 'Love thy neighbor as thyself' as its true mission—over and above every other commandment—that church will have me in its ranks. Whether it wants me or not."

"But that is the precept of every Christian," she protested. "It is . . . it is implicit."

"A little *too* implicit for my tastes. Inscribe it over the altar, and I'll be there."

That night, over supper, Mary dutifully recounted the credo for her sister, whose brow furrowed more deeply with each tenet.

"I don't understand," she said. "Is he some sort of itinerant preacher?"

"No, he merely *thinks*, that's all. In a—in a *catholic* kind of way. The non-Roman kind."

Elizabeth's eyes narrowed. "What your Lincoln *thinks* is a matter of supreme indifference to me. He must *align* himself, that is all." She gave her napkin a quick snap. "Really, if he insists on taking this line, what will he do when it comes to exchanging vows? Drag you to some bumpkin judge in Peoria? Father won't stand for it, you know."

The question of how they should be married felt sufficiently urgent that Mary raised it during their next stroll, taking care to keep all the shrillness out of her tone. But as she was learning, tone had little effect on him. He absorbed her question as if it were a point of law.

"People get married all the time outside the church," he pointed out.

"*Mine* don't," she declared.

He came to a stop then, so unexpectedly that she was caught midstep and dragged back. His eyes were ranging freely now—across the street, up to the trees—everywhere but at her.

"I guess I didn't know this would be so important to you," he said. "*Them*, yes, but not you."

"Ah!" she cried, jerking her arm free. "I refuse to let you lump me in with the opposition. I am the woman who will be your wife. The mother of your children."

"Why do you speak of children?" he asked, in a curt tone.

"Because they must be baptized, that's why. In a church. And raised in a . . ." She blurted out the first thing that came to her. ". . . in a *godly* manner."

Lincoln reached a hand round the back of his neck, gave it a scratch.

"You can pour whatever you like into their heads. But don't be surprised if it pours out again."

He gave her his arm once more and, with a show of reluctance, she took it. They were nearly to the corner when she heard him mutter: "Godly manner."

THIRTY-TWO

—◆—

EMBARRASSED, MARY WENT back to her sister to say that the issue of church would have to remain, for now, unresolved. Elizabeth answered with the full weight of her silence—a silence that now extended to any further discussion of wedding plans. No matter how often Mary raised the subject, her sister met her with the same blank smile, as if to say: *Why are we troubling ourselves?* No longer did Elizabeth make a point of asking after Lincoln or inviting him to supper. When she crossed paths with him in polite company, she gazed at him with the most benign abstraction, as though he were in the service trade. When friends asked her about the impending nuptials, she shrugged lightly and retreated into French proverb: "When the wine is drawn, one must drink it."

I know why she's so serene, thought Mary. *She doesn't think it will come off.*

And was she wrong? A wedding, Mary knew, could founder on the tiniest of considerations. One of the girls at Madame Mentelle's had broken off her engagement because she disliked her betrothed's cuspids; another took exception to earlobes. She could almost wish that her differences with Lincoln were as cosmetic, but it was dawning on her now how deeply they ran. Somehow or other, while nobody was looking, a fault line had opened up between them, and whatever silly argument they were engaged in—God, clothes, vote tallies—was merely that fault's upward thrust.

Since that day on the prairie, they had grown less intimate, not more. Perhaps Lincoln had been freer then to show affection, but in Mary's admittedly finite experience of the world, lovers *loved*. Skin drew toward skin. Mercy and her Conkling pined for each other so fiercely that, on the dance floor, they could scarcely control themselves. Even Ninian and Elizabeth, in their courting days, were altogether friskier specimens—Elizabeth used to speak, in teasing tones, of "Mr. Edwards' hand trouble." Lincoln had no such trouble. Even when he and Mary were quite alone, his hands rested on his *own* knees, lightly tensed, as though on military alert. It was true that, if she reached for him, he would reach back. For some minutes altogether, she might be able to cherish the workingman's burr of his skin, the latent strength of bone and tendon. But inevitably, he would withdraw, and with a finality that felt almost contractual. The air of abiding that she had first noted in Mrs. Francis's parlor—that she had loved him for—now savored of obligation.

In her more fanciful moments, she found herself hoping that General Harrison might bring them together. Was passion not contagious, after all? Had she not, in the early months of the campaign, longed for Harrison's election as a nun longs for Christ—chastely and to the exclusion of everything else? She had diverted some of these energies to Lincoln, yes, but if Harrison could no longer be her groom, he might still, in some symbolic fashion, lead her down the aisle to her waiting groomsman. *Be good to her*, she imagined him telling Lincoln. *She is dear to me.*

But that November, Illinois went for Van Buren. And although Harrison won enough votes nationwide to claim the prize, Lincoln would *not* be one of the electors sending him to the White House. Patronage and statewide offices would, on no account, be raining down. If anything, Illinois Democrats were more emboldened than ever, and when the statehouse opened for business in November, they lost no time in pressing their numerical advantage. As expected, Lincoln was put up for speaker; as expected, he lost. He took the defeat without a murmur, and his quiescence was matched by all the members of the Whig delegation, who trudged every day to the Second Presbyterian Church, their temporary lodging, bracing for the latest indignity.

In early December, a tiny scandal erupted when Lincoln and a pair of colleagues jumped out a window to avoid giving the Democrats a quorum.

The act was conceived in a spirit of defiance, but its actual effect was to leave Lincoln and his colleagues sprawled in a heap in the churchyard. To add to their humiliation, they had already, without thinking, recorded their votes, which made their escape not just ignominious but pointless. Mary did her best to quell her feelings, but the image of a prostrate Lincoln, jeered and hooted at by his enemies, began so to vex her that she went charging at him the moment he showed up in the Edwardses' foyer.

"What *possessed* you?" she cried.

"They locked the doors on us," he answered, sheepishly. "It got heated, and the window was *there*, and I guess we lost our heads."

"And your dignity, too, in one fell swoop. Meantime, what a gift you have bestowed on your opponents! Every Democrat newspaper across the state will be rejoicing at your downfall. The laughter will echo all the way to Lake Michigan."

He raised his face to hers now. Something sullen and obdurate had once more crept into his expression.

"Things happen," he said.

But there are some things that must never happen! That's what she was yearning to say. *At least not to you!*

How typical of a man, she thought, not to appreciate that his humiliation was *hers*. Twice over. Not to see how much of her own *self* she had staked on him: name, standing. *This* was the currency he had sent belly flopping out the window. And yet, to watch him frowning there in the Edwardses' front hall, one might have thought *she* was the one who needed to recant.

"Things happen," he said again.

IN THIS WAY, in this and every other way, the fault line widened beneath them.

To be sure, Lincoln was as faithful as ever in his offices. When business permitted, he found time to call on her at home or to take her on a stroll. Now and again, he even consulted her on a political matter. There was a bill afoot, for instance, that would cede Illinois's fourteen northern counties to the Wisconsin Territory. What did she think of *that*? She was, of course, decidedly against it (if only for the narrower range of influence it would afford *him*). He nodded, did her the courtesy of listening, but she could see that the asking itself had been a formality.

And now, with the General Assembly in full uproar, and with his practice producing its own smaller uproars, Lincoln's time was less and less his own. Even if he promised to meet her at somebody's home for supper, he was invariably late—later, even, than his colleagues in the statehouse. One evening, with the indulgence of the hostess, he had the temerity to send Joshua Speed in his place.

The night was cold, even for December, and Mr. Speed had worn against the elements a comforter, in a bumblebee pattern, wrapped round his neck like an anaconda. It should have looked ridiculous—like something he had grabbed, half seen, from his own store's shelves—but he wore it with unthinking conviction, and the frost had buffed his cheekbones down to their first principles, and his eyes looked the bluer for having wind to claw at them. He was, roughly, the same spectacle she had beheld on the night of their first meeting.

Why, you're Miss Todd. . . .

And how it pained her now to admit that he no longer had the same effect on her. This specimen for whom she had entertained furtive prospects, for whom she had even considered, if only for the space of a few minutes, throwing over Lincoln and the whole edifice of bourgeois respectability. *What a child I must have been*, she thought.

And in the next breath: *How I miss that child.*

He went to her now as if they were the oldest of friends. If he had any memory left of the spectacle he had cut at the Edwardses' supper, it had been banished. He entreated her to take an armchair close to the fire, and when she declined in favor of standing by the hearth, he unassumingly joined her there.

"I hope you are quite warm enough?" he said. "Shall I build up the fire?"

Hearing no objection, he took another log from the woodbox, jabbed it until a geyser of sparks rose up.

"Lincoln sends his regrets," he said.

"Does he? I suppose that would require him to *have* regrets."

How she hated her own voice in that moment. The carping note, the fishwife edge. *Heavens*, she thought, *how will I sound after we have been married twenty years?*

Only that prospect seemed no more likely now than being married to Mr. Speed for twenty years. Or anybody else. For want of anything else to do, she stared into the fire. Nearly relishing the way the heat annealed her face into a mask.

"Does he ever speak of me?" she said at last.

Mr. Speed seemed to consider many responses before he settled on one. "I am no lawyer, but in this event, I should probably plead attorney-client privilege." Something must have fallen in her face, for he moved at once to placate. "I meant only that whatever a friend says—about anybody, for good or for ill—it must always be held in confidence, yes? As I'm sure you understand."

She stared at the finger-shaped points of firelight, said nothing.

"He was sincerely sorry not to come," said Mr. Speed.

More silence.

"Shall I carry back some message?" he asked.

She gave her petticoats a soft gather and stepped back from the hearth. "Why should you deprive me of the pleasure of delivering it in person?"

A WEEK BEFORE Christmas, the Opdykes threw a winter-solstice ball. It was done on impulse, and the lack of time limited their décor to a few die-cut snowflakes, cotton batting round the door frame, and silver holland drawn over the carpets. But the hosts provided a full board of pheasant and ham and kept their liquor on the strong side. (By now, even Whig hostesses had tired of hard cider.) In the ballroom, the quadrilles had been portioned out in white chalk, and the windows had been thrown open in anticipation of a great horde. Yet, an hour into the proceedings, the musicians had still not taken up their bows, and the rooms were cold and underpopulated.

Lincoln had sworn upon a stack of—something—that he would be there by ten, but when the eleventh hour rang in the hall clock, he was still absent. Mary lingered in the refreshment room, nibbling on blancmange and trifle, and glancing now and then at the dance card she had deliberately held open. After a time, she wandered back out into the hall, where the first person she chanced upon was Matilda, throat and cheeks gorgeously pinked.

"Where have you been hiding?" she demanded.

"Nowhere."

Matilda gazed upon her for a time with stern eyes. "I don't know how you stand for it."

"Stand for what?"

"Being abandoned in such a cavalier fashion."

Mary blanched. "I suspect the Assembly has run late again. It often does this time of the word year."

"What stuff! I have seen easily a dozen assemblymen making merry. You must stop making excuses for him."

"What else would you have me do?"

As if she had been lying in wait for that very question, Matilda leaned in and took her firmly by the arm.

"We shall do exactly what we did before!" she cried. "Light a fire!"

The words, with their attendant echoes, left a distinct unease in Mary's soul—she remembered those long, fruitless hours of withholding in Mrs. Francis's parlor. But now, in the face of a superior resolve, she could pose only the mildest of objections.

"Some men, I suspect, may be more inflammable than others."

"Shall we test your theory?"

With a toss of her head, Matilda snatched Mary's dance card away. A mere two minutes later, she came sauntering back.

"There! I have filled it for you. No more waiting on that hayseed Galahad to pry himself free. You are liberated!"

"To do what?"

"Why, to dance, what else? Flirt. *Enchant*."

Mary winced. "That isn't done, is it? When one is—"

"When one is engaged? Puss, you may lay claim to such a distinction when that clodhopper sees fit to render you an actual *date*. With*in* the nineteenth century. Until then, neither decorum nor law can touch you."

"But what can be gained by dancing with other men?"

"Don't you see?" Matilda took her by the wrists. "He must be reminded how desirable you are."

To Mary, this was in no way a self-evident proposition. It seemed to her that, if a girl was truly desirable, her beloved should need no reminder; if she was not, no man could be manipulated into believing her so.

"And what's the use?" she protested. "He's not even here to see it."

"But he shall *hear* of it, you may depend on that. By evening's end, he will be a seething cauldron of jealousy. Why, I shouldn't be surprised if you left tonight with a date certain. Now there's no time to cavil, puss, your first partner is waiting."

This gentleman was the owner of a saddler and harness warehouse whose very breath savored of cowhide. Her next partner was a German root doctor who, within a minute, had diagnosed her with a deficiency of cinnamon, rapeseed, and gum arabic. Neither partner was the sort to foment possessiveness, but the third man on her dance card was none other than Mr. Edwin Webb, her erstwhile suitor.

"What a sight for sore eyes," she crooned as she suffered him to put his arm round her waist. "We have seen so little of you in recent months."

"Ah, well," he answered, vaguely. "Carmi."

He was more cast down in spirits than she remembered, and for several turns across the floor, she sought in vain to lift the cloud. It was only when she complimented his dancing that his eyes brightened.

"Aren't you kind?" he said. "Agnes used to say the same thing."

At once, the cloud returned, and it was left to Mary to ponder the mystery of a man who grew more in love with his wife the longer she'd been dead. Tact would have suggested leaving him to his sorrow, but when the next man failed to show, Mr. Webb immediately volunteered his services. Through great exertion, she was able to leave a smile on his face by the time the music finished—a smile that grew only slightly more complicated as he peered over her right shoulder.

"Lincoln," he said.

Mary wheeled round. Snow must have begun to fall for a couple of alien flakes still clung to her lover's hair, defying every last fire in the house.

"I wonder," said Lincoln, "is there a dance for me?"

Mary took her time coming to him. Composed the most benign of smiles.

"The card is full, as you can see. I didn't suppose you would get here in time. And then, of course, I know how little you care for dancing."

"With you, it's all right."

"Then why," she said, hearing her voice tauten, "do you seize every chance to be gone?"

"I'm working," he said, after a pause.

"Is it the state's business to which you are yoked, or your own?"

"The two are surprisingly hard to disentangle."

She stood there, for some moments, inviolably still, her eyes fixed on the ground.

"Mr. Lincoln, if you are *bored* by me in some fashion—if you find my company a *torment*—then please have the goodness to tell me now so that we may end this charade once and for all. As you can see, there are other gentlemen who would be more than pleased to take me off your hands."

Lincoln took a step closer. Lowered his head until it was only an inch or two from hers and said, in a voice of unusual tenderness: "The only company that torments me is my own."

THIRTY-THREE

ON CHRISTMAS DAY, she and Lincoln saw each other only long enough to exchange gifts. They had been consciously frugal: a watch chain for him and, for her, an Indian shawl, in a paisley pattern she was almost certain Mr. Speed had picked out.

"I shall treasure it," she said, simply.

He, for his part, stared quizzically at the chain for a second or two. Then, instead of putting it on for her benefit, he tucked it into his waistcoat pocket. Kissed her, once, on the forehead, and rested his finger on the bridge of her nose.

"The first of many Christmases to come," he said.

THEY WERE NOT scheduled to meet again until New Year's Eve, at which time they would exchange intimacy for the most public of gatherings. Lincoln's friend, Mr. Baker, was celebrating his ascension to the state senate by throwing a ball at the American House.

The hotel was Springfield's largest and grandest establishment, and the costs of entertaining on such a scale would have taxed a man even less indigent than Mr. Baker. His natural gift for oratory, however, was allied to a weakness for gesture, and he believed that Whig spirits might be revived by a ceremony that, at once, bid farewell to the disappointments of the past and embraced tomorrow's promises.

The guest list was, by design, both bipartisan and comprehensive. Springfield matrons who seldom went abroad after sunset came crowding that night onto the American House's Turkish carpets. No impediment was too great. In the makeshift dressing room, Mary found easily half a dozen ladies with babies pressed to their bosoms. With no great sentimentality, the ladies performed their maternal offices, then handed the bundles straight back to the maids. "Mind you, don't mix them up!" they called as they hurried out of the room.

Matilda and Ninian had both taken ill shortly after Christmas, so Mary had come to the ball with her sister, who was philosophically opposed to public entertainments but always morbidly curious to see if they could be brought off. "Mrs. Baker is charming—she is utterly dear," Elizabeth said. "But one can't say she has a head for logistics of this magnitude. You don't suppose she'll do anything vulgar, like stationing valets to announce the guests? Who would hear them anyway in such cavernous rooms? Oh, but I do wish Ninian were here. I know one mustn't dance with one's spouse, but I shouldn't mind a turn or two for auld lang syne. You shall have to dance for the both of us, my dear. Which reminds me, when is . . . ?" Elizabeth cast a politic glance at the carriage floor. "When is *he* due?"

"Around ten, I believe."

"Well then, we shall look for him close to midnight. Let us hope the year is still eighteen forty when he graces us."

Mary didn't bother to remonstrate; she thought midnight as good a bet as any. For some time, she wandered from one room to the next, her eyes fixed as demurely as possible before her. At last, she came to the refreshment room, which was dark except for a brass candelabra under a yellow-silk shade. Most of the champagne was gone, but there were pitchers of soda beer and lemonade and a single Windsor chair, into which she lowered herself gratefully and half shut her eyes. Whether she actually dozed, she could not afterward say, but the voice came at her as out of a deep sleep.

"Can it be? Miss Todd, alone?"

She pried her lids open. A man stood, backlit and obscured, in the doorway. She knew him at once by his outline: the massive head, the flaring neck, the whole bellicose angle of him. Mr. Stephen Douglas.

That night, he was wearing a black tailcoat with a white hothouse carnation in the lapel—a more elegant attire than was his custom, but the greater wonder was that he had been invited at all. Last March, offended by an article in the *Sangamo Journal*, he had taken a cane to Simeon Francis in the street. Mr. Francis, much the taller, had caught him by the hair and shoved him back against a market cart. Which man came away the victor depended on which newspaper you read, but the incident left Mr. Douglas with a reputation for ferocity that belied his actual size. As Mercy used to say: "He holds his ground, doesn't he?"

He held it now.

"We must dance," he declared.

What caught her off guard in that moment wasn't the lack of preliminary or the imperative ring of that *must*. No, it was the peculiar emphasis he laid on that final word. As if he weren't really talking about dancing at all.

"Ah," she stammered. "Now, do you mean?"

"When better?"

She canvassed her still-dormant brain for objections. There was nobody else on her dance card; indeed, there was no dance card. She had no particular place to be and, to be sure, nothing better to do. Perhaps the deciding factor was simply this: the dawning awareness that Mr. Douglas was so obviously savoring the prospect of her.

She nodded briefly and, with some hesitation, took his arm.

The orchestra had just finished the quadrille, and the couples in the ballroom were negotiating the complex business of whether to stay or fly. Mr. Douglas, moving unidirectionally, staked out the northwestern corner as his own, daring anybody to trespass. And he was just tendering Mary a bow when the musicians struck up again. A waltz.

With the trace of a sneer, he put his arm round her waist—in such a way that Mary thought, for the first time in her life, what an extraordinary place that was for a man's arm to be. In the next moment, they were gliding. The tempo was swifter than she expected, but he was as equal to it as she was, and as they rotated, a scent of tobacco, not disagreeable, rose from his plumped lips. And the thick humid air in the room seemed to fasten round them like bands, drawing all the available heat to her cheeks. How often she had danced with gentlemen, and how dissimilar this was from those other experiences. For he was *looking* at her, and his thoughts were nowhere else.

The song rushed to its natural conclusion, and even when their bodies were still, her skirt was still swirling round her, as though reliving the experience. She gave it a tug and, in the same instant, saw Lincoln poking his head through the frame of the doorway.

"Another," suggested Mr. Douglas.

She looked at him, looked back at Lincoln. Then she set her mouth in a grim hard line.

"Why, yes."

The tempo this time was even a hair faster, and it seemed to her that Mr. Douglas curled his arm even more tightly round her waist. To keep her from spinning off entirely, was that it? Like some escaped moon? Round and round they whirled, to the very precipice of vertigo. Once, just once, her gaze drifted toward the doorway. To Lincoln's face, still and watchful.

The music drew into a coda, and they finished somehow in the same corner where they had started. Her chest heaving slightly, Mary took up her fan and drew back to the perimeter of the wall.

"You are fatigued?" Mr. Douglas asked.

"A trifle."

"Then I shan't impose on you. For now."

She gave him a meager smile. "I really shouldn't have."

"Why not?" he asked, drawing an inch closer.

"I am—I am *answered* for, as you must know. Hark," she added, with a forced laugh, "he waits in the wings even now."

Mr. Douglas turned his head indolently and surveyed Lincoln without greeting.

"Then why is *he* not dancing with you?"

"He has only just got here."

"Meaning that he has left the field wide open and must pay the consequence." Mr. Douglas gave another of his light sneers. "Besides, wc are no longer dancing, Miss Todd, we are conversing. I believe that is a constitutionally protected prerogative."

"Which we are exercising in a rather public way."

"Would you prefer it private?"

The implications were not slow in reaching her. Nor was he slow in grasping her reaction.

"Have I overstepped, Miss Todd? I meant only to pay my sincerest respects."

With deft, unerring fingers, he drew the carnation from his lapel and, in full view of Lincoln, inserted it into the threads of her hair.

"The flower has found its native clime," he said.

He had the satisfaction of seeing the color rise up her, like sap. With a curt bow, he took a step back and made as if to depart.

"Oh, and Miss Todd? Should this impediment of yours ever be sloughed off, do let me know, will you? You deserve a man who will dance with you the whole night through."

He was in no great hurry to leave but had enough delicacy, at any rate, to exit by a side door. Mary cut her eyes toward that other doorway, where Lincoln still stood, regarding her in utter silence. And in that moment, she was overcome by the sensation that someone—no, some*thing*—had been completely unmasked.

A few seconds passed. Then he turned and walked away. And now, striding toward her, came the baleful spectacle of Mrs. Francis.

"What are you up to?" she hissed.

"I am not sure what you mean."

"I mean the tasteless spectacle with which you have just regaled us."

Mary began to fan herself in ever-longer arcs. "If people wish to misconstrue common courtesy, that is their own concern. I care little for their idle opinions."

"Oh, yes? And how little do you care for Mr. Douglas?"

Mary's free hand fluttered to the carnation nestled tightly in her hair.

"He is a gentleman," she said.

"There are many such."

"Then I shall go farther. He pays a girl the attentions due her."

Mrs. Francis's head arched up, and her eyes and mouth widened, as if she were trying to soak up each word.

"So," she said, in a more hushed voice, "this was the object of your antics. You wished to awaken the green-eyed monster in our Lincoln. Oh, you will not find it there, Mary. *Other* monsters, certainly. They are *wide*-awake now, thanks to you."

Mary tried to think back to his face, as she had just seen it, and found she couldn't, which was somehow more terrible. As if she had erased him, feature by feature. A single cool, powdery tear began to slide down her cheek.

"Come," said Mrs. Francis, taking her by the hand.

BY NOW, THE public rooms of the American House were at full capacity, and Mrs. Francis was forced to use the wedge of her left shoulder just to clear a path for them. After many blunders and dead ends and more than a few collisions, they happened upon a back stairway, lit by a single sconce. Even here, they were not entirely alone. On the upper landing, one of the guests—a man of no certain age—lay prostrate. His arm had curled itself round the newel-post, and the other now rested on his chest, from which snores of ancestral resonance emanated.

"*Someone's* been making merry," said Mrs. Francis.

She colonized the third step and, after drawing in her skirt and petticoats, motioned to the space alongside her. Mary obliged, and the instant she sat down, every last dike in her broke, and she laid her face, hot and scalding, on Mrs. Francis's shoulder.

"Dear me," said the older woman. "That's silk, you know. Oh, well, what's a little salt water among friends? But my dear, is it as bad as all that? Here. . . ."

Mary took the proffered handkerchief and tried to blot her face clear, but more tears came flooding through, and it was another two or three minutes before she could trust herself to speak. Even then, the best she could manage to say was that it was all a muddle. Yes, that's what it was. A muddle.

Mrs. Francis studied her with calm eyes. "Has he been a beast to you?"

Mary shook her head.

"What, then?"

"I don't *know,*" she cried, swallowing down one last spasm. "We never seem to agree on anything, we keep—*disappointing* each other. I look in his eyes, and God help me, I see nothing but regret."

"What cause would he have for that?"

"Oh, Eliza, I don't think he *wants* it. Any of it." She gazed down into the folds of her skirt. "I'm not even sure that he cares for me, not really. Not me or anyone."

"That isn't so."

"It *is*, I tell you!"

Mrs. Francis was silent for a while. Then she hooked her arm through Mary's and drew her closer.

"Listen to me, you ridiculous child. I have occasion to speak with our Lincoln nearly every day. Do you know the overwhelmingly preponderant theme of our talks? *You*. Oh, you do well to gape, but it is true."

"What does he say?"

"Many things. And *one* thing. He is terror-struck that he won't be worthy of you. Worse, that he will be the ruin of you."

Mary flinched as if she'd been slapped.

"Oh," Mrs. Francis went on, "he has no great fear of poverty on his own account. It has been his companion since birth. However, the prospect that *you* should be impoverished under his care, this frightens him beyond measure. That explains his distraction. That explains his *absences*. He is taking on more clients, more responsibilities. Tonight was no exception! He was tasked with drawing up a last-minute deed for Elijah Iles, the very owner of this hotel. Who sees no reason, apparently, that business can't be conducted at all hours of the year, no matter the occasion."

"But I was expecting him. . . ."

"Yes, and he should have sent word. And he should have told you why he is so often missing. But he is *proud*, this one! And he will do anything to keep you from sinking into the slough that has been his whole life."

Into the stream of snores that issued from the unconscious man, a single hitch now inserted itself. Then a moment of suspenseful silence. Then, like a reprieve, the snores poured out once more.

"But I've told him," Mary protested. "He needn't worry about money. We shall find a way."

"This is what decent men do. They worry." With a wry smile, Mrs. Francis leaned toward her. "Naturally, I advised him to unburden himself to you. I told you had far too much mettle to be daunted by pecuniary considerations. That you would *rise* to this challenge, as you would any other. As any good politician's wife *should*." Mrs. Francis's eyes fairly bore down on her now. "Only you can tell me if I was mistaken."

Joshua

THIRTY-FOUR

————— • —————

HE HAD TOLD himself from the beginning that no secret could conceal itself indefinitely. It must now and then send out tiny instances of itself, yes? The key was to keep the vast bulk of it buried, like ordnance, ready to explode at the critical moment.

And, at the same time, to create an atmosphere of utmost openness. For if Lincoln was to believe that all was well again, that things were as they had been, then it was up to Joshua to guide him there. And he had until January the first to accomplish it.

He applied himself first to the silences.

Those crevices in the day—between waking and dressing, between upstairs and downstairs, between one block and the next—that needed to be filled once more. With speech. Mindless, dispensable speech of the sort that used to be their natural province.

Joshua began with the skies. *Bit cooler than yesterday.... Smells like rain.... Not sure if that's thunder I'm hearing.* The kinds of observations that old coots would toss round the porch of a general store, expecting only the tersest of replies.

Then he turned his eyes toward the earth. *What's that fellow doing? Spading his garden? ... I wonder how those clothes can stay on the line in such a wind? ... What's at the mill door, I wonder, that's making those pigs root?*

Here he was on more fertile terrain because, no matter how banal the observation, Lincoln couldn't resist the chance to twist it. The pigs, he declared, were just Democrats, marauding through the land. The clothes, billowing in the wind, were obviously Whigs. A man who spades his own garden is a man with nobody to love him.

Under this stimulus, Lincoln's jokes began once more to creep into the conversation. He had reaped a fresh harvest from the campaign trail. There was the lady in the plumed hat who went tail up in the mud. There was Ethan Allen finding a portrait of George Washington in a British backhouse. There was the old woman who, uncertain whether her husband would defeat a bear in a brawl, decided to root for both. The language might be salty or benign; Joshua might choose to laugh or not; it hardly mattered because Lincoln was *always* amused. By the time he reached each joke's climax, the mirth had already diffused through him like nitrous oxide, until there was nowhere left for it to go but *out*, atomizing into the atmosphere.

Dinners became gradually easier, and even the evening strolls returned. In a piecemeal fashion, to be sure, and no more than fifteen or twenty minutes at a time, but nearly as free-roaming as before. The railway was still off-limits— too many associations—but most of Springfield's other attractions remained there for the taking. Taverns, saloons. The Lyceum, the Thespian Society. Even the weekly drill of the Springfield Artillery became a reliable source of entertainment.

After a time, the two men decided it was safe to resurrect the Poetical Society. One by one, the old luminaries took up their places by the well-stoked fire: Baker and Douglas, Browning and Calhoun, Logan and Lamborn. The recent election had done nothing to slake their thirst for disputation, and in this setting, sealed away from the enforced hierarchies of the General Assembly, Whig and Democrat could address each other as equals and even find unexpected alliances. Baker, one night, joined Calhoun in adumbrating the merits of Beethoven, and at the close of the conversation, clapped the other man lightly on the shoulder, as if to say, *Why can we agree on so little else?* "By God," Baker went on, stretching his arms toward the ceiling, "I've missed this."

The trickiest part came once the guests had left, when Joshua and Lincoln had to retire for the evening. Their bedtime ritual had always been a curious affair: in no way organized, dependent entirely on messages they were only half conscious of delivering. How long would Lincoln go on reading? How long would Joshua keep himself awake in anticipation? Those questions had never been asked or answered in any direct way, they had merely been *solved*.

So Joshua began by offering the one signal that was entirely within his control. Which was to say that, when they lay in bed together, he once more aligned his body with Lincoln's.

This had practical results. They no longer had to wrestle over the blanket, and Lincoln no longer had to hang his feet off the end of the bed. But more than that, the gesture seemed to *loosen* something in Lincoln. Each successive night, he came to bed a little earlier—and better disposed to talk. Even if Joshua was too tired to hold up his end, Lincoln would revert without protest to monologues. His past, of a sudden, had grown more interesting to him. One night, it was Granny Spears, an herbal healer in Clary's Grove who was stolen by Indians as a child and whose chin and nose came as close to touching as he'd ever seen. Another night, he spoke of having to sew shut the eyes of thirty hogs to get them onto a flatboat. He recalled the day he found a dozen mangled soldiers in the forest, each with a round red dollar-sized spot atop his head from where a Sauk had taken his scalp.

In the face of such reveries, Joshua had to do nothing more than listen—and even that was not strictly required. On more than one occasion, he drifted right off, something Lincoln must surely have noticed but never mentioned. There was even a night when Joshua, on the cusp of slumber, heard Lincoln say: "You *are* a comfort, Speed."

THEIR RETURN TO intimacy was, by all appearances, perfectly natural. Only Joshua knew how deliberate the project was, how often he had to say to himself: *Yes, this. And now this.* How often he heard, beating beneath every cordiality and grace note, the secret course he had pledged himself to. Pulsing to be revealed.

He knew just how far they had renewed the old trust when Lincoln asked him one night to attend a supper in his place.

"It's the Merrymans again. I wouldn't ask, but I know they're counting on a sixth, and we're sure to run late at the Assembly tonight."

"I'd be happy to."

There was a pause.

"She'll be there," said Lincoln.

Joshua imagined a whisk broom, sweeping every last cloud from his countenance.

"All the better," he declared. "I shall deploy the full arsenal of my charm."

"Don't carry it too far. We don't want her running off with you."

But Mary Todd, by the look of her, had no intention of running anywhere with anyone. She greeted Joshua cordially enough, but her eyes and cheeks had lost some of their natural luster, and her hair was flat and limp against her skull, as though it were awaiting somebody's revivifying hand. Joshua was reflexively solicitous, but when he joined her by the fire screen, she gave no sign of desiring an interview. It was something of a surprise, then, when she turned to him and asked: "Does he ever speak of me?"

THE QUESTION WAS more complex than she would have guessed, for Lincoln, out of innate tact, no longer mentioned Mary Todd by name. Whenever he wished to bring up the subject in Joshua's presence, he retreated straight into the hypothetical.

"See here, Speed. Suppose you were promised to somebody."

"Don't be macabre."

"Just suppose. Now, being promised in that way, would you care overmuch how the girl was dressed? Every minute of every day?"

"I suppose it wouldn't trouble me. So long as she weren't mistaken for my housemaid."

Some other evening, Lincoln might say, apropos of nothing: "I wish I could stop thinking of money."

"Difficult not to, isn't it?"

"When I ponder how much it costs just to keep a single body fed and clothed. Now add *one* to that number. Now add two or three. Four, even! It's—it's a geometric, a *euclidean* proposition that the money won't stretch as far as the number. And what then? What's a fellow to do?"

"Why, what generations of fellows have done before him. Lay himself at the feet of his father-in-law."

"What if he would sooner die than do that?"

"He should probably hold off on the dying until he meets the father-in-law."

Another occasion: "Speak true, Speed. Does a person's character have anything to do with the creed he professes?"

"If this is your way of telling me you've gone Hindoo . . . ?"

It was Joshua's impulse always to defuse Lincoln's vexations with humor. This was self-protective at heart, for he had come to respect the screen that Lincoln had drawn round this side of his life and had no desire to be coaxed back into old tumults. All in all, he thought it better to say too little than too much, but this did leave him in the odd position of not being able to answer a relatively simple question: Was Mary Todd ever spoken of?

As he did with Lincoln, he sought refuge in humor—in this case, a feeble improvisation about attorney-client privilege. Miss Todd declined to answer in kind, and in the light of the Merrymans' hearth, he made a surprising discovery. He had just made things harder for her, and he was sorry for it.

Sorry, yes, because the animosity he had been nursing in his soul had never specifically had her as its object. He could, in all honesty, say that he admired her—for many of the same reasons, surely, that Lincoln did—and if pressed, he would allow that she was quite as much a victim of circumstances as he. In short, there was nothing *personal* in anything he was either doing or contemplating. So to know that he had all but confirmed her worst suspicions and that she was, as a direct result, suffering—suffering alone—could afford him no joy. And when she failed to rally during supper, he could not help but think what a hard mistress Love was to those caught in her web. How fortunate was he to have been spared!

THIRTY-FIVE

—————

"WELL, THAT'S QUEER," said Lincoln, frowning down at the pages of the *Sangamo Journal*.

"What?"

"This business about your store."

Joshua paused in the act of edging his razor round his chin. "My store?"

"It says here, 'James Bell and Company is in want of funds. All whose notes and accounts have been due since the first of January, must be paid up or be sued.'"

With a steady hand, Joshua took another stroke with the razor, wiped it on the towel. "Oh, that." In no great hurry, he took yet another stroke. "If you must know, Brother Abraham, it's all your fault."

"How so?"

"You're the one who's been predicting a national bankruptcy law, aren't you? Before another year is out?"

"Yes. . . ."

"And how many debts would become *instantly* uncollectible the moment that happens? It seems to me the height of prudence to"—he ran a lazy finger along his jaw—"to get on top of the debtors *now*. While we still have some leverage." Catching Lincoln's eye in the looking glass, he tendered a small smile. "I just assumed you'd agree."

"I guess I might have. If you'd asked."

"Oh, but you're . . ." Joshua took a step back from the mirror. "You're working fourteen hours a day as it is. I didn't want to bother."

"It's no bother."

"Well, it *will* be come January when you and I take these poor debtors to court. Yes, I'm counting on you to make them *tremble*. Down to their toenails. Now, if you've finished your inquisition, I have a store to run."

THAT CHRISTMAS, he and Lincoln were consciously frugal with each other: a volume of Scott poetry for Joshua and, for Lincoln, a watch chain.

"Why, Speed," he said, "this is too good for the likes of me."

Never mind that it was silver, that it was the plainest possible design of interlocked hoops. Lincoln raised it to the window light as if it were a sultan's treasure.

"Oh," said Joshua, "I nearly forgot." From his dresser, he drew out a paisley Indian shawl, bound in a single rose ribbon. "As you requested."

Blushing, Lincoln nodded, then folded the shawl into tiny segments and tucked it inside his overcoat.

"How much do I owe you?"

"Consider it an early wedding gift," answered Joshua with a wave of his hand. "Now don't argue, she's expecting you for tea, isn't she?"

LIKE MOST OF Springfield, he and Lincoln had been invited to the Bakers' New Year's Eve ball. They had intended to walk over together, but at the last minute, Lincoln was called into business with Elijah Iles, and Joshua made the short walk by himself.

The temperature had been dropping steadily since Christmas and hovered now just above zero. The air, absent even the whisper of snow, dug with such force into every cranny of Joshua's available skin that he began to feel like he was being razed, and as he trudged the two blocks to the American House, he wondered if the same thing might be happening to his surroundings. All the familiar sights—the state capitol, Lowry's, the Globe Tavern—all the much-thumbed contents of his life in Springfield—would, at any minute, simply disappear and leave nothing but void at their back.

With his head lowered, he didn't realize how close he was to the hotel until a woman's voice came crying out of the darkness.

"There you are!"

A tiny bonneted figure, wrapped in half a dozen shawls, was darting toward him. In the mottled light of the street, he made out the pretty, pinched features of Mrs. Baker.

"Thank heavens!" she cried. "I was just saying, *Who better than Mr. Speed to keep a cool head in times of crisis?*"

To the best of his knowledge, Mrs. Baker had never seen him in crisis. She had merely been a devoted customer of his store—the kind who could be persuaded that her purchases had been her own idea. But the panic that reigned now in her eyes stirred notes of chivalry in him.

"How may I be of help?"

"Oh, where to begin?" she moaned, drawing him through the front door. "The dance cards were never printed, despite positive and repeated assurances. The shortcakes have yet to arrive. The hotel has but three bottles of champagne left over—three bottles!—not enough to last us until ten o'clock. The first violinist has taken ill, and the ballroom has not enough seats for the ladies."

She had more particulars lined up, perhaps a whole evening's worth, but Joshua's mind, cool as advertised, was already arranging each problem according to its urgency. Nobody, he assured the hostess, would miss the dance cards. As for chairs, why not just take some from the refreshment room, where guests, in his experience, rarely sat for long? The loss of a single violin mattered not at all so long as there was a double bass to keep time. The shortcakes still had two hours to arrive, and if the guests were sufficiently warm with wine, they might be beyond caring.

Which left the rather serious problem of the champagne. Perhaps one or two of her domestics might troll rival establishments to see what they had in stock? Start at the Globe Tavern, continue with Watson's Saloon, then carry on to the hotels. Offer them a bounty of twenty-five cents a bottle, if need be, just lay hands on as many as possible. In the meantime, provide the guests with as much soda beer and lemonade as they can stomach. Wet lips were less apt to grouse than dry ones.

There were more conflagrations to be put out—a hostess like Mrs. Baker lived from fire to fire—but Joshua by now had forgotten about dancing, conversing, being seen. He was of *use*. Once, just once, Baker poked his head into the room to ask if all was well. It took but a glance at his wife's face to send him scurrying back out.

Somewhere around eleven o'clock, Joshua spied a lone figure tottering toward the front door. Immediately recognizable, for all the distance that lay between them, and notable now only for its bareness against the elements. Joshua reached for his own coat and strode outside. There, in the street—hatless, coatless, mired in shadow—stood Lincoln.

"Come inside!" called Joshua. "You'll catch your death!"

Lincoln stared at him, as through a fall of snow.

"I think I'd rather walk," he said. "If it's the same to you."

With a stifled growl, Joshua snatched the comforter from his own neck and wrapped it round Lincoln's. Then stood back to ponder the very disinterestedness of that act. Perhaps Lincoln pondered it, too, for he said: "Care to join me?"

THE NIGHT WAS moonless and the way difficult, for the wagon ruts had frozen into corrugations. Silently, they picked their way along Madison, up Fourth, pausing only when they had reached the pool of light that was shed by the Matheny farm. From far off came the faintest echoes of prairie wolves. In the near distance, a herd of sheep stood sentry-like in the cold, the wool of their bodies merging with the wool of their breath.

"She was dancing with Douglas," said Lincoln.

Joshua glanced at him, glanced away.

"That's bad form, I suppose."

"I don't know what kind of form it is. I'm not even sure I mind."

"Then what?"

Lincoln's mouth folded down. "I think she could do a sight better than me."

Joshua said nothing at first, then gave a sharp tug on the comforter round Lincoln's neck.

"So you wish me to defend you to *yourself*, is that it? Very well. Abandon for a time this guise of humility. Do you sincerely consider Douglas your superior?"

"In some departments."

"Oh, for—"

"You can talk that way, but there's a—there's a quality of *assertion* that counts with certain girls, wouldn't you agree? It's—it's *aggrandizing*, it's *colonizing*, it's . . ." He paused. "I guess what I mean is he's Douglas and I'm not."

Joshua held out a single palm. "If she had wanted Douglas, don't you think she would have had him by now?"

"I don't believe she knows what she wants. All I can say is that she looked at *home*. In his arms. It looked like the most natural place she could be."

Joshua turned and stared into the sable darkness. He was tired, of a sudden.

"Damn," he heard Lincoln say. "It's cold as blazes."

"That it is."

More silence.

"I'm sorry about our pact," said Lincoln.

"Our . . ."

"Bachelorhood. Brotherhood. I didn't forget it, Speed, I didn't laugh it off, I just—I *broke* it, that's all. Without a by your leave or anything. That wasn't right."

For some minutes, neither man spoke. At last, Joshua turned round—just as a wind came down and shook the elder tree under which they stood.

"Well, never mind," he said. "What's done is . . ."

Done, he was going to say. But the cliché seemed so inadequate to the purpose that he let it die on his lips. In the next minute, a single bell came tolling from the direction of town.

"Happy New Year," said Joshua.

They stood listening until the last reverberation died away.

"We should go back," said Lincoln. "She might be waiting."

THIRTY-SIX

———

SIMEON FRANCIS WOULD not allow a mere holiday to interfere with his paper. So it was that, when Joshua went downstairs the next morning, the year's first edition of the *Sangamo Journal* was waiting, as expected, on his doorstep. He did a light inspection of the contents and, having satisfied himself of one particular, carried it upstairs.

"Here," he said, passing the paper to Lincoln. "Would you care for some coffee while you're reading?"

Joshua dropped the ground beans into the pot, tossed in some chicory root, then a handful of eggshell to keep the grounds down. He was in no hurry. He knew that Lincoln came at every newspaper in a straight line. Each column had to be well and truly digested before another could be mounted. It would be another ten minutes, at least, before he reached the third page and who knew how much longer to sift through all the mercantile news before arriving at the notice perched halfway down the page in the fourth column.

The sequence that announced this discovery went as follows: Lincoln grunted; he set his coffee cup on the ground; he muttered, almost inaudibly: "This can't be right."

"What?" asked Joshua, looking up from his own cup.

With his index finger, Lincoln stabbed the paper at its offending point. "'The co-partnership heretofore existing between James Bell and Joshua F.

Speed is this day dissolved by'"—his finger came to a halt—"'by mutual consent.'"

From there the finger would move no farther. It was left to Joshua to recite the rest from memory.

"'All who are indebted to us MUST PAY UP. Longer indulgence cannot and will not be given.'"

Lincoln stared down at the paper. "It's a typographical error," he suggested.

"No. I looked it over myself. Before it went to print."

Now, for the first time, Lincoln permitted himself a glance in Joshua's direction.

"Then . . ." His face broke into a kind of startled grin. "You're closing the store?"

"It will just have a new name. Bell and *Hurst*, if you can believe it. Our Charlie's come up in the world, hasn't he?"

"But that's—that's your livelihood, Speed."

"Don't I know it?"

Lincoln's own face seemed to disarrange itself. "I don't understand. If you're selling off the store . . . I mean, what do you propose to do with yourself?" With a broken laugh, he added: "All that *time* on your hands."

"My time will be somewhere else. As will my hands. As will I."

And to the cloud that now enveloped Lincoln's features, Joshua said: "I'm leaving, of course."

How MANY WEEKS he had spent envisioning just this moment: the upburst of the ordnance. And what a shock to see how quietly it happened. Not a blast at all but an *arresting*. Lincoln, sitting where he'd been sitting a minute earlier. The newspaper still in his lap. The coffee on the floor. The sun striking at the exact same angle through the gable window.

"Leaving," he said at last.

"Yes. Going home."

Lincoln's face still hadn't budged.

"That explains it," he murmured, almost to himself. "Why you were collecting on your debts. You were—you were putting your affairs in order so you could . . ." A spark of comprehension swam up in his eyes. "Why, you've *known* about this, Speed. For months."

"Well, of course. Something on this scale can't happen overnight, can it? The sheer volume of paper *alone*. Whole forests had to be slain."

The newspaper began to slide down Lincoln's lap.

"Of course," Joshua went on, "I had no desire to keep it from you, but my cousin's lawyer insisted on strictest secrecy. I figured that you, of all people, would understand."

The newspaper paused right at the verge of dropping—then dropped all the same, splashing like a puddle at Lincoln's feet.

"I don't doubt that it's a bit of a surprise," said Joshua. "But you know how long the family's been badgering me to come back. And what with Father gone, Farmington's become a tottering concern."

He was talking too much, he knew that. How much better to retreat into dignified silence. For even now, he could see something awakening in the other man's eyes.

"Farmington isn't a tottering concern," said Lincoln. "You told me it was worth more than a million."

"As of last *spring*, yes, but—"

"You told me you hated farming."

"The *stewardship* side of it, perhaps."

"What other side is there?"

"Well. . . ." His chest was beginning to tighten. "I don't know that I'll be working at Farmington *itself*. Louisville is just five miles away, after all. My brother's opening a practice there."

"You hate the law, too." Lincoln sat up still higher in his chair. "*And* medicine. You hate teaching. Preaching. Running for office. What exactly do you propose to do?"

He was beginning to sound uncomfortably like John Speed.

"There's bound to be something," said Joshua, as levelly as he could.

"But you have no idea what."

"I had no idea when I came *here*. Fate has a way of . . ." He lofted his palms upward.

"I see," murmured Lincoln, drawing himself up vertebra by vertebra. "This is my punishment."

"Come now," said Joshua, setting his coffee on the desk. "You're being childish."

"I don't know that I am."

"Then why are you taking it this way?"

"Which way?"

"So personally, I mean."

"But that's what you wanted," said Lincoln, with a near-ecstatic gleam. "That's precisely what you hoped I would do."

"I don't know that you entered into my calculations."

"So you admit that you calculated."

"I admit nothing," answered Joshua.

The rising note of his own voice lifted him out of his chair.

"I am not, the last I ascertained, even remotely on trial. Although if anybody in this room *should* be . . ."

"Yes?"

"Starting with counts of *perjury*. . . ."

"Aha!" cried Lincoln. "It *is* punishment. Pure and simple."

Joshua turned toward the wall. Made a point of studying the grain of the wainscoting.

"It is my own life, to do with as I wish. You *long* ago forfeited any . . ." Once again, he had to call himself back. "I neither deserve nor require any further interrogation."

"Then interrogate yourself."

"Oh, I have," answered Joshua, suddenly rounding on him. "I have asked myself what there is to keep me here. The store? It's getting by but *just*. Politics? The election's done with, and so is our party. I've made a tolerable living. I've accomplished everything I set out to do. All in all, I'd say it's time for fresh woods, yes? Pastures new."

Lincoln was silent for a long stretch. Then, squinting lightly, he transferred his gaze to the window, where the bare branches of an elm made a map of the morning light.

"Your friends," he said, quietly.

"Oh." Joshua cast his eyes down. "They'll carry on, I think. Why, look at you! You'll be married before another year is out. No time *then* for old associates, eh?" He strolled over to his desk, let his fingers scuttle along the weathered wood. "You'll find this amusing. Back in Kentucky, they've already lined up a girl for me, can you believe it? Fanny Henning, I think her name is.

They tell me she's a dear thing, but I don't know. Unlike *you*," he added with a smile, "I'm in no particular hurry. Then again, once you hit that quarter-century mark, they come looking for you. They do."

Amazing: Billy Greene's very words piping back through his own mouth. Right down to that mysterious pronoun. *They*. Who were *they*?

"So you're going," said Lincoln.

HIS VOICE WAS faint now, almost a whisper. His right arm dangled half to the floor. His head, his massive head, was bowed just an inch to the side. He looked, thought Joshua, like the martyr in a Renaissance painting: bare-throated and serene and so perversely illuminated, right there at the very pitch of darkness, that Joshua had actually to shield his eyes. Dimly, from some great remove, he heard a pounding. It stopped for a few seconds, then came back, with greater urgency.

Somebody was knocking. Knocking on his front door.

"Just a moment," Joshua answered, though his voice was too quiet to be heard through the closed window. "I'll be down directly."

In his stockinged feet, he took each step hesitantly, as though the wood might crumble beneath him, and swung open the door just as a blade of arctic air came knifing through. Taking a step back, he peered into the unnaturally bright morning light. A young woman was standing there. It took him some seconds to recognize her. One of the Edwardses' servants—the Irish one. She offered no greeting but thrust out an envelope. He had but to see the initials—*A.L.*—and to inhale the faint aroma of rose water to know who had sent it.

"FOR YOU," SAID Joshua, dropping it in Lincoln's lap.

He watched as his friend plied his large thumb to the envelope's seal and drew out the single sheet. No more than a paragraph or two, but he took his time reading, or perhaps he read it several times, puzzling out its meaning.

"She summons," guessed Joshua. And hearing no reply, he added: "You mustn't keep her waiting."

Mary

THIRTY-SEVEN

AFTER HER NEW Year's Eve conference with Mrs. Francis, Mary was in no state for further revelry. Through some combination of guile and tears, she persuaded her sister Elizabeth to accompany her home, and she was just stepping out of the Edwardses' carriage when the First Presbyterian church bell began to toll the midnight hour.

"Happy New Year," said Elizabeth, with scant enthusiasm.

Mary didn't bother answering in kind. She had always considered this the most artificial of holidays—a counter set arbitrarily on one square of the calendar when any might do. Why not March the seventeenth? August the first? She had heard that the Chinese began their year on another day altogether and had accumulated quite a few more centuries, too. But the more she pondered, the more she realized that her disaffection had less to do with the holiday than with this: An error had taken place.

Or better, perhaps, to say a whole chain of errors—she and Lincoln, again and again and in some fundamental way, missing each other's mark.

And was it too late to make amends? The words of Mrs. Francis rang even more loudly now than they had in the back stairwell of the American House.

I told him that you would rise *to this challenge, as you would any other. As any good politician's wife* should. . . .

She had just enough strength left to climb out of her chemise and draw her nightgown over her head. But she awoke the next morning with the words still fresh in mind, and as she returned her scattered garments to the closet and bureau, she imagined herself, in the same act, returning her own life to its former state, before doubt and dissent had crowded in. She would write to him this very morning. She would dapple the note with just a hint of rose water, and she would use the code names they had long ago devised for each other.

Dearest Richard,
"Welcome the coming, speed the parting guest."
In this spirit, let us welcome a new year—and new beginnings.
Come to me soonest!
Love, Molly

The only question was who should deliver the message. A male servant would be embarrassed; a scullery maid would leave some residue of her own timidity. It would have to be the Irish girl, Johanna, whose unfiltered insolence would command a certain respect.

Johanna herself was none too pleased with the errand, for the mistress of the house had already tasked her with a long list of chores. The Edwardses were throwing their annual New Year's open house, and Elizabeth was no less exacting about such an event than she was about the most formal of balls. If anything, the considerations were both subtler and more treacherous. One had to be casual, yes, but not indolent. The décor had to be relaxed but not slovenly. As for the food, it had to echo the New Year's repasts that the Todd girls had grown up with, right down to the hoppin' John and collard greens and corn bread.

It was thus for Mary an exercise in nostalgia to wander the halls of the Edwards mansion that morning and breathe in the smoky aromas of vinegar and fatback. Nostalgia, though, soon gave way to restlessness. *Soonest*, she had written. *Come to me soonest.* Yet here it was, past noon already and guests only an hour away, and no Lincoln. Was this, in effect, his answer?

At last, a few minutes before one, he was announced. She went to him at once, intent on erasing any awkwardness. "I had quite given you up!" she cried. "Never mind, you are *here*, laggard, so there will be no further complaint. Oh, but come!"

Was there something hysterical in her smile? Was that why he was so slow to take her hand?

"I'm afraid our usual parlor is off-limits," she said. "But we might snatch a brief interlude in the back parlor, if that's agreeable." Talking, talking—*hurling* herself against his quiet. "I'm not sure you've ever been there, it's really quite cozy. I don't know why it doesn't get more use. Here we are."

A fire was already at full bore, leaving beards of vapor on the window-panes. Mary, smiling, seated herself on the divan and tapped the space next to her. Again, he hesitated, and when at last he sat, it was with such a plumb-like force that the divan retreated a few inches.

"Dear one," she said, "I must speak to you of last night."

All these hours she had been granted to organize her thoughts! She wanted him to know that she had danced with Mr. Douglas only to make him angry—because he *would* insist on being late, wouldn't he? Oh, but now she knew why—and it was childish of her, she knew that now—she *would* do better—for her heart belonged to no other—that was all that mattered. All the words, all the sentiments were queued up, ready to be disgorged . . . only they were stopped in the utterance.

Stopped by Lincoln himself.

By his cheeks, drawn and riven. By his eyes, sorrowing. His very body, bowed beneath some invisible weight.

"But what has happened?" she cried, folding her hands round his. "Somebody has died, is that it?"

Her mind rooted through the possibilities. *Father . . . stepmother . . . stepbrother . . .*

"I've just been walking," he said.

"Alone?"

"Of course."

But she had written him to come to her soonest.

"Some tea might be reviving," she said. "Or refreshment of some kind. I should—I should *ring* for . . ."

In the act of reaching for the bell, though, she was stopped by something else. His watch chain.

It was not the one she had given him for Christmas. No, this was a chain she had never seen on him before.

He followed the direction of her glance, and a flush rose up along his jaw. "Mary," he said.

That was all she needed, finally. The sound of her own name, uttered in this particular tone. She grasped everything now with a near-blinding intu-ition. His air of tragedy came not from anything that had happened but from something that was *about* to happen. He had walked all those blocks not to exercise his limbs but to gird himself for this precise moment.

"Oh," she said. "Oh, no."

She rose to her feet—stood, irresolutely, for a second or two—then made straight for the nearest window. He was speaking and she was answering—responding without even thinking, for some other part of herself was furiously focused on that window. If she could but let the air in, everything might be swept away. Herself included.

From the now-indeterminate area that lay directly behind her, more words were coming. *Sorry* and *can't* and *wish* and *I* and *you*, and none of it signified, what mattered now was the window sash, which refused to budge no matter how hard she plied herself to it. Then, with a start, it roared up. She thrust her head through the opening, and the cold embraced her like a lover, and from out on the lawn came the sound of a bird flapping. Queerly off-kilter, as if the creature had broken a wing but was beating all the harder with its good wing, fluttering and circling and now diving. Straight toward her, a missile of talon and feather.

"No," she said.

Then it was upon her.

PART FOUR

Joshua

THIRTY-EIGHT

DR. HENRY INVERTED the wineglass onto the patient's bared neck and tapped the stem once with his index finger. Three black lumps dropped onto the exposed circle of skin—*stretched* themselves to their full length, as if awakening from a nap, and began inching toward the tiny pools of blood that Dr. Henry had scattered across the patient's skin. Once there, they curled themselves into apostrophes and began quietly lapping. For some twenty minutes they took their sustenance, swelling with each new draft like prunes dropped in water.

"That should suffice," said the doctor. With gentle tugs, he coaxed the creatures back into the wineglass, then rolled his sleeves back down. "He should start feeling the effects within an hour. Give him a blue mass pill before supper and another before bed. Tomorrow, we'll try him on the purgatives." He shrugged his jacket back on, buckled his bag, and, for the first time since arriving, spoke directly to his patient. "You mustn't worry, my friend. We'll have you on your feet before the week is out."

From the bed, Lincoln stared back as if somebody else was being addressed. It was only when the doctor was gone that Joshua felt free to pose the question that had been on his mind the whole while.

"Did it hurt?"

Lincoln was silent for a time. "Nothing hurts," he said.

THE DARKNESS HAD come over him slowly, then abruptly, then completely.

On New Year's Day, Lincoln had returned from the Edwards house with no visible signs of distress. Quieter than usual, but not agitated. Joshua, of course, declined to ply him with questions—that would have implied some stake in the answers—but Lincoln held his tongue, too, and whatever rancor they still felt after the bitter words of that morning was absorbed into a thick crepey silence.

Better this way, thought Joshua. *Get on with the business at hand.*

So much business! He would have to dissolve the original partnership, collect on outstanding accounts, notify customers and creditors, settle or liquefy debts, sell off backlog. Just as important, he would have to prop up the teetering edifice of Charlie Hurst, whose own credit was not as forthcoming as Joshua would have liked and whose head for business not as steady and whose lips grew tighter each day under the burden of incipient ownership. Again and again, Charlie fell back when he should have surged forward and demanded to know things that that had already been well and truly explained. Accounts, inventory, payroll . . . the details seemed to slip like sand through his brain's crevasses. *Dear God*, thought Joshua. *I shall never get clear of the place.*

All this to explain why he missed the early signs: Lincoln coming home earlier than usual, eating less, retiring earlier, staying awake later. A strange miasma seemed to have enveloped him. He had no clear sense of time and was flummoxed by even the simplest inquiries. On the night of the twelfth, Joshua was awakened by a sound that he took for an animal, trapped in the chimney. It was Lincoln, half-collapsed on the stairs, his arm hooked through the stair rail. Sobbing at such a pitch that even Charlie, on the far side of the dormitory, was roused from his sleep.

"What is it?" asked Joshua, drawing his face as close as he dared. "What has happened?"

Somehow or other, they coaxed him back to bed, but the next morning, he couldn't be roused. Hard as Joshua shook, the limbs pushed *back*. Joshua was about to check for a pulse when Lincoln's eyes shuddered open.

"It's time to get up," said Joshua, rather crossly.

Lincoln said nothing.

"The Assembly's meeting in less than an hour," Joshua reminded him.

But all Lincoln said in reply was that he *couldn't*. A word that, as soon became clear, applied to every other activity. Rising. Dressing.

Joshua left him alone for a couple of hours, thinking more sleep might help, but Lincoln's condition had deteriorated even further by afternoon. He had tried and failed to make it to the chamber pot, and he lay helpless now—speechless—in the urine-soaked sheets. Joshua sent word to Mrs. Butler, who brought over a plate of dinner, but nothing on that plate, not even the hotcake and buffalo tongue, held any appeal for him.

They were able at least to change the sheets, but there was no question of sharing the bed with him, so Joshua dragged up an old mattress and laid it on the floorboards. That night, he woke up punctually on the hour and each time, with a sudden gulp, seized the candle and swung it toward the bed. Each time, he found the same result: Lincoln neither asleep nor awake but imprisoned in some medial state. The face itself the very mask of death, but the *eyes* alive, seething. Like termites, Joshua caught himself thinking, rustling beneath a rotten floorboard.

Mrs. Butler was back the next morning, this time with compresses and towels and a bedpan and a bottle of Dr. John Mason's Vegetable Febrifuge. Lincoln consented to a little oxtail broth but only, it seemed, out of courtesy. Mrs. Butler's dismay was extreme, for she had always believed Lincoln to be criminally underfed, and he now seemed, in the space of a day, to have lost whatever flesh he had still to lose.

"What shall we do?" she cried.

Lincoln answered the question, in effect, by falling asleep—a deeper sleep than before. Mrs. Butler left before nightfall, and Joshua, lacking anything better to do, drew a chair over to the bed and sat there. An hour passed, then another. On any other occasion, he might have picked up a book or a newspaper, or even taken the dire step of making conversation with Charlie Hurst, but tonight, he required no distraction. He kept recalling—how could he not?—the time that he himself had taken ill, wandering for days and nights in the valley of the shadow of death. Had Lincoln sat just like this? Scrutinizing his face for the slightest bending toward life?

The next morning, Joshua called in Dr. Henry, who took down whatever responses the patient was capable of giving and delivered the diagnosis: acute melancholia and hypochondriasis. He was back an hour later with his jar of leeches.

Lincoln offered not a word of resistance. Even *de profundis*, he must have clung to some fledgling faith in the medical profession because there was no regimen that Dr. Henry could propose that he would blanch at. He took the mercury as willingly as the calomel. He even went against his own temperate nature and submitted to shots of strong brandy. Lacking any food to absorb the stuff, his stomach unfailingly sent it right back up, but even in the act of vomiting, he appeared to be gazing down at himself from the highest of balconies.

On the afternoon of the nineteenth, Dr. Henry and his assistant coaxed Lincoln out of his bedclothes and dropped him, limb by limb, into an ice bath. The cold traveled all the way up his spine like an electric current. Within a minute, he was trembling uncontrollably; within two, his skin was noticeably blue. Dr. Henry waited the full ten before ordering him to be taken out. He was laid back on the bed and shrouded in six blankets, and still, he didn't stop shivering for another hour. It was then that Joshua heard him mutter: "I shall have to get better, or Henry will kill me."

JOSHUA WOULD LATER look back on this as the first sign that the old Lincoln was still down there in the darkness, crawling toward a vent. Not that anyone could let down his guard. Indeed, Dr. Henry was insistent that somebody sit with the patient at all times—and that anything remotely dangerous be taken out of his reach. One morning, Lincoln, in a weak voice, said: "Shaving."

"Yes?" said Joshua.

"Downstairs. You're shaving downstairs."

"Oh." Joshua's smoothed cheeks grew a shade pinker. "I didn't want to disturb you, that's all."

"Why?"

"Why what?"

Lincoln drew in a breath. Speech was still a chore. "Why should it disturb me?"

"Well, I do *hum*, you know, as I shave. And I'm always out of tune, you've said so yourself."

With great effort, Lincoln revolved the situation in his head. At last he said: "It's the razor."

From a certain angle, this was another good sign: the operation of logic. But in that moment, Joshua shifted his gaze to the window.

"The doctor thought it best, that's all."

From his bed, Lincoln murmured something. *Juh-weh.*

"Sorry?"

"Just as well."

BY NOW, THE news of his rupture with Miss Todd had spread to the town's limits, and the only thing that remained to be decided among the citizenry was: Who had deserted whom?

Some swore up and down the break was Lincoln's idea; others insisted quite as vehemently it was Miss Todd's. Some said she had borne up under the strain with extreme great dignity; others said she had flown into a rage and flung an andiron at her faithless lover's head. The only point upon which everyone seemed to agree was that something comical had transpired.

This, in their eyes, made Lincoln's retreat from society even more comical. Passing Joshua on the street one morning, Mrs. Hardin called out with the gayest of peals. "Is your friend recovering from his duck-fit?"

The smile on her face was maternal and indulgent, and Joshua tried in vain to match it. "I don't—I'm not certain that *duck-fit* is the—"

"Now don't defend him, Mr. Speed. This is a highly unsatisfactory way of terminating his romance. He ought to have died or gone crazy, that's what I think. Tell him we are very much disappointed."

That afternoon, on his way to the bank, Joshua was stopped by James Conkling, whose eyes were no less merry than Mrs. Hardin's.

"Poor Lincoln. How the mighty are fallen, and all that."

"Perhaps that isn't—"

"Oh, come now, didn't Mercy put me through the same trot? 'Loving is a painful thrill, and not to love more painful still.' But I don't know why Lincoln's bothering with that quack Henry. Tell him to take exercise. A nice vigorous ride should cheer him up to no end."

By common consensus, Lincoln was not ailing but brooding—worse, sulking. That may have explained why so few visitors came to call. For most of that week, the only people he saw, aside from Joshua and Dr. Henry, were Mrs. Butler and Billy de Fleurville, the barber, who came twice to shave away the pile of whisker that had gathered along Lincoln's jaw and even clipped and dressed the hair for free.

On the eighteenth, Mrs. Francis arrived. She had dressed for the occasion in a black-silk dress, black shawl, and black bonnet, and Joshua had to fight down his first, uncharitable thought: *He's still alive.*

But Mrs. Francis was already charging up the stairs. "There you are!" he heard her cry. "What do you mean by putting the fear of God into all of us?"

She sat by Lincoln's bed for a good hour, voluble as ever, in no way deterred by the fact that she was the only one speaking. (When had that ever deterred her?) By the time she came back down the stairs, though, her face was grave and her glance evasive. As she slid on her glove, she murmured: "I am well repaid, you must believe."

"For what?" asked Joshua.

"My foolish meddling. Oh, it's *true*," she said, sweeping past any objection, "I *positively* should have foreseen something like this. Two such opposed personalities, they must either love to the fullest or expire in a pile of ash. There can be no middle course." She pulled on her other glove and gave a light tug to her bonnet. "I understand you are to leave us."

Joshua nodded, briefly.

"I don't know if you will believe me, Mr. Speed, but I shall be very sorry to see you go. Not as sorry as our Lincoln, of course, but all the same. Now, if you'll excuse me, I must attend to Mr. Francis's supper. You know what a *bear* he can be when he's hungry. Do keep me apprised in the meantime, won't you? And *thank* you," she concluded. "Thank you for saving him."

Joshua was about to demur when she put up her hand.

"Don't make me assign the credit to Dr. Henry. I should sooner die."

MRS. FRANCIS MUST have shared the news of her visit with at least one concerned party, for the next morning, Joshua glanced outside and found Mary Todd standing on the opposite side of the street—staring up at the window with no expectation that anybody might be staring back.

He threw on a cloak and stumbled out the door in his stockinged feet, sidestepping the clumps of snow and slush. At sight of him, she visibly tensed.

"How is he?" she ventured to ask.

"Better, I think. A little better every day."

She nodded, half to herself, then turned her gaze back to the window.

"I said things to him, you know. In the heat of it. Things I repent."

"Well," said Joshua, "you had provocation, I am sure. . . ."

"Ohh." She smiled sadly. "Neither of us is wholly blameless, I fear. But even at my angriest, I never wished this upon him."

Those same words, unedited, might have come from Joshua's mouth.

"Would you care to come up?" he asked. And when she shook her head, he added: "Shall I tell him you . . ."

"I believe the less he hears from me now, the better, don't you? Good day, Mr. Speed."

She was still standing there when he closed the door behind him.

THE NEXT MORNING, Lincoln was able to rouse himself from bed. He took a few tottering steps around the dormitory and a couple of passes up and down the stairs, gripping the rail hard. To Mrs. Butler's delight, he managed to hold down a plate of kiss pudding. That afternoon, he read a little from the *Sangamo Journal* and asked Joshua to recite a couple of pages of Byron.

There was no question of returning to the law office, but Lincoln had it in mind now to show up for roll call at the statehouse. On the morning of January twenty-first, Joshua helped him into clothes and a cloak, clapped a hat on his head, and guided him out the front door. The sudden influx of sun made Lincoln retreat like a bat, but he steadied himself by inserting his arm through Joshua's and took his first strides into the world.

On a normal day, the trip to Second Presbyterian, where the statehouse was still quartered, would have consumed no more than ten minutes. Today, with Lincoln stopping at intervals to rest, it took three times as long. Joshua couldn't help but notice the stares of passersby, any more than he could miss the looks from Lincoln's colleagues as he lurched through the door. Give them credit, though, they hurried to be of service, and when his voice proved too feeble to be heard, they raised their own to compensate.

"Never mind! It can wait." . . . "The important thing is you're back." . . . "How we've missed you, old coot!"

After the roll call, Joshua escorted Lincoln back home and eased him into the bed. Piled three blankets on top of him and was nearly to the door when he heard Lincoln whisper: "This must be how Lazarus felt."

By Friday, he could dress himself. By Tuesday, he could extend his stay at the statehouse to two hours. The following Thursday, he spent the whole day there.

When February came round, there was even talk of him returning to his practice. To hear Dr. Henry tell it—and he said this to whoever asked—Lincoln was on the road to full recovery. But nobody who caught sight of him that winter could accuse him of ruddy health. Sorrow still *rode* him, from point to point, so that at times he would stop in the street and stand there, still and attentive, as if he were conversing with it. The old jokes expired on his lips, and the new ones found nowhere to attach.

Joshua encouraged him to go walking when the weather permitted. Nagged him to eat his meals, brushed his coats, sent his boots out to be cleaned. Never once did he mention the name Todd.

One evening, with the dusk closing round them, Joshua and Lincoln found themselves sitting by the hearth at the back of the store. Lincoln sat in one chair, softly chewing on a straw, and Joshua sat in the other, taking contemplative drags of a cigar. The mood was serene enough—or, at least, sufficiently resonant of times past—that Joshua felt emboldened at last to ask the question that had been plaguing him all these weeks.

"Why did you break things off with her?"

Lincoln was not, by the looks of him, unprepared. Yet he measured each word before answering.

"It seemed the greater mercy, really. To her. To you." He shrugged. "Everyone."

"Do you regret it?"

He was quiet.

"I regret making such a hash of it. I regret being . . ." He drew the straw out of his mouth. "Well, what man could wish to be a cause of suffering?" He rubbed his thumb slowly against his index finger. "I haven't even bothered to thank you."

"Oh, don't be—"

"No, I'm overdue, Speed. When I think of all you did on my behalf, all the hours you stayed at my side. Never stinting or complaining. You stood *by* me, you did. Even after . . ." His face tightened a fraction. "I'm grateful, that's all. More than you know."

Joshua returned his gaze to the fire. "Do you remember that time I fell ill?" he asked.

"Of course."

"Do you remember what you said when—when it became clear I wasn't to die? You said, *Not on Captain Lincoln's watch*. I've never forgotten that. So, if you want to know *why*, well . . . this was Captain Speed's watch."

They were silent now for some minutes.

"When do you leave?" asked Lincoln, finally. "Leave for good, I mean."

"April."

Lincoln turned over the news in his mind, then gave a single nod.

"That's a sound plan. The roads will be clear, no ice on the river. Yes," he said. "April would do nicely." He folded up the straw into tiny sections and gently tossed it into the fire, watched it disappear in the flame. "I wish I could come with you," he said.

That was when Joshua heard his own voice, traveling the distance between them.

"Why don't you?"

Mary

THIRTY-NINE

———◆———

THE FIRST TIME it happened, she thought she'd been staring too long into the fire. How else to explain the mysterious dot that affixed itself to her eye and, far from fading, began to *lengthen* until it had described an arc? A pulsing, shimmering thing—*alive*.

Over time, she learned that, if the arc failed to resolve into a circle, the pain that had taken root in her head might still be contained. But should the circle be joined, then the ache radiating through her skull would acquire the texture of something permanent. Hours might pass, in her darkened room, before the first rays of relief shone forth, and, right to the very edge of that moment, it was possible to believe she would remain there forever, nausea rippling through her skin.

It took Dr. Henry to affix a label. "Hemicrania," he said, before adding, with a note of light condescension: "You might know it better as migraine."

How fortunate she was that he was fully conversant with the latest medical research, for the great minds at the Hôtel-Dieu de Paris were unanimous on the efficacy of hydrotherapy. "We'll begin in a small way, shall we? The next time you feel an attack coming on, you're to soak your feet in a bowl of warm water. That's easy enough, isn't it?"

After a few days, Dr. Henry pivoted toward the mustard bath. Another pivot, then, toward weekly bleeding. Mary had to lose a good two pints before she was granted a glimpse of her own future: a series of ever more violent assaults on her person, with the same negligible outcome. The very next day, she called upon her brother-in-law, the co-proprietor of Wallace & Diller's Drug and Chemical Store, and emerged ten minutes later with half a dozen bottles of laudanum. The stuff was too bitter to be drunk straight, so she cut it with raspberry shrub, and while it never eliminated the headaches, it gave her, for long stretches, the not-disagreeable sense of detaching from them—detaching, indeed, from time's axis. Future became, much to her surprise, the present, and the present future. *Yes*, she thought. *This is how my days will play out. Alone, in a curtained room.*

IN APRIL CAME the news that President Harrison had died. According to those in the know—Dr. Henry professed to be one of them—Harrison had only himself to blame. Against the strict advice of his physicians, he had lingered in the rain during his inauguration. Shortly after, he had contracted pneumonia and died within a month of becoming president.

Mary gave herself over, with an almost sensual relish, to grief. The man for whom she had staked so much was gone as quickly as a wildflower. After all the strife and alarums, all the cries for change, change, change, the old order was, in the space of a few weeks, restored—stronger than ever. What a foolish creature she'd been. Thinking politics might be redeemed by its ends.

SOMEHOW OR OTHER, she managed to go out into society. This was almost entirely owing to Matilda, who continued to regard Mary as a project of interest. If anything, the reversal of January the first had only tempered Matilda's steel. Ninian and Elizabeth had stomped from room to room, making dire noises about breach of promise suits. Matilda, by contrast, had sat silently, listening to Mary's wracked sobs before saying: "He shall pay."

Mary could not recall these words now without a spasm of guilt. Because in that moment when Lincoln had laid his mission bare—told her in that halting, convulsed way what he was there to do—the first words out of her mouth were: "It's Matilda. . . ."

The suspicion took them both by surprise, for until now, she had never knowingly entertained it. But that was what she shouted into the vacuum left by Lincoln's silence.

"You love her, say it! You love her!"

It was the only explanation her fevered brain could summon. He had found somebody younger, more beautiful, and who better than Matilda, with all her cunning *strategies*, driving Lincoln ever further away. *Matilda*, who, in a weak moment, had all but confessed her attraction to the man. *He stops just short of handsome, doesn't he? If you catch him right?* Oh, and she had caught him right, hadn't she? Dear God, it had been Matilda! Pulling every last string. . . .

"Don't be ridiculous," Lincoln had stammered. "She's not even in this."

"Liar!"

Nobody, so far as she knew, was listening on the other side of the door, but she was all too happy now, as a result, to submit to Matilda's whims. Indeed, she considered it a form of atonement to shine or not, depending on what her friend expected. And once spring dug in for good, the pair could be found as many as three or four nights a week at some supper party or ball or promenade—smiling as becomingly as ever, flirting to the brink of promise and never further.

The only trouble was that, while Mary had been looking the other way, the ground had shifted. Those old suitors—Webb and Trumbull and Shields and Gillespie—the ones who might have been counted on to step forth in Lincoln's absence were now holding off. It was as if they had long ago written off their chances and could only ply their hopes against other candidates—*younger*. Julia Jayne. Martinette Hardin. Sarah Rickard. . . .

Even Mary's own sister had ceased to groom beaux for her, having arrived at the same conclusion that Mary, by a different route, had already reached. A man could slough off the taint of a broken engagement; a woman, never. She must carry it through life, like a smallpox scar.

And so, at the ripe age of twenty-two, Mary was drifting ever closer to the eddy—while each new day, it seemed, brought a new influx of females. For all she knew, one of them might even end up in Lincoln's arms . . . and who could devise a more ironical turn of events? For, in looking back, she could see how much of her conduct with him had been premised on the idea there could *be* no other. She *alone* had the ability to see through his defects and deficits. Why, she had shouted as much in the Edwardses' back parlor.

"Do you think anybody else will ever love you? Who?"

Someone, came the answer now. Someone more complacent and forgiving—willing to love the rough quite as much as the diamond. Someone who, by her very existence, would serve as Mary's daily reproach.

For this reason, she had dreaded at first to see Lincoln abroad in society. But, as events proved, his illness was more serious than prevailing gossip had allowed for. Even when he reemerged, friends and onlookers were shocked by the change in him. "They say he walks the streets like Diogenes," reported Elizabeth. "Doom in every step." "He calls on nobody," said Matilda. "Dines nowhere. It's a lucky thing for him he loves his work so well, because that is all he has left. Even Mr. Speed is leaving. Yes, departing on the spring tide."

There was, in both women's testimonies, the unmistakable theme of moral retribution. Lincoln, by their lights, deserved every affliction that came his way. Mary envied them that certitude. When she thought back to that first of January, she had seen him laboring to do anything *but* the job he had come to do. It pained him to his core to do it, it stopped every word in his throat. Whereas the rage that rose up within her was utterly undammed. "You hick!" she had screamed at him. "You filthy, ugly *freak!*"

The words not uttered so much as vomited—from a reservoir so deep within her, she had never, until that moment, known of it. So that when Mrs. Francis came to tell her of Lincoln's condition—of how he had lain there for an hour without moving, unable to form a single sentence—Mary's first instinct was to blame herself. *Her* words had created *his* silence.

The next day, she went to Speed's store and stood for a while staring at the upstairs room where she knew Lincoln to be convalescing. So completely alone in her thoughts that it was more than a little discomfiting to see Mr. Speed stumbling out the front door. She spoke to him only so far as necessary, and thereafter, whenever she visited, she was careful to conceal herself behind the trunk of an elm.

Before too much longer, Lincoln was out and about, fulfilling his appointed rounds. Once, just once, in early February, she passed him in the street, outside Hoffman's Row. The sight nearly disabled her. But he walked on without seeing her.

. . .

AT THE CLOSE of March, Matilda came home from a supper party and, with a mysterious smile, announced that Joshua Speed had just proposed marriage to her.

"What?" cried Mary. "On the spot?"

"More or less. I was telling him what a pity it was that he was leaving us for Kentucky, and he said that he might yet consider staying on for the right person. *Is that so?* I said. *Why, yes,* he said, *but she would have to be somebody of extraordinary natural charm and vivacity* . . . and on and on, and I said, *But there must be girls of that description in your home state,* and he said, *None of your stature, Miss Edwards.*"

"Had he been drinking?" Mary inquired, a little brusquely.

"Like an Irishman after forty days in the desert. But then he drew himself up a little closer—nothing too familiar—and he spoke to me in a low tone. *I await only a word from you, and we shall be married tonight. In this very room, if you like.*"

"Why, the nerve of the man! How could he make such an overture?"

"Because he knew I wouldn't accept," said Matilda, simply. "Oh, you needn't look offended, puss. *I* certainly wasn't. Mr. Speed and I understand each other very well. In different circumstances, I think we might have been the best of friends."

Mary couldn't gauge the veracity of that claim because, to her own embarrassment, she was busy fending off this latest incursion of jealousy. Why, she wondered, had Mr. Speed never taken it upon himself to propose to *her*? Was it because she *would* have accepted?

A week later, he departed, alone, for Kentucky. As much a bachelor as when he'd arrived, seven years before.

Joshua

FORTY

———

When he was asked the hardest thing about coming back to Kentucky, Joshua's answer was simple. "The heat."

Back on the Illinois prairie, the sun had simply blazed *down*, daring you to find cover. A Louisville sun paused first to enlist everything within its reach—air, water, cloud—and from these elements, it fashioned a pall that could *not* be escaped, no matter where you hid. Even when, by all appearances, it had tumbled off the horizon, its fingers could still be felt, stifling every breeze, stopping every pore. More than once, Joshua found himself overcome in the middle of some benign chore by the sensation of his own windpipe shrinking on itself. It left him feeling absurdly convalescent, like an asthmatic down to his last teaspoon of oxygen.

And it was in these moments that he most conspicuously wished Lincoln were there.

Because Lincoln would . . . well, what? Give him a hard clap on the back? Fetch him a glass of whiskey? Laugh and remind him that nobody had forced him to come home? Some combination of all these, perhaps, but behind it all, there would have been the plain gratification of being witnessed.

Lincoln hadn't dropped entirely from view—he had been a regular correspondent since Joshua's departure—but geographical distance had introduced to their relations a new character, with each man at pains to shine. Joshua might grudgingly confess that the business of farming held no more savor for

him than it had ten years before, but he would then hasten to write of his budding real-estate partnership with James Henning—a prelude to future riches—
and he might then, in a more tentative way, speak of a budding something else
with James's sister Fanny, to whom Joshua had been very pointedly introduced.

Lincoln, on his side, was eager to show that he was working at full capacity.
His efforts to secure federal office had come to naught, but he had embraced
the law with a new zeal and had found in his new senior partner—the frowzy,
cunning Stephen Logan—the ideal mentor for honing his craft and roping
in better, or at least more lucrative, clients. In May, he had defended one of
the Trailor brothers in a locally sensational murder trial that ended, abruptly,
when the purported victim was discovered alive. A disappointed onlooker
had declared it was too damned bad to have so much trouble and no hanging. Lincoln had recounted it all to Joshua in the kind of copious detail that
suggested a mind too busy to admit of distraction. All the more surprising,
then, when at the end of that particular letter, he appended, almost as an
afterthought: *I stick to my promise to come to Louisville.*

IT COULD NOT exactly be termed a surprise. Joshua had extracted
that very promise from him shortly before leaving Springfield—had all but
insisted on it and had never—no, not once—supposed that Lincoln would
honor it.

Of course, a hardworking lawyer deserved a few weeks' holiday as much
as any man, but here was the curious part. Lincoln had not used the word
holiday, he had said only "come," a simple bit of Anglo-Saxon that left Joshua
wondering: Toward what end? Was it merely to stretch his limbs or was it to
insert his limbs, metaphorically speaking, into the coat of Kentucky—to try
it *on* and see how well it fit?

It was this latter possibility that, in the absence of any other evidence,
Joshua dwelt upon. It colored his days. He'd be reckoning up the farm's weekly
books or inspecting the harness room or trudging in his plowman's boots
through the apple orchard or watching shocks of corn lofted into the wagons,
and he would stop and ask himself: *How would it be if he were here right now?
Imagine what he would say.*

In this manner, the cord that had been severed back in Springfield began,
in Joshua's mind, to ravel itself back up. Lincoln would *come to Louisville.*

Before another year was out, he might put up a shingle—even join the burgeoning law practice of Joshua's brother. Then, having attained to that toehold, what path would be denied this former son of Kentucky? With only modest alterations in wardrobe, he might remake himself as a bluegrass legislator—run for statehouse and, from there, nab a judgeship or even, depending on climatic shifts, statewide office. With the proper guidance, he might one day cut a more commanding political figure in Jefferson County than he ever had in Sangamon.

Of course, even as Joshua conjured that future, he recognized how much of it subsisted in fantasy: Lincoln had never declared any intention of leaving Springfield. But what, after all, did his intentions signify? Who was to say he would even grasp what he most needed until it had been shown him? Until he had seen, yes, the *home* that, without knowing it, he had been seeking all his life. The columns and tapestries—the soft, summer-stunned cadences and warmly chaffing domestic atmosphere—it would all rise up before his awestruck eyes and, by its Edenic example, expose Springfield as the fractious, bitter place it had always been.

In short, it was Farmington that would have to do the wooing.

So in the weeks before his friend's arrival, Joshua devoted himself to stage direction. Mr. Lincoln would require a stout horse. His own chaise, too, if available. His guest room should be the one nearest the library, for he would almost certainly insist on reading into the night. There was no need for a cuspidor—he neither smoked nor chewed—nor a decanter, but it was imperative that his coffee be brought first thing to his room, before breakfast was even on the table: the bitterest, tarriest concoction that Sary had ever brewed. Once a week, he was to receive cans of hot water for his bath—whether or not he asked for them. His collars were to be seized the moment they came off and brought back only when they were freshly starched. The same with the boots, which were bound to be a horror, having tracked in most of the surrounding topsoil. . . .

Mrs. Speed was amused enough by this wealth of precautions to wonder if Lincoln should be regarded as visiting royalty. "Quite the opposite," answered Joshua. "He is the least assuming, least demanding person you have ever met, my dear. That's the entire point, he requires *care*. Now when it comes to conversation, I wouldn't go into politics too deeply. For the love of God, stay off the slavery question. Don't inquire after his father—the stepmother is safer ground—and if you have any pity in your heart, do not ask about his marriage prospects."

"Why ever not?"

For this was, of course, the first thing she asked any bachelor in her ken, her own son included. But when Joshua explained that Lincoln had broken off an engagement last January and had enjoyed a rather hard time of it since, Mrs. Speed gave the news all due consideration and then, with a soft nod to herself, said: "He is coming here to heal, then."

Joshua was close to laughing at the suggestion. Lincoln had already *been* healed, was stronger than ever. Strong enough to contemplate an entirely new life—or at least be nudged toward such a contemplation. But the man who arrived at Farmington in August . . . the man who, after extracting himself from the carriage, mounted the steps to the portico as though each step were twice as high as it was . . . This was not a man whom Joshua necessarily recognized.

Was it the eyes, more deeply sunken in their sockets? Or perhaps the jaw, listing a bit to one side (to favor a rotting tooth, Joshua later learned). Or the arms, seemingly out of accord with each other, or the feet dragging a fraction behind.

Or was it the general absence of tenancy? *My God*, thought Joshua. *He looks like a hollowed-out gourd. With just a few seeds rattling inside.*

Indeed, the sight of his old friend laboring under such duress was such a source of grief to him that it was left to Mrs. Speed to rush forward with outstretched hand.

"Ah, Mr. Lincoln! At last we lay eyes upon you! I hope you won't find this presumptuous, but Joshua has told us so much about you that I feel we are practically family already. Sight unseen, yes, but sight *seen* is even better. Now are you sure your journey hasn't overtaxed you? You look quite *drawn*. I can't believe you've even eaten since you left Springfield, for which I blame that dismal steamboat food. Never mind, we shall fatten you up like a prize turkey, we shall. At this very minute, I have a delicious plate of peaches and cream waiting. You won't find better peaches anywhere, I promise you!"

In this and indeed all respects, Mrs. Speed proved the best ally her son could have asked for. Over the next three weeks, she plied her guest with saddle of mutton and kidneys sauté and corned beef and blanquette of veal and flitch of bacon and larded grouse. To her inflamed maternal sensibilities, there was not enough food on Earth to pour down his gullet, and when she learned that

Lincoln's appetite had been compromised by his toothache, she dispatched him at once to her dentist. When that eminent practitioner failed to extract the tooth, she called up the full arsenal of home remedies—table salt, clove oil, peppermint tea, bourbon-soaked cotton—and when even those failed, she reminded him that peaches and cream required little in the way of chewing.

As much as she worked to revive his body, she devoted even more attention to his spirits. Her close observation had persuaded her—and Joshua was not inclined to disagree—that Lincoln needed to be rescued from Lincoln. On the excuse of showing him the grounds, she inveigled him outside for ever-longer walks. (A native Southern plant, she never wilted in the heat.) She took him in her carriage for visits to town. She demanded his presence at every parlor game: Forfeits and Lookabout and the Name Game and Squeak, Piggy, Squeak. She sent him on undemanding errands and welcomed him back like a lost child, lent him books and fitted him out with paper and ink and even graced him with a few items from her late husband's wardrobe.

And, wherever possible, she drew him more deeply into the family bosom. This, too, was a closely reasoned belief: that no man could long remain melancholy when lovely Peachy (recently married but still a flirt) teased him about his vowels or when charming Mary (that sprightliest of old maids) played for him on the pianoforte or when two-year-old granddaughter Eliza (a perfect fount of ringlets) climbed into his lap and, like a prospector, probed the ravines of his face or when, best of all, Growler the senescent bulldog followed him from room to room, trailing strands of drool. More than once, amidst the domestic commotion, Lincoln could be seen—however briefly—startling into joy, and in these intervals, the prevailing weather front seemed to realign, and a current of blood surged up beneath his skin, and his gray eyes took on a patina of soft bemusement, as if to ask: *Is this what family is like?*

It was all Joshua could do then not to put the proposal to him outright, but superstition held his tongue. The idea of Kentucky had to originate within Lincoln himself. One morning, Joshua found him walking the halls with a black leather-bound volume. Instantly recognizable, even from a distance, as Mrs. Speed's old Oxford Bible.

"I didn't steal it," Lincoln protested. "She gave it to me of her own hands. Said it was the best possible cure for the blues."

"Anybody's blues, she must have meant."

"I am largely sure she meant mine."

Joshua flushed, studied his hands. "I hope she didn't embarrass you."

"Nothing of the sort, I shall cherish it. And *her* and . . ."

He was unable to finish.

FOR THREE WEEKS, Lincoln lived the life of a Southern gentleman. His bed was turned down twice a day; fresh linen was brought in twice a week. He opened his shutters every morning and looked down upon Mrs. Speed's vegetable garden. He put his feet up on the fire irons. He rode his horse faithfully into Louisville—for the purpose, mainly, of visiting the law offices of James Speed, where Lincoln could savor both lively argument and a library that dwarfed his own by a magnitude of ten.

"If I had as many books as your brother," he told Joshua, "I might have a mind every bit as fine and subtle. Only I doubt it."

There was, to be sure, one aspect of plantation life that Lincoln never could adjust to. When he first met the Negro who'd been designated his valet, he insisted on shaking the fellow's hand and asking after his circumstances. ("And your wife? Where does she work?") Every time Cato laid out Lincoln's toilet or held up his shaving mirror, Lincoln would balk a little, and his eyes would flit from side to side, as though some wall were closing in. The smallest attentions—throwing up a sash, putting away clothes—would prompt him to half rise from where he was sitting and nod his thanks and mumble something on the order of "Not again?" or "I don't know what I'd do without you." It became such an awkward spectacle that Joshua, in a voice pitched to disguise his pique, said: "It's what Cato does, you know. It's his trade."

Lincoln was silent at first. "It would be his trade if he were paid," he said. "Or free to leave it."

Joshua did his best to shrug the remark off, but it was a strange fact that, the longer Lincoln stayed, the harder it was to avoid seeing Farmington through his peculiar lens. Of a sudden, all these—these *cogs*—that had been keeping the whole machine operating with near-perfect efficiency since Joshua was a baby now shook off their encasements and stood realized, in hard outline, against their own labor. They were beating hemp and gardening and chopping wood and churning butter and laying bricks and sawing wood and raising pigs and cattle and turkey and chickens and, inside the house, cooking and serving and polishing silver and cleaning chamber pots and carrying off laundry and carrying it back and even, upon request, dancing a jig and playing the fiddle. Some fifty-four cogs in all, retreating at day's end only to reemerge the next morning—a rite of passage so mysterious and yet so incorporated into his understanding that Joshua had never, until now, thought to anatomize it, let alone argue for it. No, that job was left to his brother James who, one night, over cigars and cognac, turned to Lincoln and, with the air of carrying on an interrupted conversation (which it almost certainly was) said: "You must agree that our Negroes are well cared for."

The gentlemen had retreated to the library, the only room in the house where Mrs. Speed could abide tobacco, and Lincoln, desiring no cigar, had wrapped his hand round some vellum-covered spine. Hearing the note of challenge in his interlocutor's tone, he turned round and said, in a guarded voice: "First, define *care*."

"They are healthy," James began, making a tabulation on his fingers. "They are well fed. They are treated fairly. They are awarded *bonuses* for exceeding their quotas. You won't find that in Louisiana."

"Very well," said Lincoln. "Tell me what happens when they don't reach their quotas. Or show themselves in the streets after sundown. What happens when the price of hemp goes down and inventory needs to be sold?"

"So you would set them all free? Is that it? Leave them to fend for themselves?"

"I think they might fend rather well if we could return them to their native land."

"Ah," said James, his voice awash in irony. "The Colonization Society rears its genteel head."

"We define care differently than you, it's true."

Lincoln was silent for a time. Then, in a different voice, he said: "You should know I was a slave myself."

"Oh, come now," Joshua interjected.

"No, I use the word with some deliberation. Until I was twenty-one, my father rented me out to whoever could afford me. I grubbed roots, I hoed corn, I split fences, I butchered hogs. In none of it did I have a speck of say. My father owned my time and wages—he owned *me*. And while I was working, *he* was out hunting and fishing and . . . doing what came naturally."

Whether through contrast or emphasis, Lincoln's eyes made a slow survey of the library, from the chandelier to the vases of orchids and coneflowers.

"If we are to speak of uncompensated labor," returned James, "then my brother and I were forced to spend nearly half of every year in the hemp fields. Father gave us no preference over the Negroes. We worked side by side with them. Swam and wrestled with them, did everything they did."

"And then you came back," said Lincoln, "to this charming house, with its fifteen rooms. And consoled yourself the whole time that your labor would *end*. And, every Fourth of July, you raised a glass to liberty—as did I, good republican. Only whose liberty were we toasting? And who, outside of our own nation, would call it by that name?"

James gave his cigar a soft twirl between his fingers. "Reasonable minds may differ," he said at length. "Perhaps we can conclude it there."

"On a subject such as this," answered Lincoln, "I should prefer not to be considered reasonable."

ONE AFTERNOON, WANTING for exercise, Lincoln and Joshua decided to take a turn round the grounds. The weather had remained markedly hot for September, and they had passed no more than two hundred feet from the veranda when, without a word to each other, they spontaneously removed their hats and coats. The heat stilled even their speech as they strolled past the salt plant, the granary. Cows, long since milked, stood sentry along the banks of the stream. A windmill made half a turn, then stopped dead.

"I believe I am melting," Lincoln announced. "And thawing. And resolving myself into a dew."

Joshua held a forearm to his brow, squinted off into the distance.

"I know just the place."

The springhouse at Farmington was built so snugly into the stream bank that the neighboring moss had, without a second thought, fanned across it and cloaked it in an emerald sward. A single door, opening at the top, gave way to a damp, grotto-like interior, in which the outlines of cider barrels and butter paddles and cream crocks were only half-visible in the shafts of sunlight. On the shelves sat buckets of fresh milk, waiting to be churned, and the walls breathed out scents of mint and cress.

Joshua shut the door after them. Peeled off his boots, rolled up his trouser legs, and plunged his bare feet into the channel of clear water that coursed across the stones. The cold met his skin like flame, rippled up the back of his legs before gathering finally as a dull ache in the root of his jaw. Lincoln by now had followed suit, and for some minutes, they sat together on the bench, the water halfway up their shins.

"Need we leave?" said Lincoln at length. "Maybe I could just tunnel my way home."

Joshua stared down through the water at his pale white feet, sole pressed against sole. "No need to speak of leaving," he said.

Lincoln made no reply. He was too mesmerized, perhaps, by the sound of the rushing stream, echoing off the walls. And it was perhaps the provocation of this silence that invited Joshua to scoop up a draft of water with his foot and send it in Lincoln's direction, catching him squarely in the left side.

Lincoln drew up in mock outrage. Kicked up an even larger draft that met Joshua in the chest.

With that, the battle was joined. For a full minute, they went at it, kicking up spume after spume—shouting louder and louder—and as the water continued to fly, the walls of the springhouse began to ring with the sound of their laughter. At last, panting, they paused to confront their mutual spectacle. Two gentlemen drenched from foot to crown, shirts sealed to skin.

"Wait," said Lincoln. "I missed a spot."

He reached out and, with his damp fingers, pressed the one dry square that remained on the back of Joshua's shirt.

"There," he said, drawing the hand away.

Joshua drew out his handkerchief for the purpose of mopping himself, but finding it every bit as damp as the rest of him, he began once more to laugh. Lincoln joined in, and it seemed to Joshua's ear that the sound they made was—by virtue of harmony, not volume—traveling far beyond the confines of the springhouse.

It could not be sustained, of course, and at last they grew quiet, save for a passing chuckle that tumbled like a loose coin from their chests. It was then that Lincoln, in a still voice, asked: "What of Miss Henning?"

FORTY-ONE

——◆——

IT WAS A strange thing. Until now, Lincoln and Fanny Henning had been, in the concourse of Joshua's mind, steamships cruising down parallel rivers. Each might now and again receive some report of the other, but they were designed by nature to keep their separate courses. Now, in the space of a second, they had swerved toward each other, and the only way Joshua could keep them from colliding altogether was to insert himself between them— an act of exertion that required just as much exertion to conceal. So it was with a sense of unusual compression that he finally asked: "What *of* Miss Henning?"

"I was only curious as to how far you'd got."

Joshua reached his hand into the water, dabbed his face. "That doesn't strike you as a rather vulgar question?"

"As I am a vulgar fellow, no."

"In that case . . ." Joshua let his fingers dance on the spring's surface. "Things have got a certain distance."

"An understanding, you mean?"

"The understanding of an understanding. Dear me," he went on, "is *this* why you've traveled such a way, Brother Abraham? To serve as my personal Eros?"

Leaning back, Lincoln dipped a finger into one of the crocks of cream and brought the finger to his mouth. "What sort is she?"

"Ah, an inquisition."

"Nothing of the kind. I am only curious."

Joshua was silent for a while, wringing out his handkerchief.

"What sort is *any* girl?" he asked.

"She might be a coquette."

"Certainly not."

"She is its opposite."

"Close to."

"Shy, perhaps."

"More quiet than shy."

"Does she sketch? Does she sing?"

"Neither that I have seen."

"Pious?"

Joshua paused. The vessels were getting closer.

"If I say yes," he replied, "you will think her dreary."

"She has wit, then?"

"Certainly."

"That's a relief. I shouldn't wish you to cleave unto a prig."

Cleave unto?

"I presume she is pretty," said Lincoln.

"One might call her so."

"Would *you*?"

"Of course."

"What is her best feature?"

"Her eyes."

"They are blue, I suppose."

"Black."

"Ah." Lincoln gave a soft nod. "'My mistress' eyes are nothing like the sun. . . .'" Then, in a voice only subtly altered, he asked: "Do you even wish to marry her?"

And here, at the very collision point of the steamboats, Joshua spirited himself back by an altogether different transport to a long-ago conversation by a railbed. With perfect recall, he heard himself uttering Lincoln's own words.

"This is what men do. Men who have reached a certain age."

Even in the crepuscular light, he could see the chevron of lines forming round his friend's eyes.

"Odd," said Lincoln, "to hear one's own idiocies circling back." He folded his arms round his chest, stretched out his legs. "Can't you make it sound a little prettier, Speed? Why not say you want to marry her because she's a dear girl?"

"That smacks of truth."

"Then what keeps you from putting some sealing wax on the whole business?"

The two men were as clothed as when they entered the springhouse, yet Joshua felt a sudden incursion of frost. The words, the cold words, that trembled on his lips were: *Why do you ask?* And it took all his sinew—all his Kentucky breeding—to declare, in the kind of nasal drawl that disguised struggle, that there were obstacles to the alliance.

"Define them," Lincoln challenged. "They cannot include your mother."

"No."

"*Her* mother?"

"She and her husband are happily oblivious in Shelbyville."

"Then who?"

"Her uncle. With whom she now resides."

"He looks down on you?"

"He merely keeps her close."

"And never suffers the two of you to have a private moment."

"Just so."

Once more, Lincoln reached back, and this time it wasn't a finger that he plunged into the cream crock but his whole hand.

"Mm," he said, licking the cream from each digit. "Let me meet this uncle."

JOHN WILLIAMSON'S DOMICILE was but a few miles from Farmington, but it had no springhouse, nor any other refuge from the heat. It took a tranquil maiden, therefore, to keep her poise in such swelter, but Miss Fanny Henning was such a maiden. Barely twenty-one, she was able to pour out orange pekoe tea for her guest as if hot liquid were exactly what the situation required. Having completed that duty, she could then cast an unhurried glance at the veranda, where the sound of two men's voices could be heard: one an insinuating tenor, the other a bass-baritone, growing ever more agitated.

"They do seem to be going at it," said Miss Henning. "Should we intervene?"

"Oh." Joshua reached for his cup and took a single polite sip. "I wouldn't presume to come between two gentlemen and their politics."

"But they might go on till dawn, at this rate. And why are they even arguing in the first place? Did you not tell me your friend was a Whig?"

"So he is."

"Then why did he pretend otherwise?"

Joshua carefully set his cup down. "Did he?"

"Why, yes. I heard him saying over supper that he was a Democrat."

"Perhaps he was just trying to get a rise out of your uncle."

"But toward what end?"

"My friend does like a good debate," answered Joshua. "It scarcely matters with whom, he can play either side."

"I suppose that is an art."

"Or a profound character flaw, you may choose."

Miss Henning gazed absently into her cup. Then she, too, set it down.

"I thought perhaps he just wanted to get Uncle John out of the room. So that we might be alone."

Joshua feigned as much astonishment as he thought tasteful. "Dear me, Miss Henning. I hope you don't think I—"

"Oh, I don't think anything. That's the problem, I am too unschooled even to be sure what is happening at any particular instant." She mustered a smile. "Yet I can't help but notice that we *are* alone."

"Yes," he said, with some feeling. "We are. . . ."

He had rehearsed the motion more than once with Lincoln, but this had not prepared him for the clumsiness that overcame him now. What should have been a graceful declension was instead a lurch, which ended with him dropping heavily to one knee and producing the tiniest of flinches in Miss Henning's black eyes.

"Mr. Speed. . . ."

Swallowing down his last misgiving, he reached glumly for her hand and bowed his head over it.

"Miss Henning . . . *Fanny*. These past few weeks have been a—a cataract to my arid soul. It seems to me that, as the poet said, you walk 'in beauty, like the night . . . And all that's best of dark and bright' . . . They—they meet in your aspect and—"

"No," she said. "You mustn't."

He drew his head back, as if she had planted her palm against it.

"Mustn't what?"

"Forgive me, I didn't mean . . . what I mean is you're not *obliged* to . . ."

"Obliged to what?"

"Well, *talk* in that way. In iambic tetrameter, or whatever it is. I don't want to know Lord Byron, Mr. Speed, I want to know *you*. I mean as *God* knows you."

He could not refrain then from glancing at the ivory crucifix that hung round her neck. *Always* round her neck, he reminded himself with a spike of irritation. He drew his hands from hers and returned himself, with as much dignity as he could, to the ottoman.

"You seem fairly certain," he said, "that God knows anything about me."

"God knows all."

"Well then, he may not entirely like what he sees."

"I shall take that as a challenge, then. To receive you as you are, from this day forth. Oh, heavens," she added. "Have I got ahead of you?"

There was something about the swell of shock in her eyes that made Joshua want to laugh. Soon enough, to his own surprise, he *was* laughing—lightly and evenly—and she was joining him.

"Well," said Joshua, "you could only have got ahead of me if I were going to use an expression like *from this day forth*."

"Were you?"

"Dear Lord, I should hope I can do better than that."

Once more, they began to laugh, and it was in the ease of their mutual release that he heard himself say, almost as if to accentuate his own joke: "But if I were to say *forever more*. . . ."

"Forever more what?"

"Well. Married."

Her lips parted by the barest fraction.

"You asked me to speak in prose," he reminded her.

"So I did."

From the veranda, the two men's voices had dwindled into a tinny drone, nearly indistinguishable from the buzzing of the fly that circled over Joshua's head. Feeling unusually damp around the collar, he rose now and took a few steps toward the empty hearth.

"I have been away from home a long time, as you know. My . . ." He glanced back at her. "My *object* in leaving Kentucky—to the extent I had one—was to make a name for myself, a life. I can see now that I was only *postponing* life. Or, rather, life's—natural progressions."

Her chin was lifted toward his, as if she were trying to catch each word in her mouth.

"It is as the Scripture says," he went on. "'When I was a child, I spake as a child . . . I—I thought as a child: but when I became'—I mean, now that I am a *man* and all . . ."

Lincoln, he thought. *Lincoln would know the verse, word for word.*

"The point is," he rushed on, "I am putting away childish things. The time has come to make a future. To have a family."

"Because that is what men do," she said, softly.

Men who have reached a certain age.

"I don't speak in categories, Miss Henning. I speak as a man who—well, hang it all, don't we get on rather well? All things considered?"

She smiled. "You get on well with my uncle. My brother, too. I don't suppose you'll be proposing to them."

It was the first hint of raillery in her. Perhaps she regretted it for at once she reached out her hand to him.

"Come," she said. "Sit."

He felt very nearly sulky as he lowered himself onto the square of sofa next to her. "I can't seem to find the right tone with you," he muttered.

"Because there is no tone you need take. You need but speak from your heart. Tell me. Are you quite resolved about this? About me?"

"As much as I'll ever be," he answered.

Conscious, as he spoke, that he was being at once truthful and deeply equivocal. And it was in that instant that he could feel Lincoln, like a joint, pressing into his rib, encouraging him to lay his hand, speculatively, on Fanny's.

"Dearest one," he said, "I shall leave my poor proposal to your tender mercies. You—you needn't say anything just yet. You may take as much time as you—"

"Yes," she said.

Then, to his surprise, she kissed him. And whispered his own Christian name in his ear, like an incantation. "Joshua. . . ."

And like that, it was done.

BY NOW, THE veranda had fallen so silent that Joshua wondered if the two men had drifted off to sleep, for the hour was late. But as he led his new fiancée outside, he found them sitting side by side in their armchairs, staring into the purpled outlines of locust trees. Companionably silent, a perfect still life, except for the trail of smoke that was curling from Mr. Williamson's pipe. It was this gentleman who first spotted the young couple and drew himself arduously to his feet and, in a voice of high comedy, declared that Illinois gentlemen surely had a queer way of seeing the world, of that there was no doubt. At which his companion rose, in mock protest, unfurled himself to his full absurd length and announced: "I come crazy all on my own. You dasn't blame Illinois."

Even as he spoke, Lincoln glanced at Joshua's hand, which rested proprietorially on Fanny's forearm. No further evidence was needed.

"Well now," said Lincoln.

FORTY-TWO

———

FANNY HAD EXTRACTED one condition from Joshua before sending him off. Until further notice, he was to keep their betrothal a secret.

Her heart, she assured him, was indisputably his, but she wished to smooth the way with her parents, the better to forestall any objections down the road. She was, of course, perfectly confident that her family would assent. Who could boast better pedigree than Joshua Speed of Farmington? Who cut a finer figure or boasted a better head for business? Who came more highly recommended by Fanny's own brother? If all went to plan, why . . .

"We might be married next spring," she whispered.

ON THE SURREY ride back to Farmington, Lincoln delivered his verdict in the most unruffled of voices.

"She's a peach of a girl. You've chosen well."

"Mm." Joshua tilted his face toward the window. "I wish we could say the same for *her*. Promise me you won't hold it against her if she backs out."

"As if that were any danger."

They were silent for a while.

"Of course," said Lincoln, "I have my own selfish reasons for rejoicing."

"Which are?"

"I won't have to worry about you anymore. I may go home in good conscience."

And because Joshua by now had fallen into the surrey's cadence—easy, unruffled—and because this rhythm was not so different from the perambulations he and Lincoln used to take through Springfield, the word *home* didn't quite register as it should. They were heading back to the dormitory over Bell & Company, weren't they? Just as they always had? But the coach gave a quick upward heave, and the word was dislodged from its original context.

"Home," he repeated.

"Just in time, too. My three weeks are nearly up. Well, don't look at me like that, I can't keep imposing on you and your good family indefinitely."

Joshua began to speak, then stopped.

"Everyone is the soul of kindness," Lincoln went on, "but I do have a fat caseload waiting for me. And what with the Tremont courts opening on the sixteenth. Then Pontiac on the fourth, Urbana on the eleventh. . . ."

And Decatur, thought Joshua. *And Shelby. Taylorville. Petersburg*. He could recite the whole circuit, by heart, in the manner of a child reciting Latin.

"But you don't understand," he protested. "There are people I want you to meet. People of *influence*. Judge Rogers and Senator Garland. Colonel Taylor's wife, the editor of the *Daily Courier*. . . ." He could hear the first querulous notes entering his voice. "For God's sake, Lincoln, you haven't been to the Oakland Race Course. You haven't set *foot* in the courthouse, which is where you'd find any lawyer of consequence. . . ."

"Oh," said Lincoln, easily, "I suspect Kentucky was glad enough to be rid of me twenty-five years ago. I haven't done anything that would change its mind."

Joshua peered at him through the coach's shadows. "You mean you'll just leave."

"Well, I'll say good*bye* first. I'm not that much of a savage."

"So it's to be like that."

"Like what?"

Joshua said nothing, for his mind was even now limning the vacancy. Lincoln would no more be seated on the far side of the dining table. He would no more ride his horse into town or let his huge hands rove through the library or stroll past the hemp house or listen to Eliza gabble or applaud Mary's nocturnes or argue out some abstruse point of law with James or scratch behind Growler's ears as the dog lay stretched round his feet. From henceforth, there would be only the space where Lincoln used to be.

And in Joshua's mind, that space began to expand and deepen until it became a vast nullity, blanketing everything round him until it seemed the night itself had been swallowed up by it.

JOSHUA WAS THE first one out of the coach, and by the time his friend had extricated himself, he was already charging up Farmington's marble steps with some partly formed idea of traveling straight to his room. But resolve failed him, and he found himself, to his own surprise, seated halfway up the steps, with Lincoln peering down at him.

"Speed?"

"Do you think . . ." He smiled sheepishly. "Would you mind fetching me a brandy? It's on the sideboard. . . ."

The rest of Farmington slumbered. Fields, orchard, barns, outbuildings. Even the flies and mosquitoes had largely retired. But out in the bluing shadows, the stream was still warbling over its stones, and the sycamores were shaking off their accumulated dust, and the earth was expelling the day's heat in coils of mist.

Behind him now, he heard Lincoln's ponderous feet descending the steps. Watched that familiar hand, setting the tumbler alongside him. Joshua drained it in a single swallow.

"I would apologize," said Lincoln. "I sincerely would, if I—"

"There's no need. You said three weeks."

With a nettled motion of his shoulders, Joshua rose now. Tottered back down the steps and stood there with his back to Lincoln, staring in the direction of the pond.

"It's just my twisty old brain," he said. "It gets things wrong sometimes. You see, I thought perhaps you might consent to stay on."

And because he couldn't look at the other man's face, he took another step into the night. But Lincoln's voice found him where he was.

"Dear me, Speed." He paused. "I mean, you can't honestly see *that*, can you? Me, a Louisville gentleman? Riding about in carriages and bowing low to the ladies? Why, they'd laugh me off the streets for the impostor I was."

Here was the main trouble: He was right. A Lincoln who actually *belonged* here would cease to be Lincoln. A self-evident proposition, or so it should have been.

"May I ask you something, Speed?"

Dumbly, Joshua nodded.

"Why did you wish me to stay?"

"Mm." He emitted a single chuckle. "Company, probably." He dug the toe of his boot into the gravel. "I know it sounds odd, living in such a crowded house as this, but one gets lonely sometimes. All the *more* so, really, for—for being right in the heart of things."

Lincoln was quiet for a time. Then, in a gentle voice, he said: "You have your Fanny now."

"Yes."

"And having finally met her and—seeing how kind she is—how devoted— well, I know she'll be ever at your side, Speed. For the whole duration. I tell you, if I were the envying sort . . ."

Joshua's boot sketched a slow ellipse in the gravel.

"And what of *you*, Brother Abraham? Who will remain at *your* side, I wonder? For the whole duration?"

"Ohh," began Lincoln, and then subsided into silence.

Joshua lifted his face to the sky, watched the moon shake off its cheese-cloth of cloud. He listened to the far-off barking of a vixen, with its trailing moan. Then he turned slowly round.

"You should speak to Mary," he said.

"Come now, Speed. That bridge has been *burnt*, well and truly."

"No. She came to see you. While you were ill. More than once she came."

Lincoln frowned softly. "Is that so?"

"She didn't want anybody to know. One morning, I actually caught her hiding behind a tree."

"Did she see you?"

"She was too busy staring up at your window."

"Sending curses my way, I don't doubt."

Joshua shook his head. "If you must know, I believe she has regrets."

"So do I." One corner of Lincoln's mouth turned up. "I'm not sure regret is the best foundation for a marriage."

"Men and women have married for worse."

Joshua planted a foot on the bottommost step.

"Just speak to her, won't you? Or at least—hold yourself *open* to such a prospect. Then perhaps I might stop worrying about *you*."

Lincoln looked at him for a time, then bowed his head an inch.

"Supposing I agree," he said. "Will you do something for me in return?"

"Of course."

"Will you write me after your wedding? I mean the very next morning. . . ."

Joshua felt his cheeks color, point by point. "If you like," he said, forcing out a light laugh. "I sincerely doubt it will be engrossing. . . ."

"I'll be engrossed."

Joshua nodded. Then he traveled the rest of the way to where Lincoln was and lowered himself onto the step until their shoulders were lightly touching. The effect was both tonic and bittersweet, for it was in just this manner that the two men used to enter Springfield parlors together. Shoulder to shoulder, like comrades walking into enemy gunfire. And for the first time in Joshua's conscious mind, the thought arose: What had they been so afraid of? What had they needed to protect each other from? And who would protect them from it now?

As if divining the tenor of his thoughts, Lincoln reached round him and gripped him by the shoulder. Held it for several seconds and then released.

"The Lincoln-Speed local," he said softly. "Remember?"

FORTY-THREE

LINCOLN DEPARTED AT noon on September the seventh, waving shyly from the hurricane deck of a steamboat bound for St. Louis.

October witnessed the formal announcement of Mr. Joshua Speed's engagement to Miss Fanny Henning. Custom would have dictated a wedding at the bride's family home, but it was the bride's dearly held wish to be married in the great hall at Farmington, and Mrs. Speed was glad to oblige. "My only hope," she told her future daughter-in-law, "is that you will be as happy in your union as I was with Joshua's father. Though I must warn you," she added, with a sly backward glance at her son, "these men take getting *used* to."

Fanny returned to Shelbyville to prepare her gown and trousseau, while Joshua spent the winter steadfastly refusing to prepare. To every inquiry about the upcoming ceremony, he returned the most indolent of shrugs. The only detail he insisted upon was that there be no lilies or gladioluses. "They remind me of funerals," he told his mother.

Perhaps by way of vengeance, those very flowers returned to him, night after night, in the conveyance of his old dream. Again and again, Joshua stood in that strange parlor, with the chairs in clean rows and the supper in the next room. A *wedding*, he told himself. Only everybody was dressed in the most somber of hues, and the bride herself was shrouded in black. As Joshua traveled down the aisle, the guests' heads wheeled his way, and as if on cue, the bride turned toward him, too, and began, with infinite care, to lift her veil. The news smote him then with the force of a lance. This was *his* wedding. His and no one else's.

In the old days, he could have reassured himself upon waking that he was in the clear. But the wedding date had been set for February the fifteenth, and the old dream now had the uncomfortable demeanor of prophesy. Something dreadful, something unspeakable, was inching its way toward him, and he had no more power over it than over the course of the moon.

A confidant might have helped him ride out his fears, but his sisters had long since grown impatient with his hesitations, and his mother would have responded with another Oxford Bible, and his brother would have replaced Christian consolation with secular proverb. "A bird never flew on one wing, Josh. A door must be either shut or open." No, if he wanted consolation, he must find it abroad, and it was in a spirit of deliverance that he now wrote Lincoln. Filled page upon page with his disquiet, all of it couched (just as Lincoln had once couched his qualms about Mary) in the abstract and conditional.

Suppose, for argument, that a man has reasoned his way into a situation—and can't reason himself out again. Can he count on love maturing over time? What if said love never materializes? May he in good conscience inflict such an uncertainty on somebody who manifestly does not deserve it?

Joshua grasped how transparent this third-person pose was, but he could find no better way to outline the dimensions of the trap that had closed round him. Lincoln, on his side, replied like the lawyer he was, rebutting each qualm.

You say you reasoned yourself into it. What do you mean by that? Was it not that you found yourself unable to reason yourself out of it? Whether she was moral, amiable, sensible, or even of good character, you did not, nor could not then know; except perhaps you might infer the last from the company you found her in. All you then did or could know of her, was her personal appearance and deportment; and these, if they impress at all, impress the heart and not the head. Say candidly, were not those heavenly black eyes, the whole basis of all your easily reasoning on the subject?

But in successive letters, Lincoln struck a different, more collegial note.

I tell you, Speed, our forebodings, for which you and I are rather peculiar, are all the worst sort of nonsense. . . . I have no doubt that it is the peculiar misfortune of both you and me, to dream dreams of Elysium far exceeding all that anything earthly can realize.

In the end, the only consolation that Lincoln seemed able to offer was the simple fact of their suffering—and the fact of their suffering *together*. In these moments, their separation felt as fresh as yesterday, and thoughts of Fanny were invariably turned to thoughts of Lincoln. And on those evenings when the pall-shrouded bride once more materialized, it was Lincoln's words, repeated like a child's verse, that lulled him back to safety:

You know my desire to befriend you is everlasting. . . .
That I will never cease . . .
While I know how to do anything.

In the second week of January, Joshua received a letter from another source: Fanny's mother.

Four pages, in Mrs. Henning's uncommonly elegant and wide-ranging hand, to inform him that Fanny had taken ill. A "slight chill" had "gripped a little hard." No more symptoms were forthcoming, and Mrs. Henning concluded by saying that she and Fanny would be seeking a temporary change of climate, the better to hasten her daughter's recovery.

Where they were going, how long they would stay, the very nature of the illness itself—all these details were passed over in silence. And indeed, the very serenity of the letter's tone—coupled with the awkward reality that Fanny herself was not writing—seemed calculated to excite Joshua's worst fears. Obsessively, he began to review the hours he had most recently spent in her company. Had she coughed in excess? Had she declined dessert or begged leave to retire early?

The next day, another letter arrived from Mrs. Henning.

> Fanny has asked me to tell you—and your dear mother—that she will notwithstanding be the blooming (and blushing) bride of your dreams come February. Dare you disbelieve? I know my daughter well enough—as one day, forsooth, shall be your privilege—as to believe her will and determination fully the match of any ill humors.

Never once did Mrs. Henning's hand waver, but it was the very determination of that charming cursive that subverted its own message. Something was wrong. Fanny Henning was desperately ill. She had been stricken with consumption or malaria or yellow fever. She would die before the spring was out, and it would be Joshua's fault. More than that, his *crime*, for was this not the very enactment of his dream? In all its inescapable logic? He would be marrying a dead girl. Dead, yes, at the very cusp of womanhood. Betrothed to—betrayed by—a man who did not love her or else did not love her enough, and it was *this* deficit, this terminal insufficiency that was now draining the life from her.

Lincoln advised him to banish his fears by staying busy, but as the days passed with no word—not even a single dashed-off sentence—Joshua's fears began to twine round him like vines. And somewhere at the back of the fear was an insidious voice, saying: *You will be free again. Free, with a lifetime indemnity against marriage. They can say whatever they want about you, but they can't say you didn't try. . . .*

One afternoon in the tail end of January, he rode back from a business trip in Louisville and found two women sitting in the parlor. One of them was his mother, who, at sight of him, began to trill like a flute.

"Oh, it's true! She couldn't stay away, dear boy! She positively had to see you!"

He had no earthly notion what his mother was saying. He knew only that the other woman was rising even now to greet him. Pausing just once to steady herself on the chair's arm before turning, by slow degrees, in his direction.

Fanny.

Alive, yes, recognizably herself . . . but, all the same, shockingly pale. Her arms diminished, her black eyes vast beyond measure. He came toward her in a slow wondering stride, his mind aflame with all the doctors who had had their way with her. All the bleedings and purgings and ice baths and heat baths and heaven knew what else. She had endured them all, she had been blistered and hammered, all so that she might come back to him—to *them*. And to his bedazzled eyes, her gallantry was like the hard, flat disklike haloes of medieval art—a testament not to any innate effulgence but to some fiercely sustained loss. Loss that was softened in this case only by the suspicion or the hope that, in the unlikely person of Joshua Speed, she had found sanctuary.

Under such a proposition, how could he fail her? For it struck him now with an unassailable force that in her sanctuary lay his.

All these thoughts, all these emotions danced on the head of a single second. In the next second, Joshua wrapped his arms round her. "Dearest one," he said.

MRS. SPEED WAS delighted to have another convalescent at Farmington. When she wasn't trundling into Fanny's room with pots of chamomile tisane or bottles of quinine-and-whiskey tonic, she was commanding Mary to wrench open the windows or bidding Peachy to scatter drops of eucalyptus oil or hiring little Eliza to dance round Fanny's bed, like an elfin princess, strewing timothy grass. Under these ministrations and the influx of sunlight from her southern exposure, Fanny grew steadily stronger.

At last the wedding day came round. And while her ivory gown, handmade in New Orleans, could not quite conceal the thinness of her arms, it did reveal against all odds the bloom that had somehow crept back into her cheeks. Mrs. Henning, it seemed, had foretold the truth. "That's what love *does*," she whispered to Joshua just before the ceremony.

THE FARMHOUSE AT Pond Settlement was still under construction, so the newly married couple spent their wedding night at Farmington.

Mrs. Speed graciously granted them the use of her own bedroom—the one she had shared with her late husband, John—and discreetly retired to a guest room at the back of the house. At the stroke of nine, Fanny, with little preamble, betook herself upstairs. Joshua spent another half hour in the library, alone, smoking a cigar and drinking brandy in roughly equal installments. Then he followed.

He found her sitting by the fire in a high-necked cotton nightgown. Not knowing exactly how things stood, he retreated behind a screen and began to disrobe. Frock coat, braces, waistcoat, pants, shirt. Finally, he removed his drawers, reaching in the same instant for the nightshirt that his mother had left on the bedpost. Then, listing a little from the brandy, he advanced toward Fanny.

The fire by now had died to a kind of fake crackle. "But you're shivering," he said.

"I'm not ill," she answered.

"No. . . ."

"I swear to you I'm not."

"Dearest, I never presumed . . ." Though, of course, that had been his first thought.

"I have never felt so well," she insisted. "Or so blessed."

"I am pleased to hear it."

"Won't you sit?" she said, pointing to the chair next to hers.

He did as she asked, weirdly conscious of his own white, bared legs in the firelight. Conscious, too, of her hair, unpinned for the first time, and her uncorseted form, pressed against the cotton fabric of her dressing-wrapper. How many nights, he wondered, had his mother and father sat just like this?

"Would you be cross with me," said Fanny, "if I told you I was a little wanting in courage just now?"

He gave her a sidelong glance, then looked away. "I would say that was entirely normal. And to be expected."

"I felt sure you *would* say that."

"Yes?"

"You see, I knew—from the first look at you—you would never be the sort to force a girl."

For some seconds, he struggled to decide if this was praise.

"Of course not," he murmured. "No gentleman would."

She nodded, almost to herself. Then, in a brighter voice, she said: "Might we play a game?"

"Now?"

"Oh, it's awfully simple. All you have to do is—well, pretend that I am *you.*"

"Pretend. . . ."

"Yes, just for a little while."

"If you like."

"Very well. I being *Joshua*—oh," she said, breaking off and looking desolate. "I can't affect your voice at all. . . ."

"Say it in your own register, then."

"You're right, that's better. I being Joshua, I say to you, *Fanny . . . Come now, you little goose, you needn't tremble. You and I may love each other any way we like. Why, we might sit together all this night—just as we are—and that would still be love, would it not? Our hearts one. Our flesh, too, for that matter. Never mind what the world thinks.*" She stared down at her hands, knotted together. "*And tomorrow, you silly goose, you might well feel differently. Entirely differently. Every day being a new day, you see.*" Her teeth closed round her lower lip. Then, like one waking from a daydream, she said: "Oh! It's your turn."

He opened his mouth a fraction, but no words sounded.

"Come now," she said. "It goes both ways, it *must*. You being *Fanny*, you say . . ."

And when still he forbore to speak, she whispered: "In your own register."

"I say . . ." Something caught at the back of his throat. "I say thank you for your understanding. . . ." He paused again. "Thank you for your patience." One last breath, exhaled like cigar smoke. "And your goodness."

All was silent for a long while, except for the last coughs of the fire.

"There!" said Fanny. "Wasn't that a sweet little game?"

He smiled, faintly, and nodded.

"And I daresay tomorrow," she added, "I *shall* feel differently."

Slowly, he eased himself out of his chair and knelt before her. He gazed into her face, and then he kissed her. Once, twice on the forehead.

"Tomorrow," he said, "I shall still love you."

Fanny took his hands, raised them to her lips. Her black eyes were shining. "We have chosen well, have we not? If nothing else, we have done that."

THEY LAY IN bed together until morning, still in their nightclothes. When he awoke, he found that his arm had grown numb from supporting the weight of her head, so he used his other arm to extract it. Then he crept into the next room and sat down at his secretary. Drew out a sheet of paper and uncapped the bottle of black ink. Held the pen over the paper, then began to write.

Dear Lincoln,
    All is well. . . .

February 25, 1842
Dear Speed:
    Yours of the 16th announcing that Miss Fanny and you "are no more twain, but one flesh" reached me this morning. I have no way of telling how much happiness I wish you both; tho' I believe you both can conceive it. I feel somewhat jealous of both of you now; you will be so exclusively concerned for one another, that I shall be forgotten entirely. My acquaintance with Miss Fanny (I call her thus, lest you should think I am speaking of your mother) was too short for me to reasonably hope to long be remembered by her; and still, I am sure, I shall not forget her soon. Try if you can not remind her of that debt she owes me; and be sure you do not interfere to prevent her paying it.
    I regret to learn that you have resolved to not return to Illinois. I shall be very lonesome without you. How miserably things seem to be arranged in this world. If we have no friends, we have no pleasure; and if we have them, we are sure to lose them, and be doubly pained by the loss. I did hope she and you would make your home here; but I own I have no right to insist. You owe obligations to her, ten thousand times more sacred than any you can owe to others; and, in that light, let them be respected and observed. It is natural that she should desire to

remain with her relatives and friends. As to friends, however, *she* could not need them any where; she would have them in abundance here.

Give my kind remembrance to Mr. Williamson and his family, particularly Miss Elizabeth—also to your Mother, brothers, and sisters. Ask little Eliza Davis if she will ride to town with me if I come there again.

And, finally, give Fanny a double reciprocation of all the love she sent me. Write me often, and believe me

Yours forever

LINCOLN

Mary

FORTY-FOUR

In February of '42, the Northern Cross Railroad did something that nobody had been sure it would: It reached Springfield.

And brought with it, in that maiden voyage, all the arguments that had surrounded it from its birth. Its advocates attributed to it such medicinal effects as circulation boosting, digestion enhancement, and nerve tranquilization; its opponents believed it would tear down the already trembling citadel of civilization. Matilda Edwards felt no need to subscribe to either side. She was merely bored (again) and wanted out for a day.

"Mary," she said, "let us make a pleasure party. Two or three of our best girlfriends. And a boy or two for spice. Not a soul over twenty-five, do you hear me? We shall pack a picnic basket and champagne bottles, and if any of the boys get too forward, we shall pitch them out at the next crossing. Yes, leave them for the cows!"

For her part, Mary had no competing invitations, and with her migraines in temporary abeyance, some still-youthful cockle in her heart warmed to the idea of a journey. For things *happened* on journeys, did they not? And if there was anything that the manicured surface of her life needed, it was that.

On the third Saturday of March, she and Matilda and the rest of their party rose with the dawn to catch the Wabasher. It came trundling in with a single fearsome whistle—like the shriek of a Hydra, thought Mary, just as it was losing all its heads. She was the only member of the group who had ridden on a railway; for the others, their enthusiasm managed to survive the screeching of the iron wheels, the plumes of ash and cinder, and the herky-jerky rhythm that kept hurling them against each other, like fish in a creel. Indeed, the greater their discomfort, the more they rejoiced. "Can you believe it?" they would say, eyes rounding. "Did you ever?" They were greeting the future head on, shaking it by its metallic hand, and the experience seemed to liberate them from present-day mores. Jim Ford, that corn-eating Methodist, made jokes about seducing farmers' daughters in the rear compartment, while Presco Wright, as authoritative as Homer, filled their minds with images of snakeheads, the strap rails that, upon coming unspiked, curled up and drove themselves through the train's floorboards.

"A friend of mine was riding this very stretch of track," declared Presco, "when a snakehead came up and struck him right under the chin. Pushed into his brain and lifted him straight *up*. . . ."

"Stop!" squealed Rachael Edds.

"Quivering and *gushing*. . . ."

"You are a beast! I shall never believe another word you say!"

"Personally," said Matilda, "I'm all for snakeheads. So long as I may designate the victims."

"You don't mean that," protested Julia Jayne. A mere sixteen, she was drinking her first champagne ever and was moved to say, more than once, that it was the most delightful concoction ever created.

"Isn't it?" said Rachael Edds, only slightly more experienced. "It makes me feel *pretty*."

At advertised speeds, their one-hundred-and-six-mile round-trip should have taken no more than seven hours, but between the fueling and watering stations, their progress was constantly halted. At one stop, the cry went up for male passengers to help pile wood into the tender. Just outside Jacksonville, the train had to pause for a half hour altogether while the engineers plugged a yard-long gap in the track. (Suspicion fell on local farmers, who were fond of making off with the rails for sled runners.) By the time the Wabasher crawled toward its terminus in Meredosia, stagecoaches were dashing past it in clouds of dust, and a man could jump out and precede it all the way into town without once having to hurry his gait.

They stopped for another half hour, then laboriously circled round and made the journey back. By now, novelty had ceased. The windows were dreary and opaque, the squeal of the wheels maddening, the infernal rocking of the car no longer sport but oppression. Jim Ford subsided into white-faced nausea. Julia Jayne, experiencing for the first time champagne's aftereffects, laid her head on Rachael's shoulder, and moaned softly in her ear. Matilda fell to drowsing, as much from ennui as fatigue, her lovely yellow-fringed head rocking back and forth like a tulip.

How puppyish they looked—and how elderly Mary felt in the act of looking upon them. At twenty-four, she had just gotten in under Matilda's age bar. Before too much longer (and there were days she could contemplate this dispassionately), she would graduate to the spinsterhood that life had apparently marked out for her. With flat appraising eyes, she peeled off a glove and stared down at her hand. Imagined each square of that fair and plumped skin blotching and fissuring with age.

Dear, dear hand.

Once more, the carriage took a lurch forward. Mary, caught off balance, reached for the underside of her seat while her eyes swept down the opposite row of seats. There, at the far end of the car, sat a straight and solitary figure, his extreme length accentuated by the black beaver hat that sat at a slightly raked angle on his head.

Lincoln.

HAD HE CLIMBED on in Meredosia? Or had he engaged in the strictly forbidden practice of crossing over between cars? Or was he perhaps even a phantom, conjured by her starved imagination? For there *was* something supernatural in his being here in this moment, undetected by any other. He gave no sign of having seen her, but the thought that he still *might*—and worse, behold her in such a solitary condition—was, of a sudden, more than she could bear. On impulse, she reached over and gave a sharp tug on Matilda's sleeve.

"Let us sing something," she whispered.

"Sing?" Matilda's drowsiness was replaced with horror. "What evil spirit has seized you?"

"It will pass the time. Come now," she said, warming to it. "Julia and Rachael! Mr. Ford! Mr. Wright! Let us make a joyful noise."

For varying reasons, and with varying shades of regret, her companions declined, so it was left to Mary to lead the way. She reached for the first song that came to mind, and through the shuddering rail car her finishing-school treble now forged its quavering path.

> As I was a-goin'
> On down the road
> With a tired team
> And a heavy load

A spark of recognition flashed from Julia's eyes. She lifted her throbbing head and began to stake out a vocal line exactly a third above Mary's. Mutually buoyed, they sailed through the second verse, accelerating as they went.

> I cracked my whip
> And the leader sprung
> I says day-day
> To the wagon tongue

By now, Jim Ford was doing the one thing he was capable of—tapping a beat on the carriage floor. Presco Wright was plunking out an imaginary banjo, and Rachael was tentatively layering in an alto harmony, and even Matilda consented to bob her head in rhythm. Together, they mounted toward the refrain.

> Turkey in the straw
> Turkey in the hay
> Turkey in the straw
> Turkey in the hay

All hesitation was banished now. It was as if the steam that propelled the Wabasher were now churning inside them. Churning in Mary, most of all, who waved her hands in time and beamed like a small sun, coaxing them on.

> Roll 'em up and twist 'em up
> A high tuck a-haw
> And hit 'em up a tune called
> Turkey in the Straw

Here, having reached their climax, they drew a collective breath as if to carry on—only nobody knew the second verse. They dangled there, in an uneasy suspension, waiting for somebody to guide them. Then, as the absurdity of their situation dawned upon them, they exploded into laughter. A sound that carried with it all the relief of passing an unexpected test and declining to be tested further.

There was a scattered applause and a murmured approval from the other passengers, and there was this additional benefit: The goodwill they had inspired (without meaning to) served to rouse their own spirits. Once more, they began to chivvy each other. Once more, Presco called up visions of snake-heads. Once more, Rachael Edds's happy squeals rang through the air. Once more, Matilda yawned. It had all gone better than Mary could have expected, and *still* she waited—five minutes, ten minutes—before casting a triumphant look toward the corner of the car.

Lincoln was gone.

THAT SUMMER, MATILDA discovered the surest way to end her malaise. She found a man.

To the surprise of all and to the dismay of many, he was not one of the hardy young swains who had crowded round her on parquet floors for the past two years but a Presbyterian classics tutor from Pennsylvania.

During his span on Earth, Newton Strong had entertained precisely two whims. The first was to quit his brother's law practice and come west to Alton. The second (and almost surely the final) was to get elected to the Illinois state legislature—for the sole reason, it was said, of following the lovely Matilda to Springfield. He was at this time thirty-two, so it was a matter of some mystery why Matilda would suffer his rather creaky wagon to be hitched to her star. Mr. Strong was, to be sure, agreeable, witty, civilized, intelligent—but in the manner of a natural history professor, not a lover.

"Why this one?" Mary was moved to ask.

The blue of Matilda's eyes was never so warm as when she said, "He smells of money. The future kind."

This was as coarse as she had ever allowed herself to be, and it signified something of a sea change in the two women's relations. Mary was no longer an amusing project—she had failed to pay out—and Matilda was now transferring all her powers of manipulation to Newton Strong. The mysterious withholdings, the punishing silences . . . They never exactly moved Mr. Strong to action, but they piqued his interest in ways that were not entirely wholesome. By summer's end, he and Matilda were no closer to being engaged than when they began, but they were near-permanent combatants, locked in a contest that might eat up the better part of their lives. It need hardly be added that they were happy.

Mercy Levering was back in town but with this crucial difference: She was now Mercy *Conkling*, with all the diminution that Mary had forecast. Too busy for gambols, too proper for larks. Mary gave up her old friend in the exact moment she heard her say, in an eerie echo of Elizabeth Edwards: "It wouldn't be proper *ton*."

All in all, confidants had grown rather thin on the ground. (And what, pray, would she confide?) Into this vacuum stepped—or, rather, tiptoed—Julia Jayne, the pious rich girl who now longed for a little low-class impiety without exactly knowing she longed for it and who had persuaded herself that Mary Todd was just the person to pattern herself upon. Day after day, Julia paid call at the Edwards mansion, seeking advice on everything from costume to dance steps to diet. Her questions were so numerous that they formed a kind of extended soliloquy, into which Mary was scarcely able to insert any reply.

"Do you think I look well in salmon? I'd like something more brilliant, but I don't know that I have the right complexion. And I do think the sash might be a little large for my figure. Do you ever have one opinion in the morning and a completely opposed one in the afternoon? You do? That's a comfort. But tell me, are my shoes too noisy? All the way here, I could hear myself going squeak like a rusty hinge. Oh, and Mr. Trumbull saw me along the way, and I was so embarrassed by the squeaking that I quite forgot to nod, which meant he couldn't nod himself, and it was all so deuced awkward, and

I don't know how to make it right. Should I write him, do you think? No, what a silly idea!"

It was the same feeling that had come over Mary in the railway car: Somehow, without her consent, she had been deputized as a maiden aunt. Perhaps she ought to have taken offense, but the larger part of her was simply grateful that somebody wanted her advice. Until now, her main claim to local fame had been getting thrown over by a man, and that story had taken on so many layers of embroidery that many townspeople believed Lincoln had actually stood her up at the altar—left her wailing there, yes, in her lace gown.

That is the closest I shall ever come to actual matrimony, she thought. *In myth.*

ONE AFTERNOON IN early August, Mrs. Francis sent her a note. *Dear Mary: It is so tiresome to be an ancient woman with nobody to talk to. Do you think you might stop by tomorrow at three?*

In truth, Mary had rather been avoiding her old friend, mainly because of the memories she stirred up. But the desire to be free of her *new* friend—for just one day—overrode Mary's reservations, and she showed up promptly the next afternoon. Mrs. Francis was already in the parlor, pouring tea from her new samovar. The two women made trifling conversation, but Mary's attention kept wandering to the old coordinates. The carpet, with the faded tea roses. The peacock feathers over the grate. The dusty waterscapes and the settee where she and Lincoln had spent all those private hours. The faintly echoing mewling of the cat. All of it now a museum that nobody would ever visit.

There came a knocking on the parlor door. "Come in," called Mrs. Francis.

In the doorway stood Lincoln.

He was just as surprised to see Mary as she to see him. He stood, as if impaled, on the room's precipice, and it was Mrs. Francis who, in a quiet but resolute manner, ushered him in and then, just before departing, gave them each a caressing look.

"Be friends again," she said. "That is all that I ask."

FORTY-FIVE

—————

BE FRIENDS AGAIN. A much easier thing to bring off in private than in public. For even a year and a half after their rupture, no Springfield hostess with any sense would have presumed to invite both Mary and Lincoln to the same function. It was left to Mrs. Francis to inveigle the two of them to her salon and to make the ceremonial gesture of bringing them together in full view of local citizenry.

"Why, Mary!" she cooed, affixing a tight grip to her friend's arm. "I believe you had a question for Mr. Lincoln."

Mary had no such question and stood gazing up rather fearfully into the ridges of Lincoln's face. Undeterred, Mrs. Francis said, in a voice loud enough to carry across the room: "Oh, my dear, you raise *such* a good point! And who better suited to address it than our mutual friend here? Now, if you'll excuse me, I have some punch to fortify."

She was gone in a trice. And with her absence, it seemed to Mary that the temperature in the room climbed by twenty degrees. The *heat* of every eye, male and female, interrogating, *anatomizing.* . . .

"Say something," said Mary.

"I will if you will."

The silence built up round them now like a cliff face.

"Your *friend*," she said. And when he gave her a blank look, she quickly added: "Mr. Speed."

He was silent some more. Then, with a ghost of his old twinkle: "You mean Benedick the married man."

"Just so," she answered, grateful for the allusion. "I have heard news of his wedding, and I confess I found it hard to imagine."

"So did he."

"The dashing Joshua Speed," she went on, a little recklessly. "In *harness*. I hope he is happy at least?"

"Most sincerely so. I have sounded him at great length on the subject."

Lincoln reared his shoulders back a fraction and briefly canvassed the ceiling.

"I did hope they might make their home here, but his life is there now. Not here."

"All the same," she ventured, "you must find it. . . ."

"Yes?"

"Well, *lonesome*. Without him."

The observation caught him off guard. He regarded her more closely.

"I admit," he said, "that I have grieved, in my way. But then, I suppose grief is one of life's natural hazards."

"Oh, it is more than that, surely, it is a direct *consequence* of life. It is the price we pay for living, for . . ." She had rushed ahead of herself. "For loving," she added, in a milder tone.

He looked at her. "But is it worth the price?"

MRS. FRANCIS MUST have continued her efforts behind the scenes because, three nights later, the two of them were asked to fill out a supper party at the Henrys', and when the meal ended, Mrs. Henry, in a voice that admitted nothing out of the usual, asked if Lincoln mightn't escort Miss Todd into the drawing room.

The entertainment that night was a pianoforte concert from nine-year-old Margaret Henry, who pounded through Beethoven and Gluck quite as if they were the same composer. Mrs. Henry, close to term with her third child, then put up a remonstrating hand and entreated her guests to talk amongst themselves while she escorted her young prodigy to bed. In this way, Lincoln and Mary found themselves once more standing by a fire, wondering a little at the mechanics that had brought them there.

"Swine," she said at last.

"You refer to me?"

"I do! You never told me you were giving up your seat in the statehouse."

The straight line of his mouth lifted a fraction. "It's true," he allowed. "The whole General Assembly is in deep mourning. Sackcloth, ashes. . . ."

"Nor have you told me your reasons."

"Oh, the people of Illinois have had to put up with me for eight long years. Surely, that's punishment enough. Besides, I like my civilian life."

"Liar."

A pearl of light welled up in his gray eyes. "Impugn a feller's integrity," he said, "and bear the consequences."

"Then let the fight be joined. Cousin John is planning to step down from Congress next year. As if you didn't know."

Painstakingly, Lincoln scraped a dollop of wax from the mantel, tossed it into the empty hearth.

"For argument's sake," he said, "suppose one were thinking of running for the aforementioned seat. What considerations might one keep in mind?"

"Speaking in the *abstract*, you mean. . . ."

"Of course."

"Then one would first look to the competition within the Whig party. There is my *other* cousin, Mr. Hardin, who has looks and pedigree. There is Mr. Baker, who has fire and oratorical gifts. Of the *two*," she said, "one might be more legitimately threatened by Mr. Baker, for he is strongest in Sangamon County, and if one can't carry Sangamon, one can't carry the Seventh District."

"Go on."

"From there, one would naturally shore up one's existing base in Menard County, while seizing every opportunity to shine in the Whig journals. A speaking tour, perhaps, on the subject of Democratic gerrymandering. Through it all, of course, one would seek to allay any prevailing concerns about one's own character. Issues of *temperament*, perhaps, or religious *affiliation*. One might also prepare a satisfying accounting of Illinois's debt crisis."

"Because?"

"Voters naturally believe that past record speaks to future performance. One would need therefore a narrative that acknowledges one's own contribution to the present problem while, in the same voice, painting oneself as indispensable to any solution, be it state *or* federal." She paused now, and with an ironical smile, concluded: "Speaking only in the abstract."

THE NEXT AFTERNOON, Elizabeth invited Mary to sit in the garden while she cut roses. It was not an uninteresting spectacle, for among Elizabeth's many talents was the ability to discern exactly when a rose had reached its fullest bloom and might be severed from its mother. Bush by bush, she took her shears and made her grave harvest, gathering rose heads as implacably as a tumbrel driver. When her basket was half full, she said: "I hear you are talking to that man again."

Mary, seated in the shade of a white oak, said nothing.

"I take your silence for confirmation," said Elizabeth.

"Why should I not talk to him?"

"Oh, I can't say." Snip went the shears. "Because he betrayed and humiliated you? Turned you into a public laughingstock? Do you consider *those* sufficient reasons?"

"He has been well punished."

"Only by his own conscience. If it had been up to me, he should have been dragged to the nearest magistrate."

Mary bowed her head an inch. "He and I were both at fault. Or is a Todd never to admit error?"

Elizabeth hooked the rose basket over one arm. "Let us put your proposition to the test. Do *you* admit you were in error when you chose him? Over my strenuous objections?"

"I admit only that it was the wrong time."

"There can never be a right one."

Having delivered that pronouncement, Elizabeth caressed a snowball bush and inhaled the aroma from a white jasmine. By the time she had peeled off her gloves, she was an altogether different creature.

"Next time, we must remember to bring Julia with us. Oh, please say you'll read to her again tonight! There is something about your cadence that enthralls her, I can't explain it. And have you noticed how Albert clamors now to join you? Three years old, and once Aunt Mary enters the room, he cannot be contained. What a *comfort* you are. Ninian and I don't know what we would do without you."

They were halfway back to the house when the thought pierced Mary like ice. *She thinks I will die here.*

AND WOULD SHE?

Could she, with any degree of conviction, declare that she and Lincoln were moving beyond that neutered middle ground of friendship?

Oh, it was true that, when they met in public now, the old teasing contrapuntal rhythms returned without any prodding, whether they were speaking of the Mormon antics in Nauvoo or the impending visit of Mr. Martin Van Buren (whom Lincoln, rather surprisingly, had been asked to entertain). Politics was once more, as it had always been, their unguent, and there were times when she could see his eyes *seeking* her across a room, as if he were already anticipating the next exchange.

Yet no matter how freely they talked, they never talked of love. Mrs. Francis, having effected their reconciliation, declined (on superstitious grounds, she said) to set up any more assignations. And who had the stomach for them, anyway? Mary and Lincoln would have to rise or fall now on their own merits—or else carry on as they were, doggedly paddling, heads straining above the waterline.

If only, she thought, they could find a campaign—something to divert their energies down a single channel. But Lincoln had pulled himself out of the hunt, and the gubernatorial contest had been all but conceded to the Democrats, as had the bulk of the statehouse races, and Sangamon County was, as ever, a shoo-in for the Whigs. In a political climate so signally lacking in suspense, it would require some ad hoc conflagration to unite them.

And then one came rushing toward them—in the form of Mr. James Shields.

Choleric, conceited, ambitious, indissolubly Irish (with the brogue to prove it), Shields was one of the most reliable deliverers of Catholic votes for the Democrats. His reward had been the plum position of state auditor, a platform he was now using to undermine both the Illinois bank and the Whigs who defended it. Lincoln and Simeon Francis decided it was time to assail Shields's character on the pages of the *Sangamo Journal,* and they had just the mouthpiece: a fictional country widow named "Rebecca" who, in a series of ribald letters, would expose Shields as the fraud and fool he was.

Mr. Francis wrote the first Rebecca letter, relatively mild in tone, but Lincoln sharply raised the volume with the second, which went right after Shields's vanity, portraying him as a deluded lecher who preyed on Springfield females. "Dear girls," cried the fictional auditor, "*it is distressing*, but I cannot marry you all. Too well I know how much you suffer; but do, *do* remember, it is not my fault that I am *so* handsome and *so* interesting."

"It isn't even a lampoon, really," said Julia Jayne, upon reading it. "That's exactly how he is. Just last week, at the Lambs', he was positively badgering me to dance with him. Couldn't believe I would decline."

Mary, too, had been obliged more than once to resist the Irishman's overtures. What a pity, she thought, that one of Springfield's "dear girls" could not speak to the indignity of feeling Mr. Shields's hand slide up her back in the midst of a waltz or smelling his tart breath when he leaned rather too close over the punch bowl. "If there were any justice," she told Julia, "*we* would write the next letter. You and I."

It was an abstract notion when she first proposed it; only further reflection gave it the texture of the real. Who, after all, was more suited to pricking the rooster's vanity than the hen? And who better to occupy the psyche of this mythical Rebecca than a nonmythical female? By penning the third letter, Mary and Julia could strike a blow both for their party and their sex.

And Lincoln would approve.

That much she was certain of, and it was this thought, finally, that drove her to pick up pen. For the rest of the afternoon, she and Julia labored in the Edwardses' library, drawing Mr. Shields and Rebecca ever closer on the page—yea, to the brink of marriage and beyond. Mary knew they were on the right track whenever Julia tried to clap the laughter back into her mouth, but as they filled the paper with line after line, it seemed to her that her true collaborator was not Julia but Lincoln. With every pass, she could feel his brown knobby hand lying atop hers, feel it so acutely that the flush spread all the way up the back of her neck. By the time she reached the closing epigram, he might as well have been sitting alongside her, flank to her flank, beaming with delight.

Ye Jew's harps awake! The auditor's won,
Rebecca, the widow has gained Erin's son
The pride of the north from the emerald isle
Has been woo'd and won by a woman's smile.

She didn't want to spoil the enchantment by showing Lincoln the letter. No, she would deliver it straight to Simeon Francis, and when it was published the following Friday, Lincoln would read these same lines in a daze of wonder and demand to know who had so brilliantly carried forth the battle with Shields—and would be all the more overcome to learn that it was *she*! Who had ever kept his interests closest to her heart.

And so, when the next issue of the *Sangamo Journal* arrived, she carried it straight up to her bedroom. Actually lay with it, pressed to her forehead, as though it might communicate the thoughts of each reader. But the hours passed—the days passed—and the only reader she could be sure of was Mr. Shields, who was widely reported to be livid—incensed. Their aim, in short, had been true. But from Lincoln she heard nothing.

The following week, he traveled to Tremont, where the Tazewell County Court was preparing to convene. That Wednesday, Mary and Julia were knitting in the Edwardses' back parlor when word came that they had a visitor. It was Simeon Francis, his face mottled, his breath coming in quick rasps.

"What is it?" asked Mary.

"Lincoln's in trouble."

FORTY-SIX

—————

For want of any other succor, Simeon Francis drew his handkerchief from his pocket and passed it across his brow, in three brutish strokes.

"I should have known," he muttered. "I should have foreseen."

"Foreseen what?" asked Mary.

"*Shield*s. The morning your letter was published, he came to me in a perfect rage. Demanded to know who the author was."

"What did you tell him?"

"What I'd been instructed to say. That the author was Lincoln."

"But who would have told you to say such a thing?"

"Who else? Lincoln."

Shields had at once fired off a hand-delivered letter to his persecutor, demanding satisfaction and insisting that only a complete retraction would "prevent consequences which no one will regret more than myself." Lincoln said no. Once more, Shields pressed; once more, Lincoln declined.

"And now it's come to this," said Mr. Francis.

"Come to *what*?"

He took off his spectacles, wiped them on his shirtfront.

"Shields has challenged Lincoln to a duel. And Lincoln has accepted."

"No," cried Julia.

"I wish I could say else."

"But it's quite absurd," said Mary. "It's *illegal.* . . ."

"Not on Bloody Island."

Until now, she had assumed the place to be mythical. A little spit of land in the heart of the Mississippi that lay outside any legal jurisdiction and had become, as a direct result, a prime spot for resolving *affaires d'honneur.* Mary tried to conjure it now in her mind, but the place that materialized—wracked by groans, soaked in gore—grew smaller the more she contemplated it, and Lincoln himself grew ever bigger, an extravagantly outsized target.

"Is it to be pistols?" she asked faintly.

"Cavalry broadswords. *That* part," added Mr. Francis, "was Lincoln's idea."

"But he's sacrificing himself for us."

"For all three of us, yes. I'm not entirely sure I'm worth it."

The air began to flutter around her, as if a pair of wings were beating in the adjoining room. Half to herself, Mary said, "We must stop it."

"I fear we're already too late," said Mr. Francis, with the most mournful of smiles. "They left Jacksonville earlier today, and they're expected in Alton tomorrow morning. That's when the whole business is scheduled to take place."

The imminence of it left a chill on the room. Tomorrow morning. . . .

"If it's any comfort," said Mr. Francis, "Lincoln has an excellent second in Dr. Merryman. Butler and Bledsoe will be there, too. General Whiteside. Between them all, surely Shields can be made to see reason—"

"But what if they all fail?"

She could tell from his face that he had not only considered that possibility, he had already converted it to likelihood. In a smaller, less secure voice, he said: "He may still come out all right. Consider those long arms. . . ."

For something like a minute, silence lay matted over them. Then Mr. Francis, looking as though the death sentence were his own, bowed to each woman in turn and said, "I just thought you should know."

He was halfway to the door when he turned back round.

"Kindly don't tell my wife. It would grieve her so."

DURING THE WHOLE interview, the two women had remained seated in an attitude that, to Mary's mind, only accentuated their helplessness before the news. At length, with a jerk of her head, she leaped to her feet and took several turns round the room, her hands mesmerically flexing at her sides.

"The stupidity of him!" she growled.

"Who?"

"Lincoln, of course! All he had to do was apologize! Could that have been so difficult? You or I would have done it in an instant if it would keep the peace."

"It is how men are, I suppose."

"Ah, yes," Mary retorted, eyes burning. "They turn a minor skirmish into an open war because they must, at all costs, preserve their fragile *amours propres*. And, in so doing, they make an even worse mess of everything. Oh," she went on, rising to her theme, "if you ask me, it is not the Dr. Merrymans of the world who can avert this disaster, it is *females*. If you and I were there ourselves, we might set this whole matter aright in the space of a minute!"

"Of course we might."

"We would only have to *explain* to Mr. Shields—in the most calm and comforting of tones—how the whole misunderstanding came to be. Shouldering, as necessary, our *full* share of the blame. . . ."

"He could hardly murder *us*," Julia pointed out.

"Of course he couldn't. Lincoln and Shields would walk away with their precious male *dignity* intact, and Bloody Island would be not a whit bloodier for all their childish posturing."

The froth into which she had worked herself was, at this point, entirely theoretical. She would forever after recall that it was Julia Jayne—in the slenderest of voices—who had made the idea concrete.

"The next train west," she said, "leaves at three twenty."

Mary stared at her. Julia's pretty, china-boned face had never glowed with such purpose.

"And if all were to go well," she went on, "we might reach Meredosia by seven. By which time, it still being light, we might get passage—"

"On a *steamer*," said Mary, advancing toward her friend. "Straight down the Illinois to Alton. There by the following morning."

What a wonder it was to her in that instant. The world's map, crimped into such negotiable folds.

"Oh, but dearest," she said, squeezing Julia's hand. "This would still be the journey of two or three *days*. Perhaps *more*. . . ."

"Never mind, I'll tell Mama and Papa we're seeing friends out west. They won't care."

"But there might be dangers," she protested. "I couldn't possibly ensure your safety. . . ."

Julia's pale blue irises deepened into something like slate.

"I hope not!"

WORKING IN SECRET gave them this much advantage: They had nobody to slow their progress or dissuade them from their course. Before another hour had passed, they were standing at the Springfield train crossing: between them, two carpetbags and a resolve that had only hardened since their last meeting.

"We shall stop this nonsense," declared Julia. "Or we shall die trying."

The journey to Jacksonville was as uneventful as they had hoped; it was during the second leg that a cow planted itself across the tracks and refused to budge. By the time they came steaming into Meredosia, indigo shadows were rolling in from the east, and there wasn't a single passenger vessel in sight. A rather dandyish fellow with a cambric handkerchief informed them that the last steamer had left a half hour before but there would be another the next morning.

"We cannot wait until then," Mary answered. Already, she was turning away and, with avid eyes, scanning the whole curve of the waterfront—just as she had once stood outside the Springfield courthouse, looking for a dray to take her home. At length, she picked out a small flickering light near the end of the wharf, where a lone figure sat upon a pile. Without another thought, she went striding down the planks.

"You there!" she called.

The man didn't appear to hear her at first. Even when she had placed herself squarely in his sights, he squinted up at her as if she were some opiate vision.

"See here, my good man. Is that your canoe?"

A wad of tobacco juice exited the left side of his mouth. "It might be."

"We are well met, then. My friend and I have need of somebody to take us downriver."

He angled his jaw toward her. "Where?"

"Alton. Or thereabouts."

"When?"

"Why, now, of course."

By way of answer, he pressed a finger to one nostril and expelled the contents of his nose through the other.

"It's a little dark to be traveling with ladies," he said.

"Have you consulted the sky, sir? It is cloudless. Have you consulted the moon? It is waxing gibbous. I see, too, that you have about you a brazier. Surely, between the moon, the stars, and the coals, we will have light aplenty."

"But I ain't rigged out for ferrying."

Ellis Hart had shown just the same obduracy when she had asked to ride in his dray. What had she done then? she wondered. Simply gone at him, probably, with the full force of her youth. It was then she heard an even more youthful voice say: "We'll pay you, of course!" Julia had crept up on soundless feet. "Handsomely." And when still the boatman still hesitated, Julia sang out, "Catch!" A coin went spiraling into the air and landed, with imperishable authority, in the boatman's palm.

"Another when we get there," she declared in her stoutest voice.

His face folded into crevices of calculation. "We'd be some hours on the water," he grumbled, "and there's nowhere for you to sleep."

"Are those your fishing nets?" inquired Mary.

Mutely, he nodded.

"Then I imagine they will make perfectly adequate pillows."

THE LAST FINGERS of sunlight were slipping from the sky as the canoe took to the open water. The boatman sat in the stern, with the brazier between his feet, and Mary and Julia wedged themselves into the bow. What with their several layers of petticoats, it made for close quarters, but as Julia declared, with insouciant cheer: "We may not live till tomorrow, but we *shall* not tumble out in the meantime."

That evening, they dined on a few crackers and a flask of cold, weak tea. Before too very long, Julia leaned her head onto her friend's shoulder and tumbled off to sleep. It was Mary who remained stubbornly awake. Chilled, despite the additional shawl she had brought—but, more than that, haunted by the possibility that they were already too late. What if Lincoln and Shields and their respective parties were to awaken with the sun's first rays? What if they were to hasten straight to the dueling ground—and from there, launch the arduous work of killing each other, bit by bit? By the time Mary and Julia reached them, there would be no one to save.

It was useless to pretend that violence was a stranger to her. She had come of age in Lexington, where the code duello ran rampant and gentlemen kept knives and pistols in their pantaloons and frilled shirts. She was not even seven when Jeroboam Beauchamp killed his wife's lover, eleven when Charles Wickliffe shot the editor of the *Kentucky Gazette*. Wickliffe himself was shot and killed not long after by George Trotter, who was spending down his days in the lunatic asylum. On and on it went, men visiting evil on each other, and women left to mourn their handiwork.

And was she to become another link in that long chain of wailing sisters? What would she do, she couldn't help but ask, when confronted with the spectacle of Lincoln's lifeless form? And now, quite as if her bereavement had already begun, the tears came juddering out of her, in jagged spasms. She was grateful for the cover of darkness, and indeed, it was the evening's innate tact, the care with which it now folded round her, that persuaded her at last to close her eyes and drift.

At one point in the night, the boat took a sudden lurch. She jerked up her head and listened to somebody fumbling in the darkness.

"What is it?" she whispered.

"Lost an oar," growled the boatman.

She had some dim notion of helping him look, but the sleep lay heavy on her limbs, and it was an inordinate relief to hear him mutter, "There you are, you bastard." Two seconds later, the canoe had resumed its soft pulsing rhythm.

She awoke some hours later—utterly convinced that she had tumbled out of the boat and was even now sinking beneath the waterline. In fact, it was just her hand, dangling in the river. With a light hiss, she raised herself up and looked round. Day—some kind of day—had broken. The sun was crouching behind great forested bluffs, and the gray of the sky was turning to yellow, and the air was dense with chatter: chickadees, blackbirds, crows.

The boat itself had been tied to a shagbark hickory sapling, and in the stern slumbered the boatman, his bare head listing softly to one side. In the probing light of morning, he looked nothing like the fellow they had waylaid the evening before. His red calico shirt sagged in loose folds from his lank frame, and his face, though dirty and sun cracked, was the face of a youth. No more than eighteen or nineteen.

She remembered then all the stories Lincoln had told her of oaring freight and passengers down the Mississippi. One night, in particular, he'd been set upon by bandits—how she had thrilled to the tale! Never once stopping to consider that he had been a boy himself then. A motherless child, yes. Just like this boatman with the trail of tobacco juice on his chin. In a trance of tenderness, she extended her hand toward his face, lightly cupped his cheek. Wild-eyed, he leaped to his feet and was in the act of raising his paddle to strike her down when reason crowded in. With a stifled growl, he jumped to shore and stood there in an attitude of embarrassed truculence.

"Had to catch a few winks is all."

"Of course," she answered mildly.

"I'll be back."

He disappeared into the forest. Whatever chill she might have felt at her abandonment was offset by the sight of Julia, thumb tucked lightly between her lips. It was enough to give Mary's tenderness a new avenue, and when the boatman returned, he found her stroking Julia's hair as if it were the silken straw of a doll.

"Here," he said, dropping a mush melon and a capful of persimmons at her feet. "Breakfast." Untethering the canoe, he took up his seat once more and pushed off from shore. "Alton within the hour," he announced.

THE RIVER BEGAN to teem now—not with birds or fish but with flatboats. Up to eighty feet in length, some of them, gliding downstream, and in the opposite direction, like floating verandas, came the day's first steamboats.

More than once, Mary feared their canoe would be swamped in some vessel's creamy wake, but the boatman picked the truest path through every maze.

It was when they passed Grafton that the water began to transform itself, by degrees, from current to tide. The Illinois shore fell farther away with each stroke, and the sky reared up. With a surge of awe, Mary recognized what lay before them.

The Mississippi.

She had traveled it more than once—felt the breadth of its shoulders—but never before had she been so *near* it, so *alive* to its essential nature. Every swell and eddy, every slap and gurgle came home to her now through the medium of her own body. Trembling, half-blind, she reached for Julia's hand and held it fast as the river gathered speed and bore them south.

By now, the sun had disappeared behind terraces of cloud, and, from the Missouri side, a fog was advancing in soft tendrils, weaving in with the last threads of morning mist on the Illinois side. Through this veil, Alton, quite unexpectedly, came rushing toward them. A topless forest: masts and spars. The town itself visible only as a necklace of lights on the overhanging bluff.

"Just like I promised," said the boatman, making once more toward shore.

Mary was silent for a time.

"In truth, sir, we had in mind a destination just a few miles on."

She chanced a quick look back. The irises of his eyes had screwed down to pellets.

"St. Louis?" he guessed.

"Bloody Island."

There was no change in his face. It was his body that tautened. "That ain't no island. That's a towhead. And you don't just run into it, you have to go a-looking for it. And it's damned hard to look when the fog's rolling in."

"Please," she said. "A man's life is at stake."

"What's that to me?"

"But it's her *husband*," cried Julia, in a burst of embellishment. "And he is in mortal danger."

"What's he gone and done?"

Mary flushed, cast her eyes down. "I suppose you could say he has defended my honor."

She could feel the boatman's appraising eye on her.

"That'll be a dollar extra," he said. "And if we hit a snag or a rock, you'll be paying for the canoe. So help me God."

It was a journey of but a few miles, but it might as well have been a hundred. The farther south they traveled, the more relentlessly the fog crowded in, until at last, it settled over their heads in a thick imponderable ceiling. Deprived of his usual coordinates and granted but a partial view of any oncoming vessel, the boatman pushed against the tide as much as he submitted to it; at intervals, he even went so far as to stop the canoe in its natural course to make sure he was in the right channel. The oaths that, all the way downriver, had been muttered under his breath were now ringing out into the damp morning air—a weave of profanity that paused only long enough for him to pass a skillet to Julia.

"Bang it against the gunwale," he commanded. "Every three seconds without fail."

"Like this?" she said, lightly tapping.

"Louder, you fool! How else will they know we're coming?"

From above, the fog continued to press down with such a geological force that Mary actually raised her hand to it, convinced it would have the feel of shale or gneiss. Soon, she thought, it would surround them entire. From what sounded like a frontier outpost, the boatman grunted: "There."

Mary squinted through the curtain of smoke. It looked like no island she had seen—nor any towhead. Just a solid wall of cottonwood timber, extending as far back as the eye could see. One might sail by it at any hour of any day without ceding it more than a passing thought. *Are you sure?* she wanted to ask. But the boatman was already angling the canoe to shore. No easy task, for the river was running high and, with some of the banks underwater, the margin of shoreline had shrunk to no more than five or six feet. Anxiously, she ran her eyes up and down the strand, looking for purchase—and was startled to find, some hundred yards down, a group of black buzzards, huddling together in a ragtag circle.

Carrion, that was her first chilling thought. They had found something dead to feed upon. But as the canoe drew nearer to land, the birds bulged out into arms and legs—elbows, collars—even, against expectation, hats.

"Let me out," she said.

"We're not there yet."

But she was already pitching herself over the side of the boat. She heard neither the boatman's vulgarity nor Julia's light shriek, for the Mississippi's gray water was now tugging at her stockings and licking the edges of her petticoats. With a burble of laughter, she hoisted up her skirt and pried one foot from the river bottom. Then the other. And came at last, drenched from knee to heel, to Bloody Island.

The buzzards never saw her come. So locked were they in their private conference that she was able to steal down the shoreline, quite unnoticed, and get within ten feet of them before one of their number turned round and discovered her.

Cousin John Hardin.

The shock was like a hand pressed against her midsection. What on earth had brought him here? His astonishment was every bit as great. The only difference was that he had some *other* astonishment, lying at the back of it. Some piece of testimony that had been waiting until this very moment, for a witness.

"My dear Mary!" he shouted. "Isn't it wonderful? They have made peace!"

His import was slow to reach her. She was too busy unmasking the other buzzards. Dr. Merryman. Mr. Butler. Mr. Bledsoe. General Whiteside.

And Mr. Shields. Neither the oily specimen of Springfield drawing rooms nor the vengeful warrior who had set this whole train into motion but a smaller, dryer figure. Shrunken, it seemed to her, by his own embarrassment.

What is it? she wondered. *What does he have to be ashamed of?*

It was then that she picked out the figure who was *not* there. The one who should have been towering over them all.

Lincoln. Where was Lincoln?

A new sound came dropping out of the fog. A great flapping of wing that whistled in her ears and stirred the air into tumult. . . .

And alongside it, and almost synchronous with it, a thrashing in the cottonwoods. As loud to her ears as if the whole forest were agitating to be he heard. Then, like an actor parting a curtain, Lincoln stepped out.

How should it be that all the peculiarities of him—the protuberances and cavities—were more pronounced for being captured unawares? He stared at her now with heavy lids as she advanced in slow strides, stopping at last within a foot's reach of him. Then, with a fury that surprised her, she began beating on him with her tiny white fists—feeling each strike reverberate in the canyon of his chest. He never so much as flinched. The only transformation was in his eyes, which glowed with an academic interest.

At last, spent, she turned away and began to stagger down the shore. Back to the *boat*, yes, though she had no clear idea what she meant to do when she got there. Commandeer the oar and paddle straight back to Kentucky, was that it? And while she was at it, perhaps she might travel back in time, to the very moment of her birth. Into her mother's womb, never to reemerge. . . .

At her back, she heard a squeaking tread in the sand. "Mary," he called. "Mary."

She had no voice to answer. No voice to tell him the things that were only just now coalescing in her mind.

He was supposed to be dead.

She had in some way counted on that. Had even, in some warren of her soul, *longed* for it.

For if she were to be the spinster that life had marked her out to be, she might at least have a *story* to carry with her. The tragic and beautiful tale of a lady who had lost her love—had knelt over his gallant body, pierced by a broadsword on a lonely island. Future listeners would weep to hear it and, in weeping, give her the dispensation she craved. Absolve her of the high crime and misdemeanor of being alone.

Her feet were foundering now in the sand—each step a greater ordeal—until at last, with a despairing cry, she sank to her knees and buried her face in her hands. From behind her, she heard his soft approach.

"Are you injured?" he asked.

"Go away. . . ."

He lowered himself into the patch of shore adjoining hers. Sat there for some time in silence. Then, with some hesitation, he reached out his hand and laid it, ever so quietly, on the back of her head.

"I believe this is the sweetest thing anybody has ever done for me."

"You mean the most foolish," she answered, in a broken voice.

"*I* was the fool, Mary. The biggest damned one that ever lived." He softly pried her fingers from her face. "Will you look at me?"

"No."

Undaunted, he tipped his head toward her. The rest of his body followed, and in some far realm of sensibility, beyond vision, she registered that he was *kneeling* before her.

"I once told you we were the two brokenest birds I knew," he said. "What I didn't see was how well our pieces might still fit together for all that. At least I *think* they might. I think I should like to try."

He took one of her hands and brought it to his chest.

"Mary Todd," he said, "would you do me the great honor of being my wife?"

FORTY-SEVEN

Of their second engagement, they breathed not a word.

Not even the souls who had assembled that morning on Bloody Island knew for a certainty what had to come to pass, and as Mary and Lincoln resumed their lives in Springfield, they were relieved to find their old habits of secrecy circling back round. By mutual consent, the wedding would be a private affair. A simple ceremony at the local Episcopal church—Lincoln, thank God, was willing—with Dr. Dresser presiding and a pair of witnesses in attendance. Family and friends would be notified at some point in the future, but the couple themselves would venture into the vale of matrimony under nobody's eyes but their own.

This resolve they clutched to their bosoms, quite as much as if it was love itself. All the more astonishing, then, that Mary should be woken on the morning of Friday, November the fourth, by her own sister.

"No," said Elizabeth Edwards.

"No what?"

"I don't care if you're marrying a Barbary ape. If there's to be a Todd wedding, it will happen here. This very night. Now get up, you little mongrel. We have work to do!"

Mary never asked her how she had found out. She merely marveled that Elizabeth's opposition to the marriage could have melted so promptly and unconditionally. Perhaps she feared unseemly gossip. Perhaps she was mindful of the lavish wedding she had thrown for their sister Frances. *Perhaps she just needs my room.*

With precious little time to spare, Elizabeth, gritting her teeth, sent to Old Dickey's for gingerbread and beer. Frances volunteered to make the supper—boiled ham—as well as the thirty-six-egg wedding cake. "I don't know that I've ever worked harder in my life," she declared as she swept into the house with two tiny children in her wake. By then Ninian had dispatched the invitations, and Julia, newly deputed bridesmaid, had shut herself in the bride's room, where she helped Mary into her white satin dress, fastened the pearl necklace round her neck and then proceeded to the equally serious business of silver brooch and pearl earrings.

"Don't cry," said Julia, as sternly as she could. "It will spoil the effect."

UPON LEARNING THAT his wedding was to be a public affair after all, Lincoln had awakened his friend Jim Matheny and asked him to be best man. Upon being informed that he needed another, he wandered into the Springfield courthouse and tapped the first man he saw, Beverly Powell. (*Thank God it was a Whig*, Mary thought later.) In the early afternoon hours, he hied himself to Billy the Barber for a haircut, then moseyed down to Mrs. Butler, who tied his necktie for him and took the precaution of reminding him about the ring. He had bought it just a few days earlier, on installment, from Chatterton's. The inscription read *Love Is Eternal.*

By the time seven o'clock rolled round, some two dozen Springfield citizens had somehow materialized in the Edwardses' front parlor. The ceremony was over so quickly that Mary remained skeptical that it had happened. For some time, she wandered through the reception, greeting well-wishers with the same rictus-smile, tossing out niceties she herself scarcely heard. She had enough wherewithal to recognize that Matilda was whispering something of extreme delicacy into Newton Strong's ear and that Mrs. Francis was weeping copiously, but because she had eaten so little, the beer went straight to her head, and she was on the lip of disorientation when Lincoln drew her to one side and, in a voice both low and urgent, said: "What do you think of Joshua?"

She hadn't the remotest idea what he meant.

"For a boy's name," he persisted. "If we were to have a boy."

In her own mind, she had already christened their firstborn son with her father's name, but in that instant, she quite forgot her resolution. She merely patted Lincoln on the wrist and, with an appeasing smile, whispered: "A talk for another time? Surely?"

THE DANCING LASTED until midnight. Then, amidst the muted acclaim of the guests, the bride and groom walked arm in arm down Adams Street to the Globe Tavern, where, for the modest sum of four dollars a week, they would be spending their immediate and foreseeable future.

It was a more disheveled place than Mary would have wished, but she had sworn at her own inner temple that she would make it work, that she would be the thriftiest and most cunning of housewives, spinning miracles of economy every day and then, at the close of each evening, turning to her husband—to Lincoln!—and saying, "You see? I did it quite on my own."

But as they climbed the stairs, the newel came right off the post, and on either side of them, the wallpaper had peeled away like rind from an orange, and from the upper reaches of the building, faintly animalistic noises echoed down the well.

"Here we are," said Lincoln in a grave voice.

The Widow Beck had already showed them the apartment, so it was hard to explain their surprise at finding but the one room in it. No partitions, no alcoves, not even an armoire. Lincoln proposed the temporary solution of standing out in the hallway while Mary undressed. In a kind of sorrowing haste, she peeled herself out of her skirt and bodice, her corset and petticoats, her chemise and drawers—folding everything as best she could, though there was nowhere left to put it—and stood at last in the thick cotton nightgown (a wedding gift from Matilda) with the drawstring at the top. Looking down, she found in her right hand the red velvet pincushion that Elizabeth had thrust at her just as they were leaving.

"Keep it right at your side," Elizabeth confided, "and as soon as anything starts to hurt, give it a squeeze. Lie still and try not to cry out. And remember," she added, with a meaningful look, "no more than twice a week. And only until you are with child."

Twice a week, Mary thought now, astounded at the very prospect.

There was no way, of course, that she could wait outside in the hallway while Lincoln disrobed, so he snuffed out all the candles and retreated to the corner farthest from the window. She nearly laughed to hear him thrashing about in the darkness, his various joints colliding with panels of wall. The surprise, when at last he reemerged in the scraps of fireglow, was how insubstantial he looked. Just a nightgown and a rather elderly nightcap, with only darkness where the limbs would be.

"Forgive me," she said. "A touch more light. . . ."

"Of course."

He dipped a candle into the embers and waited for it to catch, then returned it to its sconce. It was possible now to see him, in full, on the other side of the bed, gazing across the counterpane. She had always presumed that, under the unique compression of this moment, the entire thoroughfare of their relations would scroll into view—from that first awkward encounter in the Edwardses' spring-solstice ball, all the way down to this infinitely more awkward encounter, here in the Widow Beck's chamber. With exactitude she would chart each rise and dip and then be able to conclude that, after all, they had arrived right just where they were destined.

But in the flicker of that single candle and in the faltering glow of the fire, she found everything a perfect cloud. Lincoln the cloudiest of all, standing there in his bare legs and feet, studying her. How had they come to this, she wondered? How had they ever believed themselves known to each other? How could *anyone* be known—anyone at all—here on God's green earth?

"Well now," he said. "Well now, Mrs. Lincoln."

EPILOGUE

JOSHUA

———

November 1860

IT WAS THE last thing he expected.

He had just been ushered (grudgingly, by a pair of bodyguards) into the elegant corner suite at the Tremont House. He had greeted his old friend in formal terms, paid the necessary homage, braced himself for the most summary of dismissals. (*So good of you to come, do keep me apprised, will you? . . .*) In his mind, he was already turning back toward the door when Lincoln, to the surprise of everybody, said: "Speed, have you got a room?"

Joshua watched as each member of Lincoln's coterie—every secretary, every sycophant—turned his way.

"Well, yes," he heard himself murmur. "Four-oh-four."

"Just below, it sounds like."

"Near enough."

"Then I'll come see *you*," said Lincoln.

At once, a harassed young man in pince-nez rushed forward to explain the impossibility of such a thing, the havoc it would wreak with the schedule, but Lincoln said only: "Name your hour, Speed." There was a slight pause before he added that he would bring his wife.

"BUT IT MAKES perfect sense that he's coming to us," said Fanny. "He needs rescuing."

It was true that, for the first time since his election, Lincoln had quit the domestic sanctuary of Springfield for the brawl and tumult of Chicago. Over the course of three days, he had been swept along in a stream of political vultures (angling for office) and well-wishers (pouring unimpeded off Lake Street) and autograph seekers (one of them the mayor's son). His inauguration was only a few months off; new enemies were every day baying for his blood. Who could wonder that he should want to step out of the torrent for an hour or two—exchange his public self for a private audience?

"Imagine," said Fanny. "A man so retiring, thrust into such a hot glare. He's bound to find it all a bit deranging, isn't he?"

"You mean it's our patriotic duty to save him."

"At the very least, we might free him from his ormolu prison upstairs."

"My little philanthropist," said Joshua, chucking her under the chin. "But, of course, you're right. We must make him as welcome as possible."

"And his wife, too," rejoined Fanny with a soft frown. "Though I've read she's rather mercurial."

"I couldn't say."

"No?"

"It's been twenty years, my dear."

"What do you remember of her, then?"

"I recall her being . . ." He half closed his eyes to the tide of imagery that swept over him, and it was to keep himself above water that he reached for the first qualifier that presented itself. *"Ardent."*

The Lincolns were twenty minutes late, excusing themselves with the usual mix of masculine expostulation and feminine protest. Mrs. Lincoln was, on the whole, more cool than ardent and seemed faintly to regret the necessity of coming here. As for Lincoln, his eyelids grew perilously heavy as he leaned against the fireplace mantel. But then, rousing himself, he clapped his hands together and, in a voice of mounting purpose, said: "I have a notion. Why don't the ladies stay here in the sitting room, and Speed and I can retire to the inner chambers?"

It was clear that he hadn't rehearsed the idea with his wife, for her pupils dilated, as if under the influence of belladonna.

"We were having such a lovely time," she remonstrated.

"And you may still," answered Lincoln. "But Speed and I haven't laid eyes on each other in a coon's age. We shall be no more than a stone's throw the whole time, and Speed promises not to leave ash on the rug, doesn't he?"

"Of course."

"And I promise not to disarrange the bedcovers. There now, it's settled."

Only it wasn't, and might never have been were it not for Fanny's timely intervention.

"*Dear* Mrs. Lincoln," she said, "I'm just *longing* to hear about those boys of yours. Grown mighty as oaks, I am told. Now you must take pity on me, I'm quite hopeless with names, but I believe the oldest is *Robert*, is that it? After your father, I think. And then—oh, dear, is it *Tad*? *Please* tell me you have pictures somewhere about you. . . ."

With no further ceremony, the two men retired to the inner chamber, and even then, Lincoln was not entirely satisfied of their escape until he had pressed his ear to the door for a full minute. He turned back to Joshua and, with an approving nod, said: "Fine woman you have there."

"The finest."

Impulsively, Joshua reached into his vest pocket and, with a sense of overwhelming relief, found a cigar. Gave it a quick clip and was just lowering it to the candle flame when he heard Lincoln say: "You haven't changed, Speed. Not a hair."

Flushing, Joshua turned round. Raised the cigar to his lips.

"You are a desperate liar," he said. "I grow stouter each day."

"I was only going to accuse you of looking *prosperous*."

"Ha! Well, perhaps that's what comes of having no children to chase after."

"But you have nieces and nephews, I believe."

"A perfect horde."

"Then there's that."

"Yes."

They were quiet. From the adjoining room, Mrs. Lincoln's excitable voice could be heard, buzzing in the rafters.

"You've gotten a little hairier," ventured Joshua.

"Indeed!" cried Lincoln, swinging toward the nearest looking glass. "It was a little girl from Westville put it in my head. She wrote to say that the female sex is partial to beards, and if I were to let my whiskers grow, all the ladies would love me and get their husbands to vote for me."

"And she is vindicated. A keen political intellect."

Though, truth be told, there was something Joshua didn't quite like about the goateed Lincoln. A suggestion of foxiness, of guile. As if all those years of logrolling had been distilled into follicle.

"It's very distinguished," he hastened to add.

"Oh, I don't know." Lincoln stroked the bare spaces beneath his ear. "It's not in any great hurry to finish, is it? Perhaps by the inauguration, it will be as full as yours."

Again they fell quiet.

"Your room is comfortable?" asked Lincoln.

"Certainly."

"I suppose for five dollars a night, it'd better be."

And now *more* silence, threatening to stretch through eternity. But here was the next surprise. Without a word of preamble or apology—without possibly even knowing what he was about to do—Lincoln flung himself onto Joshua's bed.

Nothing in his expression suggested that anything out of the ordinary had occurred, and perhaps nothing had, for everything about his current attitude was just as Joshua remembered: the feet dangling over the end of the bed, the hands interlaced beneath the head, the eyes cutting straight to the ceiling. . . .

"Tell me, Speed. What is your pecuniary condition?"

"My . . ."

"Are you rich or poor?"

"I suppose one would call it satisfactory. Good, even."

"*How* good?"

Joshua eyed him. Waited.

"What I'm asking," said Lincoln, "is whether you'd be prepared to accept a cut in salary for the sake of your country. What remains of it, I mean."

In that moment, Joshua found he had the most urgent need to sit down. Only the nearest place was the bed—a square of comforter on the side opposite to Lincoln's. The mattress gave way, just a little, as he lowered himself onto it.

"Do you mean a cabinet post?" he asked, in a dazed voice.

"I do."

"Well now, I am honored. Beyond honored."

"And what else are you?"

He would later tell Fanny that he hadn't known what his answer would be. No, it was Lincoln who had told him. Lincoln's *face*, contracting into folds of regret, as though he had already divined the truth.

"With the very greatest respect," said Joshua, in a halting voce, "I fear that you don't have—within your gift—any office I could afford to take."

The folds seemed to deepen as Lincoln absorbed the news. Then, in a soft voice, he said: "You can't blame me for asking."

"Of course not. I hope you won't blame *me* for—"

"Of course not."

Silence.

"And maybe," Lincoln went on, in a lightly teasing tone, "you might think of some *other* Southerner who wouldn't be quite so impoverished as you."

"There's Guthrie," said Joshua, after some reflection. "A little on in years but a devout supporter of yours."

"Will you feel of him, then? Not by letter, if you please, but in person."

"Naturally."

"And as things *proceed*, Speed, I hope I can count on you to—oh, answer the *call*, I suppose. When the time comes. Just now, I have great need of friends in Kentucky."

"You shall have one, Mr. President. Always."

"I am most grateful."

Joshua gazed down at his hand, which was sketching a tiny semicircle on the coverlet. As though it were trying to wipe the film from a windowpane.

"I still snore like an ogre," said Lincoln.

With a stifled laugh, Joshua glanced up. "I am told I have lately developed that tendency myself."

"Thank God for separate bedrooms, eh? Our womenfolk may slumber untroubled." He gave his legs a stretch, then crossed his feet at the ankles. "Do you ever look back on those times, Speed?"

"Certainly."

"Oh, I know memory has a way of deceiving, but I recall it all now as—
an eternal sort of ferment, don't you? Rallies and speechifying—the *Poetical*
Society, remember? Ceaseless argument. Never-*ending*. We thought the nation
would perish if we stopped fighting about it." One of his fingers, almost independently of him, was sliding down his jaw. "The perfect wonder of it is that
I don't think I would have had it any other way. It seemed to me then that,
if the rest of my life were to follow the same course, why, that would be all
right, wouldn't it?"

Joshua nodded, just once, then tipped his face down.

"I'm sure I thought the same thing," he said.

He was about to say more, but he found he could no longer quite trust
himself. It took, finally, the sound of his own wife's voice in the adjoining
room—that steadfast rhythm—to call him back.

"I don't suppose there's any cause for regret," he went on. "Dame Fortune
simply had other ideas for us, that's all. Other ideas for *you*."

"She has had so many ideas," answered Lincoln, "that I've quite lost count."

His eyes shuddered down, and his body, as if answering some law of phys-
ics, tipped onto its side. Joshua took it at first for a joke, but within seconds, Lincoln's head had sunk into the pillow, and before another minute
had passed, a snore—ragged and melancholy—was rolling up from his idled
throat.

It was the old sound in all its particulars, but to Joshua's ears, it bore now
a novel enchantment. *Here* and here alone, Abraham Lincoln, leader of a
bruised and riven nation, had found a place to lay his weary head.

And perhaps it was in the interest of preserving that refuge that Joshua
now stretched himself across the bed's remaining space. Corkscrewed his own
body into the same shape as Lincoln's, stared once more into the back of
Lincoln's neck. Smelled once more that elusive scent of talc and sweat and
bear grease and who knew what else. Joshua's boots never left his feet, but
enough of the old ritual seeped through that, before he could lodge any protest, sleep had claimed him, too, swept over him like a curtain.

And then pulled away to reveal Springfield.

The Springfield of old, to be sure, and he and Lincoln were their younger
selves, out for another constitutional. Migrating the full lengths of Jefferson

and Washington and Adams and Monroe—east and west and back again. Stepping round puddles and negotiating drifts of mud. Traveling for *hours*, it seemed, and talking the whole way, though Joshua could no longer make out what they were saying. For all he knew, the most arrant nonsense was spilling out of both their mouths, and that prospect was of a sudden so subversive that he began to laugh—a giddy, mounting sound that lofted him off the street altogether and carried him, in a single breath, back to his bed in the Tremont House, where he awoke in a maze of light to find Lincoln standing over him.

Stunned, Joshua lay there, blinking. "How long have I . . . ?"

"Long enough."

Joshua raised his head from the pillow, swung his legs arduously to the floor. He had to regain his coordinates. *Fanny*, yes. In the outer room. With *Mary*. . . .

"They're still at it," said Lincoln, guessing the tenor of his thoughts. "I don't think they've missed us one bit."

Joshua nodded. "We should . . ."

He made as if to stand, but Lincoln said, "Hold off," and fumbled in his breast pocket for a handkerchief. "Here," he said. And when Joshua stared back at him, he added: "For your eyes."

In fact, the problem went further than the eyes. It extended to Joshua's entire face, which, to his own amazement, was bathed—enameled—in a coat of tears.

"Dear God," he gasped, reaching for the handkerchief. "I don't . . . I don't know what . . ."

"Probably the same wagon that hit me," said Lincoln.

And only now could Joshua's distress recede far enough to find its mirror image in the other man's face. The same grooves and reddened eyelids. The same downturn of lip and residues of salt, like tracks across a desert. Why, he thought, it was like watching a heart break twice over.

Wordlessly, he handed the handkerchief back. Eased himself to his feet.

"Perhaps another minute," he said.

Lincoln nodded, and they stood together, silent, in the half-light.

MARY

July 1882

WAS THIS HOW she would end her days, she sometimes wondered? As the Madwoman of Springfield?

Young boys, it was said, would only consent to pass her house on a dare and would, at first sight of her darkened room—blinds drawn, candles extinguished—experience an obscure but profound terror. Now and then, some concrete evidence of their presence would impinge upon her world. An arrested scream. A bark of laughter. Pebbles hurled against the glass—a rock, even. (The glazier had to be called in once a month.) Spectral moans and, occasionally, if the boys were feeling bold, a single epithet lobbed in her direction. *Freak. Batty. Crazy.*

Yes, perhaps there really *was* a distinction to be claimed here: Against all expectation, she had become a rite of passage. Survive *her*, the boys of Springfield seemed to be saying, and they would be ready for anything.

SOMETIMES SHE ENVISIONED what might happen if one of them—the bravest, it would have to be—were actually to enter the house. Tiptoe up the stairs, yes, embracing his own doom and then, with trembling hands, lift the latch on her door.

What would he find there? No hobgoblin, no ghoul. Just an infirm old woman. Wearing widow's weeds by day, peau-de-soie nightgowns after dark.

(Even now, she dressed as if she were being watched.) Confined either to bed or to an invalid chair. Incapable of even catching a fly, let alone hurting it.

Perhaps, having established this to his satisfaction, the boy would make so bold as to sit down in the armchair and ply her with questions. For surely it was curiosity, more than anything else, that would have drawn him here.

Whose house is this? he might ask.

My sister's.

Why is it so dark in your room?

On account of my eyes, you see. Cataracts and paralyzed irises and swollen corneas . . . Oh, I won't bore you with the details, but I'm nearly blind now, and the light has become a perfect horror. It hurts even to blink.

What do you do all day?

Think, mostly. Remember. Sometimes my maid reads to me. Sometimes I dictate a letter. Once in a while, there's a visitor.

Why do you wear black?

Because I'm in mourning, silly child.

A pause then.

Is it him? Is it him you mourn?

Him, yes, and many others. More than I can count. Why, once I had a boy just like you. . . .

Four boys, she might have added. Three snatched before their time. But in her confusion, they would all jumble together, and here, perhaps, was where the intruder's courage would reach its terminus, for he would gaze into those hungry dead eyes of hers and know they had no bottom.

She was sixty-two when she came back to Springfield. Bereavement, impoverishment, exile had all left their mark. So, too, infamy. She could no more escape it than blot out those three months and three weeks she had spent at Bellevue. The twelve-by-twenty-foot room . . . the locked doors . . . mail opened and discarded . . . a matron, ready at every moment with the restraints. Thank God in all His divine mercy for the gift of her sister, who, despite her own age and infirmities, had again taken Mary in. Welcomed her *home*, yes, to the old house on Quality Hill.

And how much Elizabeth had been obliged to overlook! Hasty words and ancient ruptures, but she had shrugged them all off and accepted her little sister as she was. Never asking more of her than she could give. Testifying, to whoever would listen, that Mary was *sound*. As sane as you or I. . . .

SPRINGFIELD HAD CHANGED since last she was here. Sidewalks everywhere now. Gas lamps. Twenty-two hotels, six banks, a pair of bowling alleys. Eighty saloons! And to the north of the Edwards lot, another state capitol in the works, massively scaled, dwarfing everything in sight.

And yet inside the house, everything felt arrested. The creaks and groans and smells, the whistles in the flue. All the same! Why, Mary was even sleeping in the same bedroom—the same bed. All her life she had been mocked for her presentiments, but at least one of them had come to pass. She *would* die in her sister's house.

IF ANYTHING, IT was a relief, for under the caresses of opium and chloral hydrate, she was pulling free of time's axis—journeying back night after night to the Springfield of old.

Mr. Baker, stout comrade! (Dead at Ball's Bluff before the war had scarcely begun. What had she been thinking, wearing lilac to his funeral?)

Crafty Mr. Douglas. (Expired just a few months after Lincoln's inauguration. As if he couldn't bear the thought anymore.)

Dear Julia Jayne, marrying Mr. Trumbull and then perishing at forty-two, after a brutal illness.

Matilda, lovely Matilda—or Mrs. Newton Strong, as she finally became, dropping dead in the streets of Philadelphia at the age of twenty-nine. Snuffed like a candle.

And Joshua Speed. Beautiful Mr. Speed, gone to his reward just a few weeks before. A quiet passing in Louisville, it was said, with his wife at his side.

One by one, they had preceded her to the grave, but when she thought of them now, they were in their bloom—vivid and clean as ivory portraits. There was but one figure from the past who refused to be summoned, however hard she tried.

Extraordinary, really, that a nose, a mouth, a pair of eyes that had once been as familiar to her as her own should now grow less definite each week. Yet was that not somehow in keeping with the man's life? Hadn't absence always been his most defining trait?

One night, in the act of turning down the lights, her maid asked why she insisted on sleeping on one side of the bed. Without thinking, she answered, "In case he comes back." The poor girl gasped so audibly that Mary wanted to reassure her that she wasn't being supernatural. It's just that when a woman gets accustomed to waiting on a man, it's hard to break the habit.

And from the time they were married, he was gone as often as he was present—days and nights on the circuit, on the hustings—and even when he was home, his thoughts were generally leagues away. How often, in a fit of impatience, she had demanded to know what was on his mind. How often he had responded by blinking a couple of times and murmuring ". . . Why, nothing, my dear. Nothing at all."

It was in these moments, inevitably, that she pined for him most. When he was lying on the floor in front of the hearth, stroking the dog or absently tousling Willie's hair or listening, with a half smile, to the details of Tad's frog adventure. While, on the far side of the room, she sat sewing, largely unremarked, wondering when her husband would come home.

THIRTY YEARS ON, still wondering.

THERE WAS A problem to consider.

Even if he were, by some miracle, to walk through the door—even if he were to recognize her in her shrunken, paralytic state—he might still balk at the bed. For, of course, they had never shared it.

Or any other, for that matter, once they had taken to their separate rooms. Depending on his mood or state of exhaustion, he might come calling in the early morning hours, but in those final years, they had passed their nights in altogether separate spheres: he ranging the hallways, carrying on a running dialogue with some silent interlocutor; she cocooned in her bedsheets, eyes shut, searching for Willie. *Wailing* for him some nights at such a pitch that she was sure Lincoln would hear her and come running. He never did.

So it was an obvious thing to ask: Why should he come now? When he had so much more space in which to roam? No, if she were to find him, it would have to be in the past, not the afterlife.

This, of course, was an errand to which she could devote many consecutive hours, much as she might once have labored over a piece of fancywork. The surprise was that, in sifting through all those memories, one in particular should keep shimmering to the surface. That picnic on the Illinois prairie.

So *entirely* it came back now. The rented horse and gig . . . the long journey west . . . the immensity of grass and weeds . . . that meticulously packed picnic basket and Lincoln beating out a clearing . . . and the pineapple! Dear God, how violently and ineffectually he had gone at it. Never since had she been able to look upon that noble fruit without smiling.

But what called out to her most insistently was that moment when, acting upon the maddest of whims, he had gone hunting for strawberries.

Oh, she had begged him to cease, but he *would* have every berry within reach. No matter how small, how perishable, he seized it, mashing as he harvested, so that the offering he finally presented her was nothing more than a slurry of pulp and juice. What did that signify, for, in the spirit of the occasion, she relished it from the moment it touched her tongue, savored above all the residual tingle it left on her lips, which was the same as the tingle of *his* lips, urgently imposed on hers, *devouring* her, it seemed, from sheer insatiability.

For that stretch of a few hours, at least, she had been the exclusive object of his thoughts and desires. He had *longed* for her, and it had colored his every word and deed, and if anything bore her up now, it was the memory that, over all others, he had chosen her.

And had she not rewarded his choice? For all her missteps, he could never say that her heart had faltered. He had borne her devotion right into Heaven—presented it, even, to St. Peter at the gates. *Do you see? I was loved.*

And because love must, by its very nature, create its own polarity—drawing the loved to the lover—she waited.

. . .

ONLY IT WAS hard now to distinguish waiting for *him* from waiting for death. Perhaps, in that final moment of erasure, they would amount to the same thing. His massive gnarled hand would once more fold round hers—swallow it whole—and together they would ascend, and never again would he have cause to leave, for they would be, to each other, all.

SO SHE WAITED.

EVEN ON A July night, with the flies singing their off-kilter melodies and the moths wheeling in the absence of flame, she held on, knowing herself to be enrolled in a mission. And from time to time the words of an old hymn—a hymn she'd forgotten she ever knew—would come scrolling up from the recesses of her mind, and she could hear herself singing in the quavering remnants of her finishing-school soprano.

> Come, Holy Spirit, heavenly Dove,
> With all thy quickening powers;
> Kindle a flame of sacred love
> In these cold hearts of ours.

And rumbling beneath it some nights came the old sound of beating wings. But even this had lost its terror, for what could it be but angels descending? *Reaching* with their resplendent white hands. How clearly she could imagine their touch, the ineffable light that would shine from their eyes as, in voices of tenderest love, they said . . .

Why, you're Miss Todd.

ACKNOWLEDGMENTS

I AM DEEPLY thankful to my agent, Dan Conaway, who helped rear this book from infancy, and to my editor, Betsy Gleick, who helped bring it to full maturity. Thanks also to Michael McKenzie, Abby Yochelson, Ralph Eubanks, Robert Pohl, and Justin Blandford. Chris Boesen was kind enough to lend me his migraine, and I owe a special debt of gratitude to Alden O'Brien, whose knowledge of nineteenth-century dress makes her a novelist's dream.

It was Adam Goodheart's *1861* that first planted the seeds for this book, and it was Adam himself who served as a sounding board and cheerleader during the book's gestation. Among the many nonfiction works I consulted, Jean H. Baker's definitive biography of Mary Todd Lincoln remains an amazing resource, and Charles B. Strozier's *Your Friend Forever, A. Lincoln* offers the best and most sensitive rendering of the Lincoln-Speed friendship.

Finally, a special shout-out to my brother Chris, who was my traveling companion through Lincolniana. And to Don.

COURTING MR. LINCOLN

Inside an Enigma
An Essay by Louis Bayard

An Interview with Louis Bayard

Questions for Discussion

INSIDE AN ENIGMA

An Essay by Louis Bayard

———————

ACCORDING TO THE Library of Congress catalog, 9,100 books have been published on the subject of Abraham Lincoln. Or if you like: on at least 9,100 occasions, some poor fool has tried to get the measure of him. Which raises the question of whether, at this advanced date, any other book or any other measuring is required.

And if I venture to say "yes"—even an emphatic "yes"—it's not so much because of Lincoln's undeniable historical importance. It's because of Lincoln himself and his refusal to be pinned down.

Was he the compulsive joke teller or the suicidal depressive? The honest storekeeper who traveled miles to return change to his customers or the sharp-elbowed pol who freely slandered his enemies? The defender of constitutional democracy or the dictator who imprisoned thousands without trial? The Great Emancipator or the canny strategist who saw emancipation as a tool for winning a war?

He must, perforce, be some combination of those things and of many more things, and nobody, as a result, can be surprised that after 9,100 books we still don't have a handle on him.

Even the people who knew Lincoln while he was alive never felt as though they knew him. He was, according to one advisor, "the most reticent, secretive man I ever saw or expect to see." In the words of his longtime law partner William Herndon, Lincoln was "an enigma—a sphinx—a riddle . . . incommunicative—silent."

Of all the mysteries that enveloped the man, perhaps the most profound was his choice of life mate. It certainly puzzled contemporaries like Herndon, who referred to Mary Todd Lincoln variously as a "she wolf," a "tigress," and "the female wild cat of the age." Even scholars more sympathetically inclined to her have wondered what drew Lincoln to such a complicated creature. What, for that matter, drew her to him? How did two such disparate people find each other and embark on this fraught and troubled and, at the same time, loving and enduring alliance?

As I began working on *Courting Mr. Lincoln*, these were the questions that sent me back in the time machine to Springfield, Illinois, circa 1841.

I didn't recognize the Mary Todd I found there. This was not the madwoman or spendthrift or shrew of popular imagination. This was an attractive and vivacious and intelligent young woman, unusually well educated for her era, with an abiding love for politics.

It was a passion she came by honestly. The Todd dynasty numbered governors, Scots Covenanters, Revolutionary War heroes—not to mention Mary's own father, who worked his way up from owner of a dry-goods store to legislative clerk, councilman, city magistrate, sheriff, assemblyman, and finally, Kentucky state senator.

Small wonder, then, that Mary imbibed politics from earliest infancy. If she had come up in a more modern era, she might well have staked her own claim to office, but in those pre-suffrage days, her only outlet was to find a promising candidate to marry.

And herein another mystery: why did she settle on Abraham Lincoln?

To be sure, he was a lawyer and orator of natural gifts. But he was also raw, uncouth, uneducated, still deep in debt, and on *nobody's* short list to become president of the United States. Somehow or other, Mary Todd divined his potential and never once, so far as we know, questioned her choice.

At this point, then, I had all the makings of a classic *Pride and Prejudice*-style courtship scenario, relocated to old Springfield. But it was while roaming those streets that I found another figure lurking in the shadows. His name was Joshua Speed.

Like Mary, he was a child of Kentucky aristocracy. Like Mary's father, he was the owner of a dry-goods store. And it was over this store that Lincoln lived, and it was Joshua Speed's bed that Lincoln shared for more than four years.

The customary caveat rushes in: bedding in those days was expensive, and bachelors were often obliged to share sleeping quarters. What made *these* two bachelors different was the degree of their intimacy.

"No two men were ever closer"—that was how Speed himself would later describe their friendship. Carl Sandburg, writing in the early twentieth century, went a little farther, suggesting that Lincoln and Speed had "streaks of lavender" about them. And in recent decades, scholars like C. A. Tripp and Charles Strozier have begun to investigate the nature of this relationship. Why did such an attractive man as Speed wait so long to marry? Why did Lincoln himself hold off on marrying until Speed had gone to the altar? Why did he demand that Speed write him the day after his wedding to tell him how the wedding night had gone?

These questions have generated robust differences of opinion, and I can't hope to resolve them with a single book, nor would I want to. I can only say that when I first read Lincoln's letters to Speed (one of which is reproduced in *Courting Mr. Lincoln*), I found two men actually trying to coax and coach each other into normative heterosexual lifestyles. And with that, this courtship story became a love triangle—with Lincoln himself at the center—and with Mary Todd and Joshua Speed as dual narrators, sometime rivals and also sometime allies.

The result, I hope, is a novel that honors all three parties—including the enigmatic Mr. Lincoln, who walks and talks and bleeds on these pages. At the same time, I hope it reaffirms and reanimates the essential riddle of why people come to love each other.

At one point in the story, Mary Todd asks: "How could *anyone* be known—anyone at all—here on God's green earth?" To me, it's the premise of fiction that we can, at some level, know, and at the same time never know. So as the author of roughly the 9,101st book about Abraham Lincoln, I freely embrace the speculative over the definitive, with the goal, finally, of transmitting some of Lincoln's mystery—and finding, on the other side, open hearts and minds.

AN INTERVIEW
WITH LOUIS BAYARD

by Anna Roins

Anna Roins: Mr. Bayard, we are so pleased to have an opportunity to talk to you today. Your novel *Courting Mr. Lincoln* focuses on the relationship between Abraham Lincoln and his future wife, Mary Todd—as well as his handsome best friend, Joshua Speed. Lincoln shared a bed with Speed for three and a half years, as bachelors often did in those days, while living in Springfield, Illinois. Yet, there has been some suggestion in C. A. Tripp's deeply revealing *The Intimate World of Abraham Lincoln* that the two men were more than just friends. Can you tell us a bit about why you wanted to revisit this part of history?

Louis Bayard: Over the past two decades, the scholarly community—inspired partly by Tripp—has really been grappling with the question of what Speed and Lincoln meant to each other, whereas fictional representations have been lagging behind. I figured it was time to put the subject front and center in a full-length novel.

AR: The result is a fascinating read. What was the hardest thing about writing *Courting Mr. Lincoln*? What was the easiest?

LB: Really, the hardest part of any book—for me, anyway—is finding the right voice. There's a lot of trial and error involved, and of course, the voice changes a bit as the book goes along, so you have to go back and revise accordingly. As for the easiest part, I'm still waiting to find it!

AR: Understood. You once said, "I'm always looking for the blanks in the historical canvas—the people and things that nobody really knows about." Women traditionally weren't considered important enough to be in the history books. Are there any women you might like to write about?

LB: Well, I'm currently essaying the mystery that was Jackie Kennedy, who was as far from anonymous as you can get, but she's enduringly enigmatic and interesting. And I've always thought there's a great book to be written about Shakespeare's daughters. I don't know if I'm the one to do it, but I think somebody needs to attack the commonplace notion that Shakespeare left behind no copies, no literary "heirs." I mean, how would we even know? What space would his daughters have been granted for their talent?

AR: That sounds fascinating! You have been a professional writer since 1995. Prior to that, you worked in politics as a press secretary for U.S. Representatives in Congress. In addition to novels, you write reviews and essays for the *New York Times*, the *Washington Post*, and Salon.com. What made you decide to sit down and write your first novel?

LB: I guess it was dawning on me that, if I wanted to read a particular kind of book, I was going to have to write it myself. And I do think writers write because they have to. They can't imagine doing anything else. Or they're not fit for anything else.

AR: How do you think you have evolved as a novel writer from your first book?

LB: I'm not always sure I have evolved—only because, with each new book, I feel like I'm starting over. I keep waiting for it to get easy. One thing I can say is that I write a little less than I used to. I trust the words more, or maybe I just trust the reader more.

AR: Alyson Publications, a publishing house that specialized in LGBT fiction and nonfiction, published your first book on the strength of your unagented manuscript. Later, you didn't want to be pigeonholed into a specific genre, so you branched out and looked for an agent. How many attempts did you make before you finally found one that took you on? Are you still with them today?

LB: Yeah, I did it the wrong way. Which is to say that, after a few bruising encounters with agents, I just took my work directly to the publisher. But then I conceived the idea of writing a book about Tiny Tim, and it felt immediately like a bigger idea that needed a bigger house, which meant I needed an agent. A reader of mine put me in touch with Christopher Schelling. We hit it off instantly, and then he sold the book to HarperCollins, which was where I met my wonderful editor, [the late] Marjorie Braman, and that was love at first sight, too. Looking back, I can see how fortuitous the whole sequence was, but at the time it just seemed like a natural progression. (Christopher and I parted amicably a couple of years ago.)

AR: You went from writing contemporary gay fiction into several novels of historical fiction, and along the way, came to distrust the whole notion of genre, which some consider simply labels for marketing. Is this how you feel? Is it just about voice, plot, and story at the end of the day?

LB: For me, it's the story preeminently—which, yes, will get you kicked out of certain academic and literary circles. One of the nicer trends, though, in recent years has been watching so-called literary novelists like Michael Chabon and Colson Whitehead working unapologetically in genre. So maybe those boundaries are breaking down. I do believe that being a genre writer has made me a better writer.

AR: You also teach creative writing. You once said, "That's the mistake I see in aspiring young writers. They blast you with words. They want their voices to be heard. It's hard to convince them they could be heard much better if they just pare away a lot of that stuff." What other advice would you give to new writers? What kind of writing makes you stop and take notice of some of your students and not others?

LB: Whether it's student writing or professional writing, I'm always listening for the voice. You can finesse other things—plot, character, grammar—but if the voice isn't secure, a story won't cohere.

As for what I advise student writers, it's pretty simple: Read everything you can get your grubby little hands on.

AR: Who is your first reader? Do you read reviews of your books written by readers? Do you take any notice of constructive criticism?

LB: My first reader is me, I suppose. I don't send anything out into the world until I'm feeling moderately okay with it. From there, it's my agent and/or my editor. Otherwise, I keep it pretty close to my vest. I don't even talk about it much.

For the sake of my mental health, I've weaned myself off reading my Amazon and Goodreads reviews because, being a neurotic, I tend to dwell on the bad and disbelieve the good. I do read my professional reviews in a fairly cursory way, mostly to see what's resonating for people and what isn't. Every so often, a reviewer will actually educate me about my own book, and that's almost always welcome.

AR: That's brilliant. So good to know! What is your writing day like? How much time is allocated to researching? Do you aim for a set amount of words/ pages per day? How many times does your manuscript get edited by your agent and then again by your editor?

LB: I spend two to three months up front just doing foundational research— getting to the place where I can walk around in a particular world. And then, as I write, I learn what I still need to know, which is often considerable. The whole process takes two years on average. I wish I could winnow that down, but I can't seem to.

As for my daily routine, I try to devote at least the first two to three hours to fiction. I'm not a particularly fast writer, so if I can push out five hundred words, that's a decent output. A thousand-word day is welcome but rare. I'm revising as I go along, so whatever I submit to my publisher will be more like a second or third draft. From there, maybe another two to three revisions—until I get to the point where I can't even look at the thing. I love that line of [Paul] Valéry's: "A poem is never finished, it's only abandoned."

AR: It was such a pleasure talking to you today. Thank you for your time, and all the best for your future books.

LB: Thank you!

Anna Roins is a freelance journalist and senior lawyer, previously of the Australian Government Solicitor. She studied creative writing at the University of Oxford and Faber Academy in London. Roins tries to write novels in her spare time, writes for local publications reviewing books and community pieces, and is a regular contributor to Authorlink. You can find her online at Facebook.com/anna.roins or on Twitter: @Roinsstar.

Interview reprinted with permission from Authorlink.com.

QUESTIONS FOR DISCUSSION

———

1. In the first chapter, Mary Todd is described by a fellow stagecoach passenger as "going to her future." What kind of future could a young woman of Mary's time and circumstances have expected?

2. What effect does the frontier setting of Springfield, Illinois, have on the story?

3. In one scene, Mary makes an impulsive decision to hop into a dray. Why was such an act considered newsworthy enough to mention in the local paper? What does it say about Mary's character?

4. Mary compares herself and Mercy to "soldiers," seeking to "vanquish" and "subdue." What does this metaphor say about mid-nineteenth-century relations between men and women?

5. How are Mary and Lincoln able to overcome the awkwardness of their first meeting? What commonalities do they find in each other?

6. How does Lincoln regain Mary's affections after the disastrous picnic? Does that reveal anything about the nature of their relationship?

7. Do you think Lincoln is being sincere when he says that meeting Joshua was "the greatest fortune that ever befell me"? Does that declaration change their feelings for each other?

8. This book has the structure of a love triangle, with Lincoln at the center. Whom do you think he truly loves, and how? What do you think lies at the heart of Mary's feelings for Lincoln? Of Joshua's?

9. In her conversation with Joshua, Mrs. Francis declares that Lincoln "must marry *somebody*." Do you agree? How would Lincoln's political career have been different if he'd remained a bachelor?

10. "You should have just killed me," whispers Joshua after his wrestling match with Lincoln. What is the source of this despair? How does it color his actions?

11. What does Joshua take away from his encounter with Billy Greene? Does it change his feelings about Lincoln? About himself?

12. Matilda Edwards takes it upon herself to advise Mary in her romantic dealings with Lincoln. Why does she take such an interest? Why does Mary heed her counsel? What effect does that counsel have?

13. Mary is haunted throughout the novel by the sound of flapping wings. Why does she find it so alarming? What does the sound symbolize for her?

14. The epilogue gives us glimpses of both Joshua and Mary in their later lives. How are these episodes colored by what we've already read?

15. "How could *anyone* be known," wonders Mary on her wedding night, "here on God's green earth?" Do you agree that people are fundamentally unknowable? Can fiction make people *more* knowable?

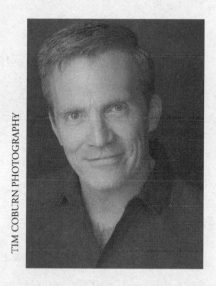

Louis Bayard is a *New York Times* Notable Book author and has been shortlisted for both the Edgar and Dagger awards for his historical thrillers, which include *The Pale Blue Eye* and *Mr. Timothy*. His most recent novel was the critically acclaimed young-adult title *Lucky Strikes*. He lives in Washington, DC, and teaches at George Washington University. Visit him online at www.louisbayard.com.